Only for a Knight

Realm of Honor

MICHELLE MILES

ONLY FOR A KNIGHT

This title was previously published.

Cover Design by Erin Dameron-Hill

ISBN: 978-1-7333887-5-7

Prologue

Lord Kieran walked through the shadowed halls of the six-thousand-year-old Dark Realm palace, his lonely footsteps echoing off the walls. Once, long ago, the palace had been shiny and new, brightly lit and welcoming.

Now it was nothing more than a shadow. A forgotten place. With forgotten folk.

Aside from his steps as he walked down the hall, he could hear the faint flicker of a torch here and there. His elongated shadow splashed along the steel-gray walls as he headed toward the throne room. He had been born to the Otherworld before it had split in two. Seelie and Unseelie. Light and Dark. And, some would say, good and evil. Whatever name was used, it mattered not.

Fergus mac Delbaíth had sat on the throne since the Dark Realm's inception, making it complacent. Almost as though those who had been banished here had forgotten what life was like when the Otherworld had been whole and all of the Seelie and Unseelie coexisted. When the Four Treasures had not been hidden away and carefully guarded by Queen Maeve.

Not for long.

Kieran had not forgotten the Beforetime, before banishment. The time when all of Fae had been joined as one. He remembered a taste of life with the Seelie. When Queen Maeve had looked at him with a warm smile and allowed him to sup next to her. When he sat on the High Council as one of the favored nobles. He had been a prince among princes. A god among gods.

All that had changed when she turned on him, no longer tolerating his outbursts, as she called them, at Council. He and his fellow Elves merely tried to enact changes to the future of the Otherworld. Changes Queen Maeve refused. He had exacted his revenge and she had cast him out, splitting the Fae into the Light and Dark Realms, and forever separating the Elves with the Treaty of Separation. From then on, he'd vowed to see the queen dethroned.

He'd been planning the siege for years. Carefully. Methodically. The immortal King Fergus would die today. The Light and Dark Realms of the Otherworld would reunite as one after thousands of years of being apart and he would lead them into their new future.

His plan had been put into action years ago when he dispatched his trusted men to find a way across the Barrier and into the Light Realm. He would not succeed without the Four Treasures and they had all been hidden by Queen Maeve. She thought putting a Guardian with them would keep them safe. She did not know how determined he was to find them.

She would soon enough.

Cormac would be returning now. Kieran exited the palace into the night where frost glistened in the air. Moonlight made the Dark side of the Otherworld glow in a blue-white veil, touching the rolling hills covered in glistening snow. Even the weather seemed to be dark and Kieran longed for the Light. Longed to touch the warmth again and step upon the earth as he once had when he was an Elven prince.

There were no reinforcements here around the Dark King's palace, for none were needed. Who would invade the Dark Realm, after all? There was nothing but thieves and murderers here. Those who had been banished from the Light to spend eternity in the frozen wasteland on the other side of the Barrier.

Kieran puffed out a breath and watched as the moisture crystallized in the air around him. He clenched his gloved hands and waited, staving off the shiver that wanted to erupt underneath his wool-lined cloak. He detested waiting on Cormac, ready to return to the relative warmth of the palace, when he saw the shadow pass over the moonlit hills and glanced up.

A large black form blotted out the stars and moon, seeming to be nothing but a great void. He watched as it took shape, the twenty-four-foot wingspan a testament to the power gliding through the air.

Nero, the black dragon, landed two feet from him, head bowing to let Cormac alight from the leather saddle. The Fomorian mage garnered more of Kieran's respect by taming the ancient creature. The ancient creature that now turned to him, red eyes peering at him with an intense glow.

Cormac patted the giant scaly neck and whispered words that

puffed in the air though Kieran couldn't hear what he said. The dragon nudged his shoulder as though to give him an affectionate pat before taking flight again.

"My lord," Cormac greeted and gave him a stiff bow.

"You have news for me?"

"I do. Could we go inside to discuss it?"

"I'm expected in court," he said. "I've not much time. Tell me what you've found."

Cormac clenched his fists and shifted from one foot to the other, his breath crystallizing in the air. "The Guardian of the Sword of Light has been located and taken."

"Where is he now?"

"The men are bringing him back through the Barrier in the Heartlands."

"Are you sure the spell you gave me to weaken the Barrier will continue to work as they come through?"

Cormac didn't hide his look of offense. "My spells have never failed when used properly."

"The risk is great, Cormac," Kieran said. "When the queen discovers the failing Barrier, she will no doubt counterattack."

"If you continue to use the magic as I instructed, my lord, you will be able to hold steady."

Kieran was still unsure but had to take Cormac at his word. "Once you have the Guardian in custody and through the Barrier, the men are bringing him here to me?"

"Aye, they will be bringing him and the Sword."

"For now, I want him unharmed. He may be the only one who can tell us how to use the Sword with the other Treasures once we get to the Stone of Destiny." Kieran relaxed his fists, happy the first step of his plan was underway. "If the Guardian fails to talk, I'm sure I can count on you, Cormac, to discover how to use them."

Cormac tightened his jaw, the muscles ticking under the skin. "I gave you my word."

Satisfied with his answer, Kieran smiled before continuing. "And what of the other two Treasures?"

"We are trying to find out who the Guardians are and where they are located. We have someone in the Light Realm helping us. It won't be long before we have them secured."

"Good. Once we have the Club and the Spear, we can make our

way to the Hill of Tara."

"And then your mighty reign will truly begin, my lord."

"My reign begins with the death of that slothful idiot Fergus. Tonight." He pressed his lips in a thin line. "Are the men in place?"

"Aye, they are. Ready to assist you."

"Then it's time I greet my king and his family. As soon as you know the whereabouts of the Club and Spear, I want to know. Once Queen Maeve realizes the Sword and its Guardian are missing, it will become more difficult to find them."

"Aye. The Unseelie have already crossed the Barrier to search for them."

"When the king is dead, we can proceed with the other plans. The Otherworld will belong to me."

"And I will do everything in my power to assist you. As I promised. I hope you can keep your promise."

"Time will tell, Cormac, if you prove yourself to me then I will. Call your dragon and bring me the news I've long awaited." He clapped him on the shoulder. "I must make haste to court. I've tarried long enough."

As Kieran entered the throne room, the scene was as it always was. The king, high on his dais, feasting on roasted fowl and sipping red wine from his golden goblet. He was flanked by his queen and his two Dark Fae princes. How had this fool become king?

Weaklings. The lot of them.

Musicians played a cheerful tune on ancient instruments. Dark Fae and Dark Elven dancers swirled, scantily clad and dripping in gold and jewels. Girls, Kieran knew, who had been bought and paid for with Dark Realm gold.

Gnomes, dark elves, goblins and the like all shared the king's feast. Faery dogs with their beady red eyes, pointed ears and short matted fur lay at the feet of the princes, panting with their long black tongues lolled out.

None of them could measure up to his strength of will or character. His goal was in sight. He could taste victory on the tip of his tongue, feel it crawling through the marrow of his ancient bones.

It had taken him time to place men he could trust throughout the court. And now as he walked toward the dais, he took note of them. Some were guards. Some were other nobles he had managed to sway to his side. Some were nothing more than common folk.

"Ah, Kieran, my old friend. You've come back to court at last. Come and join us for our evening meal." Fergus waved him toward the high table.

He could not tell the king he was busy planning his murder and as such there were many details that needed tending. He had been away from court, putting the final pieces of his plan into place. He had captured and tortured several of the Seelie nobles to find out the location of the sacred Four Treasures. One finally talked, revealing the identity of the Guardian of the Sword of Light who was now on his way here. He smiled, heard the *whoosh* of blood in his veins and felt the heavy steel of his short blade in his boot.

The king was a rotund man with a scraggly red beard and unruly red hair. He had a jovial laugh and a twinkle in his blue eyes and for that, Kieran hated him all the more.

"Good eve, my king. My queen."

He bowed, trying for all he could to remain humble even though his contempt for the man and his queen raged through him. Pulsed through him with every traitorous beat of his heart.

"We've long missed you at court, Lord Kieran," the queen said, her melodious voice ringing through the great hall. Her blood-red lips formed a beautiful smile.

His queen was not the most beautiful in the land. That title remained with Queen Maeve. Yet she managed to come in a close second. How this ugly beast of a man got such a lovely wife Kieran had never understood.

"My apologies, your majesties, for my absence. But I assure you, I am here to stay."

The queen signaled for a servant as Kieran took a seat to the left of the king. A server filled his goblet full of wine while another placed a trencher in front of him.

"What has kept you away from court so long?" the queen asked.

"I'm afraid I had personal duties to attend, my queen."

"Your absence has surely been noticed." She lifted her goblet. "Welcome home."

"Lord Kieran, I wonder, does your absence have anything to do with our last conversation?" Fergus asked. His blue-eyed gaze landed on him, pierced through him. As though to challenge him in front of his nobles here at court.

Kieran tore a slice of bread into a bite-sized piece. If the king wished to bait him…well, he was no fool. He would take the bait. And the king would suffer. "The unification of the Light and Dark Realms of the Otherworld is still a viable possibility, your majesty."

"So, you say." Fergus laughed, his large gut jiggling with the guffaw. "To attempt such a thing is folly."

"There are those who believe it is time to stop being ignored by the Light Realm. It is time to take back what was once ours by our right as Elves and Fae. We are called Unseelie because that is what the queen of the Light Realm wishes us to be called."

Fergus laughed again. "You speak as though we can snap our fingers," he snapped loudly, "and make it so, my lord. When surely you must know there is naught to be done. We are Dark Realm. It is the way of things." He waved away the thought.

"May I remind you it has been the way of things for the last six thousand years," Kieran said. His fist crushed the fresh bread into a ball. "Others here in the Dark Realm have called for change as well. There are those who are tired of skulking through the shadows. Tired of being banished to the black frozen northern lands in the Otherworld."

That gave the king pause. His cold gaze landed on Kieran, still piercing. Still challenging. "The Dark Realm has purpose. And that purpose is to be divided from the Light Realm, away from those who hate us."

"They hate us because that is what Queen Maeve wishes. She has banished us here, away from them. As punishment for whatever she deems as our crimes," Kieran snapped, his voice reedy and thin. "It's time to go into the Light. To unite the Otherworld once again."

"How do you suggest we do this?" Fergus's plump hand gripped his golden goblet so hard, his nail beds whitened. "War? Is that the way of it?"

"War is a means to an end."

A chilled silence settled over the room. The music stopped. Even the red-eyed dogs stopped panting and drooling on the stone floor. All eyes—ogre, troll and goblin alike—were on Kieran. Calm settled over him. He knew what was to come.

"Gentlemen." It was the queen who spoke. "Let us not talk of war this night."

"When should we talk about it, my queen?" Kieran asked. "When should we talk of any rebellion against the Light Realm? Is it a matter of impropriety to speak of war here in these dark walls? While we starve and wait for Queen Maeve to take pity on us, she is living in the high court of the Light. She is living as more than a queen. She lives as a goddess."

"Enough!" Fergus slammed his goblet on the scarred wooden table, red wine sloshing over the rim and his hand. "You know as well as I Queen Maeve doesn't live as such. All you have are delusions."

Kieran's world flared into a bright-red starburst. The pulse of hate throbbed through his skull, pounding the heated blood through his head. He pushed to his feet in a slow, methodical manner, his gaze never leaving the king's face.

"Delusions, my king?" He gave a wave of his hand and all those who served him came forward. Swords drawn, spears pointed. "It is you who are deluded. You are nothing but a slovenly pig feasting on food you have taken from those who serve you."

The king's face had turned ashen-white. The queen had clamped her hand on his arm. The two princes, young as they were, had no idea what was happening. But the king did. It was clear by the look of fear on his face.

"Kieran…my lord…what are you…?"

"The time for talk is over. Now we must act."

It was the signal to attack and all hell broke loose in the great hall. While his men went to work, Kieran paused and took in the disbelief on the king's face. He reveled in that, immense satisfaction seeping through his bones. When the king met his gaze, his face a ghostly pallor, he asked one simple question.

"Why?"

Kieran's response was to gut the king, slicing him from navel to neck. He fell to the ground, the gold crown on his head falling off and clattering to the stone floor. The queen shrieked, a loud, piercing sound that hurt his pointed ears. He killed her next. With her body slumping to the ground next to her husband's, he turned his rage on the princes, slitting their throats while the red-eyed dogs still sat at their feet and panted. Kieran whistled and both dogs hopped to their feet and came to him, sitting on their haunches in front of him.

A few of those loyal to the king tried to fight back, but they were killed as well. As Kieran walked toward the fallen crown, his feet leaving bloody footprints, he smirked. There hadn't been much of a fight. Nor did he expect there would be. He'd wiped out the royal family and those who would claim the throne.

The air was tinged with the metallic twang of blood. The battle was over and he could feel the *whoosh* of victory in his veins as he picked up the crown. This was the beginning. Dropping the crown on his head, he turned to his Fae, his goblins, his elves, *his* Unseelie Court now. It was then he realized he still had the bread clamped in his fist. He tossed it to the ground with a plop.

"We have wasted enough time waiting here in these dark lands, my friends," Kieran said. "Now let us take back what is rightfully ours. Let us march into the Light and fight against those who would oppress us. Follow me and I swear to you we will rule the Otherworld once again."

A cheer rang out in the great hall while sightless corpses looked on.

Chapter 1

"Sir Derron, a word if you will."

Queen Maeve, perched on an ornate silver throne, waved him forward. She pierced him with a pale-blue gaze, unwavering and unrelenting. The queen was used to getting what she wanted and Derron knew he couldn't refuse her.

He gave one last glance at Elyne as the guards led her away, her wrists shackled, to the Fae prison. Cornflower eyes locked with his and seemed to plead with him to stop the guards, sending a dagger right to his heart. Even though they both knew nothing he could say or do would change the queen's mind, the responsibility of her imprisonment weighed on him. It was because of him she was in trouble with Queen Maeve. Still, Elyne held her head high despite the undignified manner in which she was led away.

It didn't seem right imprisoning her when all she tried to do was help him and her friends in the human realm. She'd altered time to save his life, unbeknownst to him. Even after he'd broken their betrothal because he'd been smitten with a human which, of course, would never work out. He knew that, but he'd wanted to get back at the Fae princess. Now all he wanted to do was rescue her from the prison in which she was about to be tossed.

"Of course, your majesty."

"In my private chamber."

Queen Maeve rose to her full regal height, her white gown trimmed in gold flowing around her lithe, graceful body. Her youthful face with high cheekbones and cleft chin belied her ancient age. Golden hair hung in waves down her back under the silvery veil attached to the circlet of Celtic knotwork around her head.

He followed the queen's hurried steps from the throne room where the scene of Elyne's imprisonment had played out. He could hear the mutterings of the nobles speculating whether the charges were indeed true. Derron knew they were. Queen Maeve had passed down the harshest punishment she could to make an example of her daughter.

Once they were alone in her private chambers, she poured a cup of wine from a glass ewer. Silence hung heavily between them and he was loath to break it first.

"I'm sure you understand why I did what I did with Elyne." She held the cup between her hands before taking a quick sip.

"I realize she broke Fae law, but prison?" Derron asked.

"She must see my threats are not empty." She placed the cup on a nearby table and turned to him. "You're lucky I do not do the same to you."

"To me?" He gave her a faint smile. "My queen, why would you send me to prison as well?"

"You know why." Anger flashed in her eyes. "You have gone to the human realm numerous times to joust in these barbaric tournaments. You nearly got yourself killed."

"I did get myself killed, if you remember, your majesty. It was Elyne who saved me."

Elyne had gone to great lengths to save his life. She had altered history for him by sending the human, Maggie Chase, back in time. If it hadn't been for her, he wouldn't be standing there talking to the Queen of the Otherworld. He would be nothing but Faery dust. Now that Elyne had been arrested for her crimes, he had no choice. He would have to break her out of prison. It was the least he could do. And mayhap she would forgive him for his treatment of her in the human realm.

"I'm aware what happened in the past and that Elyne altered time to bring you back," she reminded him, her voice hard and bitter. "She completely defied the laws of the Otherworld."

"Aye, and she did it for me." He couldn't help but feel touched at her gesture when he found out the truth.

Maeve clasped her hands and paced the length of the room. "Let's not rehash that, shall we? I have another important matter to discuss with you."

"Is this about the Fae nobles that have disappeared?"

Back in the human realm, when he lay near death after a match with Sir Finian, Maeve told Derron several Fae nobles had disappeared but she hadn't said who or how. But he and Elyne had unfinished business in the human realm and had defied Maeve's orders and returned to help their human friends.

"Aye, it is. My spies tell me they were taken to the Dark Realm. I had intended to send you there to find out where they'd been taken." She paused, stopping at the table to pick up the wine and take another sip.

Her jaw clenched as she swallowed.

"And now?" Derron prompted.

"There is another more pressing matter. It's why I wished to speak with you alone before the Council convenes so we can decide our next steps." She put down the cup again, keeping her back to him. "It seems your father has gone missing."

Derron's heart skipped a beat. "My father?"

His father had been Guardian and Lord of the Sword of Light. A position Derron would one day inherit. But since Fae were immortal, it seemed as though it would never come to pass. His father had held the position for thousands of years while Derron skipped off to the human realm seeking his adventures and thrills. It had never occurred to him that one day he would take over that position for it would mean his father no longer lived.

Lord Malcolm and Derron hadn't always been on the best of terms. His father had wanted so much more for him, especially with the marriage to Princess Elyne. Lord Malcolm saw a great match between the two. Derron would not only inherit the title of Guardian of the Sword of Light, but also be crown prince and would one day rule the Otherworld beside Elyne.

So, when Derron had petitioned the court to have the betrothal broken, he had argued with his father and they hadn't spoken since that fateful day. Now Lord Malcolm was missing and the Unseelie were responsible.

"Is he alive?"

"I do not know," Maeve said. "My spies cannot find him."

"And the Sword?" Derron asked.

"Missing as well." Maeve turned slowly to face him, her cheeks flushed pink. "I fear the worst, Derron. No one knows where he is but we assume it has something to do with the Dark Realm. I understand there is unrest there. A new man has proclaimed himself king. His name is Kieran."

"You think he had something to do with it?"

"Possibly. We haven't much time to discuss this. The Council is ready to convene in the Queen's Chambers. Your presence is requested."

Meaning, she wouldn't take no for an answer. Derron itched to begin the quest to find his father.

Without waiting for a response, Queen Maeve headed for the door, her gown and scent trailing after her. He had no choice but to follow from her private chamber, down the torch-lit corridor to the Queen's Chamber. This was where important decisions were made regarding the state of the Otherworld. Where wars were declared. Where royal marriages were performed and men were knighted. Where criminals' fates were decided.

The oaken double doors to the Queen's Chamber soared to ten feet tall, the tops in the shape of an arch. The hinges and handles were made of the heaviest wrought iron. Two guards flanked either side, standing at rigid attention in their full armor polished to a high shine. It was likely these men never saw battle in that armor as it wasn't dented or scratched in any way. Crimson cloaks attached to their shoulders dusted the shiny marble floor. They snapped to attention when the queen approached and then bowed their heads when she paused outside the door.

"My queen. The Council has assembled."

"Open the doors, Sir Ewan."

The guard to the right of the door gave a stiff nod to his counterpart and the two reached for the heavy wrought iron handles in unison. They pulled open the doors, allowing the queen to enter. Her presence was announced immediately.

"Queen Maeve, Ruler of the Otherworld."

The men inside the chamber rose from the U-shaped table and bowed as she passed through to the throne at the end of the room. Derron had been in the Queen's Chamber before. He'd been knighted in this very room several centuries ago. He could even recall the christening of Princess Elyne when she was but a wee babe and he a young Fae. Before her father, the king, had been murdered.

"Be seated, gentlemen," Maeve said as she took her throne.

It was an oversized, ornate chair with a red-cushioned seat and back. It was so oversized she looked like nothing more than a child when she perched in it, her hands resting on the intricately carved arms.

"I've asked Sir Derron to join us as it pertains to him and his missing father, Lord Malcolm." She waved Derron to a nearby seat. "I realize the call to convene was a short one but the situation in the Dark Realm is dire. Gawaine, what have you learned?”

Lord Gawaine was the queen's High Councilor. He had always been by her side as long as Derron could remember. He had immediately taken the task when the king had died. Derron couldn't remember a time when Gawaine wasn't present within these walls.

“Fergus mac Delbaíth, his wife and the two princes are all dead by the hands of this Kieran, my queen,” Gawaine said.

“Aye and he has incited a riot within the Unseelie. His followers outnumber those who are against him,” another noble, Lord Aldun, spoke. “It seems he is killing all those who oppose him.”

“An uprising, then? Why now?” Derron asked.

“Lord Kieran has lain in wait for thousands of years, Sir Derron,” Maeve said. “Biding his time and waiting to take control, seeking revenge upon those who banished him.”

Memories flooded back to Derron of a time long past. When Queen Maeve banished the young Elf noble, Lord Kieran, to the newly formed Dark Realm, war had broken out between the Elves and the Fae. War that was settled with the Treaty of Separation.

“I'm sure you will recall Lord Kieran was responsible for the death of King Adhamh,” Gawaine said.

Queen Maeve bristled and Derron was acutely aware of the shift in her mood at the mention of the long-dead king's name.

“He's even gone so far as resurrecting dark creatures, my queen,” Lord Vaughan said.

“What do you mean by ‘resurrecting’, Lord Vaughan?” she asked, turning her attention to him.

“I mean all the creatures of the night the Light Realm have banished to the Unseelie are returning.”

The men in the room all shifted uneasily, giving each other wary glances at this news. Derron didn't need an explanation and neither did Maeve. He knew what it meant. If Kieran was awakening the darkness and shadows, it couldn't be good for the Light Realm, his father or Queen Maeve.

“So, the situation is more dire than we first suspected,” she said.

Gawaine cleared his throat nervously. “There is more. My scouts tell me in the Heartlands there is a gate. The Unseelie have somehow managed to open the Barrier here. I believe this is where they have found a way in and out.”

The Light and Dark Realms were separated by the Barrier, a

magical protective wall that couldn't be broken or removed without the magic of the Seelie who had erected the wall. The Heartlands lay between the Dark and Light Realms. The Barrier divided the Heartlands in half from north to south. It had always been forbidden for Seelie to cross into the Dark Realm and vice versa. And yet the Unseelie had managed to find a way to come through and take Lord Malcolm and the Sword.

"Dark shadows have been spotted flying the night sky, my queen," Gawaine continued.

The dragon has been awakened. May the gods protect us.

"Do you believe this is where Lord Malcolm has been taken, Gawaine?" she asked.

"Aye, I believe so. Though what Kieran plans to do with the Sword, I cannot say."

"Isn't it obvious?" Derron asked, looking between Gawaine and Maeve. "He plans to use it."

"The Sword is most powerful with the other three Treasures," Lord Vaughan stated.

"Aye," Derron agreed. "But you're forgetting anyone who wields the Sword of Light will become undefeatable in battle. What if Kieran also knows this and plans to attack the other three Guardians?"

Murmurs whispered throughout the room.

"That's impossible," Gawaine said, waving away the notion with a hand. "Even if he had all Four Treasures, he would have to know how they worked together."

"And if he has all Four Guardians," Derron said, "then he *would* know how they all worked together."

Everyone spoke at once and no one could be heard over the others.

"Silence," Queen Maeve said, though she never raised her voice. All those in the room quieted. "It is entirely possible that is Lord Kieran's plan and if that's true, then we must make sure our other three Guardians are well protected. Gawaine, I want you to send men to the Hill of Tara to protect Lord Pywll and the Stone of Destiny. Send as many men as you think necessary. Likewise, I want you to increase protection around Lord Llewelyn and Lord Udrich. The last thing we need is to have them kidnapped as well, and the Club of Dagda and Spear of Lugh in his hands along with the Sword of Light."

"Aye, my queen. It will be done."

"In the meantime, I will weave a spell to keep the Barrier closed. It may be our only way of keeping the Unseelie out while we try to find Lord Malcolm."

"What would you have me do, your majesty?" Derron asked.

"You are Knight of the Realm and Protector of the Otherworld. If anything has happened to Malcolm, then it will be your duty to become Guardian, find the Sword of Light and protect it with your life."

"My father is *not* dead." Derron was sure of it. Wouldn't he know somehow if he'd been killed? Wouldn't he sense it with his Fae magic?

"You don't know that. None of us know for certain. I need you to find out."

"How do you propose I enter, my queen?"

"We will make it possible for you to pass safely through the Barrier to the Dark Realm to find your father. There are certain protective magics the High Druid can give you that will keep you safe."

Queen Maeve wanted him to go to the High Druid? Was she mad? No one approached the High Druid unless absolutely necessary. Though, he supposed, it *was* absolutely necessary.

"If I were to go there then what? I certainly can't walk up to the palace in the Dark Realm and knock on the door."

"Gawaine, would you assume this is where Lord Malcolm is being held?" she asked, directing her attention to the lord at her right.

"Aye, I'd guess his men brought Lord Malcolm there."

"Then you will go there, Sir Derron, and bring back your father and the Sword of Light."

"I will require help, Queen Maeve," he said. "You cannot expect me to go alone across the Barrier."

"My queen." Gawaine cut a glance at Derron. "I must point out that with sending men to the Hill of Tara and the other two Guardians, I'm not sure if we can spare any others. It would leave our forces here at the palace too depleted. Should Lord Kieran launch an attack on us, I must insist we have as many knights and soldiers as possible."

"So, you mean for me to go alone? You expect me to travel across the Barrier into the Dark Realm without any reinforcements? How can I get him out of there alone? What if my father is injured? I need men. Without them, it will be nothing but a suicide mission." Derron's blood pumped, searing hot through his veins.

"We are on the brink of war," Gawaine said.

"I'm not asking you," Derron fired. How dare he answer for the queen? Gawaine may have been around for more centuries than Derron could count, but answering for the queen should still be a crime.

"I see your point, Sir Derron, of course. The quest is perilous." She considered his words as she gazed thoughtfully at Derron. "But I must agree with Lord Gawaine, Sir Derron. I cannot give you my men. I am sure, though, there are those who would follow you."

It was up to him to find his own men willing to go with him into the Dark Realm. He knew no such men. He'd been too busy frittering away his time at jousting tournaments in the human realm. There were no loyal subjects would who follow him across the Barrier. He would have to hire swords to take with him and those Fae were only as good as how much gold they were paid.

"I am sorry," she said.

"So am I. And I suppose I have no choice but to accept?"

"Your father and the Sword must be found."

He clenched his fists. "Then I will find my father and the Sword and bring them both back. And if I must go alone, so be it." He gave Gawaine a pointed glare. But, Derron thought, mayhap he wouldn't have to go alone.

"See the High Druid before you leave for the protection through the Barrier. May the gods speed your way, Sir Derron."

Chapter 2

"Hickory, dickory, dock. The mouse ran up the clock."

Scrape, scrape, scrape.

"The clock stuck one. The mouse ran down. Hickory, dickory, dock."

Scrape, scrape, scrape.

Princess Elyne repeated the rhyme she'd heard in a nursery in mid-1800s London over and over as she scraped away the dirt at the edge of her cell. The blunt rock she'd found wasn't much good and her fingertips were raw and ragged from the constant scraping but she was determined. Not that it would do her a lot of good. If she managed to dig out of the cell, she would still be faced with the wards. With no magic to break through them, she may as well forget about trying to escape.

But the rhyme kept repeating over and over in her head. The first time she'd heard it was when she'd bored of babysitting then-ghost Finian McCullough and sifted through the ages to find something more interesting to do. She spent a lot of time in London, watching the golden-haired daughters of a duke grow into lovely young women. Their governess used to tell nursery rhymes and silly stories to pass the time.

She tried not to think of the freedom she once had as she sifted from one age to the next. She'd seen the Great Pyramid of Giza built by hundreds of bronzed bare-backed workers in the blazing sun. She'd walked through the Hanging Gardens of Babylon on a spring morn, the flowers dotted with dew. She was there at the unveiling of the Statue of Zeus at Olympia.

The ancient world was by far more interesting to her than the modern world where her good friend Maggie had come from.

Elyne blew a strand of blonde hair out of her eyes and sighed, missing her friends. Finn and Maggie would likely be married by now. She hoped Maggie wasn't too disappointed Elyne hadn't made it to her wedding.

Gripping the rock in her hand to give her throbbing fingers a rest, she sat back against the stone wall of her prison. As she ran her thumb over the rock's smooth surface, she replayed the day in the throne room through her mind.

"How do you plead to these charges, Princess Elyne?" Queen Maeve, her mother, had asked.

Elyne had tried to ignore the primitive manacles biting into the flesh of her wrists. She'd focused on Derron, who stood to the left of her mother, the Queen of the Otherworld.

She so loved his handsome face. Elyne had seen a lot of handsome faces, but Derron's face was the one she saw in her dreams. She looked as close as she could, trying to discern if there was any hint of disgust or disappointment creasing his features.

Derron kept his expression impassive. He showed no emotion whatsoever.

"Princess?" Queen Maeve prompted.

The queen's voice was gruff and unfeeling. Something Elyne had gotten used to throughout her life and in some ways had learned to ignore. Her mother wasn't exactly warm and fuzzy. In fact, she was all cold steel and barbed wire.

"Is that all I get, Mother? To plead guilty or innocent and nothing more? And are these really necessary?" She held up her wrists.

Elyne's voice echoed through the cavernous throne room. The room where she had spent most of her youth and where her mother had ruled the Light Realm with an iron fist. Expressionless faces of the other royals and nobles stared at Elyne, waiting for her response. One that Elyne wasn't so willing to give.

Aye, she was guilty of using magic in the human realm to help her friends Maggie and Finn conquer the Earl of Litonshire. She was even guilty of turning back time and sending Maggie back to the fourteenth century to keep Finn from killing her beloved Derron. A lot of good that did for he very nearly died anyway. If it hadn't been for her mother and the royal healer swooping in at the last possible moment to heal him, he would have died. Again.

"Do you deserve more?" Maeve asked, ignoring her question about the manacles. "There is no trial here. You were caught in the human realm using Fae magic. You altered time. You—"

"I know what I did." As if she needed a recap of everything she'd done wrong over the last few months. "And what of Sir

Derron? Does he not get punished for his acts in the human realm?"

"Sir Derron will face his own consequences," her mother snapped. "I tire of your disregard for our laws, daughter."

"So you humiliate me in front of all the royals at court?" she asked, sweeping her hand around to encompass the entire room, her chains clinking.

"You humiliate yourself. Now, how do you plead?"

"Clearly, I'm guilty of all charges, Mother," Elyne said, a sour taste in her mouth.

"Very well then." She sounded satisfied with Elyne's answer and even smiled a little. "Your magic is hereby removed until such time as you can prove you deserve to have it back. You will spend your time thinking about your actions in the Reformatory. Your release will be upon my command."

"You're sending me to the Reformatory?" Elyne couldn't believe her mother would actually send her to the Fae version of a prison. She knew it would be heavily warded, keeping anyone out and her in.

"You seem more upset about that than losing your powers. And really, daughter, it's for your own good. Take her away."

Queen Maeve had waved to the guards who grasped her gently by the arms and led her away from the throne room, through the white marble halls of the palace. That day seemed an eon ago, but she knew in reality it had been a mere two days.

Had her life really come to this? And what of Derron? What did he think about her imprisonment? They had finally seemed to be on good terms. Despite their past, their relationship had become easier. Less unsettled. How was she supposed to prove her worthiness to get her magic back when she was stuck here behind wards? She couldn't very well do that from the Reformatory.

Elyne ran her thumb over the smooth surface of the rock, her fingers throbbing, and thought of everything she had done to save Derron's life, everything it had cost her. She would never forget the way he looked at her when he realized she'd altered time to keep him alive. The way his face had gentled and he had touched her hand.

It had all been worth it.

Glancing around the stone chamber, she could see the runes carved over the cell door and around it. She knew it was heavily warded and digging under the cell door would take nothing short of a miracle. Not to mention the constant guards standing outside her cell. Her visitors had been the servants sent to feed her. Her mother hadn't told her how long she would be stuck here but then, she didn't think her mother really cared that much. Elyne was out of her way so she could continue to run the Light Realm and not worry about what laws her daughter might be breaking.

Elyne couldn't help but wonder what the other Fae royals thought of the situation. Surely they had an opinion and if they did, when the High Council convened, would her mother even care to listen? Would they lobby for her release? She was the crown princess of the Light Realm, after all. She would someday rule them.

"And I'll show them," she muttered.

In the distance of the stone-carved Reformatory, she heard the chamber door open and close, the loud bang reverberating through the chamber. Another servant coming with one of her daily meals, no doubt. Would they notice the indention in the floor near the cell door? Would they report her for trying to escape?

At this point, she didn't really care.

Her pointed ears strained to hear the footfalls but none came. In fact, it was silent as a tomb down here. Surely someone was coming to feed her? Her heart sped up a little, throbbing with a sharp pain as she wondered why she didn't hear anything. Elyne turned her head to peer through the shadowy dimness, to see if she could see anyone outside her cell.

The man in the cloak stopped in front of her cell, turning toward her. Her heart sped up as she peered beneath the hood for a face but saw nothing but a shadowed chin. He paused, standing with his arms at his sides, peering into her cell. All the hair on the back of her neck stood at attention.

"Who are you?"

Despite her determination to make her voice strong and hard, it quivered with fear. The man whisked off his hood and gave her a wicked grin. Elyne gasped.

"Derron! You scared me half to death. What are you doing here?"

"Busting you out."

He produced a flat disk with intricate Celtic knotwork on one side. He placed it first to the left of her bars, then the right and then over the cell door. The runes around her cell glowed a soft burnt orange. A moment later, the door clicked open. Derron swung it wide and stepped across the threshold.

"How did you get in here? Where are all the guards?"

He stepped farther inside, his mouth quirking in a grin as he reached down to help her to her feet. "I have excellent resources."

"I guess so." She tossed aside the smooth rock and brushed the dirt from her hands.

"It's the least I could do after what you did for me at tourney."

She flushed, her cheeks burning hot. Before she could respond, he took her hand in his and kissed her fingertips.

"I did the only thing I knew to do," she said.

"And for that, I am eternally grateful. Now, come. Let's get you out of this dank place."

"I hope you know what you're doing. When my mother finds out, she'll be furious. Are you certain about this?"

His face relaxed into an easy smile. "I think you're worth the risk."

"Where are we going?"

He stopped so fast, she nearly ran into the back of him. "*We* aren't going anywhere together. I have to leave."

"Then I'm coming with you. I have no place to go. What am I supposed to do? I can't go back to court and I don't have any powers. She took them away."

"You can't go where I'm going."

"Where is that?" she demanded, using her haughty tone.

"My father is missing, Elyne."

His words hit her like a fist in the gut, so hard she hadn't even noticed he failed to answer her question. *The Sword of Light?*

"When? How?"

"No one knows exactly when, but his disappearance was first discovered while we were in the human realm. The Sword of Light is also missing."

"How could this happen?" Elyne asked. "He's a Guardian. He has the gift of sight. He would have known someone was coming for him."

"Unless the Unseelie used their dark magic and killed him."

"You think he's dead?" Elyne refused to believe he was dead. Why would someone kill him? The Sword of Light was useless without the other Four Treasures of Fae. "They took the Sword."

"Aye, and if he's not dead, then they're holding him prisoner until they can figure out how to wield it," Derron said. "Your mother has asked me to find my father, bring him and the Sword of Light back before something happens to either one of them."

"Are the other Guardians in danger?"

"Maeve thinks so. She's ordered royal guards to keep watch over them at all times. She's worried, Elyne," Derron said.

Elyne had never seen her mother worry about anything. She'd always led the Light Realm with confidence, masked her feelings from everyone. Elyne had grown up thinking her world was safe and secure under the watchful gaze of the Queen's Guard and ruled by the iron fist of Maeve. Now she wondered what had happened to that security.

"Maeve doesn't want to take any chances. She and the High Council think my father has been taken to the Dark Realm."

"I'm coming with you."

"You cannot. It's too dangerous."

"I can and I will. I can't let you go alone, Derron."

"I'm not going alone. I intend to hire a few good men to go with me since your mother can't seem to spare any of the Queen's Guard. And your mother has requested I visit the High Druid for protective magics."

"The High Druid? You're not serious." When Derron's expression didn't change she blew out a heated breath. "You are serious. I'm going. You got me out of prison. Where do you think I'm supposed to go?" She shook her head. "You're stuck with me now."

"I hadn't thought of that." He looked her up and down before he heaved a heavy sigh. "I suppose you're right. You can't go back to the Light Realm."

"And I can't sift to the human realm. In fact, I can't do any Fae magic until I prove to her I deserve to have it back. How she expected me to do that in prison, I have no idea."

"I don't think she truly meant to keep you here, Elyne."

She gave him a look of disdain. "It's been two days, Derron."

"I believe she intended to free you. Eventually. Feel free to thank me for getting you out. However, I should have thought this escape plan through better, I suppose."

"What's to think through? You did a fine job. You got me out and now I'm coming with you."

"Mayhap I'll sift you off to Maggie and Finn where you'll be safe," he suggested.

"Maggie wants to spend some serious alone time with her hot Scottish husband. I doubt she'd want me to crash her party."

"I'd rather you be someplace safe," he argued.

"I don't want to go someplace safe." She folded her arms across her chest and looked like a petulant child.

He heaved a sigh. "Are you sure you want to go with me? It will not be a pleasant journey."

"I'm tougher than you think. What's the plan?"

"There's a gate in the Heartlands leading through the Barrier to the Dark Realm. That's where I'm going."

"Mayhap I spoke too soon," she said.

He chuckled. "Still want to go?"

"It's either that or go back to prison and I'd really rather not do that." All her life, she'd been told to avoid the Heartlands, that Seelie were not allowed to cross the Barrier into the Dark Realm. Yet here she was about to do just that. Provided, of course, Derron allowed her to come.

"Then I suppose that's settled."

Her heart fluttered against her rib cage. His eyes softened, his lips parted, and for a moment she thought he intended to kiss her. She could count the days she'd dreamed of this moment, waiting for him to come to his senses. Was she still hurt he'd broken their betrothal? Aye, of course. Could she forgive him? Aye, absolutely.

"Come on, then. We have a High Druid to visit. And then we'll be going to the slums."

"Why the slums?"

"Why, my dear, it's where the mercenaries are."

Chapter 3

"I still can't figure out how you got past the guards or the wards," Elyne said.

Derron had taken her by the hand and led her through the dank tunnels of the prison. She knew there should be guards flanking each doorway but none were present. Derron had somehow encouraged them to leave their posts. The wards were another matter altogether. How did he get past them? Even Fae magic-breakers couldn't crack the seal that secured each cell. Only her mother could allow the wards to be removed.

"Are you going to tell me?" she asked.

"No."

"Fair enough."

She would find out from him eventually how he managed it.

Once they were past the main cellblock, Derron led her up the winding stone staircase. Up and up and up they went until they finally made it out of the dungeon. Again, there were no guards.

"Where have they all gone?" she asked.

"I sent them away." Derron flashed a wolf smile.

"Aren't you sly?"

"I do try, princess."

Derron snatched a torch from a wall bracket, still holding her hand, and led her through the narrow stone corridor toward freedom. This was too easy. There was no way he was going to walk in, unlock her cell door and walk out. Was there? But yet, there was still no sign of the Queen's Guard. Still no sign of anyone at all.

Elyne knew beyond the doorway ahead was the courtyard and then they would leave the Queen's Palace for the slums. She'd never as much as set a toe outside the Queen's Palace in the Otherworld. The "travel" she'd done was when she sifted to and from the human realm and then when she followed Derron from tournament to tournament.

At the oak door he paused, gave her a glance and a smile before pushing it open. The iron hinges groaned objection as the door swung open and freedom beckoned. It was nighttime in the Otherworld, the sliver of a moon glowing brightly in the indigo sky. A blue-white veil descended on the courtyard, bathing it in soft light. Glittering stars twinkled in silent merriment. It was a clear, crisp night. Elyne shivered.

"You're cold."

Derron placed the torch in the bracket outside the doorway to the prison and slipped off his cloak. He draped it around her shoulders, the warmth of his body heat immediately enveloping her. She didn't want to notice he wore the garb of a Guardian— black pants tucked neatly into boots polished to a high shine, thick tunic with long sleeves, a sword at his waist as well as a dagger strapped to his thick thigh. No, she didn't want to notice that at all.

"Thank you."

"I think it might be best if you wait for me while I visit the High Druid," he said. "It could be dangerous."

Shadows played across his handsome face, softening his features. A wave of hair fell across his forehead, his pointed ears barely visible.

"It's dangerous for me to stay behind. Once my mother finds I've left the prison, she'll search for me. I cannot stay in the palace. I'm not afraid of the High Druid."

"I can take you someplace—"

"No," she said emphatically.

"As you wish, princess." He bowed with a flourish.

"Don't mock me, Derron."

"I would never dare, sweet princess." His grin was accompanied by a wink. "Come along then. We have much to accomplish in a short amount of time."

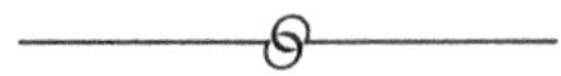

The High Druid's dwelling didn't seem appropriate for a man of his stature. It was a nondescript little cottage on the edge of the palace grounds. Gray smoke curled upward in lazy drifts from each chimney on either side of the house. Golden light flickered in each window.

"Are you sure about this?" Elyne asked.

"Getting cold feet? You're welcome to say behind if you wish."

"No, thanks."

Derron knocked on the door, his knuckles rapping heavily against the dark oak. It seemed odd to be standing outside the door of the High Druid, waiting for him to answer. The High Druid didn't accept callers unless one was expected or summoned. An eternity passed before the door finally swung open.

For years, Elyne had heard of the High Druid though she couldn't recall ever having seen him in person. He looked like every other wizened old man in court, sans beard. Standing taller than she, he had silver hair that hung to his waist. It looked as though it had been combed until it shone. His eyes were the color of moonlight, giving him a rather ghostly appearance as he peered at first Derron then Elyne. She knew he was ancient and his face should have reflected it, though she spied only a few crinkles around his eyes and mouth. He had aged well all these long years.

"You must be Sir Derron," he said. "Queen Maeve said you'd come."

"Aye, she sent me."

The High Druid stepped aside and allowed them to enter, closing the door softly behind them and then turned to her. He took her hand in his, kissed her knuckles. "Welcome, Princess Elyne. I heard you were imprisoned. Did I hear wrong?"

"No, you did not." She wasn't going to share how she got out. It wasn't any of his business and she didn't want to take the chance he would tell her mother.

Inside the cottage, there were floor-to-ceiling bookshelves along one wall crammed with all sorts of books. Some had tattered covers. Others looked new and pristine. Cluttered along the shelves were jars of various herbs. Some jars held unidentifiable things. Things Elyne didn't wish to know about at all.

A fire crackled in the oversized fireplace, heating up the small room. And in the middle was a large wood table with a scarred top and chairs. Two of the chairs had ancient-looking papers with yellowed edges piled in them. One had a bundle of material in it.

"Queen Maeve told me of your journey, Sir Derron," the High Druid said. "I understand you're to visit the Dark Realm in search of your father. 'Tis a dangerous journey, that."

"One I'm willing to take."

"And one that could cost your life. How honorable of you." His smile unnerved Elyne. "I'm to give you something that will allow you to cross the Barrier."

"That was the plan, aye," Derron said. He shifted from one foot to the other, impatient. "The sooner I can go the better."

"I have several things that could help you," the High Druid said. "First, a concealment cloak." He reached for the bundle of cloth on one of the chairs, held it up. "This will hide your presence."

"I'm not sure what good that will do me," Derron said.

"It will merely hide you should you have a need. Take it. I must insist." He shoved the cloak at Derron, who had no choice but to accept it. "Now for something to help you across the Barrier. Let me see…"

"That could come in handy," Elyne pointed out. Derron scowled at her.

"Your grace, I'm here for the protective magic—"

"I know what you're here for." He shuffled toward his oversized and overstuffed bookshelf. "Don't interrupt, laddie."

Elyne stifled a snicker behind her hand while Derron shot her another look of annoyance. She knew he wanted the High Druid to get to the point but there was no rushing the man. She watched the elder run his bony finger across the spines of his books and mutter under his breath.

"Aha! Here it is."

He pulled a large voluminous tome from the bookshelf and tossed it to the table with a loud *thud*. When the High Druid opened the book, the aged leather spine crackled. The gilt-edged pages were yellowed from age and the man flipped them with care, still muttering under his breath.

"The Barrier, laddie, was erected over six thousand years ago," he said. "It's not something to be taken lightly. If you want to get through it without dying, then you will be patient." He pointed to one of the pages to hold his spot as he looked up, his gray eyes meeting Derron's. "How many in your party?"

"I'm not certain. My men haven't been assembled yet."

"That poses a slight problem but I can work with that. And the princess?"

"I'm going," Elyne said.

"Dangerous journey for a fair princess."

"I am not afraid of what is on the other side of the Barrier."

"Ah, my sweet princess, you should be. You both should be." He glanced between the two of them. "Lord Kieran wakes the sleeping beasts."

"What does that mean?" Elyne looked from the High Druid to Derron, who shifted uncomfortably from one foot to the other. "What sleeping beasts?"

"What his grace means, princess, is Lord Kieran awakened the black dragon," Derron said.

"God's teeth." The swear she'd heard so many times in the human realm seemed appropriate now.

The High Druid turned back to the book. "You should make yourself at home. This will take some doing."

Absently, he waved toward one of the fireplaces where there were two wooden chairs with Celtic knotwork carved along the back and the sides. Elyne looked at Derron who, though he didn't seem all that thrilled by the prospect, nodded agreement. Sitting down by the warm fire, she couldn't help but watch the light flickering across his face. She forced herself not to stare.

As they sat in amicable silence, she wondered what she could do to repair their relationship. Maggie had let it slip that Derron had petitioned the court to break their betrothal. Hearing that had hurt her, cut her to the core. To get back at him, she had gone to the High Court, told them he was jousting. To make them see he too broke Fae law. Now she regretted those actions. It had ultimately severed their marriage contract.

"I wish you'd reconsider," Derron said.

The sound of his voice in the silence startled her out of her deep thoughts. For a moment she thought he'd heard her thoughts, and then immediately shoved them aside.

"I'm going," she said. "I thought we'd settled that already. You know why I can't stay here."

He turned his gaze from the fire to her. The look he gave her sent her stomach plummeting to her shoes. She wasn't sure exactly what she saw in his face. It looked like a mixture of concern and adoration and it made gooseflesh rise on her arms.

"I couldn't leave you in the prison." A slow smile spread, his eyes lighting. "But your mother will have my head if anything happens to you."

"Then see that nothing happens to me, sir knight."

He chuckled at this. He stood, drew his sword, and then bent down on one knee. "I swear by my sword to protect you with my life, fair princess."

Elyne flushed to the roots of her hair. She cleared her throat. "Well, then if you swear it upon your sword, I suppose I have to believe you."

"Aye, you do."

He stood and sheathed the sword, his gaze back on her, making her uncomfortable. He looked as though he intended to say something else as he took her hand in his. His fingers were warm. She focused on his knuckles, the way the skin tightened as he gripped her hand.

"Elyne, I—"

"The spell is complete," the High Druid announced.

Her heart sank to her toes as Derron released her hand and stood. "Good. Then we can be on our way."

"Not before I explain how this works."

Elyne rose and followed Derron back to the High Druid, her heart pattering wildly in her chest. What had he been about to say? To do? He had reached his hand toward her. He had something in mind to tell her until the High Druid had interrupted. Curse him.

The High Druid held a small vial with a cork in the top. Inside was fine sand a pale shade of pink. He handed it to Derron.

"Faery dust. Use it when you are ready to enter the Barrier. Uncork it carefully and sprinkle a few grains of sand over your head. The dust will make you invisible, protecting you and those who follow you into the Barrier. However, it will protect you for a short time while in the Unseelie side."

"How long?"

"A few hours at best. Once it runs out, you will no longer be protected."

"What if I can't find my father in that time?"

"I would suggest not being on the Unseelie side. If you are, however, then you must get out as soon as possible. The longer you linger in the Unseelie world, the more difficult it will be for you to get out. And I can assure you the Unseelie will not let you go so easily."

"That's the best you can do?"

"The Barrier is ancient, laddie. There is no real magic that can destroy it."

"But there's a tear in it. That's how the Unseelie have been entering the Light Realm."

"Aye, a tear. Should the Barrier fall…well, I wouldn't want to think of what could happen to our world or the human realm should it fall."

"That doesn't inspire a lot of confidence, your grace."

"If I had more time, Guardian, I would be able to concoct something a little more suitable. However, given the time constraint, this is the best I can do. Guard it well and may the gods be with you."

Chapter 4

"Fool!"

Derron practically shouted it the moment they were out of earshot of the High Druid and his cabin. Elyne hurried after him, panting to keep up.

"He offers me a cloak and a vial of magic as protection in the Dark Realm? How am I supposed to find my father in few hours? It's not possible. I don't even have any men from the Queen's Guard. This is an impossible task."

Elyne had no words to comfort him. She wasn't sure what to say. She hurried to his side and took his hand in hers. He stiffened for a moment before relaxing and then squeezing her hand, as though to say everything would be all right. She was about to offer words of comfort when a man's voice stopped her.

"Sir Derron, I must speak with you, if you please."

Derron stopped short and Elyne came to a sudden halt beside him. They both watched the tall, lean figure approach. In the moonlight, his light-colored hair shimmered as though sprinkled with starlight. He had a regal look about his face, his ears more pointed at the top than either of theirs. He wore tall black boots, black pants neatly tucked into the tops, a white tunic and black cloak held together with a silver clasp in the shape of a triskelion spiral. Everything about him told Elyne he was unmistakably Elven.

"You hold me at a disadvantage, sir," Derron said.

"You are the son of Malcolm, Guardian of the Sword of Light," the man said and bowed deeply to Derron.

"Aye." Derron said the word slowly as though unsure of what to make of the man.

"My name is Eldrin emar'Rudul."

"And what does an Elven ranger wish of me?" Derron asked.

His pretty face broke into a smile. "You've heard of me, I see. I've come to help you find your father."

Elyne wondered how the ranger, Eldrin, knew so much about the Fae and the goings-on at court. She searched her memory for any rumors she may have heard about the Elves, but nothing came to mind. Mayhap because she'd spent a good bit of time in the human realm. It seemed perfectly reasonable Derron, as Knight of the Realm and Protector of the Otherworld, would know Elven rangers. But even so, she gave him a questioning glance.

At the mention of his father, Derron stiffened slightly. Elyne wouldn't have known he had done it if he hadn't tightened his grip on her hand.

"What do you know about my father?"

"I know your father and the Sword are missing. I know they have been gone for quite some time. I know the Queen fears war and cannot give you any men from her Queen's Guard to accompany you."

"How do you know all this?"

"There are whispers at court, my lord. The realm fears the worst. Since the queen cannot give you an army, I give you myself."

"Why?" Derron didn't bother to hide the suspicion in his voice. "You are Elves. What business do you have with my father and the Fae court?"

Eldrin smiled, thin-lipped. "I realize our races have not been amicable in many years. But I assure you it is not the way all of us think. News of the slaying of the Dark King and his family has traveled quickly. We know who has proclaimed himself ruler. He was once one of us. A Woodland Elf who craved power. We banished him to the Dark Realm eons ago. We had thought he would perish there, as most Unseelie do. We believe he means to take control of both Light and Dark Realms. Should the Otherworld fall, the Elves have no interest in seeing him come to power. It is in our best interest to see Queen Maeve remain as ruler."

"Then mayhap you should be telling the queen instead of me."

"We've attempted to speak with the queen on numerous occasions. She refuses the Elves' requests to meet with her."

"Why would she do that? The Elves are part of her domain."

"I know not, my lord. Mayhap she is still bitter about the war between Elves and Fae. At any rate, it is why I come to you. To offer help."

"She refuses you and *still* you wish to help?"

"Aye, my lord."

"Why?"

"Because we know Lord Kieran is now a Dark Elf. And we wish to make sure he never makes it out of the Dark Realm."

Derron looked the Elf up and down, his gaze thoughtful as he considered him joining them. "So be it. First, stop calling me 'my lord'. I don't like it. If one of those Unseelie hears you call me that, I may as well paint a target on my chest. Second, I hope you know what you're doing."

"As do I, Derron." He bowed low and then, as if seeing Elyne for the first time, extended his hand to her. "Princess, your beauty rivals your mother's. I'm enchanted."

Elyne slipped her hand into his as he bowed low. Derron scowled.

"Enchanted?" She wasn't sure what shocked her more. The fact he said he was enchanted to meet her or the fact he called her more beautiful than her mother.

"It is a wise Seelie who knows the princess and heir to the throne." Eldrin continued to hold her hand.

"That'll be quite enough." Derron intervened, giving the Elf a little shove and taking Elyne's hand back.

"My apologies. I didn't realize she was spoken for."

"I'm not," Elyne said quickly. Derron, after all, had broken their betrothal and despite her feelings for him, she wanted to see him squirm. If only a little.

"If you're coming with us, then let's go. I'm heading to the slums to hire mercenaries."

"That will not be necessary," Eldrin said. "I can provide the men. There's no need to hire those who want nothing but gold and offer no loyalty."

The Elves were a proud race and, some of them thought, superior to the Fae. They looked down on those who wanted to profit from fighting for coin instead of fighting for a cause. Elyne wasn't surprised to hear the Elven ranger wanted nothing to do with the mercenaries in the slums. And quite frankly neither did she. They were trouble and the last thing they needed was more trouble.

"You can offer loyalty to me and Queen Maeve?" Derron asked. "For nothing in return."

"All we ask for in return is that our lands remain safe. Come with me to the Woodlands. There, we will gather supplies for the journey."

Eldrin led the way through the courtyard and Derron and Elyne fell in step behind him.

"He's certainly accommodating," she said.

"I don't like it." Derron narrowed his eyes, his gaze on the Elf's back.

"You think he's not telling you the truth?"

"Elves rarely do anything without wanting something in return, Elyne."

"But he said he wants his lands kept safe."

"I know what he said."

She could hear the mistrust in Derron's voice and glanced at the Elf in front of them, his shimmering hair fell to his waist. She'd never had many dealings with the race of Elves. She'd never had a reason. But she also had no reason to distrust Eldrin, either. At least not yet.

"He's offering supplies and men. Mayhap he merely wants to help."

"I'll believe it when I see it."

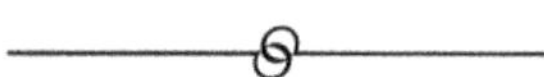

Eldrin led them to the Woodlands, the forest that lay to the north of the Queen's Palace. Elyne had seen the dense trees from atop the palace walls, but never ventured there. She'd preferred to do her traveling by sifting from human realm to Otherworld, not traipsing through thick trees with sweat rolling down her back.

The legends she'd heard about the Woodlands proclaimed it a magical place, even to the Fae, who were forbidden to cross into the forest. She supposed with Eldrin as their escort, though, they would have no problems with that.

The Woodlands Forest was home to the Wood Elves, a race as old as time and Tuatha dé Danann alike. Thousands of years ago, they'd warred for rule of the Otherworld. They'd fought bloody battles with each other over the Queen's Palace, bleeding the ground red until finally the Fae defeated them and the Treaty of Separation could be formed between the two races. The Fae claimed the Queen's Palace while the Wood Elves built their cities in the forest.

Elyne considered Eldrin. As an Elf, he took a chance coming to the Queen's Palace to seek Derron and form an alliance with the Fae knight. She assumed what he said about her mother remaining in power was true. The Elves were not fond of those Unseelie in the Dark Realm either. Once an Elf was banished there, he became known as a Dark Elf, forever forbidden from the Light Realm.

At the edge of the forest before the line of trees, a wooden fence with a gate blocked their way. Elyne had never seen this before and didn't even know it existed.

"The forest is gated?"

"As it has been for many centuries," Eldrin replied.

"I've never seen it before."

"That's because you are a Fae."

"How do you explain it now, then?" she demanded.

"You are in my protection and in the presence of Elves, your highness. You can see it now because I've removed the magic that hides it," Eldrin said.

As they neared, the gate opened to allow them to pass through and closed behind them. There was no one on the other side of the gate. It opened and closed by itself. It must be the work of Elven magic. Both races were known to possess magic. How Elves used it, though, was quite different from the Fae.

A tall man emerged from the trees to greet them. He wore a long white tunic, white pants and tall white boots. His hair was the color of spun gold and hung to his waist. The sides were pulled back to reveal his pointed ears. His eyebrows slanted upward over narrow pale-blue eyes. His high cheekbones and carved face reminded her of Fae royalty.

"Eldrin, why have you brought these…Fae…here?" The word *Fae* on his tongue sounded as though it burned like acid.

"Have you not heard, Lord Navin? The Dark King is dead. The Unseelie plan an attack on the Light Realm."

"And?"

"This is Sir Derron, Knight of the Realm. And this is Princess Elyne, heir to the throne of the Otherworld."

"Fae nobility." Lord Navin's tone matched his look of disdain. "I am not moved by their titles, Eldrin. Tell me what they're doing here. 'Tis forbidden."

"The Unseelie plan to attack, my lord. If they attack the Light

Realm, then our own realm is at risk. Do you want to see them destroy the Woodlands?"

"You expect me to believe Unseelie can come into the Light Realm? They cannot cross the Barrier."

"But they have," Derron said, speaking up now. "And they will again. They've kidnapped my father."

"Lord Malcolm? Guardian of the Sword of Light?" Surprise flickered in the lord's eyes as he looked at Derron.

"Aye. And I go to find him and bring him back."

"You mean to cross the Barrier?"

"There is a way through in the Heartlands. And I have the High Druid's magic to protect me and whoever travels with me."

Lord Navin looked at Eldrin again. "You plan to go with them?"

"Aye, I do. And others who wish to join us."

"Nay. I cannot allow it. No right-minded Elf would join forces with a *Fae*."

"Excuse me, my lord," Elyne said, unwilling to stand by and allow him to insult her race. "Your race survives because we Fae allow it. We gave you Wood Elves the Woodlands Forest."

"Aye, after you nearly committed genocide," Lord Navin flared back. "Why then should we help you? I cannot allow it, Eldrin. The king will hear of this."

"I brought them here because we can help," Eldrin said, standing his ground. His face flamed bright red, the tips of his pointed ears pink. "We have men and supplies. And aye, the king *will* hear of this."

Eldrin made to shove past Navin but he stepped in front of him. "Do not make me arrest you, Eldrin. It would be most unpleasant for you in the Hollow."

He gave the lord a *try and stop me* look and took another step toward the trees. Navin put his forearm against Eldrin's chest and gave him a shove backward.

"What is the meaning of this?"

The voice boomed from behind them and the two Elves dropped to their knees, heads bowed. Derron and Elyne exchanged a look of curiosity. She glanced at the newcomer and saw he was similar in stature to Eldrin and Lord Navin. Tall and lithe wearing a crown of green leaves. He wore a winter-white robe trimmed in silver thread lined with white fur over a richly embroidered tunic, black pants and shiny black boots.

King of the Woodland Elves.

"Your majesty," Lord Navin said from his kneeling position, head still bowed.

"Eldrin, I sensed these Fae the moment they crossed the gate. Why have you brought them here?" The king gave Derron and Elyne a cursory glance before turning his attention back to the Elf ranger.

"Your majesty…Father, if I may rise?" Eldrin asked.

Elyne blinked as she looked between the two. The king was Eldrin's father? She'd had no idea.

"Aye."

Eldrin stood while Lord Navin remained on the ground. Elyne thought that most curious. They had to ask permission to rise? And had to bow until he gave it? Mayhap the Fae court should do something like that. There would be less insolence.

"I've brought Sir Derron and Princess Elyne to the Woodlands to gather men and supplies."

"To what end?"

"The Dark King is dead—"

"Aye, I know. I received word this morning." He waved his hand as though it were old news.

"If I may, your majesty?" Derron asked. The king's cold gaze flickered to him.

"You are not my kind and yet you wish to address me?" the king asked. He narrowed his dark eyes, and then gave one stiff nod. "Very well. Proceed."

"My father, Lord Malcolm, has been kidnapped by Unseelie. Queen Maeve has sent me to find him and return him and the Sword of Light to safety."

"Oh, aye, I know all about the disappearance of your father, the rip in the Barrier, everything. I tried to warn Queen Maeve when I first noticed the weakness in the Heartlands but she would not listen." His accusatory gaze lingered on Elyne. "Nor would she allow me to meet with her."

"My apologies, your majesty," Elyne said. "I'm sure my mother intended to meet with you."

"Pish-posh on that, girl," he snapped as he glowered at her. "She had no intention of speaking with the Elves. That's why I sent Eldrin." His gaze shifted back to his son. "I assume you're here because you've offered our help?"

"Aye, Father, I have. With your permission, I've come to gather a few men and some supplies."

The king didn't respond right away. An uncomfortable silence hung in the still air between them like an oppressive heat. Elyne glanced at the king, who had his dark gaze fixed on Eldrin.

"Very well. See to it, Eldrin. I trust you to select your men wisely."

"Thank you, Father, I will."

The king turned on his shiny boot, his robes fluttering with a flourish. As he headed for the trees, he said, "You may rise, Lord Navin."

When he disappeared into the forest, Navin rose to his feet and reeled on Eldrin, snatching him by the collar of his tunic and shoving him against a tree. In the flurry of action, Navin had pulled out a dagger, the point now at the base of Eldrin's throat.

"You insolent ranger," he hissed. "How dare you?"

Eldrin gave him a cool look, as though he were unconcerned with the point of a dagger pressing into his skin. "Does it bother you the king gave me his permission to gather men?" He smirked. "I would have asked you to come along, but now that you've expressed such a disinterest, I think not."

"I've swallowed your insults long enough, *ranger.*"

Elyne watched as Derron, clearly losing patience with the situation, drew his sword and pointed it the small of Navin's back.

"Stop, please," Derron said. "My father's life is at stake and you two Elves stand here and bicker with each other. I've not the time. Eldrin, if you wish to help me, then I would appreciate it if we could get on with it. If not, then Elyne and I will be heading to the slums to hire mercenaries."

Elyne suppressed the scowl she wanted to give him. She'd rather stand here and watch the Elves fight it out any day.

"Hire your mercenaries, then," Navin snapped, never taking his eyes off Eldrin. She could clearly see the hate emanating off him in waves. "Elves have no interest in your fight with the Unseelie."

"You will have an interest if they cross the Barrier and invade, like Queen Maeve thinks. Release him, Lord Navin," Derron said.

"Aye, release me," Eldrin said, his mouth quirking in a slanted smile. "These Fae have no interest in our Elven quarrels."

Navin removed his dagger and sheathed it at his waist. Derron removed his sword but held it at the ready at his side.

"I don't know why our father granted your request, Eldrin, but I will make it my mission to find out and change his mind." With that, he stalked off into the forest, leaving the three of them.

"What a cranky arse," Elyne said.

"My apologies," Eldrin said. "My brother and I have never quite seen eye-to-eye. And now he intends to make it his mission to petition our father to stop me from going."

"*That's* your brother?" Elyne glanced where Navin had disappeared, as though she could still see him. She wondered what sort of family dynamic they had.

"With all due respect, Eldrin," Derron said, "we haven't time to discuss your family problems."

"Quite right. Come. Let us go into the forest and speak to the other rangers. I know several who will be willing to assist us."

Eldrin led them from the gate where the tussle had happened and the king had disappeared through the thick trees into the Woodlands Forest. Something made her shiver, gooseflesh blossoming on her arms. She gripped her elbows, hugging herself. The trees seemed to have eyes. The forest was enchanted after all. She had long been told that since she was but a wee Fae. She longed for her powers. One never knew what the Elves would do, knowing there were Fae trespassing in their forest.

The trees' trunks were at least a hundred feet in circumference and even smelled old. Older than time itself. She knew they had been standing as long as there had been an Otherworld. Longer than that even. They stood since the dawn of time. Even Man had not come to destroy these trees. Ancient redwoods, oaks and tree species she'd never seen before cluttered the forest as far as she could see. And in between those trees were shadows that danced to and fro. Mischievous sprites and tree nymphs, distant cousins to the Elves, flitted through the shadows.

Elyne was not fond of sprites or tree nymphs.

They moved deeper into the forest and the trees morphed from mere trees to homes. The Elves had been crafty carving their homes into the trunks. Candlelight twinkled and flickered inside them. As they passed through, curious Elves stepped out of their homes to see the two Fae. They would sense them in their domain, of course, knowing they were forbidden to cross into the forest. Young and old alike, they all wanted to get a glimpse of Derron and Elyne.

Elyne held her head high as the crown princess. Even so, she edged closer to Derron.

He chuckled, deep and low in his throat. "Fear not, princess. You are safe with me. These Elves will not hurt you."

"I'm not afraid of them." She was suddenly irritated that he knew her motives and could read her so easily.

They followed Eldrin to a stone structure nearly camouflaged by leaves. It was hard to see where the trees ended and the stone began. Ivy climbed the walls, curving upward and disappearing into the foliage. Seeing the structure in the midst of the forest seemed strange and yet wonderful all at once.

Through a large oaken door, they entered a small hall dimly lit by filtered sunlight through slats in the roof. A giant redwood grew in the center, the trunk so large it took up nearly the entire hall as it shot upward and disappeared. Elyne craned her neck to look up at it, but couldn't see the top of the tree.

"This is Ranger Hall," Eldrin said. "My brethren will join us shortly."

"They knew you were coming?"

"I told them to meet me here and hoped that you would be with me." Eldrin smiled.

It was clear to Elyne that Derron wanted to ask more questions. He didn't get the chance when several other Elven rangers entered the hall. They were similar in height and stature to Eldrin.

"Eldrin, you risk much bringing a Fae among us. It is forbidden," the first one said.

"I told you, Firdaras, I had intended to speak with Sir Derron about his father. He is here now. And he requires our help."

"Why should we help the Fae?" one asked. "They have never helped the Elves."

"As I explained before, Kerhar, the Dark King has fallen. The Unseelie Court has been overtaken. Our realm is in danger."

"That is a matter for Queen Maeve," Firdaras said.

"Queen Maeve has sent me to find my father," Derron said before Eldrin could respond. "Eldrin, I came here on good faith. Your 'brethren' refusing to help is now a waste of my time. Princess Elyne and I will be going."

"Wait, Sir Derron. Aye, your father's life is in danger and that's why I brought you here," Eldrin said. He turned to the group of

Elven rangers. "We are Elves, aye. But our very existence is threatened by this new Dark King. A man who was once an Elf like us. Lord Kieran was long since banished to the Unseelie Court by Queen Maeve and now intends to invade the Light. We, as Elves, cannot allow that to happen. If he does, he will destroy everything and everyone in his path. I ask you all for your help. Come with us across the Barrier to find the Sword of Light and the Guardian."

"How do we know this threat isn't a fabrication of the Fae?" another asked.

Elyne had had enough. "This is no fabrication. I am the crown princess, heir to the throne of the Seelie Court. Sir Derron and Eldrin speak the truth."

"Princess Elyne." Firdaras bowed to her.

The others followed suit. Clearly, they hadn't realized who she was until she told them. She was tired of the bickering. Eldrin was trying to get them help and there was opposition every step of the way. She huffed out a breath. If she had her magic, none of this would be happening.

"Rise, rangers," Elyne said.

"Your word is as good as your mother's. If the queen believes there is a threat, then so do I."

"This is an outrage, Firdaras. How dare you side with the Fae?" Kerhar asked.

"I side with the Fae when our lives and our homes are in danger," Firdaras said. He turned back to Derron. "How do you intend to cross the Barrier?"

"We've now explained this more than once," Elyne snapped. "There is a place in the Heartlands we can cross. Are you Elves with us or not? If not, we must be on our way."

"You intend to travel with us, princess?" Firdaras asked.

"I go where Sir Derron goes," she said.

She wasn't about to have some Elves tell her what to do. Not now. She'd been through enough with her mother and now Derron. She was going and that was final.

"I'm aware of the risks," she said before any of them could object. She glanced around Ranger Hall, taking care to meet each and every gaze of the Elves in the room. "Your king has agreed you would assist us. You are the bravest and best of the Elven warriors. You would not be a ranger if that weren't true. Our Fae and Elf bloody history was long ago. Now I'm asking you, as princess of the realm, to join with us and keep our Seelie Court safe. If Queen Maeve falls, then all is lost. I ask you to protect the Light by joining us and helping us find Lord Malcolm and the Sword of Light."

Derron grasped her hand and squeezed, as though to tell her he was proud of her. She wasn't sure if her inspirational speech would sway them. But if it did and it worked, then they could at last be on their way.

Firdaras bent on one knee and took her free hand in his. He gazed up at her, his clear blue eyes serious. "You have my bow and sword, princess. I pledge my arms to thee."

Her breath caught in her throat at his words. An ancient oath. Words that had not been spoken in thousands of years. Since the Elves and Fae were one.

Firdaras rose and stepped aside, looking at his brothers as though giving them a silent nudge. One by one, they all knelt on one knee, took her hand and pledged the ancient oath. One by one, the group that was three expanded to a small band. Ten Elven rangers, a princess and a Fae knight.

Bring it on, Lord Kieran. We are ready for you.

Kieran's steps echoed as he walked through the halls of the palace, winding his way down to the dungeon where the prisoner was kept. It had been days since the former dark king, his wife and the princes were removed from his court. But a lot had happened. He had taken control of the palace. Those who resisted were killed.

In the past few days, he learned of a coup attempt to have him assassinated. His informants were loyal, though, and let him know about it before it could happen. His justice was swift and public, letting others know their fate should they decide to rise against him. He would not tolerate their rebellion.

It had been shortly after that when Cormac brought news of the prisoner's arrival. Kieran ordered his men to question him to find out how to wield the Sword of Light. To no avail.

When questioning did not work, he ordered the prisoner tortured. The man was resistant even still. He would not break. No matter what horrors they did to him. When Kieran received the news, he knew he would have to handle the matter himself.

Now, as he descended the stairs, he knew what the outcome would be should the prisoner refuse to help. He smiled at the mere thought.

Cormac greeted him at the bottom of the stairs, holding a torch. The yellow, garish light flickered off the mage's face as he gave a nod of greeting.

"My lord, you have come to see the prisoner?"

"Aye. Has he agreed to cooperate, Cormac?" Kieran knew the answer to this question already, but he posed it anyway.

"Nay, my lord. He has refused and proven his high tolerance for pain. We've tried many tactics but he has resisted all of them."

"Indeed? Who knew the old Fae would be such a challenge?" He smiled. Kieran was not afraid of a challenge. "Open the cell."

Two guards stood as sentry on either side. A primitive cell. Though without magic or any other means, those imprisoned weren't likely to escape the dark throes of the dungeon. One of the guards twisted the key in the door. The hinges groaned as it swung open.

Kieran entered followed by Cormac, still holding the torch. He put it in the brace near the door, the light flickering over their captured Fae lord.

He'd been badly beaten. His face was nearly unrecognizable it was so bruised and bloody. One eye was completely swollen shut. He leaned against the stone wall, his head at an awkward angle, his knees drawn up. The once-shiny blond hair was now a tangled mess caked with blood and dirt. His clothes were soiled and torn. Instead of fingernails, he had bloody stubs. His hands were shackled together, as were his ankles.

"Lord Malcolm," Kieran greeted.

"Come to welcome me to the Dark Realm, Lord Kieran?" Despite the torture, the man still had a clear, baritone voice. "I can't say it's been a pleasant stay."

"You do know why you're here, don't you?" Kieran asked.

"So I can spit in your face? I'm not sure I have any spit since I've been denied food and drink but I'll try to muster it up."

"You've been most uncooperative," Kieran said.

"You've been most inhospitable." Malcolm held up his shackled wrists.

"We have the Sword," Kieran said, ignoring his retort. "If you want to live, you'll help us."

"And if I don't? Help, I mean." Malcolm tipped his head back, peering at him with his one good eye. "At this point, I think my life may be expendable."

"We have other ways of discovering how to wield the Sword." Kieran's men were close to gaining two of the other Four Treasures. Once he had the Club of Dagda and the Spear of Lugh, all he would need is the Stone of Destiny under his feet to take control of the Otherworld. And then he would be invincible.

"The other Guardians have no knowledge of how to wield the Sword, just as I have no knowledge how to wield the Spear or the Club." He cocked a grin, his lips spreading over his once-white teeth. Now they were stained red. "You'll not discover it from them. Nor will you be able to overthrow Queen Maeve."

Bloody fool. The Fae Guardian underestimated his determination and his power.

"I find you very perceptive, Lord Malcolm," Kieran said, maintaining a cool, level voice. "Or did you discover our plan by other means?"

"Your men were clumsy," Malcolm said. "Had I not been caught unawares I would have killed them all. I have to hand it to you, Kieran, you were well prepared. Your men didn't give up. But I knew why they were after me when they took the Sword. You realize the queen will never allow you to take over the Otherworld."

"Time will tell, my lord." Though Kieran kept his voice calm and steady, his blood surged with boiling anger that his men were so stupid and inept. "I will ask you directly. Tell me how to wield the Sword."

"That's not asking." Malcolm gave him an evil smile before spitting out a clot of blood. "I'll never tell you."

"Then I'm afraid you leave me no choice. If you will not assist me, then I will have to find someone else who will."

Malcolm's chains rattled. "Stay away from my son."

"Oh, do not despair, my lord. I don't intend to send men after him. By a wonderful twist of fate, Queen Maeve has decided your life is worth something. She's sent your son to find you, so he is coming to me. All I have to do is bide my time and wait. And once he's here he *will* tell me how to wield the sword. By then, I will have the other two Treasures. The Barrier will be destroyed. The walls between the pitiful human realm and the Otherworld will fall and I will be ready to depart for the Hill of Tara."

"You will never succeed. The others won't tell you how to wield those Treasures, either. And then where will you be?"

"I'll have three dead Guardians."

Lord Malcolm became so still, Kieran wasn't sure he still breathed.

"Don't look so surprised, Lord Malcolm. Did you not think I would kill you and the others? Now that you realize the gravity of your situation, will you assist us?"

"You can threaten to kill me, Kieran, but I will not change my mind. And even if you *do* kill me, my son will avenge my death and become the rightful Guardian of the Sword of Light."

Kieran chuckled. "You dare threaten *me* when I am not the one in chains? How thoughtless of you, Lord Malcolm." He turned to Cormac and spoke loud enough Lord Malcolm could hear him. "Kill him. And then send a message to our dear Queen Maeve, won't you? Select whatever body part she might recognize."

"I am not afraid of death, Kieran."

The Dark King pinned him with a withering stare but spoke once again to Cormac. "Since our lord is not afraid of death, Cormac...*make him afraid.*"

Chapter 5

After much argument and discussion, Derron and Eldrin decided it would be best to wait until morning to begin the trek to the Barrier. Which was fine with Elyne. She was exhausted and looking forward to a few hours rest before beginning the long journey. Eldrin allowed Derron and Elyne to stay in his tree home and they had agreed to meet back at Ranger Hall at first light of day.

Eldrin's home wasn't grandiose in any way. It was carved into the hollow of a giant tree. Torches flanked the wooden door with iron hinges. The Elven ranger pushed open the door and Elyne and Derron followed him inside. It was small, quaint, cozy. A fire burned low in a nearby hearth. A small cast-iron pot sat on a hook over it. He went to the pot, took it off the fire with a cloth and set it on the nearby table. They shared a pot of tea, a wheel of cheese and some bread. Afterward, he took the two Fae to a small room furnished with a bed, an oversized chest, a rocking chair with a cushioned seat and a candelabra with six candles burning brightly.

"I hope you will find the accommodations suitable," he said. "In the morn, we will break our fast and then head back to Ranger Hall."

But Elyne hadn't really heard him as she was fixated on one thing. *The bed.*

Did the Elf expect them to *sleep* together? Her stomach cramped.

"Your hospitality is much appreciated, Eldrin. The princess and I thank you."

When she didn't respond, Derron nudged her. "Oh, aye, we do. Thank you, I mean."

"I bid thee good night, then."

Eldrin closed the door with a snap, leaving her alone with Derron. She backed up to the bed and perched on the edge, her stomach roiling with nerves. Derron yawned and stretched. He sat in the rocking chair and kicked off his boots, then stood and unstrapped his sword from his waist, hanging it over the back of the chair. When he started to pull off his tunic, she jumped to her feet.

"Stop."

Surprise washed over his face as he paused with his tunic midway. "Why?"

"You can't undress here. In front of me."

He chuckled. "Don't tell me, fair princess, you're shy."

"Shy, no. It's just that…that…" She pulled her gaze from his hardened abs back to his face. "You can't do that."

The smile in his eyes ignited with a sensuous flame. "Why not?" He dropped his tunic and inched toward her.

Elyne huffed out a breath. She tried to back away. "You know why."

"What are you afraid of?"

"Nothing." *Everything.*

"I won't hurt you." One corner of his mouth pulled upward as he reached her, sliding his hands around her waist. "I can promise you that."

"There's one bed." Even to her ears, she sounded ridiculous.

He laughed out loud then and released her. "Is that what you're worried about? Fear not, fair princess, your virtue is safe with me." He bowed with a flourish.

When he stood, she punched him as hard as she could in the shoulder.

"Ow." He put his hand over the spot she'd hit. "Was that entirely necessary?"

"How *dare* you make fun of me?"

"I wasn't—"

"You can sleep on the floor for all I care."

Elyne shoved passed him and stomped to the bed, jerking back the blankets. She kicked off her shoes so hard, one flew across the small room and smacked into the wall with a thud. Sliding under the covers, she pulled them to her chin and turned on her side, squeezing her eyes shut.

"Good night, then."

His voice sounded sheepish. She could hear him blowing out the candles, one by one, plunging the room into total darkness. His weight sank in the other side of the bed, as far from her as he could get. But he didn't slide under the blankets. He lay on top of them, not moving.

Elyne knew it would be a very long night with Derron next to her.

Her sleep was restless. When the morning came, she sat on the edge of the bed and slipped on her shoes. Glancing behind her, she watched Derron still sleeping. His face looked peaceful. Calm. She regretted her outburst from the night before. When he stirred, she turned away. She combed her long locks with her fingertips.

"Good morrow, princess."

His voice was still thick with sleep as he rose from the bed. She heard him pulling on his boots.

"Good morrow."

He walked to stand in front of her, strapping on his sword. "About last night—"

She sprang to her feet and smiled. "Forget it."

Before he could answer, she flung open the door. He followed her away from the room. The two of them found Eldrin already awake. In the center of the table were several shapes wrapped in a soft cloth and tied with rope.

"Good morrow," he greeted. "I've gathered a few things to take with us on our journey." His hand swept the top of the table. "Once we've eaten, we can be on our way."

The rest of the morning was awkward at best between Derron and Elyne. But they managed small talk with Eldrin as they ate, and then headed back to Ranger Hall. Several of the men were already there, each one with his own pack of supplies for the long trek. After a round of morning greetings, the men gathered together at the table, looking at a map of the Otherworld and deciding the best route.

Elyne, still a bit smug after the rangers had pledged their allegiance to her, watched as Derron conferred with Eldrin and the others. What was the best way to go? How would they get there without being detected by the Unseelie? If there was a way for them to get in through the Barrier, how many Unseelie had been sent through?

She could see Derron's frustration in his face and when he

raked his hand through his dark-blond hair. At last, he pulled out a dagger and stabbed the map in the middle, quieting the Elven rangers.

"We need to get here," he said, pointing to the dagger. He'd placed it over the Barrier in the Heartlands where there was a way in. "I don't care how we get there but we must make haste. All this bickering is getting us nowhere."

"Aye, Sir Derron, I agree," Firdaras said. "But we must be cautious, too. We can't expect to walk directly to the Barrier. With the Unseelie on the move, the roads will be dangerous."

"The roads may be dangerous, good gentles, but Lord Kieran plans to attack," Derron said, his tone impatient. "There will be other dangers to concern ourselves with, especially if he already has possession of the Sword of Light."

She longed for her magic, though at this point she wasn't sure what good it would do. She doubted it would make the Elves and her Fae knight get along any better. Elyne huffed out a breath. If she left it to them, they would do this all day and never make a plan. She had to intervene.

"Most of the roads are protected by the Queen's Guard," she said. "If we stay on them, we should have safe passage."

"All the way to the Barrier?" Kerhar snorted. "I think not."

"Aye, all the way to the barrier, Kerhar." She gave him her best withering stare. The one she'd perfected ages ago and inherited from her mother.

"We will trust her highness," Eldrin said. "And use the Banríon Road." He slung his supply pack across one shoulder. He already carried his bow and quiver of arrows on the other.

"The main road?" Kerhar asked. "Are you mad? Lord Kieran will surely have his Unseelie all over it by now. Taking the Banríon Road will lead to certain death."

"You don't know that," Elyne snapped. "You assume the Unseelie have already invaded. If they have, Kerhar, my mother would surely know about it. She has not mobilized for war."

"War? You do not know what you speak of, princess." He practically snorted his response, as though she were a child who knew nothing.

"Aye, I do," she said, irritated by the ranger's acid retort. How could he imply she wouldn't know what it meant for the Unseelie to cross the Barrier? "You know as I do that if numerous Unseelie have crossed into the Barrier, it is an act of war. It is forbidden for them to come into the Light as it is forbidden for us to go into the Dark."

"Yet we go anyway."

She held her arms ramrod straight at her sides.

"Enough! It is the only way, Kerhar," Eldrin said. "If we go through the Woodlands, it will take more time. Time we cannot afford."

"I disagree. It is safer—"

"The princess and I will follow Eldrin on the Banríon Road," Derron interrupted. To make sure the others knew he meant business he snatched his dagger and sheathed it. Then he grasped Elyne by the hand. "You are welcome to join us."

Kerhar gave Derron a look of death, though Derron didn't seem to notice. He followed Eldrin out of Ranger Hall. The other rangers trailed one by one. But Elyne was acutely aware of the glare Kerhar gave her as he passed by and out. Derron fell in step beside her as they brought up the rear.

"It won't do, princess, to anger our allies."

"You anger them as well," she pointed out.

"Aye, but I'm not a Fae princess." He winked.

"Bampots, all of them," she said, though she took care to keep her voice down. She knew Derron was right but she'd grown tired of their bickering. "Your father's life hangs in the balance and all they can do is fight over which road to take."

He chuckled. "You are quite right. Their sworn oath is keeping them from deserting us. How did you do that? I know you have no magic, so you couldn't have coerced them into it."

Elyne knew he referred to the ancient words they'd given her as they knelt at her feet and kissed her hand. She wasn't entirely sure how she managed that. Truthfully, she was as surprised as he was but she didn't want to let him know that. She flashed a bright smile, fluttering her lashes and lifted one shoulder in a coy half shrug.

"I'm sure it was because I'm so charming."

This made him laugh out loud, showing off his deep dimples on either side of his kissable mouth. It sent her stomach plummeting to her shoes to see the joy in his face. Something he hadn't had in far too long. As least since his last joust in the human realm when he nearly died…twice.

Derron slid an arm around her shoulders and pulled her close as they walked. She stumbled, falling into him a lot closer than he probably intended. She could feel the warmth of him pressing through to her skin, delighting every sense she had. Her pulse quickened as he leaned toward her and kissed her on the cheek. Disappointment quickly followed when that was all she got. A sisterly peck.

"You are truly delightful, your highness," Derron said.

"I wish you wouldn't call me that." Irritation clawed through her. Mostly because he didn't take her in his arms and kiss her thoroughly. As though she were the last Fae woman worth kissing.

"Why not? Isn't that your rightful title?"

"It is, but it's unnecessary for you to continue to use 'your highness'."

"You don't seem to mind when the others call you that." Before she could answer, he asked, "Would you prefer 'princess', then?"

"No." She pouted, clenching her jaw tight and trying not to pucker her lips. Still, she was incensed. And he still held her so close she could feel his pulsing heart. Or maybe that was her imagination.

"'Your worship'?"

Now he was teasing her. She flushed to the tips of her ears, her face burning hot.

"Not that either, I gather. How about 'your grace'? I suppose I could bend the rules of address this once and call you that. Would that do?"

"No." She punched him in the ribs to get away but he still held fast. "Let me go."

He stopped walking so suddenly she stumbled again. This time he turned to her, grasped her arms and pulled her close. So close, her hands rested on his chest and she knew for certain she could feel his heart pounding through his tunic. Their eyes locked, his searching hers. Heat flooded her. Something she'd not known…well, ever. And especially for Derron.

It had been much too long since he'd looked at her like that. Ages, in fact. When he had tried to court her and all she wanted to do was run away from him. She'd wanted nothing to do with him. She had been such a fool to reject him. And why had she? She thought she hadn't been in love with him. How wrong she was.

"Elyne, then. How about I call you Elyne?"

She liked the way her name sounded on his tongue. Oh, he'd said it before. But usually with *princess* attached to it. Rarely her name. And never looking at her like that.

Her gaze focused on his lips, perfect for kissing. The deep-set dimples on either side. The scruffy blond whiskers shadowing his jaw and cheeks. Neither of them wore their glamour here in the Otherworld to hide their true Fae features. His ears were tipped like hers, his blond hair fell over his forehead in thick waves and she longed to run her fingers through the silken strands.

"You may call me Elyne."

His gaze landed on her lips, paused, and then lifted back to hers. He wanted to kiss her but he was afraid. Mayhap as afraid as she was for him to kiss her. That would mean they had deep feelings for each other and since they'd made such a mess of things with the broken betrothal, she wasn't sure where that would leave them.

"Then 'tis what I'll call ye."

She blinked in surprise as he released her and resumed walking. For that brief moment, his lilt came out so clear it took her aback. In fact, she couldn't recall ever hearing it. He masked it so well.

"Are you coming, Elyne?" he called over his shoulder.

Elyne fell in step beside him. "Shouldn't I be armed as well?" She steered the conversation as far from the two of them as possible. She didn't want to acknowledge the desire Derron had managed to stir inside her. All she wanted to do was ignore it.

"You? Armed? Why?"

"All of you are armed," she said. "You have a sword and a dagger. And I have no magic."

"Fear not, dear prin—Elyne. I promise to keep thee safe."

She scowled at him. *Mocking me again.* "Are you denying me a weapon?"

"Can you shoot a bow?" he asked, giving her a sideways glance. Even though he tried to keep his face passive, she could see the underlying smirk.

"Nay."

"Wield a sword?"

"Nay."

Derron chuckled. "Then, pray tell, what sort of weapon do you wish for?"

She'd never laid her hands on a weapon before but it seemed silly to be traipsing through the Woodlands Forest with nothing but her wits. She would feel much better if she had something within reach. Mayhap some sort of blade she could keep on her person. Something that could replace the fact she had no magic. She may as well be running around naked.

She looked over Derron, noticed the sheath tied to his thigh and knew that's what she wanted.

"A dagger." Aye, that would make her feel better to have one. "I know how to use that."

"A dagger?" He splayed his fingers. "You have any ideas on where to get one? I don't see Thuluke's Weapons Shoppe here."

Her gaze landed once again on his dagger. He put a possessive hand on it. "You want mine. Of course, you do."

"You could spare the dagger."

"I could, couldn't I?" Smiling, Derron unsheathed his dagger and handed it to her. "I expect you to take good care of that. It was a gift from my father."

"It will be safe with me." She ran her finger along the pearl hilt, admiring the iridescent colors dancing along it.

"Have any idea how to use it?"

Elyne blinked. "Not exactly."

Grinning, he stepped behind her, wrapped his long fingers around her thin wrist. "Allow me to demonstrate."

Derron's body pressed against her back, molding to her easily. With her wrist in his hand, the delicious warm skin pressing hers, it was difficult for her to concentrate on his words.

"Thrust like this." He pulled her arm back and then pushed it forward. "Aim for the heart. If you miss that, then the neck." Heated breath cascaded over her nape. His woodsy scent filled her nose.

"Why?" she asked.

"Best way to kill a man, princess. How does it feel?"

Splendid. Though she was certain he meant the dagger in her hand. "It feels like a dagger."

He chuckled and released her. "You'll need this, too." He untied the sheath from his thigh. "But a lady, nay a *princess*, shouldn't keep that in plain sight."

"Why not?"

"She is more lethal with a hidden weapon."

A mischievous light twinkled in his eyes, making her heart do a quick *ka-thunk* in her chest. Derron knelt at her feet, his gaze still on hers. When his hand went up her skirt and rested on her calf, she nearly came undone. Slowly, he slid his hand along her leg, pushing up her skirt to reveal an expanse of creamy white skin. Her heart throbbed, pounding wildly in her chest and ears. Her breath caught in her throat.

Elyne watched as he tied the sheath to her thigh in the same manner. She'd swear she could still feel the warmth of his skin on it as he secured it in place.

"There. The dagger?" He held his hand up for it.

She placed the pearl hilt in his palm and he deftly slid it into the sheath. All the while keeping his hands in constant contact with her leg.

"That should do it." Derron rose to his full height.

He had two inches on her, his hair brushing his forehead as he gave her a wicked smile. He knew what he was doing and he liked doing it. She liked him doing it. Why did he touch her so intimately when they'd been at odds for so long? He'd gone to the court to have their betrothal broken and now this?

"Feel better, princess?"

"I—"

But that was as far as she got when an arrow went zooming between them and buried in the ancient oak beside her head. Derron immediately went into action. Grabbing her, he pulled her to him and dove to the ground, landing with a muffled *oof* with her on top of him. She could hear the Elf rangers shouting, but they spoke in Elvish and she couldn't understand what they said.

Eldrin had his bow at the ready and fired off shot after shot to the unseen attacker in the woods. And then he held up one hand and shouted, "Hold your fire!"

Derron stood and helped Elyne to her feet. Firdaras and Kerhar hauled a young woman out from behind a bush and dragged her toward Eldrin.

"We found our attacker, Lord Eldrin," Firdaras said, nodding to the girl.

"Allanna," Eldrin said on an exasperated sigh. "Why did you fire on us?"

"I had to get your attention somehow," she said, her eyes flashing.

"What are you doing here?"

She was short and petite, her hair the color of gold and worn long, hanging over her shoulders and down her back. She didn't wear the traditional garb of a female Elf. She wore pants, soft suede boots that laced to the knee, a black tunic and cloak with the familiar Elven triskelion clasp. She held her bow in one hand, a quiver of arrows across her body. Her face looked as though it had been carved from porcelain, so smooth and perfect were her features. She had wide bright-blue eyes, a small thin nose, high cheekbones and thin pink lips.

"I want to come with you," she said, gazing intently at Derron.

"Are you mad?" Eldrin asked. "You can't come with us. Go home where you belong."

"But *she's* coming." She nodded toward Elyne, her voice full of jealousy. "Why can't I go?"

"She is the crown princess of the Fae. You are but a *child*. You have no business here."

"But I can fight. I can shoot a bow and arrow better than some of these rangers." Her face scrunched in anger as she glanced between Firdaras and Kerhar. "And I know how to fight with a sword. Can't I go? I know you're going to kill the Dark King. I want to come. I want to help. I want to kill the king."

Eldrin sighed again. "You can't help, sister. Now go home. I don't have time to take you back. Father will be wondering where you are."

"Father wants me to dress like a girl and learn to dance and sew. I want to be a ranger like you. Please, Eldrin. Please let me come along. I can help you."

"Dancing and sewing is what you should be doing." Eldrin's face turned a pale shade of red as he held his temper. "And there's nothing you can do to help us."

"You know there is, Eldrin. You're being stubborn. You know I have the—"

"Enough," Eldrin snapped, cutting her off.

She clamped her mouth shut. Her lips pressed together in a long, thin line.

"You can't come. I don't want to worry about you, too," Eldrin said.

"But you're all in danger."

"Aye, from the Dark Elf," Eldrin agreed. "All the more reason you stay here."

Elyne decided to step in. The girl seemed harmless enough. "I don't see what the problem is. Why don't you let her come along? You can hold me responsible for her well-being."

"Princess, we already have enough liabilities," Derron said.

She narrowed her eyes at him. "You mean *me*. I'm a liability?"

He quickly backpedaled. "No, no. We have a large party already. Adding another will slow us down that much more."

Allanna's youthful face fell into a pout. Elyne propped her hands on her hips, her brows raised. "Are you saying that, as a girl, she would slow us down, Sir Derron? And if that's true, then does that mean I slow you down as well?"

He flushed and swallowed hard.

Eldrin huffed out a breath. "All right, Allanna, you can come along. Odds are you'll follow us anyway even if I send you home."

Allanna smiled wide. "You know me so well, brother."

He sighed, resigned. "If anything happens to you, Father will have my head."

"It's not me you have to worry about. I'll be all right. You'll see. Nothing will happen to me."

"Aye, I'm sure you will."

Chapter 6

The journey through the Woodlands Forest and to the Banríon Road seemed longer than a day. By midafternoon, they were all weary from walking. Allanna had taken up her place next to Derron. Elyne didn't mistake the adoring looks she gave him. The way she fluttered her long eyelashes up at him.

"What is the Queen's Palace like?" she asked. "I've always wanted to see it."

"I'd gather it's not much different than your father's palace," Derron said.

She scowled. "My father's palace is built in the trees. Not at all like the castle built of stone with all the high turrets. Won't you tell me about it? Are there many servants? Is there music?"

"Mayhap you should consult with Princess Elyne," Derron said, nodding in her direction. "She knows all about life at court."

Allanna gave her a sideways glance before turning her attention back to Derron. Clearly, she was uninterested in conversing with Elyne. "Don't you? You're Knight of the Realm and Protector of the Otherworld."

"He may be those things," Elyne interjected, hurrying to catch up to them, "but he spends a fair amount of time away from court."

A flicker of annoyance crossed her youthful face before she decided Elyne's information was interesting enough to warrant a response. She directed her next question to Derron. "Are you chasing dragons?"

He laughed. "Dragons? I'm afraid those have been long lost to the shadows, my young friend."

"Queen Maeve put them to sleep there long ago," Elyne said. "Even before my time."

"That's not true," Allanna said. "They still fly the night skies."

"Allanna, enough." Now Eldrin joined them, the agitation clearly marring his face. "You know those are nothing more than falsehoods. Forgive her, Sir Derron. My sister has quite a fanciful imagination."

"I do not." She pouted. "I saw them."

Elyne came to an abrupt halt. "You've seen them?"

"Aye, I have. A large black one with red eyes and sharp, white teeth."

"As I said, my sister has a fanciful imagination." He snagged her by the arm and tried to pull her away but Allanna remained rooted in place, refusing to move. They glared at each other, each not wanting to give in to the other.

Elyne exchanged a glance with Derron, her blood running cold. She'd heard the tales of the great onyx dragon. The one that had nearly destroyed the Otherworld before the queen banished it to the shadows. Could it be Lord Kieran disturbed the dragon's slumber and awoke it from the shadows? If so, that would not bode well for them, especially on the brink of war.

"Derron…"

"We have no proof," he said quickly. "Merely her word."

"I saw it!" The young Elven girl pulled her arm from her brother and stepped toward Derron, both hands in fists.

"Allanna—"

"No, Eldrin. It was flying in the night sky. *I saw it.*"

"When?" he challenged.

"A few nights ago." She flushed.

"You were locked out again, weren't you?" he asked, the anger evident in his face. The tips of his ears turned pink.

She turned her attention to her wringing hands. "I…I went exploring. I didn't make it back in time before the gates were locked. Don't tell Father!"

"You left the boundary of the Woodlands?" He growled, a guttural sound deep in his throat. "We will stop here for a short rest before pressing on. You will come with me, Allanna, so we can discuss why you shouldn't be leaving the confines of the palace."

As Eldrin led away his younger sister, Elyne couldn't help but worry about what she'd said. "Do you think it's true, Derron?" she asked.

"I can't say. I'm not going to disbelieve her, though, until we know for certain."

"How will we get proof Kieran has the dragon?"

"I don't know, Elyne, but I think anything is possible." He

picked up a water skin and headed toward the nearby spring. He gave a nod for her to follow. "However, there was mention of awakening of the shadows when I attended the Council."

"But how? How could he? He has no magic powerful enough to break my mother's spell."

"That, my princess, is the big question. Isn't it? He must have someone working with him. Which also means we've underestimated him. He's more powerful than we thought."

And if that were true, then there would be no stopping him. A shiver went up her spine, leaving her cold.

"What are we going to do?" she asked.

"We'll have to get to the Barrier sooner than later," he said. "But with this big party, it will take longer to get there than I had hoped."

"I shouldn't have come." She fixed her gaze on the ground. "And I shouldn't have offered to vouch for Allanna either."

"No," he said quickly and stopped walking. He turned to her, tilted her chin up and forced her to look at him. "Eldrin is right. A girl that headstrong would have followed us. I'm glad you're here. You understand our situation." As he said this, he glanced toward the group of Elven rangers.

She understood. He meant she was the only one of his kind. Not that the Elves didn't get it, but they had no love for the Fae, as the Fae had no love for the Elves. One thing they could all agree upon was Lord Kieran had no place in the Seelie realm.

"I worry for your safety, though, Elyne. Yours and now Allanna's. If anything should happen—"

She put two fingers on his lips to silence him. "Nothing will happen to us. Not with you here."

"I hope you're right."

"I'm always right, Sir Derron. You should accept that by now." He grinned as she kissed him on the cheek. "Come on. Let's go find that fresh water."

At nightfall, they had found a tavern and an inn along the edge of town with plenty of room for them all. The adoring looks Allanna gave Derron irritated Elyne, chafing her already raw nerves. After their bow and arrow lesson, the young Elven girl had rarely left his side, taking up permanent residence next to him and chattering senselessly.

"It's your punishment for taking responsibility for the she-elf," Elyne had whispered. Derron let out a soft groan of annoyance.

But as the sun drifted toward the horizon and night fell across the Otherworld turning the pale-pink sky black, the rangers and Fae made it to the Rocking Horse Inn.

"Elves and Fae traveling together?" The innkeeper looked them all over with a critical eye.

"Do you have room enough for all of us?" Derron asked, not bothering to explain their situation. He waved toward the group.

"Oh, aye, I do, if ye are willing to share. I'll put the ladies in a separate room together."

"That won't be necessary," Elyne said.

"Perfect," Derron said, ignoring her. "Could we trouble you for ale and mayhap some food? We'll pay, of course."

She shot him a look. The last thing she wanted to do was share a room with the young Elven female who'd been batting her eyelashes at Derron since the moment she'd joined them. Mayhap, though, it would be a good opportunity to set the girl straight on that account. Derron belonged to no one. And if he *did*, it would certainly be Elyne.

"Aye, o'course. Make yeselves at home in the tavern. My lady-wife will be along shortly to serve ye."

Travel weary, they all headed into the tavern where long, well-worn tables and benches were placed in front of a roaring fire that heated the entire room. Elyne kept close to Derron as they sat. A moment later, an oversized woman bustled into the room. She served ale and mead and promised to return minutes later with the beef stew she'd been cooking all day.

"Sharing a room with that girl is the last thing I wanted to do," Elyne whispered into Derron's ear.

"Aye, princess, I know. But you can't very well be sharing with me, now, can you?"

"And why not?" She noted he called her princess again. Mayhap old habits were hard to break. She tried not to let it bother her.

"We are not betrothed."

Hearing that was like a knife to the heart. She all but winced, looking away from him and staring into the dark ale in front of her. She could have pointed out they were once betrothed but that was in the past and done. Now they were nothing to each other but sometimes friends. And even then, she wasn't sure that's what they were. True, he had released her from the prison but that wasn't indicative he had any remote feelings for her.

Elyne sighed, resigned to the truth. "I still don't like it."

"You shared a tent with Maggie at the tournament," he pointed out.

"That was different. I *liked* Maggie." And she missed her. Something she didn't really want to admit either. She missed her friend and Finn. And the hustle and bustle of the week-long tournament that had pulled them all together.

Derron chuckled. "Maggie grew on you."

Elyne didn't want to admit that either. Why was he pointing out all these painful things to her? Was he punishing her for some reason?

The innkeeper's lady-wife returned with bread bowls full of thick beef stew and placed them in front of everyone. Despite her hunger, Elyne wasn't interested in sitting with Derron and the rest of the Elves. The room seemed stifling and constricting. She needed to get away from them. She needed some air, even though she'd been out in the air all day long. She rose, stepping over the bench.

"Where are you going?" Derron asked, looking up at her.

"I'm not hungry anymore."

She headed from the tavern and stepped outside. Nearby, she heard the whinny of a horse. The stable was to the left of the inn and she decided she could stand to spend some time with something that didn't talk back. She found three horses in the stable. One whickered as she approached and picked up a brush. She swept her hand down the mare's black mane.

"Bet you don't have any trouble with men, do you?" Elyne asked.

The mare snorted, bobbing her head once.

"That's what I thought. Lucky girl."

The rhythm of brushing the horse's neck was calming. Almost therapeutic.

"Who needs them anyway? They are more trouble than they're worth."

"Elyne?"

She jumped at the sound of Derron's voice and looked back

over her shoulder at him. "Why aren't you with the others?"

"Why aren't you?" he asked. "I came to check on you."

"You don't need to check on me. I'm fine." Though, in truth, she really wasn't. He'd hurt her even though he hadn't meant to.

"Was it something I said?"

Why did he persist in making her talk to him? "Not at all." She wouldn't look at him. Just kept brushing.

"I think it was. I didn't know you missed Maggie so much."

The horse snorted, as though reading Elyne's thoughts. "It has nothing to do with Maggie. I needed some air. That's all." She needed to get away from him. Couldn't he see that?

"You've never been good at hiding your emotions from me, Elyne."

His voice was dangerously close. She knew he stood right behind her. She continued to brush, her hand making a long, sweeping motion along the mare's neck.

"Is this about the betrothal?"

She would rather die than admit to him that's what hurt her so much. She forced out a laugh. A pathetic attempt at one. "Don't be foolish, Derron. Our betrothal has been broken for quite some time. I'm at peace with that."

"Nay, I don't believe you are."

His hands landed on hers, halting her. He took away the brush, set it aside and then turned her to face him. She didn't want to look at him. Didn't want to feel anything for him. She tried to convince herself he'd destroyed that when their promise of marriage was broken. He cupped her chin, tilted her head up so she had to meet his gaze. A scorching gaze that seemed to say he wanted her.

"I thought that's what you wanted," he said.

"*You* wanted it. You intended to carry Maggie off to the Otherworld. Remember?"

And all the other fair maidens who flung themselves at him. She recalled with great detail how they offered their favors to him, waving opaque champagne-colored cloth at him, begging him to choose them. He always had one or two ladies fair at the tournaments.

"Aye, I recall that. An apparent lapse in judgment. I must have been drinking too much mead. Finn would have never allowed it anyway." His grin showed off both dimples. Dimples that made him famous and melted the knees of many a lady.

"Things had already been set into motion, Derron. You didn't really want to marry me. As I didn't want to marry you." That may have been true at one time, but now she wasn't so sure. If her mother reinstated their betrothal, she would accept it without complaint.

"Is that true, then?" he asked.

"You know it is."

"Then you would feel nothing if I kissed you?" A dangerous gleam ignited in his eyes. Elyne could see the beginnings of a faint smile. A teasing smile.

A curious swooping pulled at her stomach. "That's right. I'd feel nothing."

"Mayhap I should test that theory," he suggested. He leaned dangerously close to her, his lips a breath from hers.

Her mind screamed no, but her mouth said, "Mayhap you should."

Derron cupped her face, his hands warm and gentle. When his mouth connected with hers, her stomach turned into a roaring fire, exploding through her in a burst of heat and flame. Singeing her from the inside out. His lips were like velvet as they lingered on hers, tasting her, sipping her like honey wine. Her head fell back and her body went limp as he pulled her into his arms. She didn't fight him. She couldn't. Her arms slipped around his neck as he deepened the kiss, his tongue delving into the recesses of her mouth. She sighed, their breath exchanging as their souls touched.

Never in their long history had he kissed her. She wanted it to last forever. She wanted him to proclaim his love for her then and there. She just wanted him.

Sir Derron. Protector of the Otherworld. Knight of her heart.

The thought startled her so suddenly she broke away from him, stepping out of his arms and as far away as she could get. Her lips were still damp. Her heart still throbbed from wanting.

They stared at each other a long moment, his lips parted, his chest rising and falling with quick breaths. It had affected him, too. His face even looked a bit flushed. He broke their gaze and raked a hand through his hair.

And then he smiled. As though the kiss hadn't affected him.

"Did it prove your theory, then? Did you, in fact, feel nothing?"

How dare he ask her that when he knew otherwise? She held her head high, giving him her best snootiness. "I felt nothing."

Even as she said it, her heart panged with longing. Longing turned to guilt when his smile faded. He had wanted her to tell the truth. He wanted to know he affected her deeply. Why the lie? Why couldn't she tell him how she felt when she knew he wanted to hear it? Because he'd hurt her. He'd shredded her heart when he petitioned the court to break their betrothal. He had destroyed hope for a future.

"Very well, princess. We have a long journey ahead and an early morning. I bid thee good night."

He left the stable. With his every step, her heart wept a little harder. She had lost him once again.

Chapter 7

Elyne spent the next several hours with the horses. By the time she left the stable, the night was cold and still. The moon shone brightly down from the inky blackness. She paused, gazing up at it. If she hadn't been standing there, she wouldn't have seen the large black shadow move across the sky.

She stood perfectly still, watching it as her breath plumed in the air. She couldn't stop the shiver that racked her body as she realized it was no shadow. It was a dragon.

A great black dragon. The very one Allanna had mentioned earlier that day and insisted she'd seen. She hadn't been telling a story. She had been telling the truth.

The beast glided, its wingspan so large it didn't need to flap them but every so often. Its head turned, the red eyes locking on her for a brief moment. A scream caught in her throat. But the dragon continued its flight over her, past the inn and back toward the direction they had come earlier that day.

Elyne gasped as she realized where the dragon was headed.

The palace. The darkness had been released.

She had to warn them and bolted into a run, her legs pumping hard as she burst into the inn, the door cracking against the wall as it flung open. She pounded up the stairs and paused. Which room was Derron's? She didn't know. Standing on the landing, trying to catch her breath, she considered opening each and every door until she found him.

She didn't have to. A door flew open and he stepped out, sword in hand ready to fight. He relaxed when he saw her.

"Elyne, what are you—"

"A dragon is flying toward the palace."

"What?"

"A dragon. A great black dragon, Derron. It's headed to the palace now. I have to get back to my mother. I have to go!"

"Hold on a minute."

By now, the Elven rangers had poked their heads out their doors to see what the commotion was. Even the young female Elf wandered into the hallway, yawning. Derron gripped Elyne by the shoulders to calm her. It took sheer strength of will not to fall into his arms.

"I *saw* it, Derron. My mother is in danger. The entire palace is in danger."

"Even if we left now, we would never make it in time," Eldrin said. He stepped up next to Derron. "The palace is more than a day's walk from here."

"Then I need a horse. There are some in the stable. Let me go." She tried to break free but Derron held her fast.

"I won't let you go alone. If the dragon is flying toward the palace, then it's already too late. Lord Kieran has surely released other creatures from the shadows and unleashed them," Derron said.

"I don't care. I have to go back. My mother—"

"Has her entire Queen's Guard as well as the High Council. She'll be fine." His hands tightened on her shoulders to press his point.

"No." She couldn't stop the tears watering her eyes. Or the emotions bubbling up through her. There was nothing she could to do help. If the palace fell under attack, she would likely be killed or taken prisoner, too.

"What's all this?" The innkeeper stood at the bottom of the stairs and shouted up at them. "What's all the commotion?"

"Someone left the door open." This from the innkeeper's wife who was out of view but behind the portly man.

"Nothing," Derron called back. "Everything is all right. Everyone back to bed."

"Everything *isn't* all right, Derron, and you know it." Anger flamed deep in the pit of her stomach, burning through her.

"Shh."

"Do not fecking shush me." She ground the words out through her teeth.

The Elves wandered back to their rooms, doors shutting quietly and leaving them in the hall.

Derron slid his arm around her shoulders, pulling her along toward his room. The bitter taste of fear was in the back of her throat as she forced one foot in front of the other. Despite knowing Derron and Eldrin were right, she didn't want to accept that as the truth. She and Maeve had never really gotten along but she hadn't wanted anything to happen to her. She thought her mother would always be queen, ruling the Otherworld as she always did. It had never occurred to her Maeve might not sit on the throne one day.

Derron led her into his room, shut the door and then held her. He still grasped the sword in one hand while he hugged her to him, his woodsy scent from the afternoon wafting over her. She hadn't noticed it before when they'd kissed. She was too busy focusing on his mouth on hers. But now she took comfort in it, inhaled his scent as she closed her eyes and imagined a different world that didn't include Lord Kieran or the threat of her mother's murder or…war.

"I have to know if she's all right, Derron."

"If we go back now, we will lose more time getting to the Dark Realm."

Anger swelled through her, shattering her momentary peace. "My mother for your father?" She pulled out of his grasp and gave him a shove. "Is that how it is?"

"No, of course not, Elyne. But the Queen's Palace is well protected and so is Queen Maeve. If the Council thinks she's in danger, they'll take her to a safe place. You know this as well as I."

She crossed her arms over her chest. She knew Derron was right, but she was still stubborn enough to argue with him. "What if they can't get to her in time? What if something happens to the entire Council? Then what, Derron? The whole of the Otherworld is…" She paused, her breath hitching. "In my hands."

By the gods, she would rule then.

He tossed the sword to the ground with a clatter, and then gripped her by the shoulders. "Nothing is going to happen to her. Do you hear me?"

"You can't be certain of that."

Her bottom lip quivered. Her eyes burned hot with tears. She didn't want to cry in front of him. It would show her weakness and her fear, things she would be forced to face. She was terrified of ruling the Otherworld, which was the last thing she wanted to ever admit.

"No, but I can be certain that one dragon does not a war make."

He had a point. She'd seen one dragon. She hadn't seen anything or anyone else. But that didn't mean the Unseelie weren't on their way. If Lord Kieran had raised one of them, there had to be more. There *would* be more.

"I'll send one of the Elf rangers to find out what's happened. Would that make you feel better?"

It was his way of appeasing her. Reluctantly, she nodded. "Aye, it would."

"Good. Now, why don't you get some rest? We leave at daybreak."

She hugged her elbows. "I'm not going to share a room with that elf-child."

"Then stay here with me."

He suggested it so casually she blinked as though she hadn't heard him right. It was the last thing she expected to hear. She stared at him, the blood rushing out of her head so quickly she thought she might faint. She glanced at the narrow bed with the straw mattress.

"I'll sleep on the floor."

He bent to pick up his discarded sword and re-sheathed it. Then settled down with his back against the opposite wall, his feet crossed at the ankles, and closed his eyes. "Good night, princess."

Elyne slipped under the scratchy cloth blanket. She feared sleep wouldn't come after all the stress of the day but her eyes drifted closed and soon she was fast asleep.

The first twitter of birds woke her. She blinked her eyes open, acutely aware of the warmth behind her. That wasn't the thin blanket she'd curled up under. In fact, it was much like the hard curves of a man. The soft snoring in her ear gave it away, too.

When had Derron climbed onto the narrow bed with her? She certainly couldn't recall that. His arm was draped over her as he spooned her. He stirred behind her.

"Good morrow, princess."

Elyne shoved his arm off and sat up, tugging her fingers through her tangled hair. She scooted to the end of the bed.

"What are you doing there?" She stumbled as she tried to get off the bed, her feet tangling in the blanket.

"I got cold. Didn't think you'd mind." He stretched and yawned.

She turned to look at him and noticed that at some point, he'd shed his tunic. She had seen him shirtless once—in the hospital tent at tournament when he'd been injured and Seamus had come to cure him. His chest was sprinkled with dark hair and a line trailed down his perfectly carved abs. His biceps curved into thick muscles. He'd managed to keep himself toned during all those jousting tournaments he loved so much. The image sent her senses reeling.

She struggled to get out of bed when he snatched her and pulled her back down, hovering over her.

"What's your hurry, princess?" He gave her a devastating grin.

It unnerved her to have him so close, especially after that searing kiss they'd shared hours before in the stable. His body was warm, his hot skin pressing against her, burning through her gown.

"I thought you were going to dispatch one of the rangers back to the palace."

"Aye, I already did. After you fell asleep last night."

"You did?"

"Mm-hm."

His lips brushed hers, teasing. Toying. She hadn't even known he'd left her.

"He sent his fastest rider. He borrowed one of the stabled horses and sent Aranion. The ranger should be arriving at the palace any time now."

"Why didn't you tell me?" It was hard to concentrate when he nuzzled her neck, placing long, slow kisses on her skin.

"Because I know you. You would have tried to go yourself. I could never allow you to travel back to the palace alone with the threat of war looming. What if something happened to you?"

"I…could have taken one of the Elves." Her eyes fluttered closed, her heart throbbing an erratic beat.

"I think not."

Heat pressed all around her, into her. Warmth spread from the center of her core outward as Derron continued to slay her with his kisses. His hand moved from her shoulder over her breast, caressing her there. Her cheeks flushed hot, and she knew she should push him away. Stop him. But she enjoyed his hand there far too much.

He continued to kiss her, nibbled her earlobe. When his hand moved lower, she flinched. This time she did shove him away and scrambled out of bed away from him and stood, her back to him. It took several deep breaths to get her pulse under control.

She'd spent so much time pining for him and wanting moments like that and now she didn't know how to handle them. How could she tell him she had never been with anyone? She was too ashamed to admit it. That and she was far too worried about her mother's well-being to enjoy any sort of pleasure. She flushed again, her cheeks burning hot. She couldn't let him see her like this.

"Something wrong?" he asked. She didn't mistake the twinge of hurt in his voice.

"No, I…we haven't time for that. We should go."

Behind her, she could hear the rustle of material. She didn't want to turn around and see him half naked again. It would send her over the edge. Once he was properly dressed, his sword strapped to his side, he opened the door. Silence settled between them, the tension now thick. He wouldn't look at her. Probably because she'd wounded his male ego.

She followed him out of the room and down the stairs to the common area. There were several of the Elves, including Eldrin, already there, breaking their fast on thick slices of brown bread and tankards of mead and ale. Elyne could smell some animal roasting on the open fire and her stomach rumbled in response.

"Princess, we have a long journey ahead. Why don't you ask the innkeeper's wife for provisions? We'll pay for them, of course," Derron said.

"You're giving me something to do so I'll stay out of the way. Aren't you?" she asked, her hands on her hips.

"'Twas that obvious, aye?"

Rolling her eyes, she made for the kitchens to speak to the owner's wife. Derron clearly wanted her as far from him as possible. She had definitely injured his ego. Now it would be more work to soothe it. With a huff, she stomped toward the kitchen.

Queen Maeve paced the length of her private chamber, her hands fisted. She awaited word of the other Guardians, hoping they were all right. The message the dragon brought the night before was a warning from Lord Kieran. She knew that. But she hadn't expected the warning to be so gruesome. Lord Malcolm, Guardian of the Sword of Light, was dead.

They were lucky, though. The dragon could have attacked.

They had braced for a full-blown war. But the messenger merely dropped the basket moments before the dragon turned and winged away, leaving everyone perplexed as to the arrival. Until they looked in the basket.

She'd lost track of time now. For all she knew it could be morning. She'd been unable to sleep. Unable to rest or quiet her mind. Fear had been something she hadn't experienced in a long while. Fear for her kingdom and her people. Fear that the Unseelie had found a way to truly come into her realm and destroy everything she'd guarded for the last six thousand years. Everything she'd sworn to her dying husband King Adhamh that she would defend and protect.

Gawaine had sent his messengers. She'd told him not to return until he had news from all three Guardians. Whether they were alive or dead, she needed to know. He had complied and left her, though she wasn't truly alone. The guards flanked the doors outside her chamber. She was to be escorted around the palace at all times. Even guarded with men at her bedside while she slept.

How would she get the message to Derron? For that matter, how would he take the news? He would be devastated, of course. And she would have to make him a lord in addition to knight. Knight of the Realm and Protector of the Otherworld…now Guardian of the Sword of Light. Lord Derron. It disturbed her greatly she would have to present this news to him and soon, for she preferred to tell him herself. She didn't want to send it with one of her men. It seemed too impersonal. His quest to find his father would be halted.

And yet the Sword was still missing, in the hands of the barbarian. She despised asking him to change his quest to seeking the Sword of Light, but she had no one else she trusted to send.

The door to her chamber banged open suddenly, startling her. She jumped, her heart palpitating a quick tattoo. Several men swarmed through the door, making her step backward away from them. Two guards flanked a man—no, an Elf—followed by Gawaine, who had a stern look on his face.

The Elf wore riding clothes—soft pants, boots, tunic, vest and cloak. He carried an empty quiver. She assumed her men confiscated the bow and arrows when he arrived. He must have struggled for he had one red eye, threatening to turn black as it swelled.

"My queen, forgive the intrusion," Gawaine said and bowed. "This Elven ranger was captured trying to get into the palace."

"I was sent by Sir Derron," he spat as he struggled against the guards who restrained him.

"Don't believe him, your majesty. Sir Derron would never ride with an Elf," Gawaine put in. He cast a disgusted sidelong glance his direction.

"He would and he is. Ten of us, all Elven rangers, have agreed to help him find his father in the Dark Realm. We pledged our fealty to Princess Elyne by swearing the ancient oath to her."

"Princess Elyne?" Maeve repeated, shock rolling through her. "That's preposterous. She's in the Fae prison."

"Nay, your majesty," the Elf said. "She travels with Sir Derron. She worried for your safety when she saw the dragon fly toward the palace last eve and requested I come to make sure all was well."

Silence lingered between them as the queen stared at the Elven ranger. Elyne had broken out of the prison? How? When? And why hadn't she known about it? It had been heavily warded and heavily guarded. If she had somehow managed to slip out, she surely would have known. Unless… Did Derron have something to do with it? She couldn't understand how he would know how to get past all the wards. Getting past the guards would be easy for him. He was a smooth talker and could get them to do his bidding. Mayhap he was more persuasive than she gave him credit.

"Release him," she ordered.

Gawaine didn't bother to hide his astonishment. "My queen, is that so wise—"

"I said release him. Now."

The guards let him go. The Elf smoothed his hands down the front of his tunic. "Many thanks, your majesty."

"Gawaine, go check the prison. I want to know if what…" She paused. "What is your name?"

"Aranion," he said.

"I want to know if what Aranion tells me about my daughter is true."

"Your majesty—"

"Go. Now." She dismissed Gawaine with a flick of her wrist. His face flushed red as he left her private chamber. "Guards, leave us. I wish to speak with Aranion alone."

They both hesitated, clearly not wanting to leave her alone with an Elf. She was aware of the hatred that had long stood between the two races. And yet they'd pledged an ancient oath to her daughter. She needed to know more.

"Remain outside the door if it will make you feel better," she said.

They shuffled out, closing the door with a snap behind them. Queen Maeve poured two tankards of wine and handed one to him.

"You travel with Sir Derron and the princess."

It was not a question but he answered it as though it were.

"Aye." He accepted the tankard and took a small sip, as if testing it for poison. To show she meant good faith, she took a long draw from her cup.

"Tell me how this came about."

"Eldrin brought him to us in the Woodlands and asked our help. We'd heard of the slaughter of the Dark King in the Unseelie Court."

"Then even the Elves realize the gravity of our situation," she said. "And you all agreed?"

"Aye, all the rangers agreed to go along with him."

"And the princess?"

"We pledged our swords and bows to help her find Lord Malcolm and the Sword of Light."

"By speaking what oath?" she wanted to know.

"We all knelt at her feet and pledged our arms to her."

Her eyebrows rose. She knew this ancient oath and was surprised the Elves still remembered it. It was an oath that had died long before the Elves and the Fae warred. When Elves and Fae still lived as one in harmony. But what surprised her most was that her daughter knew of this oath and had somehow persuaded them to swear it.

"Why would Elven rangers be interested in helping the Fae?"

"Our leader, Eldrin, requested our help. Should Lord Kieran invade, even our homes will be at risk."

Mayhap all was not lost, then, if even the Elves knew what dangers this uprising in the Dark Realm posed.

"I should like to meet this Eldrin someday. He sounds wise beyond his Elven years." She took another sip before placing the tankard on her desk and perching on the edge. "And my daughter saw the dragon coming toward the palace?"

"Aye. Sir Derron sent me here to make sure all was well."

Mayhap there was hope for her daughter yet and she wasn't quite as selfish as Maeve thought.

"I'm afraid all is not well," she said. "The dragon came with a message from Lord Kieran. A rather gruesome one at that." Pausing, she collected her thoughts as the ranger looked on, waiting for her next words. "I'm afraid I have terrible news for Sir Derron."

"If you have terrible news, then it must have to do with his father."

She nodded. "He's been murdered. Cut into small pieces and brought to me as a warning. There wasn't…much left of him." She swallowed the bile that rose in her throat. "Lord Malcolm is dead."

Speaking the words aloud made her stomach clench. She knew it was true, of course, but she hadn't said it to anyone yet.

"By the gods…" he whispered and closed his eyes as if in silent prayer.

Gawaine returned then, one of the guards opening the door for him. She could see the answer about Elyne's disappearance etched in his face before he even said it.

"The prison is empty, your majesty. Princess Elyne is nowhere to be found and none of the guards know where she is."

"That's because she's with Sir Derron."

Anger rolled through her quickly, followed by relief Elyne was safe. How did she think she could keep Elyne imprisoned? What disappointed her most was Derron had a hand in it. How did he get past the guards and the wards? Though, now that she considered everything that had happened, she shouldn't be surprised. Derron would never have left his beloved in prison. It was unwise to think she could keep them apart.

Fear for her daughter trickled through her. Elyne was with Derron on a dangerous journey. She took small comfort knowing the knight would keep her as safe as he could from harm. In time, the two of them would realize the love they had for each other. It would take more than a Fae prison to keep them apart.

"With Lord Malcolm's death, the guardianship falls to him. I must tell him the news in person and then anoint him the new Guardian." Maeve rose to her full height.

"Surely you jest, your majesty. You cannot think to leave the security of the palace walls to find him somewhere on the road to the Dark Realm," Gawaine said.

"No jest, Gawaine. I'm going. And Aranion is coming with me."

"I simply cannot allow it." He stood in front of the door, blocking it as though keeping her inside. "It's far too dangerous, especially after the message we received."

"It's why I must go to him now," Maeve said. "I intend to sift there."

"I am not comfortable with that, your majesty. Especially with your magic so depleted."

She gave him a cold look. She was quite aware of the state of her magic. She'd used most of it to protect the Barrier from the Queen's Palace. She was also quite aware she weakened with every passing day. It wasn't enough to stop her from sifting.

"I appreciate your concern, Gawaine, but I intend to go anyway. Now tell me, have you received word about the other Guardians?" She changed the subject abruptly but she knew Gawaine would not let it go so easily.

He seemed taken aback by the sudden change. "Not as yet. That's why you must stay here, my queen."

"I won't be gone long," she said and patted his shoulder. "Come along, Aranion. Let us go find my daughter and the future Guardian of the Sword of Light."

Chapter 8

They'd traveled all day on the Banríon Road. Since the Elven ranger hadn't returned from the palace, she hoped it wasn't a sign that he'd been captured or—worse—killed. If she had her magic, she would sift to the palace herself. But under the circumstances, she conjured images of the Elf's demise on the road.

"Don't worry," Derron said, using his most reassuring voice. "I'm sure your mother is fine or we would have heard by now."

That was true. News of the slaughtered queen would have traveled quickly in the Heartlands. But even so, they were in such a remote area, it would take days for the news to reach them. Maybe even weeks.

Derron found another inn and tavern along their route in which they stopped for the night. It was fairly rundown compared to the one they previously left. The two buildings were dilapidated—one looked to have once been a stable with a caved-in roof and the other seemed to be the main building with lamplight dancing in the smudge-covered windows. A grubby sign hung out front but no one could read what the name of it was through all the dirt.

"This doesn't look so welcoming," Derron said.

"Let's keep going," Elyne suggested.

"I'm afraid we can't. We need a roof over our heads, even a rundown one."

"I don't like this."

"Neither do I."

And yet, Derron opened the door and stepped inside the inn. The interior was almost as dirty as the exterior. Cobwebs hung in every corner. Dust caked the floors, tables and chairs. The stench of something dead and rotting permeated the air. A hearth remained unlit and cold. There didn't even seem to be embers glowing there, almost as though the owner never expected visitors.

"Hello?" Derron called.

Somewhere upstairs a door slammed. Heavy footsteps pounded the creaky floor and staircase. A potbellied, balding man appeared at the top of the stairs. He chewed on the stub end of an unlit cigar, his tunic soiled, his breeches tattered from age. He peered down at them before descending the stairs, each step a labor. He paused in front of Derron, looked over the group. He had a scruffy salt-and-pepper beard that would have surely matched his hair if he had any and a squinty gaze that landed on Elyne and lingered there.

Derron took her by the hand and pulled her closer.

"What'd ye want?"

"You have rooms available?" Derron asked.

"What do ye think?" he retorted with a snort.

"I think you have a bad attitude. We require rooms. There are thirteen of us."

"Fifteen gold pieces a night. For each of ya."

"Fifteen?" Elyne asked. "That's highway robbery."

He leered at her. "Fifteen is the going rate, sweetheart. Take it or leave it." He leaned closer to her, the stench of his unwashed body wafting over her. "Or we could take it out in trade."

Derron nudged her aside. "We'll take it for the fifteen a night. I don't have enough coin but I can get it to you."

"If ye don't have enough, then no rooms." He ran his tongue over his lips as he looked at Elyne again. She could see his black stumps for teeth and shuddered with disgust.

"Do you know who we are? I am the crown princess of the Otherworld. Sir Derron is the Knight of the Realm, Protector of the Otherworld. You can be assured we will get your coin for you."

Recognition flickered over his dirty face as he stood a little straighter. "Now that ye mention it, ye *do* resemble the queen." He bowed his head then. "Beggin' ye pardon, yer highness. I meant no disrespect." He wiped his sleazy grin off his face and bowed low.

"If you meant no disrespect, then put your eyes back in your head and wipe the drool off your chin," she snapped. "We'll be taking the rooms now, Mister…what is your name, sir?"

"You may call me Orin, your highness."

"See to the rooms then, Orin. We tire from our journey and are ready to rest."

She waved him away. Orin scuttled back up the stairs.

"Nicely done, princess," Derron said. "Now let's hope the rooms look better than downstairs."

"I highly doubt that, Sir Derron."

She was certain the beds would be full of fleas, the blankets ratty and worn, the windows dirty and the floors covered in dirt. Still, it was better than sleeping outside.

Elyne had been correct in her initial assessment of the rooms. The floors were dusty and the windows covered in grime. However, she was wrong about the beds. Despite their worn appearance, there were no fleas in the straw mattresses. The blankets were a bit scratchy and a little worn, but overall it wasn't as bad as she thought it would be.

Derron knocked on her door before opening it.

"Are you comfortable, princess?"

"In this place? I'd say I'd rather sleep on the floor, but under the circumstances that doesn't seem like a grand idea."

He laughed. "My room isn't much better. My apologies for the accommodations."

She snorted. "It's not your fault. We needed a place for the night. This was better than nothing, I suppose."

A knock sounded on the door, making Elyne jump. She hoped it was the Elven ranger returning with news of her mother. But when Derron opened the door, the hooded figure shoved him aside and entered. Derron immediately drew his sword.

Before he could get out a warning, the melodious voice said, "You wouldn't stab your queen, now would you?" She whisked off her hood to face them both, her shining blonde hair like a halo.

Elyne gasped. Derron sheathed his sword and gave her a deep bow, which was expected of him. But Elyne would be damned if she bowed to the woman who stuck her in that awful prison. Yet she couldn't deny her relief at seeing her mother unharmed.

What was she doing here? How did she find them? And, more importantly, what would Maeve do to her now that she knew she was free?

"Mother." The word came out on a rough whisper. She had intended to make it bold and strong, but sounded like a weakling.

"Hello, my daughter." Her gaze flickered over her from head to toe. Somewhere in those three words, Elyne could hear the unspoken chastising. *My errant daughter who has managed to break the laws of Faery and manage to get out of Fae prison.* Her gaze cut over to Derron, a look of disdain on her fair features. "Did you have anything to do with this?" She wagged a finger at Elyne.

"I'm afraid I don't know what you mean, my queen." He gave her his best innocent look and flashed a grin. If Elyne didn't know any better, she would have believed him.

"Hm." The queen sounded unconvinced. Because she was no fool, she knew better. She would rightly suspect Derron would have rescued her. Even her mother was not unaware of their rocky relationship, but she would know Derron wouldn't leave Elyne there. Elyne waited for her mother's explosion, but it never came. She peered at them with a scowl.

"What are you doing here?" Elyne demanded, unable to stand the silence. All her previous worry for her mother's safety melted away with her sudden unwelcome appearance.

"The Elven ranger you sent arrived yesterday. It seems you saw a dragon coming toward the palace and feared for my safety. How kind of you." Her tone dripped with disdain.

Elyne stiffened. Even now, Maeve could still regard her with contempt. When she'd worried about her safety and how she would continue on in the Otherworld without her. "How did you find us?"

"The Elven ranger you sent, Aranion, helped me locate you. I come with news," the queen said. "I would have sent a messenger, but I thought it would be best coming directly from me."

"It is about my father?"

Elyne could see the color drain from Derron's face. His forehead creased with worry and she knew, as he did, that Queen Maeve would seek him out for one reason.

"The dragon Princess Elyne saw carried a message. I'm very sorry to tell you, Sir Derron, your father has been murdered. I'll spare you the grisly details of this death."

"Tell me," Derron demanded, but Maeve shook her head. "I must know."

She pressed her lips together in a straight line before exhaling a heavy sigh. "He was…cut into several pieces."

Elyne's stomach clenched into a tight knot, the bile rising to her throat at the thought of another Fae—a noble—being slaughtered like that. Derron stood completely still. Not breathing. Not even blinking. Elyne placed a hand on his arm for comfort but he didn't acknowledge her. Didn't even look her way. She prayed to the gods Lord Malcolm had already succumbed to death before that atrocity had been inflicted upon him.

"The Sword?" He forced the words through pale lips.

"Still missing, I'm afraid." It was the first time Elyne had ever heard genuine sorrow with a hint of fear in Maeve's voice.

"Lord Kieran still has it," he said, now through gritted teeth. "I will kill him for it."

"I had no doubt you would, Derron." She paused, as though choosing her words carefully. Her youthful face that belied her ancient age took on a look of grief, her mouth drawing down in a slight grimace. "You know what I must do. Every Treasure must have a Guardian and you are the heir."

"Was. Was the heir."

She closed her eyes briefly and nodded. "Aye, was the heir. I'm truly sorry for your loss." Maeve glanced from him to Elyne and back again. "Why don't I give you a moment?"

It was quite possibly the most sensitive thing her mother had ever done.

Maeve slipped out of the room, closing the door softly behind her.

"Derron…I'm so sorry."

Derron stepped away from her and stood at the grimy window, staring out into the void that was the night. The glass reflected his face back to her and she could see the pain and despair, his normally bright-blue eyes hard and dull. Full of rage and hate and sorrow. But it wasn't the night he saw, Elyne knew.

"I will avenge him, Elyne." His voice sounded strained, hard.

"I know." Hearing his pain clenched her heart. She wished there was something she could do. She knew, all too well, how difficult it was to lose a beloved father.

"Kieran's blood will be on my sword before this war is over."

"I believe you."

He turned to her, his eyes meeting hers. And somewhere in the depths of those pale-blue pools, she thought she saw the mist of tears. He would never allow her to see that deep emotion from him, though. He would mask it and keep it hidden.

"You know what will be asked of me now," he said.

"A lordship and the title of Guardian."

Her nails dug sharply into her palm. In that one moment, their relationship shifted from one of playfulness to one of all seriousness and all business.

He'd lost the life he'd once had. The carefree one where he could go to the human realm whenever he wanted, joust in tournaments and woo the ladies fair. That life was gone now with the death of his father. Now he would have to take a more responsible role and remain in the Otherworld. Now he would become the Guardian of the Sword of Light.

Derron took a deep breath and gave a curt nod. "Tell your mother I'm ready."

Reluctantly, she opened the door to find her mother waiting outside in the drafty hallway. Their eyes met and Maeve gave her a nod and entered the room.

"It seems I've come ill prepared. May I borrow your sword?" she asked. Nodding, Derron unsheathed it and handed it to her, hilt first. "Kneel."

Derron took a knee in front of his queen. She tapped one shoulder then the other as she spoke.

"I, Queen Maeve of the Otherworld, name you, Derron, son of Malcolm, Lord and Guardian of the Sword of Light, Protector of the Otherworld, Knight of the Realm. Henceforth, you shall be called Lord Derron and assume all the responsibilities and duties of each title forthwith. Do you accept these duties and titles?"

"Aye, my queen, I do."

"Rise, Lord Derron." He came to his full height and she handed the sword over to him. She took him by the shoulders and placed a kiss on each cheek. "I wish it could be under better circumstances, my lord."

"Aye, your majesty. As do I."

"Rest, now. In the morn, let us convene your Elven rangers and discuss our next plan of action."

"You're staying?" Elyne interjected. She hadn't meant to sound like a petulant child.

"Aye, my daughter. I'm staying in this dreadful place. I hadn't intended to but under the circumstances, I believe it's necessary for me to stay and discuss our strategy with Lord Derron." She glanced around the room, at the walls and ceiling with a critical eye. "This ramshackle building can barely be called an inn." She shuddered. "I'm going to talk to the owner and see what can be done about it."

She whisked open the door, leaving behind the scent of jasmine and a flutter of her fur-lined cloak. Derron and Elyne stood side by side, watching her go. His fingers laced with hers.

"Stay with me tonight," he said.

She knew he wouldn't want to be alone and even though they wouldn't discuss the death of his father, it would weigh heavily on his mind. She turned toward him, slipped her arms around his neck. "Of course."

He kissed her, his warm lips meshing with hers with a bit of passion. She hadn't expected that and it momentarily took her aback. But she couldn't deny him. Not when he needed her. She could taste the hint of ale on his tongue from their pitiful supper earlier that night.

When he broke from her and took her by the hand, she knew she wanted more than a kiss here and there. She wanted to be with Derron. But how could she tell him that now? It wasn't the right time. And yet he led her to the small narrow bed and climbed in, pulling her down next to him.

Elyne curled against him, his arms around her. She could hear the beat of his heart and feel the warmth of his body radiating over her. Instead of more kisses, though, he held her close and immediately went to sleep.

Chapter 9

Strips of sunlight filtered through the dirty window into the room and splashed across the wood-slatted floor. Elyne blinked her eyes open when the bright light pressed against her closed eyelids. She lay there, feeling Derron's arms still wrapped protectively around her and listening to his heavy sleep-induced breathing in her ear. Dust particles danced around each other in the streams of light, as though they had choreographed the routine on purpose.

Elyne couldn't stop the stab of pain in her heart when she thought of how Derron must feel losing his father. She too had lost a father, albeit many eons ago. Mayhap that was why her mother had turned so cold and unfeeling. She was a young Fae when he died, barely old enough to remember. Even so, she could still hear her father's voice in her head as though it were yesterday, telling her stories of their ancestors, the Tuatha dé Danann, and how they came to the Otherworld, taking it over from the Fir Bolg. Back then, she had no idea he had embellished most of the stories to include a strong-willed woman. Looking back, she knew it was what he wished for her.

She was definitely strong-willed, much like her mother. Her disobedience—refusing to follow the laws of the Otherworld for the mere fact they were the laws—came from her father. He had often defied the laws when he needed to fight for a cause. She got her inherent mistrust of others from him, too. He had been skeptical of others until they gave him a reason to trust them.

When he died, he left a void so large in her life it was as though a black chasm had opened at her feet. He would have approved of Derron, even if she didn't. She had been such a fool to refuse him that first time so long ago. Now she could not ask for more from him with such a large burden hanging over him. Guardian of the Sword of Light, Protector of the Otherworld, Knight of the Realm...how many more titles did a Fae need?

He stirred behind her and she slid from under his protective arms and out of the bed before he came fully awake. It reminded her much of the previous time when he'd managed to snag her, toss her to the bed and hover over her. When he had that playful look in his eyes. She wondered if she would ever see it again.

"Good morrow, fair princess." His voice was still laced with sleep as he rolled over to look at her.

She stood at the window, as far out of his reach as she could get. "Good morrow. I trust you slept well."

He yawned. "Not at all."

The pain snapped through her. She understood. His sleep had been erratic, tainted by dreams that weren't so pleasant. No doubt he dreamed of the death of his father.

"Come, then. Let us break our fast. My mother will want to convene sooner rather than later."

"Aye." He flung off the shabby blanket and rose, stretching his arms before snatching up his sword and strapping it to his side. He'd slept in his traveling clothes.

So, had she.

She looked down at her rumpled dress and wished she had something fresh to don. She smoothed the wrinkled skirt as best she could and dragged her fingers through her hair, trying to comb out the knots.

As soon as Derron opened the door, they could hear her mother berating the innkeeper. He glanced at her, surprise evident on his handsome features.

"My mother wasted no time getting to work," Elyne said with disdain.

He grinned, showing off his dimples, and extended his hand. "Let's see what hell she's causing, shall we?"

Downstairs, Queen Maeve chastised the innkeeper, who stood before her in a soiled tunic, breeches with a frayed hem and boots that should have long since been retired. Sweat beaded his bald pate and upper lip as he stood there at the mercy of the queen, listening to her go on and on about the poor conditions of his business.

"You call this stew? This is nothing but slop. It's not fit to feed the pigs." She slammed down the bowl on the wooden table, a thick brown substance sloshing over the side. "You can't expect anyone to pay for this, nor for a room in this pitiful excuse for a building you call an inn. It's drafty, dirt cakes the windows and there is a hole in the roof." She pointed upward. "And the stable is no stable at all. More like a ruin."

"Mother," Elyne said, interrupting her tirade.

She swept her skirt aside and looked at Elyne, giving her a once-over. "Ah, there you are at last. Both of you. This inn is no place for anyone to stay. I've ordered Lord Gawaine to bring adequate supplies to outfit the entire company."

"Company?" Derron asked. "There are a dozen of us, my queen."

"Not anymore." She waved in dismissal and turned to the door, flinging it open. Outside, in the early morning light, the landscape had been taken over by a sea of tents. "Your army, my lord."

"You brought an army?" Derron asked.

"We can't very well fight a war without one, now can we?" Maeve asked. "My war council will be here shortly. Eldrin," she called and waved him toward her. He bowed to the queen, despite the fact that she wasn't his ruler. "As soon as Gawaine arrives with our tents, I want you to see to it personally this building is demolished. It's a disgrace."

The innkeeper opened his mouth to object, clamped it shut again. His face flushed as he pressed his lips together in a thin straight line. But Elyne saw.

"As you wish, your majesty," Eldrin said with a nod.

"Mother, you can't demolish the building. What about the innkeeper? His family?"

"Oh, he has no family to speak of. He's nothing more than a con man taking advantage of the poor and starving." She flashed the innkeeper a scornful look, one Elyne had seen numerous times. "He'll be relocated."

By that, she meant *prison*. Elyne shuddered. She would never wish that awful place on anyone again after having been in it.

"I've ordered him to return your gold." Maeve produced a small leather pouch and tossed it to Derron, who caught it one-handed. "Once Gawaine arrives and we've all been properly fed, we will discuss how we are to regain the Sword of Light."

"I thought you wanted a small group to try to get the Sword back," Derron said.

"All that's changed with the death of Lord Malcolm," she said. "Eldrin, bring your rangers. We will find appropriate accommodations for you all."

Queen Maeve stomped out the door. Eldrin and his sister Allanna followed in her wake.

"That's just like her to take over," Elyne said, propping her fists on her hips. "I can't believe she managed to have an entire army sifted here by morning."

"She's the queen," Derron said. "She can do whatever she pleases."

"Aye, well…I don't have to like it."

"Nor I. It seems we're going to war." He sounded grim. "I had hoped we could avoid it."

"If she's bringing the entire war council here, then who's minding the castle?" Elyne wanted to know.

"'Tis a good question. Let's go find out." He headed for the door and Elyne trailed after him.

But Maeve was already in the encampment, Eldrin and Allanna at her side as she ordered where she wanted the camp set up, where she wanted the tents. Eldrin nodded, laughed at something she said that amused him. She flushed, cast her eyes downward. And to Elyne's great horror, she saw the Elven ranger *flirting* with her mother. The queen of the Otherworld.

"You go ahead," she told Derron, unable to stomach the sight of her mother flirting shamelessly with an Elf. "I'm sure you don't need me to plan your war."

Which left her with nothing to do. If she had her magic, she'd sift away from here. Mayhap to visit Maggie and Finn. Derron laced his fingers with hers, stopping her from fleeing.

"Elyne—"

"I'm going for a walk. Let me go, Derron." She slipped her hand out of his.

Thankfully, he allowed her to go without any argument.

By nightfall, Queen Maeve managed to turn the small, out-of-the-way inn into a hustling, bustling camp. The inn had been demolished as she commanded. All that remained was a pile of rotting wood and broken glass, which would be torched. The innkeeper had been apprehended and taken away. Shackled as a prisoner in one of the tents, no doubt.

Lord Gawaine arrived along with the entire war council. Elyne learned they had left a few soldiers at the palace. The rest of the staff and servants remained until they returned. It was odd to think of the Queen's Palace as nearly deserted. It all seemed so surreal.

The command tent, as it came to be known, housed a large table big enough for everyone. Derron had insisted she join them, even though she objected. But he convinced her that as crown princess she had every right to be at the meetings and needed to know what was happening almost as much as he and her mother did. Begrudgingly, she agreed.

"The death of Lord Malcolm cannot go unanswered," Queen Maeve said that night at the meeting. "We must retaliate."

"Agreed," Lord Gawaine said. "But how do you propose we attack an enemy we cannot even get to?"

"We invade the Dark Realm," Lord Roderick said. He had served her father as well and been a fixture in the court for as long as Elyne could remember. Tall with dark hair that brushed his collar and a face covered with a scruffy beard and mustache, he embodied everything a knight should look like to her.

"You don't mean to march up through the Barrier," Lord Vaughan said. "It is forbidden for any from the Light to enter."

"Unless the queen allows it," Lord Roderick replied.

"Entering the Barrier is not an option," Gawaine said. "Lord Kieran is after a much bigger prize than the Sword of Light. He will come to us."

"How can you be so sure?" Roderick asked.

"Lord Malcolm is dead," Gawaine said. "The Sword of Light is in his possession. We all know that if he gains control of the Spear and the Club, he will be headed for the Hill of Tara to the Stone of Destiny next."

"Where he can proclaim himself High King," Maeve said.

"To proclaim himself High King would mean there would have to be no ruler of the Otherworld," Roderick put in.

All fell silent as the weight of his words sank in. Elyne shuddered. He implied her mother would have to be dead—that mayhap Lord Kieran would kill her himself—for there to be no ruler of the Otherworld. Maeve remained quiet for a long moment, the silence stretching between them all.

"Aye, I've no doubt that is his plan," she said at last. "He wants me dead, as he wanted my husband dead. He may expect to find me in the Queen's Palace, waiting for him. Alas, I will not be." She smiled then. A thin-lipped smile that seemed strained.

Maeve had not spoken of her husband's death in centuries. Hearing the words slip from her lips startled Elyne and made the memory resurface with a vengeance. She had shoved the memories of that day into the dark recesses of her mind but now she faced them. She recalled the blood on her hands as she tried to pull her father from unconsciousness, how she had blamed herself for the attack because she had begged him to take her to the Whispering Wood, to the calm pool of Loch Moreen. He hadn't taken her there in so long because, at the time, there was unrest in the Light Realm and he didn't want to stray too far from the Queen's Palace.

But Elyne had begged and, being the accommodating father he was, he gave in and took her. And that's when the ambush happened. Deep down, Elyne suspected her mother had never forgiven her, even though she said she didn't blame her. It happened. They were attacked by the Dark Elf. Elyne narrowly escaped with her life but it cost the king's. Maeve had been the last one to see him alive before his soul faded to the gods.

Now Elyne carried the burden of guilt and the helplessness of having no magic. Her life couldn't be more useless.

"We're overlooking the other fact that for there to truly be no ruler of the Otherworld," Roderick said and paused, oblivious to the horrible memories playing out in Elyne's mind. He cut her a glance and despite being lost in memories, she saw it. "The princess will have to be dead as well."

A loud *ka-thud* sounded in Elyne's chest at his words. It was something she hadn't considered either. That Lord Kieran intended to wipe out both her and Queen Maeve. She should have realized this when he murdered the Dark King and his entire clan in one fell swoop. The war had really begun long before that, though, when he masterminded the attack on her own father. Her hands turned cold at the thought and she bit her lower lip. Derron grasped her fingers in his, holding her hand and squeezing to reassure her.

"Then we'll make sure that won't happen," Derron said and pinned Roderick with an icy stare. "Having them here with us instead of at the palace is for the best."

"I'm staying but I want my daughter someplace else. Someplace safe."

This stunned Elyne out of her silence. "What? No. I'm not leaving."

"You are the next in line for the throne," Maeve said. "If anything should happen to me, you would immediately become queen. I can't have you here in danger."

As Elyne started to reply, Derron squeezed her hand again. Hard. She clenched her jaw as he addressed her mother.

"Your majesty, I believe it's best if she remains here. She'll be safer under guard of the Fae army than hidden somewhere. Should we fail, and Kieran does take over, then he will find her."

And kill her anyway. His unspoken words hung in the air between them.

Maeve pursed her lips into a thin line. "It is against my better judgment. She may stay, then. Now, gentlemen, I suggest we get back to the matter at hand," Maeve said, steering the conversation away from the morbid. "We know Lord Kieran has the Sword of Light. I have sent soldiers to protect the other Guardians."

"It will not be enough."

Eldrin's quiet words filtered through the air. Everyone had forgotten the Elven ranger sat with them, listening to them until now. Allanna sat next to him, joining them at the insistence of her brother. He laced his fingers and leaned his forearms on the table.

"Kieran has proved he will kill to get what he wants. He wants the Spear and the Club. He will have them," Eldrin said.

"How can he wield them?" Roderick asked. "Does he know how?"

"If he makes it as far as the Stone of Destiny and climbs to the Place of Crowning," Maeve said, "then all he'll need is the ancient spell and…" She paused, swallowed hard.

"And no ruler." Elyne's stomach quivered.

"Then how do we stop him?" Derron asked.

Eldrin glanced at his sister, who sat quietly. He gave her a nod and she flushed, color staining high in her cheekbones.

"Allanna is a seer. She has seen the future."

"You tell us this now?" Derron snapped.

Elyne understood his anger. Eldrin hadn't mentioned it when Allanna joined them in the woods.

"Forgive me, Lord Derron," Eldrin said. "Her flashes come sporadically. In the last few days, she has been able to discern the future."

"Tell us what you saw, child," Maeve said.

"He will capture the Spear and the Club. There will be a great battle at the Stone of Destiny." Allanna spoke so softly it was difficult to hear her. She kept her eyes downcast, not looking at anyone.

"There's more," Elyne said. "She's afraid to tell us."

Eldrin glanced from Maeve to Elyne, and then nodded slowly. "She saw the death of both the queen and the princess."

Chapter 10

Night blanketed the Dark Realm, an inky blackness pressing over the land, threatening to suffocate them. Kieran had felt that way for days with no news regarding the location of the Guardian of the Spear of Lugh. It was the second piece he needed to make one more step toward his ultimate goal. And so far, his men had not been able to deliver.

He took a sip of the bitter ale and swilled it around his mouth, tasting defeat. *No, I will not accept that.* He had come too far and waited too long for this moment. It was within his grasp. He couldn't give up. Not yet.

A brisk knock on his chamber door interrupted his thoughts.

"Come."

The door swung open and Cormac entered. Cormac, who had proven useful with his list of Unseelie contacts, his ability to wake the shadows and summon the creatures of the dark, and his bottomless wealth. Kieran idly wondered how much longer he would be useful to him.

He did not offer the man a tankard of ale or words of greeting. Cormac clasped his hands in front of him and shifted from one foot to the other in the shadowy light.

"Well, what news?"

"My king, Queen Maeve has left the palace, leaving it relatively unprotected."

Kieran pinned Cormac with an icy stare at this bit of news. It was not the news for which he had been waiting. Irritation clawed through him.

"And this means what to me, Cormac? I wanted information about the Guardian of the Spear of Lugh and I have heard nothing. Instead, you bring me this? That the Queen's Palace is deserted?"

In his drunken stupor, he threw the tankard of ale he'd been sipping at Cormac. Cormac ducked, the brass cup flying over his head and clanging against the floor. Ale splashed across the stones.

"It means, my king, that the Light Realm is ripe for invasion." Cormac's voice was hollow and thin. Yet his eyes pinned him with a glare that said he was not intimidated by his temper. A quality Kieran had once admired. Now it merely annoyed him.

Kieran rubbed his forehead, squeezing the skin between thumb and forefinger. "What it means is the queen took my message a little too seriously and has deserted."

He looked at his second-in-command, who stood with his arms hanging listlessly by his sides. He sighed. He hadn't meant to scare the queen away. Merely send her a strong message he intended to take the other Treasures, no matter the cost. Now he would have to find her to kill her.

"What sense does it make to invade an empty palace?" Kieran asked.

The ale pounded in his veins, making his head throb. He hadn't meant to drink so much, but after days of hearing nothing about the other Guardians, frustration had set in. He'd taken it out on the available wenches but he'd managed to use up most of them to the point they were no longer of value.

"If we take the palace, your majesty," Cormac's voice was slow, patient as though he were speaking to a child, "then we can force those who remain under our control and spread out our army out from there. We can use the palace as a base of operations. There would be no stopping us then."

Kieran had been reaching for the brass ewer for a refill and a fresh cup as Cormac spoke but now halted. How was it he hadn't thought of that before? He'd been so focused on the Treasures he hadn't thought to take over the Queen's Palace. And why would he? It wasn't part of his ultimate plan. He had intended to rule the Otherworld from his own designated location. Not her palace.

"My scouts are, of course, continuing to search for the Treasures. I've ordered them to find the queen and her daughter as well."

Her daughter. Princess Elyne. She was but a girl the last time he saw her when he'd murdered the king. He had been a fool to spare her life then. He should have killed her when he had the chance. Should the queen die at his hands, he would have to contend with the princess trying to thwart his quest for the throne. He would have to kill her as well. Mayhap Cormac still had a use.

"As soon as you know where they are, I want to be informed.

As for the palace…" He sat back in his silk-draped chair, ran a hand over his three-day growth of beard. His skin bristled against the stubble. "Tell me your plan for taking control of the Queen's Palace, for surely you have one."

"I do, my king. We break through the Barrier, enter the Light Realm with our army. We are over twenty thousand strong. Some could be directed to the palace while the others go with you to the Hill of Tara."

"Where I proclaim myself High King."

"Aye, your majesty."

Cormac had clearly put a lot of thought into this. More thought than he, himself, had. Anger flared through him. Anger and suspicion. Was Cormac hiding something? Would he try to take over once Kieran had achieved his rule of the Otherworld?

"What's in it for you, Cormac?"

"My king?" He genuinely looked confused as his forehead creased with concern. "I don't follow."

Did he take him for the fool? Of course, he followed. He knew exactly what he meant. "You wouldn't have put so much time into thinking through the plan had you not wanted something in return. What is it?"

Cormac's expression hardened, a chill settling in his cold blue eyes. "I want you to release my family."

Ah, so there it was. "Never. They are all traitors to my cause."

"A crown you do not have," he fired back.

"Do not cross me, Cormac, or you will end up like Lord Malcolm."

"Do not threaten me, Kieran, or you will lose all the funds I've provided. Not to mention my unique assistance."

Kieran knew the man referred to his magical abilities. He didn't like to be threatened and scowled. "How do I know you will maintain your loyalty to me should I grant your request?"

"How do you know I won't if you don't?"

Clever. He had a response for everything. If Kieran didn't need him, he would kill the man where he stood. Cormac was fearless, unthreatened and willing to push back. Though he held value to Kieran, his family was expendable.

Kieran chuckled then and clucked his tongue. "A threat for a threat. Is that it, Cormac? Is that how you intend to control me? I am far more dangerous than you give me credit."

"I know how dangerous you are," Cormac said. "And I do not fear you."

"That is why I will allow you to live. If you want them to live, you have no choice but to continue to help me."

"If you kill my family, I will kill you, my king."

Kieran sized him up. Cormac knew, as he did, he needed him and his money. Of the Dark Realm, he was the only one who had agreed to fund his war. But Cormac's wife, his parents, even his children, had been against Kieran from the beginning. They had tried to convince Cormac to stop funding him and when they became a nuisance, Kieran took them into custody to force his hand.

"I will release your family once I'm proclaimed High King as ruler of the Otherworld and the kingdom is secured. Until then, they will remain in the prison along with the others."

"As collateral to your war." Cormac bit the words out.

"We will go with your plan," Kieran said, ignoring his last statement. "Send ten thousand to the palace. The others will come with me as we begin our trek to the Stone of Destiny on the Hill of Tara. I suspect I will find Queen Maeve's men waiting for us there. As for the Barrier, how do you intend to breach it?"

"I have the assurance of a dark mage that he can break through it."

"Very well. Make it so." He dismissed Cormac with a wave of his hand.

"I have more information, my king."

With Cormac's pause, Kieran's blood heated another notch. "Well?"

"Queen Maeve has sent soldiers to the Stone of Destiny. It and the Guardian are both heavily guarded."

"Does she think to intimidate me?" He scoffed. "As soon as the Barrier is down, I want to launch a full attack on both the Stone of Destiny and the Queen's Palace and anyone else who gets in the way. I will accept no failure. Kill the Guardian of the Stone of Destiny for all I care. The man is useless to me. See to it, Cormac."

When the man continued to linger, Kieran huffed out a breath and snapped, "Is there more?"

"Aye, there is. You wanted information about the Spear of Lugh and the returning scouts tell me they've located it."

Kieran's eyes narrowed. "You've known all this time and failed to tell me right away?" Growling, he picked up the ewer of wine and threw it at the man's head. He had good reflexes, though, and ducked. The ewer crashed to the floor behind him. "You should not have withheld this information."

Cormac remained silent, staring at him, his face passive. His cool exterior was a calm façade.

"Ah, but I see. It was the only way to make me agree to release your family." He leaned back in his chair and ran a hand over his chin. He would make sure to keep a close eye on Cormac from now on. "You are more cunning than I give you credit, Cormac. If you've located the Spear, bring it to me at once."

"And the Guardian?"

"Kill him." He shrugged. "Now that you've found the ancient spell to use with the weapons on the Stone of Destiny, we know how to wield them. It makes no matter to me if he lives or dies."

"As you wish, my king." He turned on his boot heel and headed for the door.

Elyne had taken to her tent, feigning sickness. When Allanna— or Eldrin rather—had announced the death of her and her mother, a stab of fear hit her heart. The girl explained her visions were never very clear. She could not see the why or the how, only the what. Which meant there was a way their deaths could be avoided. Derron and the others were certain of it. Elyne was not.

She'd demanded her mother return her powers so she could fight, but Maeve had refused, stating she had yet to perform one selfless act.

"This is not the human realm, Elyne, where you can simply alter time at your whim and pick the outcome of your choosing," her mother said after denying her request.

Elyne fumed. "If you give me my powers back, then I *can* perform one selfless act. And it has nothing to do with altering time."

"No," she said simply.

And Elyne knew what was unspoken. *It had to be on her terms.*

So Elyne had left the council meeting after that, no longer interested in hearing about the planning of a war that could potentially wipe out most of the Light Realm. She found her tent, not far from her mother's, furnished with a narrow bed, a large chest with clean gowns inside, a six-foot candelabra. She lit the tapers, the yellow-gold light flickering shadows over the canvas. Sighing, she climbed on the bed, covered herself with the available blankets and curled into a ball.

She must have drifted off to sleep for the next thing she realized, Derron shook her awake. She rolled to her back and looked up into his eyes full of concern.

"Are you all right?"

"Fine," she said tersely.

Was she fine, though? No, not really. She preferred not to think about the fact her death had been prophesized.

"I've not seen you in hours. I was worried."

Elyne shoved off the blankets and climbed out of the bed, pushing her fingers through her hair. "I was tired."

"Elyne." He grasped her by the shoulders, turned her to face him. "Do not let Allanna's vision bother you. It won't happen."

"How do you know that, Derron?" To her chagrin, her voice hitched on his name. The lump was there in her throat before she could stop it. "None of you know that for certain."

"*I do.*" And he shook her a little with his words. "I know for certain."

"How?"

"I won't allow anything to happen to you."

The valiant knight. She smiled. He played the role well as Protector of the Otherworld, Knight of the Realm, Guardian of the Sword of Light. Despite his reassurance, though, he couldn't promise her nothing would happen to her. If there was one dragon, there had to be more. What would stop Lord Kieran from sending a dragon into their camp, breathing fire and killing them all?

"You're mother has protected our camp," he said, as though he could read her thoughts.

She shrugged him off. "He is Unseelie. He can breach that protection. My mother's power is not infallible."

"You left before we discussed our plans," Derron said, dropping his hands by his sides. He didn't attempt to touch her again. "Your mother has sent scouts. Lord Kieran is still in the Dark Realm behind the Barrier."

"But for how long? If he's managed to take the Sword of Light, what's to stop him from getting the Spear of Lugh or the Club of

Dagda? And then he'll be headed to the Stone of Destiny." She hadn't realized she'd been pacing until Derron snatched her by the arm and pulled her to him. He hugged her, hard. So hard, it nearly squeezed the breath out of her.

"We will be there to stop him. Maeve has sent troops to the Barrier."

"It won't be enough."

Tears burned her eyes. She couldn't remember a time when tears had threatened her so much. She blinked them away, trying to keep them at bay. Derron wouldn't know why it affected her so. Why Lord Kieran's advance and threat made her want to hide away. She should have stayed put in the prison, where she would be safe. Where he could never find her.

"You don't know that," he said.

"Aye, I do! He murdered my father right in front of me, Derron. It's why he was banished to the Dark Realm. And now he comes for me and my mother. He will not stop until he has what he wants. He will never stop."

She *hated* the sympathetic look he gave her now. The way his eyes softened. The way his shoulders slumped a little. She hadn't wanted to mention it. Didn't want him to know her torment with the threat of Kieran looming. He'd killed Derron's father, too. Why should her pain—albeit from long ago—be any more important than his?

"Aye, I know."

It was all he said. All he needed to say. And only when he wiped a tear from her cheek did she realize they'd fallen.

"You must think me awful." She couldn't stand for him to look at her like that anymore and pushed away from him. "When he's murdered your father as well and not so long ago."

"No, princess. I don't. I think you're trying to be brave and strong. I think you want me to be brave and strong. I can't do that for you if I'm silently grieving for what is lost."

His words stabbed her heart. "I ache for you and your loss."

"Aye, I know that, too." He cupped her face, his thumbs stroking her damp cheeks.

How did he know? Could he read her so well? Was she that transparent? She thought for a moment he was going to kiss her but he smiled at her. His eyes misted with tears he blinked away. How could he go on? She had never seen him openly weep and she never wanted to see that. It might unhinge her. Derron had always been the strongest man she'd ever known.

"I believe you need a distraction," he said.

"A distraction?"

"Aye, something to entertain you. To occupy your time. I have an idea." He gave her a conspiratorial grin.

"And what is that?"

"I will fetch Lady Margaret for you."

Her heart skipped a happy beat. "Lord Derron, you know she will never leave Sir Finian's side. Nor will he allow her to go with you alone."

He laughed. "Aye, I know. 'Tis why I intend to bring him along as well. And mayhap Sir Drake. 'Twould be nice to have them back with us again, aye?"

"For what purpose?"

"Why, dear princess, for a grand banquet, of course. I trust you can put one together on such short notice?"

"With the help of my mother. I don't think she'd be happy if I asked her about that in light of our current situation. She has other pressing matters on her mind."

"You should ask. A banquet would be something we could all enjoy."

"I'm not so sure she'll approve."

"I'm sure you'll think of something, then."

"And how am I to explain why they're here? You know how my mother feels about the humans. She will not be happy to see them, especially here in the Otherworld, where it is forbidden."

"Ah, you see, I've already thought of that. Sir Finian and Sir Drake can fight with us once we face Lord Kieran."

"You think they'll be willing to risk their lives for us?"

"We risked our lives for them in the human realm," he pointed out.

Elyne wanted to point out that Sir Drake hadn't been mixed up in the problems she and Maggie caused at the jousting tournament in Middleham. She kept it to herself, though, biting her bottom lip.

"Aside from that," Derron continued, "I will make sure the humans have a high resistance to Lord Kieran's dark magic."

"And how do you intend to do that?"

"Once they step foot into the Otherworld, they instantly become immune to any magic. They will see us in our true form.

No glamour will be able to hide us."

Elyne narrowed her eyes at him. "How do you know this?"

"Trade secret." He flashed a brilliant smile. "I can't tell you everything, princess. Now, can I? Some things must remain a secret."

"It would be nice to be in on some of the information." She folded her arms over her chest. "Do you think you can convince them to come back with you?"

"Sir Finian will be the most difficult to convince, but I'm hoping his lovely lady will help me persuade him."

Elyne laughed. "If Maggie has a chance to step foot in the Otherworld, there will be no stopping her."

"Exactly my hope, your highness." He winked. "I'll leave you to set up the banquet field while I fetch our dear friends."

Derron kissed her on the cheek before leaving. Since she wasn't too keen on asking her mother for help, she'd go to the only other person she could trust. Eldrin.

Chapter 11

Eldrin turned out to be quite helpful. When Elyne mentioned to him the plan of having a banquet with music, food and dancing, he immediately organized his fellow Elven rangers to help. Allanna had the light of excitement in her face as she followed her brother around, asking questions and begging to help.

"You don't even know how to dance," Eldrin said. "You skipped classes from Master Randir."

"But you can teach me, Eldrin," she said. "Can't you?"

He paused, giving her a look of annoyance. "I've tried before. You stepped on my toes and wouldn't let me lead."

"Then how about I play an instrument?" she suggested.

"Allanna, I know you have never had an instrument in your hands before. Why would you think you could do that now?"

"But I can learn," she whined.

"Actually," Elyne put in, "I'm sure we could find someone from my mother's court to teach you. She has the finest musicians and dancers in her employ."

Eldrin flashed a look that read *you're not helping*. Elyne gave him a bright smile. He sighed, resigned. "Very well, then."

Allanna squealed happily. "Oh, thank you!"

"Why don't you find Lord Gawaine? He'll be able to direct you to our musicians," Elyne said.

She nodded, a bright smile on her face, and hurried off with her wavy hair bouncing behind her.

"You're welcome," Elyne said brightly.

"That girl is incorrigible," Eldrin said on a sigh. "I fear there is no hope for her."

"Mayhap there will be yet, Eldrin."

"What is the meaning of this?" Queen Maeve shouted across the encampment. "A banquet, Princess Elyne?"

"Aye, Mother. I'm sure you are familiar with them," Elyne said, propping her hands on her hips to confront her mother. Eldrin managed to slink off, avoiding the confrontation. *Coward.*

"We cannot have a grand banquet here. Not now when we're about to go to war."

"As I understand it, Mother, the war hasn't happened yet. What's the harm in having a little fun beforehand?"

Her mother's response was to purse her lips.

Elyne resisted the urge to roll her eyes. "The men are restless. It's something to keep them entertained. It will allow them all to have a little fun while waiting to confront Lord Kieran. If you reinstated my powers, I could organize more efficiently."

It wasn't a formal request, more like a suggestion. But one Elyne hoped her mother would agree to do. It was, after all, in the best interests of everyone. Maeve immediately shook her head.

"No, absolutely not. And throwing a banquet is not a selfless act."

Elyne tried not to allow the anger to consume her. She took a deep breath before replying. "What do I have to do to prove myself to you, Mother?"

"You have to show me you aren't so self-serving. Everything you did in the human realm was just that."

"Need I remind you everything I did was to save Derron?"

"No, you needn't," she snapped. "Whose idea was this banquet?"

Elyne tasted the bitterness of defeat. *So be it.* "It was Derron's."

"Well, then I'll take it up with him. Where is he?"

Elyne refused to tell her he'd headed off to the human realm to retrieve her human friends. "I'm sure I don't know, Mother. Mayhap finding someone to play some music."

While Derron was off to sift Maggie, Finn and Sir Drake to the Otherworld, Elyne worked on setting up the banquet. They needed enough tables for everyone, so she talked several of the knights into helping her build crude ones. She asked Lord Gawaine to bring the Cauldron to help take care of the food—it would never go empty. She also managed to find enough knights and guards who were willing to play their instruments and put together a makeshift band. It was coming together quite nicely.

It had been months since Elyne had seen Maggie and Finn. Since the end of the tourney in Middleham, when she'd promised her human friend she would take a letter to Maggie's father. She'd never had the opportunity to do that, for shortly after tourney,

Queen Maeve had arrested her, put her on trial and thrown her into the Fae prison. She would have to explain that to Maggie when she arrived and hope she would understand that, under the circumstances, she hadn't managed to make it back to the human realm.

Now Derron returned with the three humans trailing after him. Elyne had never been so happy to see them. Maggie hadn't changed one bit. She wore her long auburn hair pulled back from her face, hanging in waves over her shoulders and down her back. She wore a gown of royal blue, belted at the waist with a gold braid and looking the part of the wife of a laird. Her eyes lit with happiness when she saw Elyne.

Maggie embraced her in a tight hug when she saw her.

"Ellie, it's so good to see you. I've missed you."

Ellie. She'd forgotten that was Maggie's nickname for her and grinned. "Welcome to my home."

"And what a spectacular home it is. I've never seen the sky that shade of pink before." Maggie glanced at the sky before giving her a long once-over. "This is a great look for you." She wagged her finger at each pointed ear.

Elyne laughed. "You see me without my glamour here in the Otherworld, do you?"

"Yes, and I'm surprised it's not blinding me like it did in the human world. Why is that?"

"I would guess because you are in my realm now, my lady."

"We're old friends here. No need to be so formal. You must catch me up on everything. I understand Sir Derron is now *Lord* Derron."

"Aye, he is. I'll tell you the whole story soon enough."

Because at the moment, she saw Queen Maeve stomping toward them through the campgrounds. Elyne braced for the coming storm.

The queen stopped short and looked at Maggie, then Finn and finally Sir Drake. It seemed to take a moment before recognition registered on her face, and then she turned a pale shade of red.

"What are *they* doing here?" she asked.

"Queen Maeve—"

The queen quickly cut off Derron. "Humans are strictly forbidden in the Otherworld. You of all people know this, Lord Derron." She looked at Elyne, then. "Did you have anything to do with this?"

Before Elyne could respond, Derron said, "No, she didn't. It was all my idea. I brought them here."

"And you'll take them back immediately."

"No," Elyne said, taking a step next to Derron. "He won't."

"You defy me again, my daughter. This is not helping your case."

"I brought them here to assist with the war effort, your majesty," Derron said. "When we fight at the Hill of Tara—and I'm certain we will—Sir Finian and Sir Drake will be invaluable to us."

"What can *humans* do to assist us?" Queen Maeve wanted to know. "They have no use here in the Otherworld. They are all but worthless."

"Gee, thanks," Maggie said sourly.

"On the contrary, Mother," Elyne said. "Sir Drake and Sir Finian are two of the best knights I've ever seen. I would want them on my side in a fight."

"They cannot help us here. Take them back," Maeve said.

"With all due respect," Derron said, "I believe they can help us. They stay."

She paused, mulling this over. A dark shadow of defeat fell over her face. "Since you're so determined, Lord Derron…they can stay. About this banquet—"

"Well underway and in hand, your majesty," Derron said. Elyne knew what he was doing. He wasn't giving Maeve a chance to kill the idea and for that, she could kiss him. "The men's excitement over something enjoyable to do is evident in their assistance with the preparations."

"I don't deny that the idea is a good one, but we are preparing for war."

"War, aye. They shouldn't have to think about it every moment."

"It is against my better judgment," Maeve said.

"Aye, I understand. I am sure you will enjoy yourself as well."

She glanced from him to the field and back again. "Very well, Lord Derron. I will allow it."

"Many thanks, your majesty." Derron bowed, showing her more respect than she was due. At least in Elyne's opinion.

Once the queen was gone, Maggie blew out a breath. "Whew.

She's a tough nut to crack, isn't she?"

"You have no idea," Elyne muttered.

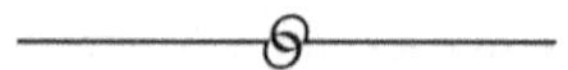

Elyne took Maggie, Finn and Drake through the encampment—what Maggie had immediately dubbed as Tent City of the Otherworld—to their temporary homes. They all had quarters close to each other, to Maggie's apparent delight. She hooked her arm in Elyne's and chattered away about life with the Scottish laird as they walked. Finn and Maggie would be in one tent, Elyne in the one directly across from them, which was reminiscent of their days at Middleham, and Sir Drake next door.

Maggie planted a kiss on Finn's cheek. "I'm going to catch up with Elyne. I'll be in after."

He patted her cheek with affection before ducking into their tent. Maggie led Elyne into hers. When she asked Elyne about her father and if she'd delivered the letter, she cringed.

"You didn't take it?" Maggie asked, looking crushed.

Elyne couldn't stop the wave of guilt washing over her. "I haven't had a chance yet."

"I understand."

Though it was clear by her tone of voice she didn't. Her face fell, her eyes welling with tears.

"I have a legitimate reason, though, as I was imprisoned upon my return to the Otherworld."

"You were imprisoned?" That immediately changed her expression, the letter forgotten. She looked at Elyne with concern, taking her by the hand and leading her to the bed to sit down. "What happened? Your mother?"

Maggie was no fool. She could guess what might have happened once Elyne and Derron returned to the Otherworld after the tournament in Middleham.

"Aye, my mother. She stuck me in prison and took away all my magic. She was quite unhappy with my meddling in the human realm."

"To help me. And Derron." She squeezed her hand. "I'm sorry, Ellie."

"'Tis nothing to be done about it. She put in me the Fae prison and warded the cell to keep me in and others out."

"How did you get out then?"

"Derron came to my aid."

"I knew it!" She blurted it out, smiling broadly. "I knew he loved you."

"I'm afraid it's not that simple, my lady."

"Don't 'my lady' me. It *is* that simple. He loves you. You love him. What's the problem?"

"The problem is Lord Kieran is trying to invade the Light Realm and take over. He's already killed Derron's father, making him the Guardian of the Sword of Light. Now he's after the other Guardians and me and my mother. He will kill us all to get what he wants."

"Derron won't let anything happen to you or Queen Maeve. I'm sure of that."

"I have my doubts. The elf-girl saw it in her dreams."

"What elf-girl?"

Maggie creased her forehead in confusion. Elyne had forgotten she didn't know everything that had gone on in the Otherworld since they'd parted ways.

"I will explain later."

"You shouldn't let all that get in the way of your feelings for Derron," Maggie said.

"You don't know how difficult this is for him. And me. Lord Kieran killed my father, too."

Maggie bit her lower lip. "I didn't know."

"Nay, you wouldn't have. 'Twas a long time ago when I was a girl."

"Do you want to talk about it?"

Elyne considered this. She had never confided to anyone her thoughts and feelings about that awful day. Maggie had been more of a friend to her than any Fae in the entire realm. She certainly couldn't convey her feelings to her mother, who had hated her from the moment her father had died.

"When I was a girl, my father and I would ride out to the Whispering Wood. We'd sit by the calm pale-blue waters of the Loch Moreen and have a picnic. It was always the two of us. He taught me how to fish in the loch."

"You? Fish?" Maggie giggled, covering her mouth. "I can't picture it."

"Do you want to hear this or not?"

"Yes, of course. Pray continue."

"There had been some unrest in the realm. I learned later it was Lord Kieran. He was nothing more than an Elven ranger then, living in the Woodlands. The Elves and the Fae have had an uneasy alliance for centuries, so when the Elven King came to my mother for help, she listened.

"Lord Kieran was a menace, even then. My mother's solution was to banish him to the Dark Realm. Before the Elven King could act, Lord Kieran left the Woodlands and found me and my father. He murdered him there in the Whispering Wood on the banks of Loch Moreen. Killed him with several arrows. Right in front of me."

Elyne hadn't realized Maggie held her hand until she squeezed her fingers so tight it hurt.

"How awful."

"I believe he would have killed me, too," Elyne said. "But something stopped him. I don't know why he spared me that day."

"And you never will," Maggie said. "It's not your fault."

"It is. If I hadn't been such a petulant child, we would have never been in the Whispering Wood that day. I would have never seen him murdered right in front of me. I felt so helpless. I wish I could have saved him."

"You have to let that go, Elyne. What happened, happened. And there's nothing you can do to change the past."

It still pained her. She should have never asked her father to take her there that day. And then he would still live. She wondered how different her life would have turned out.

"He murdered Derron's father, too. Cut him up and sent the pieces as a message—a warning—to my mother."

Maggie swallowed hard. "God, how awful. How is Derron handling it?"

"He does not grieve."

"Then you have to help him through that. You of all people know how he feels right now. You can offer him some comfort."

"He told me he had to be strong and silently grieve for what was lost. He means to lead the men against Lord Kieran."

"Then time is of the essence, Elyne. You should tell him how you feel about him. It's time you stop pining away for him and do something about it."

"There is something about the Fae you don't understand, so

telling me to do such a thing is against all that is proper."

"Proper shmoper. Since when do you care about what's proper?"

"Since I am now in the Otherworld and abiding by my mother's rule."

"Well, that does make a difference," Maggie said. "Though I've never known you to follow the rules, Ellie. What is this mysterious thing I don't know about the Fae?"

"When we choose one another, it is for life. It is known as the bonding."

"So you're waiting to bond with Derron?" Maggie asked.

"Aye."

"And you've never…bonded…with any other?"

Elyne flushed, her face burning hot. This was a conversation she had never had with anyone else, nor did she really want to have. Yet this was Maggie and Maggie could ask her anything and she would answer. Maggie was the only person Elyne was completely at ease with. "Nay."

"Oh." She smiled. Beamed actually. "That is so sweet."

"Hardly," she scoffed and rose to pace the small confines of the tent.

"Clearly, he feels the same for you. I've seen it in the way he looks at you. But, wait, what about all the ladies at the tournament?" Maggie asked.

"Humans don't count," Elyne said, her mouth pulling down in a grimace.

"Right. Of course. Should have known. We're a lower life form than the Fae." Her tone was laced with sarcasm.

"Don't be cheeky."

"Cheeky is my middle name," Maggie said and flashed a bright smile. She flung an arm around Elyne's shoulders. "I'm famished. What do you have to eat around here?"

Chapter 12

By the time they emerged from Elyne's tent, it neared dusk. Elyne had taken the opportunity to change out of her soiled gown. Her mother had taken into account her need for fresh clothing and had them brought with the soldiers. Her initial choice—a plain gown in black—was nixed by Maggie and replaced by a sapphire gown in crushed velvet that hugged her curves. Maggie swept up the sides of her hair away from her face and pinned it securely. She proclaimed her "soft and pretty" as they headed out of the tents.

Finn waited outside the tent, his arms crossed. He wore his long hair plaited, one on either side of his face, his pale-green tunic setting off the silvery color of his eyes.

"*Och*, there ye are lassie."

Maggie stood on tiptoe to kiss him on the cheek. "We had some catching up to do."

Sir Drake emerged from his tent and joined them. "I'm glad to see I'm not late to the party."

"Not at all." Maggie smiled warmly.

"It is an honor to be here, your highness." Drake bowed low to the princess, then took her hand and kissed it. "Imagine my surprise when I learned you and Sir Derron are of the fair folk and royalty at that. I thought you existed only in faery tales, not in real life."

"The Fae are quite real, Sir Drake," Elyne said.

"I'm honored to know you, princess."

"It is I who am honored to count you among our friends."

"This seems like old times, doesn't it? Sir Drake escorting you, Ellie, while I'm on Sir Finian's arm." Maggie patted Finn's arm affectionately.

"I do hope Lord Derron won't mind, your highness." Sir Drake gave Elyne a winning smile and held out his arm.

"I'm sure he won't." Elyne slipped her hand on his arm as she led the way through the tents. "He's a bit preoccupied at the moment."

Elyne filled in her friends about everything that had happened since returning to the Otherworld, with Kieran and the Four Treasures. When she told them the Dark Elf intended to slay the queen—and her—Maggie's look of shock immediately went to one of anger.

"Then we will have to stop him. And I'll help," Maggie said.

"*Och*, lass, ye'll do no such crazy thing. Ye have already given me enough gray hairs."

"I'll help if I want to," Maggie argued.

"I can assure you, princess, we will assist any way possible," Sir Drake said.

"We can discuss it all later," Elyne said, hoping to diffuse an argument between the two. "I'm famished."

The Fae and Elves had transformed the encampment. It really was Tent City, Elyne thought, as they walked past rows and rows of them. Queen Maeve had used her persuasive powers to build a giant tent that was the heart of their operation. Several six-foot candelabras were placed throughout the tent, giving it a warm, inviting glow. In the center, a giant black cauldron sat on a crackling fire.

On the other side, another table, though this one wasn't for feasting. Several rolled-up maps were scattered around the surface. The queen, Lord Gawaine, Derron and a few others from the Council stood around it, looking down at a map that Gawaine held unrolled.

"What is that?" Maggie asked, nodding toward the cauldron.

"The Cauldron," Elyne said, pointing to it. "It will never allow us to go hungry."

The men and ladies dipped from the Cauldron, the level of the thick and hearty stew inside never getting lower. Several of the Elven rangers including Eldrin and his sister Allanna sat at the banquet table, feasting on the stew in a trencher. All managed to wear their best finery. Even in this time of war, the queen had managed to bring along a few servants who kept tankards full of ale or mead. Derron headed over to greet them.

"Ah, the lovely Lady Margaret and her Scottish brute, Sir Finian, have decided to join us," Derron said.

"Scottish brute, Lord Derron?" Maggie chided. "Can't you two call a truce?"

"I admit I'm disappointed you chose him over me." Derron captured her hand and kissed it.

Finn slipped her hand from Derron's and tucked it into his elbow. "I'm sure ye'll get over it."

Derron laughed. "I have other ladies fair that interest me. Well, one lady."

His gaze flickered to Elyne before turning back again to the two of them. Elyne hadn't missed it and her face flushed. In the last few days, she blushed more than she had in her entire life.

"He means me," Allanna announced. She had made her way across the feasting tent and paused next to Derron, looking up at him adoringly. "Right, Sir Derron?"

Maggie raised an eyebrow as she glanced at the young Elf.

"'Tis Lord Derron now," Elyne corrected, bristling as Allanna latched onto Derron. The girl had been a constant fixture during their trek. "Or hadn't you heard?"

Allanna ignored Elyne as she turned her attention to Maggie, Finn and Sir Drake. "You must be the humans. We heard humans were here."

"Lady Margaret and her husband, Sir Finian," Elyne said. "And this is Sir Drake Attenborough of the human realm."

"I think I should be insulted by being called a *human*," Maggie said and chuckled.

"I've never met a human." Allanna pinned her gaze on Sir Drake, then on Finn.

"This is Lord Eldrin's younger sister, Allanna of the Elves," Elyne said.

Maggie wrapped her hand around Finn's muscled forearm protectively. "And I've never met an Elf before. First time for everything, I suppose." She plastered a smile on her face, though Elyne could tell she strained to keep her voice normal. "Lord Derron brought us here at the princess's request."

With Maggie's protective gesture, Allanna turned her attention back to Sir Drake, who couldn't seem to take his eyes off the young Elven girl. He immediately seemed smitten with her. Elyne knew she would have to intervene sooner or later, especially if the knight decided to court her.

"You know the humans?" Allanna asked, looking wide-eyed with awe at Elyne.

"Aye, I do."

"How?" she asked. "How do you know them?"

"I've been to the human realm," Elyne said.

"What's the human realm like? Is it as fearsome as in all the stories?" Allanna asked. Her gaze turned back to Drake, the tips of her ears turning pale pink.

"There are stories about the human realm?" Maggie asked. She glanced between Allanna and Drake, a mischievous glint in her eyes. Elyne knew that look all too well. "I should like to hear a few of them."

"Forgive me, my friends." Eldrin arrived at Allanna's side, taking her hand in his and pulling her away. "My sister shouldn't be bothering you with such nonsense."

"She isn't bothering us." Maggie stepped away from Finn and hooked her arm into the young Elf's. "Come, Allanna, and tell me all these stories you've heard of us humans."

"You shouldn't encourage her," Elyne said.

"And why not? Everyone needs a little of that now and then." Maggie winked as she led the Elf-girl away.

Elyne huffed out a breath. "Your pardon, my lord ranger. My friend, Maggie, loves people. More than she should at times."

"Aye, and gets herself in a wee bit of trouble," Finn said. "She canna help but meddle in other's affairs. I've told her to mind her business whilst here."

"She clearly didn't listen." Elyne pursed her lips together, watching the two in animated conversation. Every few seconds, Allanna would fling a glance their direction. "Mayhap I should intervene before—"

"Maggie means no harm. She's a lovely person and wishes to help people." Derron caught Elyne's arm and stopped her from breaking up Maggie and Allanna. "Let her be."

Elyne knew what he meant. If Maggie spent any time with Allanna and learned there was a hint of interest in Sir Drake, she would do everything in her power to get the two together. It was clear too Sir Drake had more than a passing interest in the girl. This meant, ultimately, if Allanna's attention was directed to Sir Drake, she would no longer be interested in Derron.

"I will allow it," Elyne conceded. "For now."

A small group of musicians took up residence in a corner of the massive tent. They played a joyful tune, one Elyne had learned to dance to long ago. She met Derron's gaze and her stomach flipped over in response. If they were alone, she would step into his arms and kiss him. But she couldn't do that here, under the watchful gaze of her mother.

"Come, friends, let us feast and enjoy the calm of the evening," Derron said.

As they made their way to the Cauldron, Allanna walked over, her hands clasped in front of her and her eyes cast downward. Elyne waited for her to talk to Derron, but she approached Sir Drake.

"Would you dance with me, sir knight?" she asked.

"Allanna." Eldrin's tone was on the brink of anger.

"I would be honored," Sir Drake said and bowed to her with a flourish, making her blush. "But you'll have to teach me the steps. I've not danced to this before."

"That would be my honor, sir knight," she said.

Eldrin flashed the knight a look of surprise as he took his sister by the hand and led her to the dance floor.

"Maggie works fast, doesn't she, Sir Finian?" Elyne asked.

"Aye, ye have no idea." He sighed.

"Let them dance," Derron said. "What harm will it come to?"

"Harm? Just to Sir Drake's feet," Eldrin said. "My sister is quite fanciful, Lord Derron. She tends to get herself into trouble."

"Sounds like someone else I know." He cut a playful glance at Elyne, who scowled at him.

"Then she's a good match for Sir Drake," Maggie said cheerfully, joining them. "She's a very outgoing young girl. Sir Drake is older, calmer, grounded. He'll keep her feet firmly planted on the ground while she keeps her head firmly in the clouds. And he longs for love."

"Ye canna be matching an Elf with a human, lassie," Finn said. "'Tis not the way of things."

"Aye, my father will never allow it."

Maggie propped her hands on her hips. "Sometimes, though, you can't help who you love. Clearly, these two like each other well enough. She told me as much."

"Her father is the king of the Elves, Maggie," Elyne said and stared at the two as they danced, holding each other close and looking at each other as though they were the only ones in the room.

Maggie huffed. "Well…that's a pickle, isn't it?"

The night seemed to last forever. After Sir Drake and Allanna danced, they sat together and supped from the Cauldron. Elyne could see how much they liked each other by the way they laughed and talked. Queen Maeve had long since retired, exhausted from the day's events. Maggie regaled them all with tales of how she came from the future and ended up in Finn's arms followed by their adventure at the last jousting tournament. Allanna listened intently.

"I want to know more about your future," Allanna said.

"She doesn't have any more stories to tell because she made it up," Eldrin injected before Maggie could reply.

"I come from the twenty-first century," Maggie said. "And I promise you I'm not making that up. My father and best friend are still there. Probably wondering where I am." She glanced at Elyne, as if reminding her of the promise she made to take Maggie's letter to her father. Elyne would still honor that promise…as soon as she could. "Elyne can tell you. She brought me here."

Allanna's head swiveled in her direction, her eyes wide. "You did?"

"I'm afraid she's telling the truth. I did bring Maggie back in time."

"But not without a good reason," Maggie said. "Would you like to tell them or shall I?"

Elyne flushed, her face burning so hot she thought she might faint. No, she didn't want to tell them. Not that Derron didn't already know, but she didn't want to have to explain her reasons here in front of everyone. Most of all him.

"Why? Why did you do it?" Allanna leaned toward her, waiting for her next words.

"I did it for my own amusement," Elyne lied. "My mother hasn't forgiven me for it yet."

"That's not it." Maggie took another swig of her mead. "And you know it, Elyne."

"Mayhap the lassie doesna want to discuss it," Finn said, gently. He patted her arm, trying to steer her away from the conversation.

But Maggie would have none of that. "She did it for love."

Allanna blinked owlish eyes as she looked at Elyne. "For love?"

The way the Elven girl said it was almost as though she couldn't believe Elyne, the hardened crown princess of the Otherworld, could be in love. Elyne didn't dare look at Derron, for she could feel his heated gaze on her, pressing into her. She knew what that gaze would tell her—that his feelings for her ran deeper than he was prepared to voice. And if she looked into his eyes and saw that tenderness, those feelings of such deep caring, she may crumble. She glared at Maggie with her best *would you shut up* look.

"Come on, lassie. 'Tis clear ye've had too much to drink." Finn hauled Maggie to her feet.

Elyne breathed a sigh of relief. At least *he* understood.

"No." Maggie pouted. "We're still telling stories."

"Nay. Yere coming to bed. 'Tis late. Ye can tell them more tall tales on the morrow."

Finn all but dragged her away. Eldrin took that as his cue to leave as well.

"Come, Allanna. It is time for us to retire as well."

"I wish to stay." She leaned her chin in her hand and gazed up at Sir Drake. "I'm not tired yet."

"Nay, you must come now or I'll send you back to the Woodlands with a message for Father."

Allanna took the threat seriously and sprang to her feet. Sir Drake rose as well and before the Elven girl could escape, he took her hand in his.

"Until the morrow, my fair maiden." And he kissed the back of her hand with a gentle kiss.

Elyne struggled not to roll her eyes. Allanna flushed as her brother led her away. Drake never took his gaze off her until she was completely out of sight.

"I bid you both a good night, my friends," he said, bowing low to them.

"He's quite taken with her, isn't he?" Derron asked once Drake was out of earshot.

"Aye, much to her brother's dismay."

"It will be difficult to keep them apart, I'm afraid. They've already formed quite an attachment."

"The Elven king will never allow the match. Drake is human," Elyne said.

"You may be right, princess." Derron got to his feet and held his hand out to her. She slipped her fingers in his. "But as someone said, you can't help who you love."

Derron echoed Maggie's words. Words Elyne knew to be true. She had lived them for centuries. She couldn't help loving Derron, even when she thought he was dead. Even when she turned back time, sent Maggie to the thirteenth century to alter history and save his life. She would do it all over again.

"Allow me to escort you, my princess. You must be exhausted."

She nodded and they walked out of the tent into the cool night air. The moon hung close to the horizon, like a big fat ball. It bathed their encampment in blue-white light. So bright it blotted out all the pale stars. A cool breeze tickled her skin as they walked and she tried hard not to shiver. Sensing her chill, Derron wrapped an arm around her shoulders.

"I know what Lady Margaret was trying to get you to say. When she wanted you to tell Allanna why you altered time."

"You do?" she asked.

"Aye, I do." He stopped, turned her to face him. "She wanted you to say you changed time for me."

Her heart pounded wildly as she looked into those depthless eyes of his. Of course she altered time for him. He knew it as well as she did. She'd said it before when Maeve's healer came to him. She didn't want to say it again.

"Lady Margaret likes to play matchmaker," Elyne said, sidestepping the subject.

"That she does." He cupped her face. "Tell me, Elyne. Say those words to me again."

No was the first word that came to mind. She would rather fall on a sword than tell him those words again. It hurt her heart too much. She didn't know if they could ever be together again. If they could mend their relationship enough to put aside the past and go forward into the future where all that mattered was loving each other. She wasn't ready to give him her heart. Not yet.

"Tell me," he urged as his lips brushed against hers.

Blood whooshed in her head, drowning out every sound other than Derron's breathing. The entire world fell away from them, making it seem as though they were alone.

"I did do it for love," she whispered.

He kissed her again. "For me?"

"For only you."

His mouth captured hers as he tasted her, their tongues dancing together in a sweet and tender kiss. Elyne's knees threatened to buckle and it was then she realized Derron held her. His arms had enveloped her, pulled her so close she could feel the beat of his heart against hers.

She had all but told him she loved him. She could have slapped her forehead for letting him coerce her into saying the words to him. Judging by the passion of his kiss, she knew he wanted more and her heart wasn't ready for that yet. She pushed away and stepped out of his arms.

"Good night, Lord Derron," she said, taking a step backward.

"Princess Elyne, I—"

"I can find my own way. I'll see you in the morning."

She didn't wait for a response. She picked up her skirts and hurried away.

Chapter 13

The birds sang Elyne awake the next morning. When her eyes blinked open, she shoved off the coverlets and quickly dressed in a gown of pale pink with long, flowing sleeves. She pulled her hair back into a decorative snood. Assuming Maggie and Finn would still be sleeping, she headed to the main tent, butterflies in her stomach.

She didn't know why but it made her nervous to see Derron that morning. She had enjoyed that kiss way too much the night before when they had stood under the stars and pretended no one else in the world existed.

Derron was absent as others made preparations for the day's coming banquet. In the distance, she could hear the whinny of a horse. She ventured past the main tent to find her mother had constructed a stable where the demolished inn had been. Inside, there were warhorses.

Elyne headed back to the main tent to break her fast at the Cauldron. There she found her mother with Lord Derron, Gawaine and Eldrin. They all had grave looks on their faces as she approached and she immediately knew something was dreadfully wrong. Derron broke away from them and intercepted her as she approached.

"What's happened?" she asked.

"The Spear of Lugh has been taken," Derron said, leading her away from them.

"When did it happen?"

"We found out this morning," Derron said. "The Guardian is dead. Lord Kieran now has the Spear and the Sword."

"What about the Club?" she asked.

"Safe for now as far as we know."

"But you think Lord Kieran is getting closer to the Club," she said.

"He's ruthless. He'll kill anyone who gets in his way. Doesn't matter who."

This wasn't news to her, of course. She was aware of the Dark Elf's brutality. Derron suddenly clamped a hand on her arm and dragged her along behind him. She started to question him when she saw it—the dark shadow moving across the morning sky. The great black dragon flew directly toward their encampment in the middle of nowhere. As Derron dragged her along she never took her eyes off the beast.

When it landed in a nearby copse, he stopped, watching as the wings fluttered the tops of the thin trees as though they were made of paper. Shouts could be heard through the encampment as men took to their posts. Riding on the back of the black dragon was a man, his ears distinctly pointed. She wondered if this was Lord Kieran or a messenger. Moments later, he emerged, carrying a small round basket covered with a swath of leather. Elyne suspected what was in that basket and pressed a hand against her queasy stomach.

"Who is that?" she asked.

"I don't know," Derron said as they watched him approach.

Gawaine, Eldrin and the queen stood next to them.

"Cormac," Queen Maeve said. "He's the one who brought me the message of Lord Malcolm."

Cormac paused, holding the basket and peering directly at the queen. Elyne knew he stood at the edge of her protective bubble, unable to penetrate it. He flipped aside the leather covering, reached in and pulled out the head of the Guardian of the Spear of Lugh.

Elyne looked away, focusing her attention on her mother and trying desperately not to dry heave. Her mother's expression was impassive yet the color had drained from her face. Her lips had practically turned white as they formed a thin line.

"Your Guardian, Queen Maeve," Cormac shouted so she could hear as he held up the head.

She balled her fist and started toward him.

"Where do you think you're going?" Gawaine asked, panic in his voice.

"To greet this murdering brigand," she said.

"Not without me, you're not." Gawaine fell in step beside her.

"Or me." Derron released Elyne's hand and followed suit.

As Elyne watched, Eldrin, Sir Drake and Sir Finian joined them.

Elyne didn't want to be left out. She fell in step with them.

"We must be cautious," Maeve said. "He is Lord Kieran's personal messenger."

"There is nothing to trust about him," Derron said.

They paused a few feet from him. Cormac's dark glittering gaze touched on each one of them.

"Your guards, Queen Maeve?" Cormac asked, his voice holding an edge of sarcasm.

"State your business," Gawaine snapped.

"Isn't it obvious?" Cormac pinned him with his sharp, assessing gaze before glancing back to Maeve. "I come with a message." He held up the head, the eyes drooping, the mouth hanging open in a sickly manner.

"Your Lord Kieran has a peculiar way of sending messages," Maeve said.

"*King* Kieran wishes you to know what he is capable of," Cormac replied. "It is a matter of time before we find the third Guardian, the one who wields the Club of Dagda."

"You will never find the third Guardian."

"I think we might." He cocked a smile, placing the head back in the basket. "Once we have all the Treasures, a new High King will be proclaimed at the Stone of Destiny."

Maeve lifted her chin, looking at him as though he were nothing more than a nuisance. "A bold statement, indeed. Go back and tell your master he will never become High King. Not so long as I live."

Cormac laughed. "Oh, but my sweet queen, you shall not live long." He took a threatening step toward her and every man but Gawaine pulled a sword, ready to defend her. One brow lifted, but he still remained unconcerned with the men. "I wouldn't use the word *never* so carelessly, if I were you."

"You can threaten me all you like," Maeve said coolly, lifting her head and jutting out her chin. "But even if you kill me, there is an heir to take my place."

Cormac's gaze flickered to Elyne, her heart ramming hard. "As if King Kieran will allow her to live either."

"Do not threaten my daughter." Maeve's voice held an edge Elyne had never heard, one of fierce protection. "Go back and tell your king if it's a fight he wants, then it's a fight he'll get."

He chuckled. "We shall see you on the Hill of Tara at the Stone of Destiny, then, your majesty. In a fortnight. May I suggest you be prepared to battle?"

He dropped the basket at his feet, bowed with a flourish, and sauntered back toward the copse where the dragon waited.

"What a pompous ass."

Maggie's voice startled everyone. Elyne hadn't realized she'd followed and overheard the entire conversation.

"Gawaine, I want you to begin preparations to move the encampment to the Hill of Tara as soon as possible. We must beat the Unseelie there."

"Aye, your majesty. It will be done."

"What about tonight's banquet?" Elyne asked.

"It is no longer important. We have far more imperative things to worry about than that folly. I need you and Lord Derron to come with me."

"Where are we going?"

"To awaken the dragons, my daughter."

Awakening the dragons was not something Maeve took lightly. It had been centuries since they were part of the Otherworld. The queen had put them into shadow long ago. But now there was a need and, frankly, Elyne was excited to see them take to the skies once again.

"I will sift us to the dragons, awaken them, and then we will fly out."

"Why do you need us to go with you?"

"Do not challenge me, daughter," Maeve said. "You will do as I tell you."

"That's always the way it is with you," Elyne said. "Always doing what you bid."

Anger flashed across in her face and Elyne knew she pushed her too far, especially in a time like this when two Guardians were already dead.

"Ladies, please," Derron said. "You want us to go with you, your majesty, then that's what we'll do."

"The dragons reside in a place that is…unpleasant," Queen Maeve said. "I need protection." Her icy gaze landed on Elyne. "Should I fail, then it will be up to you, my daughter."

"I don't know how to awaken the dragons, nor do I have the magic to do that."

"Should I fail," she repeated, putting emphasis on each word, "then you will."

Maeve didn't wait for Elyne to reply. She sifted them from the encampment to a cold, dark place. Sifting with someone else—especially with no powers—was never fun. It left Elyne feeling dizzy and sick to her stomach. That was the first thing she noticed.

The second thing Elyne noticed was an icy wind pressing against her exposed skin, chilling her to her marrow. She blinked to focus on her surroundings, but all she saw was a glacial landscape with rolling hills covered in snow. Past the rolling hills a great mountain reached for the pitch-black sky. Sun did not live in this land. Only shadow. Only darkness. Elyne shivered and hugged her elbows, her nail beds turning blue.

"This is the shadow," Maeve said. "It will behoove us not to linger here long. Lord Derron, you may want to have your sword ready."

He wielded it, the metal *shinging* against the scabbard as he held it aloft. "Why is that?"

But there was no need to answer as they saw the giant hairy beast barreling toward them. It had giant paws and coarse white fur that stood straight up on its back. Its red eyes peered at them as though they might be a tasty morsel. It snarled as it ran, drool dripping off each razor-sharp tooth. Elyne had heard of such beasts in bedtime stories her father told her. She had never seen one until now. Even still, she recognized the winter wolf, knew what it was capable of. It could tear them to shreds in a matter of seconds.

"Steady, Lord Derron."

Maeve's voice was calm. She didn't even shiver in the cold wind. The woman didn't even have one goose pimple on her exposed arms.

"If we don't move, it will not see us as a threat," Maeve continued.

But Elyne wasn't so sure. She stepped closer to Derron, hovering behind him. The wolf pounded the icy ground and then came to an abrupt halt in front of them. It was bigger than Elyne had imagined it would be, its head standing waist high. Queen Maeve stepped toward it, held down one hand in front of its snout.

The wolf sniffed her hand, inspecting her to see if she were something tasty to eat or someone to trust. It must have decided the latter for it licked her hand, and then sat down at her feet, looking up at her with those red eyes.

"Good girl," Maeve cooed. "You may put your sword away now, Lord Derron. Come. We must make haste to the dragons."

The queen trekked across the frozen tundra, the way the wolf had come. The wolf rose to its feet, panting and padding along beside the queen, as though it were her pet. How did the wolf trust her mother so quickly? They should have been ripped to shreds according to all the stories her father told her.

Elyne didn't want to ponder this too long, for she knew her mother had secrets she would never know. Mayhap that was best. She clutched her arms to her body, trying to keep any more warmth from escaping but it was no use. She was freezing.

They crested one hill and came down the other side, now faced with the giant mountain in front of them. Once they neared, Elyne could clearly make out the dark opening and knew it was a cave. She also knew they would be going inside where the dragons lived. All the dragons from her childhood dreams and faery tales.

"There are other creatures that live in the shadow with the dragons," Maeve said. "We must tread quietly so they will not notice us."

"Why did you put the dragons in shadow?" Elyne asked.

"Long ago, before the walls of the Otherworld had been erected, dragons shared the land with Fae, Man and Elf alike. The Fae, Elves and others of our kind lived in perfect harmony with the dragons, but Man found value in their teeth, skin and bones. They hunted them to the brink of extinction," Maeve said. "It was when I put them all into shadow they maintained their lives, their lineage."

"How did Cormac get the great onyx dragon?" Derron asked.

"The dragon is called Nero, though I know not," Maeve said. "I suspect Kieran must be more powerful than we thought. He must have some way to come here to the forbidden lands and awaken them from their deep slumber."

That frightened Elyne. If Kieran were truly that powerful, then what could stop him? She suspected there was more to him than they knew, or would ever know.

"He would have to be powerful, wouldn't he?" she asked.

Maeve nodded slowly as they paused outside the caves. "Aye, my daughter. He would."

A cold shiver ran through her, jarring every bone and every tooth in her head. Her mother didn't have to explain, she already knew what was at stake now. If he had the power of the dragons, what other power did he possess? It terrified her. She inched closer to Derron and slipped her fingers in his.

"Into the dragons cave we go," Maeve said. "I would advise you both to stay close."

Elyne wouldn't have to be told twice. And she certainly wouldn't be wandering off in that dark place. Her mother reached for a torch nestled in a bracket outside the cave. She pulled it out and waved over the top. A warm, glowing flame sprang to life. She gave it to Derron and reached for a second one on the other side of the opening, lighting it.

The winter wolf started to follow, but Maeve put her hand up to stop him.

"Stay," she commanded.

The wolf sat on his haunches and whined as though wanting to come along.

"Guard us well, my friend." She patted his head and took her first step into the cave.

The glow from the torch reflected off the arctic walls of the narrow passageway, illuminating it in an eerie glow. She and Derron followed Maeve, the coldness seeping farther into her bones. The passageway opened into a huge cavern peppered with stalactites reflected by a pool of smooth-as-glass water. There seemed to be a pale, ethereal glow about the cave and it wasn't coming from their torches.

The place was calm, quiet and dusted with shadows. As Elyne squinted into the darkness, she thought she could make out shapes and the light glistening off scales. Maeve stepped to the edge of the pool, holding her torch aloft. Derron stood behind her, one hand on the hilt of his sword. Elyne was left with nothing to do but stand next to her mother, shivering.

"Ambrielle," Maeve called softly. "I release you from your slumber."

A long silence ensued. So long Elyne wondered if there even was a dragon in the cave.

And then she saw it. Two eyes blinked open and stared at them.

Maeve saw them too and turned toward the beast. She bowed low and placed a hand on her dragon's nose.

"Speak to me, as you once did," Maeve said. "Let me hear your voice."

Nay, I speak only to your minds. You disturb my slumber. Why? the dragon asked in a deep, gravelly voice.

Her gaze landed on Elyne and Derron before turning back to Maeve. Mayhap to ensure they all understood she would not speak aloud to them. It was considered an honor to hear the great voice of a dragon.

"We need your help."

Why should we help you? When you've sent us here in the dark place for all eternity?

"I sent you here for your own good, Ambrielle, you know that. If I hadn't, you'd all be extinct."

The dragon snorted, a puff of smoke emitting from her snout. Then she moved, lifting and rising and taking a step toward them into the light. The ground shook beneath their feet and Elyne grasped Derron's arm to keep steady. When the dragon emerged into the light, Elyne could see the deep-emerald scales reflecting the light. Gold eyes peered at them with curiosity.

'Tis true. You did. Six thousand years we've waited in shadow. Though I do not know why we should help you. We could stay here in our darkness with our treasures.

"You could. But our lives are threatened," Maeve said. "The Unseelie have risen and are trying to destroy our kind. I believe the Dark King uses one of your kin to battle us. Twice now we've seen the great onyx dragon, Nero."

Ambrielle tipped her head to the side in question.

"If I die," Maeve said, "then any hope of you awakening again will die with me."

Nero flies with the Dark King?

"Aye."

If we should help you, then what will you give us in return? Ambrielle asked, her voice rumbling through all their minds.

"Freedom," Maeve said. "Freedom to roam the skies of the Otherworld once more."

The dragon *hmmed* deep in her throat and pondered the offer. She stretched her great wings as far as they would go—each tip touching one side of the cave. *To fly again. 'Tis a tempting offer.*

"I will release you from slumber for the rest of your days," Maeve said. "What say you then?"

There was silence again. As Elyne glanced around the cave, she could see two more pairs of eyes peering toward them. Ambrielle nodded then.

We accept your terms.

The other two dragons emerged from the shadows. One an azure, the other a striking silver that reminded Elyne of pale moonlight.

"Thank you, my old friend." Maeve placed a hand on Ambrielle's snout again and patted her. "Will you carry us back to our encampment?"

I should be honored, my queen. Ambrielle turned her gaze to Elyne and Derron. *Who has come with you to awaken us from our slumber?*

The azure dragon nudged Elyne, startling her as she snorted hot breath over Elyne's face. She had never thought she'd stand so close to something so big, yet here she was. And she wasn't certain she wanted to actually ride on the thing.

"My daughter and crown princess of the Otherworld," Maeve said, gesturing to Elyne. All three dragons bowed low. "She will take my place someday. You will follow her as you would follow me."

As you wish, my queen, Ambrielle said.

The great dragon turned her gaze on Elyne, peering at her in a way that made her feel as though Ambrielle could read her innermost thoughts. Elyne shifted from one foot to the other.

She is as strong as you, my queen. Fierce and confident, if a bit arrogant. Yet she has a strong moral fiber. We would be honored.

Maeve gave Elyne a look she couldn't read, which made her more nervous than she had ever been before. Usually, she could read her mother's moods by the way she treated her, talked to her, looked at her. Now she wasn't so sure. Her gaze flickered away and then to Derron.

"This is Lord Derron, Knight of the Realm, Protector of the Otherworld and Guardian of the Sword of Light," Maeve said.

The silver dragon emerged from the shadow to stand next to Derron. Unlike Elyne, he didn't seem bothered by their overbearing presence at all.

Ambrielle turned her gaze on Derron, giving him the same once-over she had given Elyne.

He is fearless and charming. Loyal and noble. A true Knight of the Realm. We are Ambrielle, Aura and Luna, Ambrielle said. Aura being the azure dragon and Luna the silver one. *We will come to your aid, my queen. We have chosen our Fae riders.*

Aura nudged Elyne. Apparently, the azure dragon had chosen her. Elyne wasn't sure whether to be terrified or honored.

"I will open the cave," Maeve said, "and we will take to the skies. Dragons, take your positions." She turned to Derron. "Give me your torch, Lord Derron."

The silver dragon walked to the far side of the pool, nudging Derron to follow. Maeve nodded, as though silently telling him he should do what the beast wanted. He handed her his torch and followed the dragon. Aura hadn't moved, apparently already in position. The three dragons stood as though at the apex of a giant triangle.

Queen Maeve stood at the edge of the pool, inches from stepping into it. She held one torch in each hand, staring across the water and chanting something softly under her breath. Elyne couldn't hear her. She had no idea what she was saying. Then Maeve tossed both torches into the water. They immediately snuffed out with a sizzle, extinguishing the yellowish light in the cave.

"Let there be no more shadow. Let there be light," Maeve said.

One or two bubbles popped in the pool. Slowly at first until it turned into a rolling boil. The ground rumbled beneath their feet. Maeve stepped to Ambrielle, placing her hand on the beast's shoulder. Ambrielle dipped her head, hiding the queen from sight. Azure did the same to Elyne as did Luna to Derron.

Stalactites cracked and fell to the ground with a thunderous roar, some landing in the once-peaceful waters of the pool with a splash. Overhead, the cave broke into giant fissures, the rock parting and letting in the pale light of the outside world. Elyne gasped and stepped closer to the dragon, who held her head down and puffed out her heated breath.

It is the great opening. We have long awaited it.

A new voice boomed in Elyne's head, making it throb. She pressed her fingers against her forehead, realizing then Aura mind-spoke to her.

I will protect you from harm, princess. You may trust in that.

She stood under the great azure dragon as the cave fell into pieces around them. As they watched and waited for its opening. When the dragons would be free. The waters in the once-calm pool crested over the broken stalactites as well as broken pieces that had once been the ceiling. It filled up the shallow pool quickly until there was no more pool and water crested the small banks, sloshing over their feet.

Elyne hugged closer to the dragon, unhappy her feet were now not only cold but also wet.

"Alight!" Maeve shouted this over the din of the rumbling cave.

Aura lowered her neck as far as she could to the ground. *Come, princess. This place is no longer safe.*

Elyne didn't need to be told twice. She hoisted herself onto the back of the dragon and watched as her mother and Ambrielle lifted into the night sky, followed by Derron and Luna. When their turn came, Elyne's breath caught in her throat as the great dragon lifted off, the beat of her wings as loud as the beat of her heart.

Up, up, up they went into the night sky. Into freedom.

Chapter 14

The ride had been exhilarating and Elyne was sorry to see it come to an end when they landed in the encampment to gaping spectators. Aura leaned her neck low to the ground to allow Elyne to step down. Her feet had barely touched the ground when Maggie came running to her.

"I don't believe it!" Maggie looked up at the dragon. "I thought when your mother said you were going to wake the dragons it was a metaphor for a trebuchet or something."

"This is Aura." Elyne patted her neck. "The silver one is Luna and the emerald one is Ambrielle."

"Wow. All my life I thought dragons were nothing more than a myth."

"The queen put them into shadow to protect them from hunters," Elyne said.

"I never thought it possible. Then again, I'd never met an Elf either until I came here. This truly is a magical world," Maggie said.

Elyne glanced around the encampment, saw that most of the men wandered around, talking. But there was a frenzied undercurrent, a tension in the air Elyne could feel. Her feeling further confirmed when Gawaine intercepted Maeve right away.

"There's been some news," Maggie said.

"What is it?"

"Lord Derron, a word," Queen Maeve called.

Gawaine and Eldrin were at her side as Derron joined them.

"What's happened? What's wrong?"

"Kieran broke through the Barrier and invaded the Queen's Palace," Maggie said under her breath. "The walls were breached."

Elyne's stomach twisted in a sick knot. "Casualties?"

"There were no survivors," Maggie said.

Elyne pressed her hand against her swirling stomach, her knees threatened to buckle. Her home was now overrun with Unseelie. The palace she would have one day inherited was most likely gone.

And all the servants left behind, innocent Fae, slaughtered in cold blood. Maggie grasped her by the arm and led her away. They sat on crude stools in the middle of camp.

"That means the entire palace is under Kieran's control," she said. "He knew my mother left it unguarded."

"Ellie, I'm so sorry," Maggie said.

"He took advantage of our weakness."

Elyne pitched forward, putting her head in her hands. It took all her strength to keep from heaving for the second time that day. All around her it seemed her world was crumbling, the life she once knew altered in a way that could never be changed back. At least her mother and the Council hadn't been in the palace.

"The war is beginning," Elyne said, her voice muffled against her hands.

"Let's not think about that right now. Let's think about that tomorrow."

"I have to think about it now," Elyne said. "Derron will be fighting. My mother will be leading the war effort. We are not prepared for war, Maggie. Not the Seelie Court."

"Why not?"

"We've never had a need for an army. We have always been at peace so our numbers are thin." She sat up quickly, the blood rushing to her head so fast she saw pinpricks of light. "What fools we are! All this time Lord Kieran has been preparing for war, building an army, searching for the Guardians. He's planned this for years. No, centuries. And what have we done?" She looked at Maggie, shaking her head. "We've done *nothing*. Derron frittered away his time in the human realm at jousting tournaments. And I followed him, meddling in human affairs."

"If you hadn't meddled in 'human affairs'," Maggie did air quotes, "I would have never met Finn. For that, I will be eternally grateful. And anyway, what's done is done. You can't undo it. Things have been set into motion and they can't be changed."

"You should go home, Maggie. You and Finn and Sir Drake. My world has changed and not for the better. My world is broken."

"Not broken." Maggie patted her hand. "A temporary setback. We'll stay. The men will fight."

"What are you going to do here?" Elyne asked.

"Hold your hand and worry with you. But I have no doubt the Fae *will win*. I'm sure of it."

"I hope you're right."

"Have you talked to Derron yet?" Maggie asked.

The abrupt change in subject stopped Elyne. She glanced his way to see him currently embroiled in a conversation with her mother. "About what?"

"Don't play dumb. You know about what. How you feel about him."

She crossed her arms, pretending ignorance. Maggie had been trying to get the two of them together for a while now and Elyne was sure her human friend would be up to her matchmaking in no time. "I'm sure Derron knows I'm fond of him—"

"Fond?" Maggie shook her head. "Are you kidding me?"

"*Fond.* That's it. Nothing more." They both knew she lied.

Maggie snorted. "Sure, okay. If that's the way you want it."

"Now is not the time for that."

"There is never a convenient time for love, Ellie."

Maggie was right but Elyne wasn't ready yet to face her feelings for him or the impending battle that lay ahead. She much preferred to lock away the feelings she had for Derron and deal with them later.

What if he doesn't survive?

It was the niggling voice in her head that insisted on nagging her. The one that always had the bad news and gave her the what-ifs. She hated that voice and shoved it away with vehement disapproval.

Derron was a survivor. He would always be part of the Seelie Court. She couldn't imagine life without him. He had survived every jousting tournament—no, that wasn't right. He *hadn't* survived until she had turned back time to save him. Derron could die like all the rest of them. The very thought made her stomach cramp.

"I have to deal with that in my own time, Maggie," Elyne said finally. She ignored the voice in the back of her head telling her Derron could die. "Now is not that time. And I don't want to talk about it anymore!"

She quickly got to her feet and dashed off. She thought she heard Maggie mutter a "Geeze, okay," as she hurried away.

She headed directly for her mother, Gawaine and Derron, joining the trio near the main tent. They were discussing strategy.

"We cannot go back to the palace now, my queen. It's far too risky," Gawaine said.

"Those who were left behind are all dead. Nothing can be done for them, your majesty." Derron had a dark, sorrowful look on his face. A different one than when he learned of the death of his father. It pained her to see him in such a state. Her stomach cramped again.

Elyne had never seen her mother distraught. Her forehead creased with the stress of everything and for the first time, Elyne noticed lines in her youthful face. Despite that, she still maintained her cool.

"If we counterattack now, it will be nothing but a death mission," Derron continued.

So her mother had wanted to go back to the palace and try to retake it. Even Elyne could see the folly in that and she was no strategist. With Kieran's men in the palace and all their people slaughtered, it would be silly to go back there.

"The palace may be lost to us now, but we will regain control of it," Maeve said. "How many soldiers do we have?"

"Three thousand," Gawaine said.

"It will not be enough. Lord Derron, do you think you can talk with Eldrin about recruiting the Elves to fight for us?" she asked.

"I can ask him," he said. "But Elyne and I had a difficult time trying to convince the rangers to come along. We will have to speak directly to the Elven King."

"That shouldn't be a problem, since Eldrin and Allanna are his children."

"We can try," Derron said with a half shrug. "We'll need someone to act as messenger."

"I'll go," Elyne volunteered, not waiting for anyone else to respond. "I'll go talk to the king."

Derron's head snapped toward her and she could hear his sharp intake of breath. His eyes glittered with surprise and a hint of pride. She knew he would try to talk her out of it but she wasn't going to let that happen. Leaving for the Woodlands would be the perfect excuse to put some distance between her and Derron. Being in the same encampment with him was becoming almost unbearable.

Maeve gave her a look of disbelief. "You?"

"No, Elyne." Derron shook his head.

"I convinced the rangers to pledge their swords to me. I can convince the king."

"What makes you think you can be so persuasive?" Maeve asked.

"Because I can," Elyne snapped.

"It's too dangerous," Derron said. "You can't go. I won't let you go."

Thinking fast, she said, "I won't go on foot. I'll take Aura. She can fly me there, to the king. Eldrin can go with me if you feel that uneasy about it."

"Unacceptable," Maeve said, sounding and looking as snooty as she possibly could.

This was Elyne's chance to prove to her mother she could be responsible, she could be a leader. This was her one selfless act. And Maeve was trying to squelch that. Elyne's eyes narrowed. "Why not? You don't think I can do it?"

"Actually, no, I don't."

"I *will* do this, Mother. I can speak to the king on your behalf. And if you don't allow me to go, then I'll go anyway. With or without your consent."

Fire flashed in Maeve's eyes. Elyne was tired of the way her mother treated her. Tired of trying to prove anything to her. She would prove *this* to her and show her she could be the crown princess and future ruler of the Otherworld. She would do this.

"Elyne, Kieran's dragon—"

But she held up a hand to stop Derron. "I'm well aware of Nero, Lord Derron. Now, shall I ask Lord Eldrin to come with me or not, Mother?"

"What makes you think you'll be successful?" Maeve wanted to know. She crossed her arms in a familiar gesture Elyne had often imitated. Elyne made a mental note not to do that again.

"Because I believe the Elven King will want to help us. He's aware Lord Kieran murdered the Dark King. He doesn't want his people to be annihilated any more than you or I do."

"If this is a ploy to get your powers back—"

"No ploy, Mother."

"Very well, then. Go, Princess Elyne and see if you can form an alliance with the Elven King."

"I object to this, your majesty," Derron said, the tips of his pointed ears turning hot-pink with his anger. "You cannot allow her to go."

"'Tis done, Lord Derron. She goes." Her gaze flickered back to her. "But if you fail, then do not bother to come back."

Elyne clenched her fists, watching as her mother turned on her heel and stalked off, Gawaine following at a frenzied pace in her wake. Elyne couldn't hear what he was telling her but judging by the way he talked with his hands, she knew he was objecting, too.

"That's it then," Elyne said.

She didn't wait for Derron to reply. She hurried off to find the azure dragon.

"Princess Elyne," he called.

She ignored him, picking up her pace and walking so fast her leg muscles objected. She could hear his boots hurrying after her. She didn't want him to catch up to her. She didn't want to explain to him.

"Elyne," he called again but still she refused him. When he finally caught up to her, he snatched her by the arm and spun her to face him. "Why are you doing this?"

"Because I have to." She jerked her arm away and started off again. "She will never respect me, Derron, if I don't do this. Never."

"That's not true, Elyne. Your mother loves you—"

"Don't give me that speech," she snapped. "My mother doesn't trust me. She thinks I can't do anything and mayhap she's right. I intend to prove her wrong."

"You don't have to prove anything to her."

"You know that's a lie as well as I do. I have to prove to her I'm worthy of the title of crown princess. It's the best chance we have to survive."

"Why you, Elyne?"

"Because if I don't, she'll find someone else to inherit the realm. You, for instance."

"Elyne, that's preposterous. I have no right to the crown. You know that."

"A simple law change will fix that."

"You're determined to do this?"

"I am."

"Then let me go with you."

"No." She stopped, turned to him and put her hand on his chest. She gave him a push. "Go away, Derron. Back to your council meetings and war planning. Aura and I will go to the king."

"What about Eldrin? I thought you intended to take him with

you."

"I never intended to take him with me," she corrected. "I'm going alone."

Elyne walked away from him, half expecting him to follow her. He didn't. And when he didn't and she realized she really was going alone, her heart ached a little more.

Chapter 15

Stupid. That's what she was being, Elyne thought as she walked toward the faery mound where the dragons hid. She had no clue how to convince the Elven King to send troops to help the Fae cause. He would probably laugh at her, tell her to go home to her burning palace. The Elves had no interest in fighting and hadn't in thousands and thousands of years. Their last fight had been against the Fae and that hadn't turned out so well for them, had it?

She bowed her head, her chin on her chest. "Gods…give me strength." She whispered it in the wind, a silent little prayer to help her through her latest foolishness. She needed strength from the gods, or anyone. Strength to carry on and make it past this war. Should they survive she would tell Derron she loved him. If he rejected her then, she would know it wasn't meant to be.

Hello, my friend.

Aura's voice was in Elyne's head before she saw her. Looking up, the dragon stared at her with those golden eyes. Aura blinked slowly, nodding as if in greeting. The way she sat reminded Elyne of a cat. Her front legs were straight, her back legs tucked up close to her body and her great tail with barbs on the end curled around her. The gossamer wings were flattened against her, seeming to be invisible next to her shiny scales.

"Aura."

You have need of me?

"Aye. I want you to take me to the Elven King in the Woodlands. King Urdithane."

The Elven King? Thousands of years have passed since we have spoken to the Elves.

It sounded more like rumination than an objection. "Then you'll take me?"

I will fly you there, aye.

"Good. The sooner we go, the better. I'm on official palace

business."

Aura lowered her head and allowed Elyne to climb up on her back at the base of her neck. Elyne gripped the scales, leaning down close to her as Aura stood on all fours, spreading her beautiful iridescent wings. As her wings went up, she crouched and pushed off from the ground, straight up into the pink sky singed with afternoon light.

When Aura took to the air, it made Elyne's stomach clench and she held on as best she could. The flight to the Elven King would be a short one for the dragon with the twenty-foot wingspan. Looking down, she watched the world flash by in browns and greens and gold. Every now and then she spied the rich blue sparkling waters of a loch, sunlight glistening off the smooth glass surface.

As they approached the Woodlands, she could see the crumbling walls of what was left of the Queen's Palace. Of course, she would see the palace as they passed overhead. How could she forget? It hadn't occurred to her and now, remembering the fate of the palace once more, she had to see for herself the destruction. She had to know if it was true.

"Fly near the palace," she shouted into the wind. "But not too close. I don't want them to see us."

As you wish, princess.

Aura banked right and headed directly for the palace, keeping her distance as best she could. It wouldn't be hard to spot the azure dragon, though, so they had to be cautious. Aura seemed conscious of that as she kept her wings gliding through the air.

As they neared, Elyne could see the outer walls had been breached, the ground scorched black. Broken wooden ladders scattered around the outside, a battering ram that had burned itself out from the retaliation fire, abandoned trebuchets and catapults outside the walls pointed at the palace. A fire smoldered somewhere within the walls as indicated by the gray smoke wafting upward in lazy curls.

Upon seeing the destruction, she could understand why no one had survived. Her throat constricted with thick tears, her eyes burning. The once-beautiful palace had been reduced to barely more than a ruin. What would become of the Fae now? If they couldn't retake it and defeat Kieran, then they would have no ruling seat.

We will rebuild. We will survive.

Aye, you will, Aura said in her head.

So the dragon could hear her thoughts, too. Elyne shuddered as gooseflesh rose on her arms and the hot tears spilled down her cheeks. Seeing the destruction doubled her determination to recruit the Elves.

"To the Elven King, Aura." Elyne whisked away the tears. She didn't need the king seeing her in that state. She needed him to see her strong, powerful and unwavering.

Aura banked left, back toward the Woodlands, toward hope. From their vantage point in the sky, Elyne could see the Elven king's home. He lived high atop the giant sequoia tree, his home carved not into the trunk but built around all the thick branches and limbs.

Elyne had never seen anything like it, either in the human realm or her Fae world. She had never ventured that far into the Woodlands to see how the Elven king ruled. But here, she could see the seat of the king and knew he would be inside, presiding over his court as her mother would be presiding over hers had none of this happened.

Intricate footbridges went from one tree to another. She could make out rope ladders, many basket systems that went up and down from one level to the next. Elves were hard at work yet pausing to stare at them as they neared.

There would be no place for Aura to land in the treetops, Elyne realized. So she would have to get close to one of the bridges and step off.

"Get close to the top of the king's palace there." She pointed to the bridge she had in mind. "Then get somewhere safe until I have need for you."

When you are ready, call for me.

Aura slowed her flight the closer she got to the trees, but the wind from her wings still blew away leaves and shuddered branches. Elves paused to watch and point at the great creature hovering in midair as Elyne swung one leg over and prepared to step off. She took a deep breath, hoping she wouldn't plummet to her death.

You will be safe. I will catch you if you fall.

Grinning, she patted Aura and pushed off the beast's neck. She stuck out her foot with a tentative step and reached for the rope handhold at the same time. But when she brought her second foot up, it slipped on the edge of the wood. She lost her footing completely and started to fall, gasping and grabbing on to the handhold with both hands. The rope burned into her palms.

Behind her, she could hear the dragon try to reposition to get under her and nudge her back onto the bridge, but Aura was too big and trees were in the way.

Elyne tried to pull up and not panic. She thought she could hear shouts and screams from below her, but she was too attuned to the flapping of Aura's wings and the pounding of her own heart to really notice.

A hand clamped down on her wrists, holding her in an iron grip. She looked up into the handsome face of an Elf. He had pale-green eyes and pale silvery hair. He hoisted her up in one swift move, pulling her over the rope handhold. He smiled, his teeth straight and white and perfect. He held her a moment longer than necessary. She finally wiggled out of his grasp, stumbling backward onto the bridge, her heart in her throat.

"Thank you."

"Your dragon is beautiful," he said, though he never took his eyes off her.

He wore the classic Elven band with the woven silver knotwork on his head. His fine clothing was a brocade doublet with swirls in a rich silvery thread. His shirt was fine white linen, the voluminous sleeves ending in cuffs fitting perfectly at his wrists and buttoned with two silver buttons. His black breeches were tucked neatly in a pair of black shiny boots with buttons up the outer leg.

Aura, you may go now. Elyne mind-spoke to the dragon and shooed her away.

Aura turned, crashing through limbs and trees, before disappearing into the sky.

"My name is Princess Elyne, I am crown princess of the Otherworld." No sense wasting any time. "I must speak with your king immediately about a serious situation."

He merely smiled a quiet smile, his perfectly shaped lips forming a narrow line. "Ah, the Faery princess. I knew you were no Elf."

"Aye, I am Fae. I thought that readily apparent by my introduction."

He chuckled, a deep rumble in his throat. "Indeed. I can take you to King Urdithane, but he doesn't often agree to meet with…Faeries."

"I am no ordinary Faery," she quipped. "And I come with an urgent message from Queen Maeve. My mother."

"We have no interest in your Fae wars or battles," he said.

"Mayhap you should allow the king to make that decision." It took great restraint to keep her tone even. "I believe you will have an interest when your trees are torched and your homes have burned to the ground."

"As you said, an urgent message from Queen Maeve. Follow me, then."

He started down the footbridge that wound upward around the giant trunk of the tree. As Elyne followed, it occurred to her he hadn't bothered to offer his name, nor had she asked. She would once they reached the king and she could properly thank him for his help.

The bridge ended in front of two giant wood doors in the shape of an arch flanked by two soldiers in full dress. Each one had a quiver on his back, held a bow in one hand and had a sword strapped to his belt. Though they didn't look deadly, Elyne guessed they would quickly take the head off any intruder. Her guide pushed open the doors and led her inside, the guards not bothering to stop him. They each gave her a curious glance as she followed the Elf inside.

Somewhere in the distance, she could hear flute music and the faint strumming of a harp. A few voices rose up in song while others laughed. The polished wood floors reflected the torch light, the walls nothing more than the inside of the trunk. The palace was redolent with the smell of the earth, damp leaves, freshly cut grass and sunshine. An iron bracket adorned every wall and column, holding a blazing torch with a white flame.

As they walked deeper into the heart of the tree, the music and laugher and singing become louder, clearer. She could see another doorway like the one they'd entered. Double doors with a high arch. Beyond that, a warm glow lit up the room. The throne room. Her heart stuttered in her chest. She, crown princess of the Otherworld, was about to enter the throne room of the great Elven King.

Once they crossed the threshold, the shiny floor was covered with a plush garnet rug leading directly to the dais where the king sat on his throne, which looked as though it too had been made from the ancient tree. The twisted, knotted wood curved into a high back, the arms and legs gnarled. The whole thing was draped in a matching garnet cloth. The king presided over his court with a flask of ale in hand.

As people took note of them walking toward the king, the music, laughing, singing and voices fell silent. All eyes were on the Fae princess as she approached the king.

If you fail, do not bother to come back.

Her mother's harsh words rang in her ears as she made the final steps to the bottom of the dais. Her guide paused, stepped aside and Elyne did something she had never intended to do. She knelt, bowing her head in respect. The king sat a little straighter, placing his ale aside and peering at her with keen interest. He leaned his elbow on one knee, giving her a good once-over before running his hand over his chin.

"Whom have you brought to me, Andahar?" he asked at last. "Is this Princess Elyne I see?"

"Aye, Father, it is the crown princess of the Otherworld, as she so pointedly told me."

Elyne didn't appreciate his condescending tone, nor did she appreciate the fact that the Elven prince hadn't bothered to announce himself when he rescued her from a certain plunging death. She glanced at Andahar and could clearly see the resemblance he had to Allanna and Eldrin. She looked back at the king, wondering how many children the man had.

"Rise, your highness." The king stood, waving her to her feet. "There is no need to bend the knee to me. Your family was once a friend to mine."

Low voices muttered throughout the court, as if trying to decide if the king had truly lost his mind. The Fae were not welcome in the Woodlands, yet he seemed to welcome her. Something about his words dislodged an ancient memory, one that Elyne had buried long, long ago.

"I come with a message from Queen Maeve, your grace," Elyne said, standing to her full height.

His brows rose over those dark, searching eyes. He stepped down off the dais to stand in front of her, peering at her with curiosity. "Why would Queen Maeve send me a message?"

"We have a common enemy. If I may have a word with you?

Alone?"

Gasps filtered through the room as though asking for a private audience with the king was unheard of. Next to her, Andahar laughed but the king never looked away from her. His gaze narrowed, the curiosity replaced by wariness.

"Shall I grant her request, Andahar? Would you like to hear what the princess has to say?"

"Aye, Father, I think we both should."

Elyne flushed hot. She gritted her teeth, trying to maintain her cool. It took all her strength not to lash out at them.

"Come then, your highness, to my private chamber so that we may speak." He glanced around at those gathered in his court. "Alone."

He held out his hand to her in invitation. Not hesitating, Elyne placed her fingers in his. The king was exactly as she had remembered him from their brief encounter in the Woodlands, when Eldrin brought them there to plea for help from the rangers. But there was something else familiar about him, some thread of memory that kept threatening to surface she hadn't quite grasped yet.

King Urdithane led her to a small chamber off to the side of the grand throne room and closed the door softly behind them. The floor here was covered with more of the plush red carpet and a small seating area with four chairs that looked inviting. The king waved her to one chair, and then sat across from her. Andahar sat next to her.

"Before you tell me what's so urgent, your highness, perhaps you can tell me where I might find my daughter, Allanna. She seems to have disappeared from the palace."

"If you're asking me, then surely you must already know." Irritation clawed through her. Couldn't he allow her to get right to the point?

He chuckled, a low sound deep in his chest. "I do know. I knew she slipped out of the palace to follow Eldrin and his men. She's always been a wild sort. More interested in weapons and warfare than dancing and sewing. I'm going to have a time marrying her off. I knew as soon as she heard about the quest to the Barrier, there would be no keeping her away."

"Do you not fear for her, your grace?" she asked.

"Of course, I do. What father wouldn't?" He sighed then,

resigned. "The comfort I take in her being away is I know she will be safe under Eldrin's careful watch. But you didn't come here to talk about my daughter. Tell me what is so urgent, your highness."

"You know of the death of the Dark King in the Unseelie Court," she said.

"Aye, I do indeed." He poured three tankards of red wine. Picking one up, he passed it to her. "But this is not news. We knew of this long before now."

Elyne took the tankard, but her stomach was too knotted to drink. "Aye, I know. You recall that Lord Derron, Knight of the Realm and Protector of the Otherworld, and I came with Prince Eldrin to your Woodlands to ask for help."

The surprise was evident on Andahar's porcelain features. "Father? I knew not of this."

"Aye, I do recall. I allowed him and his rangers to accompany you on the voyage to the Barrier to stop the Dark King. Has that not happened?"

"Why was I not told of this?" Andahar demanded, as though his father had not spoken.

Elyne rushed to answer the king, cutting off his response to the prince. "Because, your grace, we received word Lord Derron's father was captured and murdered by Lord Kieran."

"This means nothing to me. I do not care for your Fae troubles." He sipped his wine, proving to her the news was of no consequence to him.

"You should care," Elyne snapped, trying to maintain her cool. "Shortly after we learned of Lord Malcolm's tragic and gruesome death, the Guardian of the Spear of Lugh was also captured and murdered. Lord Kieran now possesses both the Sword of Light and the Spear of Lugh. The Club is within his reach and, we believe, he intends to make haste for the Stone of Destiny once he has those three Treasures in his grasp."

King Urdithane glanced over the cuticles of his fingers, clearly bored with the conversation. "Why should we assist the Fae any further? You have our rangers' help. And as I understand it, they have pledged their fealty to you."

"It will not be enough against an army ten thousand strong," Elyne said. "My mother bade me come to you and ask for help. Surely you understand we are all headed for war. If you do not help us, then Lord Kieran will annihilate every one of the Fae. He's already butchered those who remained at the Queen's Palace and taken it over."

"The Queen's Palace has fallen?" Andahar asked, turning his attention to Elyne. Apparently, his previous questions had been forgotten for the moment.

"You really must stay on top of current events, my son," Urdithane said. "I knew of the attack."

"And you did nothing?" Elyne asked. "You allowed Kieran to murder innocent Fae—"

"It is not my position to interfere with Queen Maeve and the Fae."

She clenched her jaw until it ached. How could she get through to him?

"My mother and her war council are making camp along with several thousand troops in the Queen's Army. Had she been there when the palace came under attack, she would have been killed, too." Saying the words aloud made Elyne's throat constrict. Tears threatened but she refused to allow them to fall. She would not cry here in front of Elven royalty.

"I have no interest in helping you," King Urdithane said.

Anger flared inside Elyne. How could he be so lackadaisical about it? How could he sit there and pretend he didn't care about what happened to them? Her hand tightened around the tankard until her muscles ached.

"Your grace, do you not understand? If Lord Kieran manages to get to the Stone of Destiny with the other three Treasures, he will be able to proclaim himself High King of the Otherworld. That includes your Woodlands and any of the other Elves who inhabit the Seelie Court. With my mother and me dead, Kieran will be the one who rules. He will not turn a blind eye to your tree homes. If you rise up against him, he will march on your forests and burn your trees to the ground. He will destroy everything and everyone you hold dear. He will kill you and your family without blinking an eye."

"Father…" Andahar's voice was quiet and timid.

Elyne glanced at him. His forehead had creased with concern and worry and question. Hope rose in her. If she couldn't convince the king, then mayhap she could convince the prince. She rushed on before either of them could speak.

"There was a time, long ago, when the Elves and Fae were one.

When we fought side by side and lived in peace. I beg you, King Urdithane, to allow that time once again."

"Why should I? When the Fae nearly wiped out all the Elves?" His words seared her, flaying her flesh. "I remember those lost days, princess. I remember them well. And it was because of your mother…your Fae queen, that we are now forever divided."

That was news to Elyne. She made a mental note to delve into that subject further. She opened her mouth to speak when he cut her off with a wave of his hand.

"Do not speak to me of alliances, princess. You Fae do not honor them."

Insulted, she stared at him with fire burning in her gut. "Is there nothing I can say to convince you?"

"Nothing." He pressed his lips together in a straight line.

"Even if I give you my word as crown princess?" It was a last-ditch effort. She could feel the hope dwindling to nothing more than burning embers.

"The word of a Fae means nothing to me," he growled. "Go back to your battles and leave us."

"But Father—"

"No, Andahar."

When the king spoke those last two words, Elyne knew his decision was final. He would not change his mind. Slowly, she rose to her feet and placed the ale on a nearby table. With her heart in her throat, she walked to the door, her hands shaking from both anger and fear. Her mother had said if she failed not to come back. So where did that leave her? If her father were here…

Her father… He would know how to handle this stubborn king.

And then she remembered…when she was but a girl and her father still alive, the Elves and Fae were not at odds. She paused at the door, remembering Urdithane's words. *Your family was once a friend to mine.* The memory clicked inside her and surged to the forefront of her mind. Urdithane and her father, King of the Fae and the Otherworld, had been friends.

After her father was killed by Kieran and her mother took over the Otherworld with her steely hand, the Elves and Fae became at odds. Before she reached the door, she turned back, looking at the king and the prince.

"My father once ruled the Otherworld," she said, her voice hollow in the room. "He was also murdered by Lord Kieran. That is why you banished him to the Unseelie Court. Whatever happened between you and my mother…I can assure you I do not share her views of the Elves. I believe there can be peace and harmony between our races once more. I have always believed that and I always will. Even if you do not."

She reached for the door, her hand on the handle as she twisted it. The door cracked open, letting in a shaft of light from the throne room.

"Wait." King Urdithane's voice stopped her. "Wait, please, Princess Elyne. I've been too rash."

Elyne closed the door and turned back to him, standing there with her heart pumping wildly. Did this mean he was changing his mind? Would he help her?

"I always admired your father. We had a very amicable relationship. Unlike the queen and I."

"I remember you," Elyne said. "In the Beforetime."

"Ah…the Beforetime. Is that what you call it?" His smile was cold and bitter. "Before your mother accused the Elves of premeditating the murder of the King of the Otherworld and sent us all down a path of destruction. Before we had to invoke the Treaty of Separation."

Elyne flushed. Although she knew Kieran had once been an Elf, she didn't know her mother had accused the Elves of such a thing. She would have to find out the truth from her once this was all over.

"You didn't know, did you?" he asked. She shook her head. "I cannot fault you for that, then, can I? Prince Andahar, do you concur?"

"Aye, Father, I do."

"I do not agree with how your mother rules the Otherworld. I never will. However, I believe you have a genuine heart. I believe you would keep your word to me if you gave it to me."

"Aye, I would." Things had quickly spiraled out of control. She feared the king would ask something of her that she could not agree to. Then what would she do? Make the pact and hope her mother would honor it?

Urdithane ran his hand over his chin, his skin bristling against the pale whiskers. "We must help the Fae. For them and our kind as well. I believe that is our duty now in the face of war. Especially since one who was once our own invades the Seelie Court. Is that something you would agree upon, Prince Andahar?"

"Aye, Father. I believe Princess Elyne is right in that we will be destroyed as well as the Fae. There is a reason Lord Kieran was banished to the Unseelie Court and is now a Dark Elf."

"Indeed. It will take some time to gather men, princess, but we will send them to the Stone of Destiny," the king said.

The sudden relief that washed over her made her feel faint. "You have my grateful and heartfelt thanks, your grace."

Thank the gods, he had agreed to help her. Now she could go back to her mother with her head held high, knowing she had quite possibly saved them from the Dark Elf. She would take her leave of him, call Aura, and head back to the encampment.

"On one condition," he added.

Panic stabbed her like a sharp dagger. It was what she feared would happen. She was not authorized to negotiate a deal with him. Only to ask for his assistance. Then again, her mother did say not to return should she fail. She would have to handle this with care.

"I will do what I can for you, your grace."

"No. I want you to give me your word," he said.

At some point when she had her back to him, he had put down the wine. Now his long, slender fingers curled around the arms of the chair, his nail beds turning white. Now she understood the speech about how he knew she would honor her word, putting her in a place she didn't want to be. She knew whatever he asked, she would have to agree and she would have to give him her word. And somehow, she would make it happen, with or without her mother's help.

"I want you to agree to remove the Treaty of Separation so the Elves and Fae may coexist as they once did."

Fecking hell. She couldn't agree to that. If she did, her mother would have her hide. The Treaty of Separation had been in existence for thousands of years. It wasn't something that could be broken overnight. There would have to be negotiations made, agreements, politicking. She hadn't the stomach for any of that.

"If you give me your word, I will honor it as the truth and I will give you four thousand men to fight your cause. But the lives of Elves will not go without this cost. We will not bleed with the Fae for nothing."

"The Treaty cannot be broken without my mother's consent.

She will wish to negotiate."

"Do you think I don't know this? I intend to negotiate with your mother…but not without you. You will be present for each meeting and you will make sure the Treaty is abolished for all time."

He leaned forward to press his point, one elbow on his knee. Prince Andahar glanced between the two of them, his initial look of surprise turning to one of smugness. He didn't know the king had planned such a thing, yet he approved of it. And why wouldn't he? To be able to mingle once again with the Fae would empower both their races.

Gods. How can I not agree? Saying no would mean she could not return to her mother triumphant. Saying yes would mean she could return to her mother but with a steep price. She met the king's dark gaze, lifted her head a little higher and smiled.

"You have my word, your grace."

Chapter 16

And so the price was set.

Elyne mind-spoke to Aura to return as Andahar escorted Elyne out of the palace back to the footbridge where they had met. No words had passed between them since leaving the king behind. Elyne had no more words to give the Elves. She had no idea how she would handle this with her mother.

"You can leave me here," Elyne said, pausing on the footbridge and looking out over the treetops. Her hands gripped the rope, her fingers tightening around the roughened handhold.

"You can call your dragon from here?" he asked.

"I have already called her. She will come and take me back to our encampment. Will you send word when the men have been dispatched to the Stone of Destiny?"

"I will see to it personally." He paused. Though she didn't look at him, she could feel his hesitation and saw him drag his bottom lip through his teeth, as though he were choosing his words carefully. "I didn't know how your father was killed, princess," he said, his voice soft. "I am truly sorry for your loss."

The distant memory came crashing back to her. "It was a very long time ago." She turned to him then. "I didn't know my mother blamed the Elves for his death. I thought she blamed me."

"Why you?"

"I was with my father when Kieran killed him. The Dark Elf let me live, though I don't know why. I thought my mother held that against me all this time."

"Mayhap she was looking for someone other than Kieran to blame," he suggested. "Grief will do that to someone. I'm sure she never blamed you, though."

But she blamed the Elves.

Her mother's grief was something she had never considered. Elyne had never seen her cry, not once, since the death of her father. Though, in retrospect, the queen had the Otherworld to rule. She had no time for her grief. She had to remain strong in his absence. A small piece of Elyne could forgive her and remove the longstanding grudge between them. She understood so much more now.

"Thank you, Prince Andahar, for your help."

He took her hand, kissed her knuckles. "Thank you, princess, for agreeing to abolish the Treaty of Separation."

The dagger of fear stabbed her heart again and she immediately shoved that aside. She would deal with that much later.

"I gave King Urdithane my word," she said, sounding more confident than she felt.

Her mother would not like this new agreement. *So be it.*

The *whomp-whomp* of wings in the distance hinted that Aura had returned. As Elyne looked into the distance, she could see the giant dragon headed for them.

"May the gods speed your way," the prince said.

She nodded thanks as he stepped back. Aura crashed through the trees, disturbing leaves and limbs. She hovered by the footbridge as close as she could. Elyne noticed the dragon had a saddle and reins, which was definitely something new.

"I see your dragon has made friends with the Elves," Andahar said, nodding toward the harness and reins. "That saddle is Elvish."

Elyne tipped her head in question to the dragon. "Did you enjoy your stay, then?"

They gave me this for you, princess. They call me the Ancient One.

If Elyne didn't know any better, Aura was smiling. She reached for the reins and pulled herself onto the dragon's back. She wanted to ask why they gave her these things, but she didn't want to voice it in front of the prince. Were they being kind to her simply because she was a Fae princess? Or did they know she came to ask for help from the Elves?

"Farewell, Andahar."

"Until next time, princess."

Aura maneuvered her big body and turned toward the sky, leaving Elyne with the last image of the smiling Elven prince.

You were successful in your quest, my friend?

"I was," Elyne answered.

Will the queen be pleased?

Queen Maeve pleased? In all her years she wasn't sure if the queen was ever pleased about anything. Elyne patted Aura on the neck. "Let's hope so."

Daylight waned, turning the sky from pale pink to a burnt orange. Derron paced the main tent from one end to the other, his hands behind his back. He couldn't eat or rest until Elyne was back safely. Queen Maeve had disappeared after her harsh words to her daughter, not to be seen for the rest of the day. Gawaine made an appearance to bring her food, telling them the two of them made preparations to move the encampment to the Stone of Destiny.

Derron understood the stress the queen must be under. They were shorthanded by too many to fight against Lord Kieran. They all knew that. But to tell her own daughter not to come back should she fail to get help from the Elves enraged him.

He'd told her as much. She'd given him an icy stare.

"It is not your place to tell me how to treat my daughter," she had snapped.

"What if she doesn't come back?" he'd fired at her. "Then what?"

"Then the Elves have refused to help us and we are on our own." Her tone was icy cold.

"And what of Elyne, your majesty? What happens to her? You intend to leave her alone? She could be captured by Lord Kieran. Or worse. She could be killed."

"Elyne made her choice to go." Her eyes narrowed as she said it, her tone changing from icy to flat and unconcerned.

Derron looked at her with disbelief. How could she toss the princess away as though she were nothing more than yesterday's garbage? He didn't understand it. He would never understand their strained relationship. Since Elyne's father had died, the queen and her daughter had drifted further and further apart. Almost as though Maeve blamed Elyne for his death.

"One of these days, your majesty, you will end up alone."

"I am already alone." Her words left a frost on the air.

Derron left her to wallow in her self-pity and returned to the tent to pace. Not even Maggie's sunny outlook could console him or soothe his dark mood. The men gave him a wide berth and left him alone. It was probably for the best since all he could think about was Elyne and her safe return.

He heard the wings of the dragon before he saw it and hurried from the tent to look up into the now inky sky. Aura flew home and on her back, Princess Elyne. He breathed a sigh of relief to see her coming back unharmed and sooner than he expected. Her quest to get help from the Elves must have been successful. His heart hammered hard in his chest with the anticipation of news she might bring.

As the dragon neared, it garnered quite a few onlookers. Several of the Fae soldiers filtered out of their tents as well as a few of the Elven rangers including Eldrin and Allanna. Even the queen stepped out of her tent to watch her approach. Aura landed quietly and bent her head to allow Elyne to step off. The princess slid to the ground with grace. She turned back to Aura, said something to her and patted her on the neck. The dragon gave her a friendly nudge before lifting off back into the night sky.

Elyne's gaze landed on Derron first, then her mother. She lifted her head a little higher. Her mother strode to her with long steps, her grown flowing around her. Eldrin and Allanna joined them.

"You've returned, I see," Queen Maeve said, her tone cool.

"I have," Elyne replied, her tone equally cool.

Elyne's stance matched her mother's. Both with feet apart, arms folded across chests. The princess with a defiant look on her pretty face. The queen with a look of cool acceptance on hers. Had she not expected the princess to come back?

"Does this mean you've managed to get the Elves to agree to help us?" Maeve asked.

"King Urdithane and Prince Andahar will send four thousand men to the Stone of Destiny in less than a fortnight."

Derron couldn't stop the smile that broke out on his face. She had done it. "Well done, princess."

"Very well, then. Lord Gawaine, the camp leaves for the Stone of Destiny at first light."

No *thank you* or *well done* or any sort of praise from the queen. She didn't bother to wait for a reply from Gawaine either. She turned on her toe and headed back to her tent.

"As you wish, your majesty," Gawaine said to the empty air the queen left behind. He turned to Elyne and bowed deeply. "Our most heartfelt thanks for your efforts, princess."

"I'm sure my mother feels the same way."

Even Derron could hear the bitterness in her tone. Gawaine

took his leave of her, following after the queen to make the necessary preparations.

"You spoke to our father?" Eldrin asked.

"Aye, I did. And your brother," Elyne said. "Your palace is a beautiful one, Prince Eldrin."

"I'll be sure to pass along your compliments when I next see my father," he said.

"Forgive me for prying, but why did you become a ranger? No taste for life at court?"

"Prince Andahar is first in line. Whereas, I am not," he said simply. "I chose this life."

"You didn't tell him about me, did you?" Allanna squeaked. "That I was here?"

"No, I did not." No, she didn't tell the king his daughter was with them since he already knew the truth.

The girl blew out a breath. "Thank you, Princess Elyne."

"It is I who thank you and your kind." Her gaze flickered back to Eldrin. "Your father was not so easy to convince but once he understood the situation, he agreed to help us."

"I do hope that will not be forgotten," Eldrin said.

"I gave him my word, your highness, as he gave me his."

He gave a nod of understanding. "Come, Allanna. We must pack our belongings and make ready to leave in the morn."

The others filtered away with the two Elves, leaving Derron and Elyne alone again.

"I'm glad you're safe," he said. "And that you came back."

"Did you think I wouldn't?"

"I didn't know," he said honestly. "I hoped you would. I worried you wouldn't."

"I didn't take my mother's threat lightly, Lord Derron." She clasped her hands in front of her, looking tired and haggard. He could see the fatigue and stress lines at the corners of her eyes. "I'm sure she hoped I would not return."

"She doesn't think that." He tried to wave away the idea. "Sometimes she doesn't realize how she treats you."

"It matters not, Lord Derron. Her opinion of me hasn't changed in centuries. Nor will it, I suppose."

"How did you convince the king?" he asked, abruptly changing the subject. He suspected Elyne was right about her mother, but he didn't want to hurt her any more by discussing it.

Indecision flickered across her face. She dragged her bottom lip through her teeth, as though she wasn't sure what her response should be. Then she gave him a winsome smile. "Did you forget how charming I am?"

He laughed. "Come now, princess. It was not your charms that convinced the king. I'm sure of it." He knew she wasn't telling him everything as he took her by the arm and led her away, back toward the tents. In the distance, Gawaine shouted orders to remove the ones that weren't necessary and one by one, the tents fell flat to the ground.

"The king and I came to an understanding," she said. "And agreement."

"What sort of agreement?"

"I can't tell you. Not yet."

"Why not?" He stopped her, turned her toward him and held her by the shoulders. "Elyne, if there's some promise you made to the king, then I have to know."

"I will tell you and my mother in time."

"I don't understand why you can't tell me now."

"Because you are Knight of the Realm, Protector of the Otherworld, Guardian of the Sword of Light. If I tell you, then it will be your moral obligation to tell the queen. And I can't have you telling the queen yet. Not until the war is over."

"Elyne…"

"No, Derron."

She was adamant. He knew with her stubborn streak she would divulge the information when she was ready. What she didn't realize was two could play that game. He would find out another way. The last thing they needed was to be blindsided by some promise Elyne made to the king.

"Very well, then," he said and released her.

She blew out a breath. "Thank you for understanding."

"I am glad you're back and unharmed."

"Why would the Elves harm me?" She looked taken aback.

"It's not the Elves I worry about. It's the spies. What if you had been captured by Lord Kieran? We would have never known."

The thought of Elyne in the hands of that madman made him sick with dread. He shoved it away, not wanting to visualize what could have been. Something he said made her face fall, turning serious. She reached for him, slipping her hand in his.

"I saw the Queen's Palace," she said. "Or what was left of it."

"You flew over it?"

"I had Aura take me over it."

"Elyne—"

"I know it was dangerous. But I assure you, we exercised great caution. I had to see it for myself. I had to know how bad the destruction was."

"And how bad was it?" He was almost afraid to ask.

"Awful." She whispered the word.

He could surmise from the threat of tears in her eyes what she saw. "Was it completely destroyed?"

"The shell of the palace was left but most of it had been burned to the ground. They used a battering ram to break through the front gate. The walls had been destroyed." She gripped his hand hard. "There wasn't much left and it was overrun with Unseelie."

"We'll get it back, Elyne. I vow to you we will return it to its former glory." He squeezed back to show her he meant it.

"I hope so."

Her gaze locked on his and he could see the pain behind her eyes as she rapidly blinked away the tears. Seeing her home destroyed—the only true home she'd ever known—must have been hard for her. He wished there was something he could do now that would help. He cupped her face, never releasing her gaze.

"I really am glad you're safe."

"You said that already." Her words were barely above a whisper.

"Aye, I did."

Without waiting for a response, he touched his lips to hers. She responded immediately, her velvet mouth accepting his kiss without resistance as she had in the past. As if she wanted him to kiss her. He savored the sweet recess of her mouth, his tongue dipping in. She tasted like honey wine and smelled like wind and sunshine. And something happened then that was most unexpected.

Elyne slid her arms around his neck and pressed closer. Every curve of her body molded to his. She shivered. His arms encircled her, holding her closer, keeping her safe next to him. Through the material of her gown and his tunic, he was aware of the unmistakable pump of her heart hammering rapidly, matching his beat for beat. Almost as though their bodies had tuned to each other.

His kisses moved from her mouth down her neck. "Come with me to my tent, Elyne." He breathed the words against her skin. His tongue danced over her swiftly beating pulse.

Elyne flinched in his arms and she tried to move away. She was no simpleton and knew what he implied without saying the words. He wanted her. Under him. On top of him. Next to him. It didn't matter. All that did matter was taking her to his bed and making slow sweet love to her. He wanted to feel the quiver of her body under his, know every inch of her from head to toe. Kiss every expanse of milky-white skin.

Her hands landed on his shoulders with a little push but he wouldn't let her go. He tightened his grip around her, refusing to release her. His mouth was still doing a dance on her neck, nipping her earlobe. He thought for sure he heard a small mewl escape her throat before her fingers dug into his shoulders, her nails pressing through the cloth of his tunic.

"I cannot."

"You can." He pulled her closer, held her steady.

"No, Derron." She shoved harder, breaking the circle that enclosed her. She stumbled backward, her lips damp from kissing and her cheeks flushed. "I cannot."

He'd never felt so robbed in his life as he looked at her standing out of reach. All he had to do was take two steps and take her once again into his arms. He could kiss her into compliance but he didn't want that. He wanted her to come willingly. Mayhap he had misconstrued her return kisses as the same thing he wanted.

At least, that is what he told his wounded mind. He wanted to ask her why not, wanted to know why she wouldn't acknowledge her feelings for him. All she had to do was tell him. She clasped her hands in front of her and pressed her lips together.

"As you wish, princess." Derron inhaled deeply, exhaled slowly in an effort to get his body under control.

"Please don't misunderstand," she said, her voice so quiet he could barely hear her.

She looked as though she wanted to say more. She took a step forward, placed one hand on his chest and kissed him quickly. Her lips barely brushed his before she moved away. He didn't even have time to process that before she hurried away.

Elyne rushed through the tents, searching frantically for her own. Her heart pounded a rapid tattoo in her chest, her breath hitched in her throat. All she could think about was Derron, the way he kissed her, pulled her into his arms. The way he asked her, his mouth on her throat, to come to his tent with him. She knew what he wanted. She wanted it, too. But something held her back. Something kept her from going with him.

She wasn't ready. How could she ever be ready for a man who was much more experienced in the ways of love than she? Would he decide he didn't want her if he knew?

All this went through her mind as she ran, skittering at last to a halt. Her chest heaved as her breath seesawed in and out of her.

"Ellie?"

Maggie's voice startled her. She pressed her hand against her chest.

"Are you all right?"

"Aye. I'm fine."

"You don't look so good." Maggie took her by the arm and led her into a nearby tent—her own. Was Maggie coming to find her and happened upon her? She didn't know. Not that it mattered. She was glad to be in her own tent, away from Derron and her mother. "Come sit."

Elyne allowed her to lead her to the narrow bed. She sank into the soft mattress and took a deep, calming breath.

"I heard what you did," Maggie said. "That you went to the Elven king."

"I did." Elyne didn't want to elaborate. She was still busy thinking about that kiss and Derron.

"That was very heroic of you, Ellie."

She glanced up and met Maggie's gaze, wondering if the human was mocking her. She could tell, though, her friend meant it as she had a look of sincerity on her face. She perched on the edge of the bed next to her.

"It was what I had to do. Nothing heroic about it," Elyne said. "At least, my mother doesn't think so."

"Don't let her unkind words wound you. She doesn't mean it."

"Everyone keeps saying that but what you do not understand is that she does mean it. Or she wouldn't say it."

"I believe she is very proud of you. She's afraid to admit it."

"I disagree. She blames me for my father's death."

"I can't see how she would," Maggie said. "Especially after you managed to get help from the Elves."

"The Elves…" She snorted. "Nothing comes without a price, Maggie."

"What do you mean?"

She stood, prowled the small tent. "If I tell you something, you must swear you will never reveal it to anyone."

"I can keep a secret."

Elyne flashed an *I don't think so* look. She hoped she could trust Maggie to keep it to herself, for she had to tell someone. Mayhap she merely needed the reassurance that she did the right thing, not that Maggie could tell her that but it would ease her conscience.

"You mustn't tell anyone, Maggie. Even Finn. *Especially* Finn. The man is so honorable he'd run right to Lord Derron."

"I promise I won't."

"I did get the Elven king to agree to help us but it was on the condition I agree to abolish the Treaty of Separation."

Maggie knit her brow. "What's that?"

Her human friend would have no knowledge of the problems in the Otherworld. She quickly explained the short version to her so Maggie would understand. The more she told her, the wider her eyes got.

"Oh dear," Maggie breathed when Elyne had finished. "And you haven't told your mother this?"

"How could I? She wasn't exactly thrilled I'd returned and she didn't even thank me for getting the aid of the Elves."

"When do you plan to tell her?" Maggie asked.

"I'd thought after the battle at the Stone of Destiny. Provided we win."

"You don't think she'll be upset?"

"Of course she will but she'll find anything to be upset about." Elyne propped her hands on her hips. "I can't help that. But if the Unseelie wipe us out on the Hill of Tara, then what does it matter? My mother and I will both be dead and Lord Kieran will attack the Elves anyway."

"And if you win on the Hill of Tara?" Maggie asked.

"Then I'll face that when I have to." She flopped back down on the bed next to Maggie. "The king wants me to be involved in the negotiations."

"And the queen won't like that either," Maggie said.

"Definitely not."

"So why did you tell me?"

"I had to tell someone," Elyne said. "Else I'll go mad."

"Oh, Elyne. I definitely wouldn't want to be in your shoes. What if you hadn't agreed to the condition?"

"He would have refused to send the men. He doesn't care for my mother."

"Understandable," Maggie said. "But all things considered, Ellie, I think you did the right thing. I've heard Lord Kieran's army is ten thousand strong and the Fae are seriously lacking in that department. I don't know much about warfare, but I do know the odds wouldn't be with you if you didn't have help from the Elves."

It was nice to hear, even from a human, that she did the right thing. Would her mother like the terms? No. Would she be upset Elyne kept it from her? Absolutely. But she couldn't risk telling her yet lest her mother refuse the offer.

"I'm glad you think so, Maggie."

"Now. What about you and Derron?" Maggie asked, abruptly changing the subject.

Elyne laughed. "Always the matchmaker, aren't you?"

"You and Derron are perfect for each other. It would be a shame if you didn't get together."

"Lord Derron has bigger things to worry about than me."

Even as she said the words, she couldn't stop remembering those kisses or the invitation to his bed. The invitation she had refused. *What a fool I am.*

"Yes, he was quite beside himself while you were gone," Maggie said.

"He was?"

"He kept a watchful eye on the sky from the time you flew away to the time you flew back."

"How do you know?" Elyne narrowed her eyes in suspicion. Maggie hadn't been present when she returned from the Elven king.

"I have my ways." She gave her a conspiratorial grin. "I can assure you, though, it's true. He loves you so much. I don't know what's stopping you both from falling into each other's arms."

Elyne flushed, the heat flashing through her entire body. Had

Maggie seen them together? She would feign innocence.

"It's not a good time for that sort of thing," Elyne said, shoving aside the warm feelings of need. "The Guardians are disappearing one by one and now we're to meet the Unseelie at the Hill of Tara."

"So?" Maggie asked. "It's never a good time to fall in love but people do it under all types of circumstances. Look at me and Finn."

"You and Finn are totally different than me and Derron."

"I beg to differ," Maggie said. "Do I need to give you a push in Lord Derron's direction?"

"No. I don't need any help in that department and I'll thank you to keep out."

"As you wish." Maggie held up her hands in surrender and then got to her feet. "Since we leave at first light, I think I'll get some sleep. Sleep well, Ellie."

"You, too."

When Maggie left the tent, Elyne lay on the bed, staring up at the canvas until she finally drifted to sleep, falling into dreams of dragons and Elves.

Chapter 17

Elyne's sleep had been restless so she left her tent long before the dawn came. She decided to put her sleepless night to good use and help direct the teardown and packing up of the encampment. Her mother must have had a sleepless night as well, for she was out shouting orders to the men, too. Elyne did her best to keep clear of her. She wondered, though, if this was the way their relationship would be for eternity. Strained, uncomfortable. Would they ever make amends?

Mayhap when the queen is on her deathbed.

A sobering thought. She and Elyne both could be dead on the Hill of Tara if Kieran had his way. And then he would be High King. They would both have departed this world at odds with each other. Once everything was done, then mayhap she could try to repair their broken relationship.

Elyne needed to get away. She decided she would ride ahead with Aura and scope out the Hill of Tara to find a place to build their new camp. As she approached Aura, though, she could see a man talking to Luna. She could tell by the sound of his voice and the way he stood it was Derron. Her heart flipped in her chest. Her stomach fell to the bottom of her shoes. She wasn't prepared to see him yet, not after leaving him a few hours before. She halted in her tracks, watching him talk to the big beast, patting her neck.

He looked dashing—though he always did—in his black breeches and knee-high boots. The boots had long since lost their high shine and now were covered in dust and muck. His shirt was soft suede in a pale brown and over that he wore his cloak with the triskelion clasp at the neck. His golden-blond hair fluttered in the breeze and it was then she realized how long it had gotten. The ends now brushed his shoulders. He wore a three-day scruff of beard and when he tilted his head just right, she could see his five o'clock shadow illuminated in the early morning light.

It took her breath away how stunningly handsome he truly was.

When he looked up, their eyes met. Her knees threatened to turn to jelly. It took all her strength to keep her feet in place when she really wanted to run to him, fling herself into his arms and kiss him senseless.

"Good morrow, princess," he greeted and gave her a nod.

"Good morrow, Lord Derron." She dipped a quick curtsy.

Had their relationship taken yet another turn as they exchanged formal words? She watched his hand stroke Luna's neck. The dragon fluttered her gossamer wings, ruffling the air around them. If the beast had been a cat, Elyne was sure she'd be purring.

"I've been getting to know Luna better," he said. "She loves wild strawberries. Did you know that?"

"Most dragons do," Elyne said. "It's their favorite snack."

Luna dipped her head in a nod and snorted, white steam curling from her nose. She nudged Derron, as if to tell him she wanted something. Elyne glanced around, wondering if Aura was nearby. She didn't see the great azure dragon though.

"I was thinking I should take Luna and fly to the Hill of Tara for a little reconnaissance. See where we can move the campsite before Kieran gets there."

Elyne blinked surprise. "I was thinking I should do that with Aura."

"It seems we both have the same idea, doesn't it?"

In the distance, she spotted Aura coming in for a landing. Elyne braced herself for the rumble of the earth, but the dragon was light on her feet. She landed without so much as a sound and lumbered toward Elyne, head down, and nudged her in greeting. She still wore the harness and reins the Elves had given her. Elyne patted her neck in greeting.

Derron grinned and Elyne wanted to melt. "Fancy harness you have there."

"When I visited King Urdithane, it seems the Elves took a fancy to Aura. They fashioned this for her. Makes riding easier."

"Mayhap you should use your powers of persuasion and secure one for Ambrielle and Luna, too." It sounded like more of a suggestion than a request.

Even so, Elyne didn't know the king all that well, despite the promises they'd made each other. She wouldn't be so bold as to ask the king for such a thing.

"Mayhap we should ride together with Aura." She didn't know

what made her say it but suddenly she couldn't bear the thought of not being next to him.

He considered her words, his gaze thoughtful. "Are you certain you want that?"

Pain stabbed her heart. Had she hurt him last night with her refusal? "Aye, I'm certain."

More certain than anything in the world. To fly together, away from the war and death and destruction if for a moment would make her forget everything. Mayhap it would make him forget everything, too. Then things could get back to the way they were before.

"Will the queen miss you?" he asked.

"The queen and I aren't speaking to each other at the moment. I doubt she'll know I'm gone. Shall we ride?"

Aura hunkered as close to the ground as she could while Elyne climbed on, Derron following. His body curved against her as he settled into position. She was acutely aware of his pressing thighs, warm and inviting. He reached around and took the reins in his hands.

"Off we go, then, princess."

To the Hill of Tara, Aura.

By your command, my friend.

Derron's body tensed against Elyne as Aura took flight, her wings beating the wind in that tremendous *whomp-whomp* sound Elyne had grown so familiar with and so fond of. At the horizon, the morning sun peaked over the edge of the world, burning the night sky from inky blackness to a pale pink. How she loved sunrise in the Otherworld. She had forgotten how much she missed it when she was off to the human realm. She hoped once all this was over and done with, they could restore the Queen's Palace and enjoy the sunrises once more.

With Derron at my side.

Elyne warmed to the thought, enjoying the fantasy of having him beside her, watching the rebuilding of the great palace.

His love for you is great, my princess.

Hearing Aura's words in her head made her jump. How did the dragon know that? Elyne thought each one picked their own rider and attuned their thoughts to that one Fae.

I am ancient. I know many things, Aura said.

And you know Derron loves me?

Aye, I do. He thinks about you often and wishes to make amends for whatever heartache he has caused you.

Elyne knew the reference was to the kiss they'd shared. That and Elyne's disappearance shortly after his invitation to his tent. So he was sorry. And he wanted to make things right between them.

She was touched.

Do you not love him? Aura asked.

This from a dragon. Elyne nearly snorted. How did such a beast know the hearts of the Fae?

We love too, my friend, and mate for life.

Then again, Elyne surmised, the dragon did understand.

I do love him, Elyne said. *But I'm afraid.*

When hearts are involved, there is nothing to fear.

Wise words from a wise one. Mayhap the dragon was right.

The flight to the Hill of Tara hadn't taken long from their campsite. As they flew over the land and the villages, they could see the destruction Kieran had left behind. Small towns were no more. Houses had been scorched and burned to the ground. Dead Seelie Fae littered the ground. Elyne sucked in a sharp breath at the sight, for as far as they could see, there was nothing but death. She could say nothing, do nothing but point.

"I see it," Derron said in her ear.

"Awful."

"We'll make him pay for what he's done to our people."

Elyne prayed to the gods Derron was right and Lord Kieran would meet his end soon. Up ahead, she could see the Stone of Destiny—a stone monolith rising out of the ground and stretching upward to the sky. It stood about twenty feet high with stone steps roughly hewn into one side. Once the rightful ruler of the Otherworld was proclaimed, the Stone of Destiny would glow with a faint golden light. Even as they approached, Elyne could see the stone did not glow.

"The Stone?" Derron asked.

"It's not glowing," Elyne said.

Her heart did a *ka-thud* in her chest followed by a wild beat. Fear spread through her in a sickly feeling, cramping her empty stomach. If the stone wasn't glowing that meant either her mother was dead—which she knew was not the case—or Lord Pywll, the Guardian of the Stone, was dead. And worst of all, the men that had been sent to protect the Stone of Destiny were all dead.

Her worse fears were realized when they saw the headless body of Lord Pywll, the green hillside stained a dark red under what was left of him. Sickened at the sight, Elyne took a deep breath to keep from heaving.

"He's dead." She said it aloud to confirm her fears. "They're all dead."

"Let's go back," Derron said. "It's not safe here."

He was right. Kieran had left men behind to guard the Stone of Destiny, knowing all too well if he abandoned it after killing the Guardian, Maeve could take it. And he still had one more Treasure to find.

They gathered the attention of some of the men below. They grabbed their bows and arrows and fired off a few shots into the sky. Aura banked, arrows missing her by a narrow margin.

Take us somewhere safe, Aura.

The dragon complied, heading back toward their camp. She landed far from the threat on the edge of a silvery loch. Elyne slid off the saddle, her feet landing on the cold, hard ground. Derron followed after her. She fell to her knees at the water's edge and dry heaved until she couldn't anymore.

"Are you all right?" he asked.

"I need a minute." But her voice quivered and her hands shook as she dipped into the cool water and splashed it over her heated face, trying to swallow back the bile that threatened to rise again.

"If we had been there," Derron said, his voice gentle, "we couldn't have saved him. And we would have been killed, too."

"I know."

He crouched down next to her. "There is something I don't understand. If Kieran was here with his men, why not name himself High Ruler? He'd already killed the Guardian."

"Because…" Elyne paused, trying to control her racing pulse. "He needs all four Treasures together. And he needs my mother's blood." Allanna's prophecy raced into her mind. *She saw the death of both my mother and me.*

Derron stared at her a long, silent moment. "What do you mean…your mother's blood?"

Derron hadn't remembered his folklore. Elyne blew out a deep, shaky breath and launched into the explanation.

"For one to become High Ruler, the previous ruler must already be dead. If not, then a blood sacrifice has to happen. By that I mean Kieran will need to kill my mother and let her bleed into the ground around the Stone. Now the Stone is silent. It's not glowing. So to make it glow again he would have to kill Maeve, wield the Sword, Spear and Club together and step upon the Place of Crowning. There is an ancient spell that must be chanted and whoever has stepped upon the Stone of Destiny will be named High Ruler of the Otherworld."

She wasn't sure, but she thought she saw his face pale.

"We should go back. Warn your mother."

"She already knows. And Allanna saw it in her vision."

Derron glanced over his shoulder. Next to them, Aura lapped at the water. "I'm not comfortable with this, Elyne. I don't even have my sword."

"An unprepared knight?" She gave him a coy smile as she rose, and then lifted her skirt to reveal the dagger he'd given her when they'd started their trek to the Dark Realm. She'd worn it every day since. "I'm not."

"Cheeky girl." He ran his hand up her calf.

She slid it from the sheath and handed it to him. "Does that make you feel better?"

"I'd feel better if we were heading back to the camp."

"I agree. We should. It's not safe here with all the Unseelie crawling over the land." She headed toward Aura, Derron falling in step beside her.

"I'm glad you've come to your senses about that. Why do you suppose Kieran left the Stone of Destiny instead of waiting for Maeve to come to him?"

Elyne shrugged. "He needs the Club. He may already know where it is. We have heard nothing about Lord Llewelyn. That means one Guardian still lives."

"Your mother told Cormac he would never find him," Derron said. "It could be she expected Kieran to kill Lord Pywll and sought Lord Llewelyn and moved him to safety."

"Then what of the Club?" she asked.

"What if your mother took the Club away from Llewelyn? What if she's keeping it close to her? That way she would know it was safe and in her hands. Completely out of reach of Kieran and his men."

"Then someone close to her could be Guardian of the Club?" she asked.

"It's possible. She could even have it. And if that's true, then the queen is in more danger than we realized," he said.

"If Kieran tracked your father and Lord Udrich easily, then he must be close to finding Lord Llewelyn. I'm sure he was enraged when he killed the man and found no Club."

It made sense to kill the Guardian of the Stone of Destiny. He was the easiest target. But the Sword of Light had the most power. Mayhap why he went after that first. Wielding the Sword would give the holder ultimate power. Make him undefeatable in battle, even without the other Treasures.

Elyne pressed a hand against her roiling stomach.

"She has him close, then," Derron said. "She knows who he is and that he has the Club. All this time, it was right under our noses."

"We have to get back to warn her," Elyne said, hurrying toward Aura.

"Will she listen?"

"She'll have to."

She and Derron climbed on Aura's back and headed back to the campsite. Elyne kept her eyes on the sky, looking for the black dragon. She knew if she saw it, they would be in trouble. Still, she couldn't help but glance down at the world below. That's when she spotted the Elves. A long line of them, some on horseback and some on foot, heading toward the Hill of Tara. Her heart skipped a happy beat. The Elven king had kept his word and sent the soldiers. They were outnumbered two to one and Elyne knew once the Elves arrived, they would do away with Kieran's men with ease.

Derron patted her shoulder and pointed. He'd seen them, too. She nodded, smiling at him. He smiled back.

There is hope yet.

When they arrived, things were in upheaval. Most of the camp had been dismantled in preparation for moving to the Hill of Tara. But there was something else at work. Some other underlying form of panic. She spotted the queen right away, her Council surrounding her as well as Eldrin and a few of the other Elves. Several pairs of eyes lifted to the sky when they heard the dragon coming and waited for Aura to land.

Elyne and Derron slid off her back and hurried to the queen's side to find out what was happening.

"Another Guardian dead," Gawaine said. "And at the Stone of

Destiny."

Elyne spotted the covered basket at her mother's feet and knew immediately Cormac had already paid them a visit. That sickly feeling crept over her again, knowing the Guardian's head was in that basket.

"We have come from the Hill of Tara and the Stone of Destiny," Derron said. "We saw the death and destruction there."

"That and the Stone is not glowing," Elyne said.

"So it begins." Maeve's gaze flickered to Elyne. "Leaving the camp to go to the Hill of Tara without my consent was dangerous *and* stupid."

"It was my idea, your majesty," Derron said. "Elyne came along to help me find a suitable place for the new campsite."

"And did you find one?"

"I believe we will be best suited on the south side of the Stone of Destiny. Where the Guardian and the men were killed."

"Very well, then. We'll plan to meet the troops there. Send word, Lord Gawaine."

"By your command, your majesty."

"Princess Elyne and I also saw the Elven troops heading toward the Hill of Tara on our flight back."

The queen stood very still and quiet, almost as though she had turned into a statue. "So King Urdithane kept his promise to send troops." No one missed her gaze flickering to Elyne and then back again to Derron. "There is hope for us yet."

Her words echoed Elyne's thoughts as they flew back.

"Even so, with the Guardian of the Stone of Destiny dead, it's only a matter of time now before he finds the Guardian of the Club of Dagda," Gawaine said.

"That won't happen." Maeve gave him a pointed look.

They sized each other up for a long moment. Elyne saw the flicker of trust in her mother's eyes. She glanced to Gawaine, who had set his jaw, a muscle ticking there. Almost as though the two of them shared the secret location of the Club.

"I can assure everyone here the Club of Dagda is safe. As is the Guardian." Again she gave a pointed look at Gawaine.

Lord Gawaine must be the Guardian of the Club of Dagda.

If they were trying to keep it a secret, neither of them were doing a good job. Elyne could tell from the looks they kept giving each other her suspicion was right.

"What do you intend to do, my queen?" Lord Vaughan asked.

"I intend to continue to the Stone of Destiny. This is where Lord Kieran will make his final stand. I will meet him there. Ready the Queen's Guard. I want them sent ahead, for all the good that will do. The Guardian is already dead. Hopefully, they can reach the Stone of Destiny before Lord Kieran does and keep it protected."

"If I may, my queen," Gawaine said. "Wouldn't it be easier to sift us all there? It would thereby ensure we reach the Stone before he does."

"It would, aye," Maeve said. "But I've used most of my magic to maintain what is left of the Barrier, for all the good it's done. Kieran's magic is powerful and I'm weakened. Sifting us there will further diminish my powers and I must conserve all I can for the final battle with Kieran."

Warning bells went off in Elyne's head. She had no idea her mother had used a counteroffensive to Kieran's magic to destroy the Barrier. Fear gnawed at her. With her mother's powers weakened—and she not having any herself—who would defend the Stone of Destiny should Queen Maeve fail?

"What about the humans?" Derron asked.

"They will be well protected, since you insisted they be part of this war. Using a minor spell, I've placed protection from dark magic over them. Kieran's darkness will not hurt them."

"Your majesty!" One of the queen's men ran through the encampment toward her. Everyone turned to see him barreling through, not stopping for anyone. When he halted, his chest rose and fell as he tried to catch his breath. "My queen, Lord Kieran is trying to break down the walls between the human realm and the Otherworld."

"Can he do that?" Gawaine asked, his voice becoming a high-pitched squeak.

"Apparently, he can. And we have grossly underestimated him," Maeve said. She looked at the solider. "What else do you know, Ewan?"

"My spies tell me he is confident he will defeat you at the Hill of Tara. All the while, the walls well be coming down, allowing his Unseelie to pour into the human realm."

"Total domination, your majesty," Derron said.

Elyne's heart hurt. She had never expected it to come to this.

Their world was never meant to bleed into the human realm and it sickened her to think of the destruction the Unseelie would cause, not to mention the loss of human life.

"He intends to rule over both realms," Derron added.

"We will have to make sure that doesn't happen," Queen Maeve said.

"How?" Gawaine demanded.

"I do not know yet," Maeve said.

"What about the High Druid? Can't he help us?" Elyne asked.

Everyone looked at her, making her feel as though she said something she shouldn't have. Maeve stared at her a long, thoughtful moment. As though she were considering what she'd said.

Elyne and Derron had visited with the High Druid before they left on this journey. He had given them a couple of things they could use. He'd already given Derron the concealment cloak and the vial of Faery dust. If he could give them those things, then why couldn't he help them keep the walls from coming down?

"I'm afraid it will take more than the High Druid to help us," Maeve said. "One is not enough. We'd need an entire clan. We haven't time to gather them."

"Why doesn't someone raid Kieran's camp and get back the Treasures?" Lord Vaughan suggested. "Surely he keeps them close to him at all times."

Maeve was already shaking her head. "No. It's too dangerous. I'll not risk more men to get the Treasures back. We will get them back soon enough."

But the idea sparked something in Elyne. She chewed her lower lip, considering it. Aye, it would be dangerous, but *she* could do it.

"Then what do you propose we do?" Gawaine asked.

"We go to the Hill of Tara, Lord Gawaine, and we win."

Traveling to the Stone of Destiny took far longer on foot than by dragon or sifting. During their trek, Elyne had heard more towns and villages had been destroyed—burned to the ground and all inhabitants murdered—as Lord Kieran marched his way to the Stone of Destiny on the Hill of Tara. He had left a bloody warpath in his wake. Things were not looking so good for the Fae with the

Guardians dead and the unknown location of the fourth. All Kieran needed was that Club and he would be able to wield all the power.

Unless I can stop him.

Once they arrived at the Stone of Destiny, Lord Kieran's men would soon follow. True, her mother said getting them back from his camp would be too dangerous. But no one else had the cloak and the Faery dust. And she had a dragon that could take her there. It *could* be done.

With Aura's help, I can make it happen.

When they arrived at the Hill of Tara, the Fae troops were already making camp. Elyne spotted the Elves too, who had taken up residence next to them. As though they had already decided the Treaty of Separation was no more. Had King Urdithane told them? Or was that something he would wait to announce until after the battle was done?

Elyne knew she should tell Derron. He would offer some words of wisdom. But she couldn't risk him going to her mother without her consent. It would jeopardize everything.

As usual, her mother worked with great authority as she organized the campsite. The main tent was erected—the one where the war council would convene and where the Cauldron had returned to the center on a fire pit. This is where the Elves and the Fae would mastermind the battle against the Unseelie and Lord Kieran.

And so it begins.

She had almost forgotten Maggie, Finn and Sir Drake were with them until she saw them again. Maggie came bounding up to her and hugged her tightly.

"What's that for?" Elyne asked.

"You looked like you needed it. Finn told me Lord Kieran intends to break the walls between the human realm and the Otherworld," she said. "I'm…frightened, Ellie."

"You should be. If he breaches the walls and they fall…I shudder to think what will happen to the human realm."

What Elyne didn't say was if that happened, then she, her mother and all the rest of them would likely be dead. A sickening thought and one she shoved away quickly. She couldn't dwell on that.

"What about my father?" Maggie asked, her voice faint. "Will he be all right in the future?"

For a Fae who could sift, time in the human realm was not linear. The Dark Elf could end up in Maggie's time to wreak havoc. Elyne saw her face drained of color, knowing Maggie worried about her father's safety.

"The Unseelie leave no survivors."

"I don't understand why he would do that." Maggie's words were hot with fire. "Why kill everyone? There will be no one left to rule!"

"Aye, I'm sure that is his plan," Queen Maeve interjected, startling both of them. She fixed Elyne with a hard stare. "My spies tell me Lord Kieran will be here by dawn. The camp is now six thousand strong with the arrival of the Elvish army."

Even though Elyne wanted to tell her *I told you so* she held her tongue.

"You negotiated with the king to bring them here," the queen continued. "For that, I thank you. Well done, Princess Elyne."

Stunned, she stared at her mother, watching as the queen stalked away.

"Wow," Maggie breathed. "She actually thanked you."

"I can't believe it myself," Elyne said.

"There is hope for the war…and there's hope for you and your mother, Ellie."

"I pray you're right, Maggie."

Chapter 18

It had taken some searching, but Queen Maeve found what was once known as a faery mound deep in the earth. It had long since been deserted and was overgrown with foliage, yet it offered the perfect place for the dragons. As a makeshift cave, it would house them during their stay at the Hill of Tara. This was not the most ideal situation for them, but they accepted it with grace.

Elyne accompanied her mother to the faery mound. She found several wild strawberry bushes nearby, which made the dragons more willing to settle into their temporary home.

"What happens to them once the war is over?" Elyne asked.

"I have no intention of putting them back into shadow," Queen Maeve said.

This both pleased and startled Elyne. "What's to become of them?"

"I would hope the hunters have long since given up."

"And the black dragon?"

"Nero is what he is called," Maeve reminded her. "Most likely, he will be terminated during the battle."

Terminated? Her mother's choice of words was less than desirable. Elyne didn't want to see any creature as beautiful as a dragon—even the black one—destroyed.

"Come, daughter. I want you present in the next war council meeting. It will be our final planning session before we attack."

"You intend to attack Lord Kieran now?"

"We must strike when he least expects it."

As they returned to the main tent, which wasn't far from the faery mound, Elyne wondered if Lord Kieran would be expecting them to strike first. Waiting in the tent was Prince Andahar, Eldrin, Lord Derron, Lord Gawaine, Sir Drake, Finn and the war council. They were seated at a long wooden table, tankards of ale scattered about and a large eight-candle candelabra in the center blazing brightly.

"Gentlemen, thank you for waiting." Her mother took her seat in the middle of the table. She indicated to Elyne to take the empty seat next to her. "I especially would like to thank Prince Andahar for coming on behalf of King Urdithane."

Andahar nodded toward the queen but his eyes were on Elyne. He gave her a friendly nod of greeting. She would have to make sure and speak to the prince about the agreement she'd made with the king. She didn't want him discussing it with her mother before she'd had a chance to talk to her first.

"We have six thousand Fae and Elves and even a few humans," Maeve gestured to Finn and Drake, "who have joined us in this fight. For that I am most grateful. However, Lord Kieran's army is still ten thousand. I would ask you, gentlemen, how we have a hope and a prayer to defeat the Unseelie. I have spoken to many of you who believe we should strike first."

"Aye, my queen, we should," Gawaine said. "We hold the element of surprise. While Lord Kieran's army marches here, we can prepare for attack."

"Wouldn't he be expecting that?" Elyne asked.

All heads swung in her direction. She could feel her mother stiffen next to her, heard the soft intake of her breath, and knew she had annoyed her by speaking out. But hadn't she wanted her there for a reason? Was she supposed to sit idly by and say nothing? Better to be seen than heard? Elyne's blood boiled at the thought. How did her mother ever expect her to learn if she didn't participate in any of these meetings?

"Princess Elyne, you make a valid point," Derron said.

She flushed hotly at his formal address.

"Princess Elyne knows nothing of warfare," Gawaine said, scoffing at her.

"What if she's right? Lord Kieran would be prepared for an immediate battle," Derron said.

"Are you suggesting we wait him out?" Gawaine asked, his words searing. "We would be an easy target."

"Gentlemen, please, let's discuss this without shouting at each other," Maeve said.

"I'm not shouting," Gawaine said. "I'm merely stating I believe it is folly to not make a move. He has ten thousand men."

"Aye, we've established that," Derron snapped.

"Well, since the princess brought it up, mayhap she has a

solution?" Gawaine said.

"The *princess* is sitting right here. And I would appreciate it if you didn't speak about me as though I were not," Elyne said.

Her mother visibly relaxed and blew out a breath. Elyne stole a glance at her, saw a faint smile on her lips and one eyebrow raised. Did she approve?

Did it matter to Elyne? Not particularly. She pressed on. "I merely stated it seemed to me Lord Kieran would be expecting an immediate attack. Mayhap we send someone to negotiate."

"Negotiate what? The terms of our surrender?" Gawaine's voice cut through her.

"Negotiate a truce to avoid unnecessary bloodshed," Elyne fired back. Lord Gawaine was really getting on her last nerve.

"I believe bloodshed, princess, is a foregone conclusion." Prince Andahar spoke for the first time, his voice calm and soothing amidst the heatedness. "Or else you would not have come and asked my father for help. Wouldn't you agree, Prince Eldrin?"

"Aye, I would, my brother."

Elyne flushed, embarrassment heating through her. Gawaine was right—she knew nothing of warfare and battle. She should keep her mouth shut.

"However," Andahar continued, "the princess has an interesting idea. Sending someone to speak to Lord Kieran on behalf of the Seelie could buy us more time to prepare. It is simply impossible to plan an entire battle in less than a few hours, which we're trying to do now."

"Agreed," Maeve said.

Surprise flared through Elyne as she glanced at first her mother, then Andahar. His glittering eyes met hers.

"We are ill-prepared," Maeve said.

"You agree we should delay?" Gawaine asked, sounding rather put out.

"Aye, I do," Maeve said. "Whom shall we send, then? I do not believe I should be the one to go. It will give Lord Kieran too much opportunity to behead me."

"No, you shouldn't go," Derron agreed.

"I will go," Andahar said. "It is the best option for all of us as it will show Lord Kieran that the Fae have the Elves for allies."

"I'm sure he already knows that," Maeve said. "His spies are as prevalent as my own. However, I'm not opposed to the idea that you go. I suggest you take several guards."

"I volunteer," Eldrin said. "As an Elven prince and ranger, I cannot allow the future king of the Elves to go without me."

"Thank you, my brother," Andahar said.

"I would like to accompany them as well, my queen," Derron said.

"As Knight of the Realm and Protector of the Otherworld, I agree it is your duty, Lord Derron. I need you here, though."

"Staying here will not keep me safe, your majesty," Derron said. "I intend to go and confront the Dark Elf who murdered my father."

She considered his words, never taking her eyes off him. "Understood, Lord Derron. I won't stop you. I'd request you talk to Lord Kieran to try to settle this peacefully. I doubt he'll be willing to give himself up, though."

"He won't surrender, no," Derron agreed. "But that's not our objective anyway."

"See if you can get us at least another day," Maeve said. "Now, the hour grows late and it's time for me to retire. In the morning, I want my negotiators ready to ride out to meet Lord Kieran before he has time to get settled. Once that meeting is done, we will gather again and begin planning. Gawaine, I want you and the council to develop some battle tactics and have them ready for me by the time Lord Derron and the Elves ride to meet Lord Kieran."

"As you wish, your majesty."

The queen had just ordered the war council to spend their night planning the war while she got her beauty sleep. A pang of sorrow for them went through Elyne.

As Queen Maeve rose, the men stood, too.

"I bid you good night, gentlemen," she said.

Most of the men dispersed as she walked away. But Lord Gawaine trotted after her, catching up to her. Elyne overheard a snippet of their conversation.

"Are you certain this is the best course of action, your majesty?"

The queen's reply was inaudible but Gawaine's sour face was all the answer Elyne needed. She approached Derron then, waiting until no one else was around before she talked to him.

"Derron, are you sure you want to do this?"

"Aye, I am." He gave her his best winning smile, touching the side of her face with gentle fingertips. "Are you afraid for me?"

"I don't like it," she said. "He could kill you right then."

"He could," Derron agreed. "I doubt he'll try, though."

She thought of the Treaty of Separation and the promises she'd made to both Prince Andahar and King Urdithane.

"Is there something else?"

"I…there is…something I need to discuss with you. Alone." She glanced around and saw all those wandering through the tent were intent on their conversation. Elyne needed to tell someone, even if it was Derron. Mayhap she could persuade him not to tell her mother. She feared, though, Andahar would tell him and she couldn't have Derron learn that from the Elven prince.

"Then come." He took her hand and led her away, winding his way through the maze of tents until he stopped outside one that she assumed was his. He led her inside, the candlelight flickering on the canvas in soft shadows. "Now, princess, tell me."

"When I went to see King Urdithane, he was not so easily persuaded to help us," she said. "I had to make…certain promises to him to gain his trust and allegiance."

Alarm flickered through is eyes. He folded his arms across his chest. "What sort of promises? Did you have to promise him your hand?"

"Gods, no. Nothing like that." But she loved that he seemed jealous.

"Then what?"

"Urdithane wants to abolish the Treaty of Separation."

His brows rose toward his hairline, his eyes widened as he stared at her a long, silent moment, his face impassive. Her stomach did a sickening flip-flop before sinking to her toes.

"Say something, please."

"You promised him to abolish the Treaty." Derron's tone was steady.

Elyne's shoulders slumped. "I did."

He blew out a breath. "Oh, Elyne…"

"My mother doesn't know and I don't want her to know. At least not yet," she said, her words so fast they nearly ran together. "Don't tell her, Derron, please. I beg you."

"She has to know, Elyne."

"I know she does but if you tell her now, I'm not sure what her reaction will be. She may tell the king to take back his men and then where will we be? They have no love for each other."

"That much is for certain. How could you make such a promise?"

"I believe you were there when Queen Maeve told me to not come back if I didn't succeed." She pressed her lips together in a thin line, a bitter taste in her mouth. "The king also requested I be a part of the negotiations."

Derron ran a hand through his thick blond hair as he paced the short length of the tent. "When do you intend to tell her?"

"When we have the Four Treasures safely returned and Lord Kieran is dead."

"And if that doesn't happen?"

"Well, then, we won't have to worry about the Treaty of Separation, will we? We'll all be dead."

Elyne couldn't stop the threat of tears that stung her eyes. She turned away from him, refusing to let him see her cry. His warm hands landed on her shoulders, pulled her to him.

"We will succeed." His words were soft in her ear as he leaned down to her. He kissed the top of her head.

"How can you be so sure?" She whispered it, her throat tight with tears.

"Because we have the help of the Elves, thanks to you." He turned her to face him. "I won't tell her yet. You have my word. But once this is all over, we will need to speak with her about the terms. Prince Andahar, I assume, knows?"

"He was there with the king. That's why I had to tell you before he did. I didn't want you to find out that way."

"Thank you, princess, for telling me. For trusting me." He cupped her face, searched her eyes.

Elyne knew what he wanted. She stood on tiptoe and kissed him softly on the lips. "Good luck tomorrow."

With that, she slipped out of his arms and left.

Chapter 19

Derron saddled up with both Elven princes. He gripped the reins tightly as they looked across the field. In his other hand, he held the banner of peace, a white cloth with a green triskelion across it. Had the banner been scarlet, it would have signified war.

Lord Kieran's camp sprawled acres of land. Everywhere he could see there were pointed tops of tents and more going up even as he watched. Sir Finn and Sir Drake joined them, trotting up on either side of Derron, who gave Finn a questioning glance.

"We canna let ye go it alone," Finn said. He glanced over the two Elves with a look of curiosity.

"I thank you both," Derron said. He glanced at his small band of brothers. He hoped the two Elven princes, two humans and a Fae lord would stand a small chance against Lord Kieran. "Let's ride."

Clutching the banner in one hand, he kicked his horse into action and they all bounded across the field. They paused halfway and waited in the shadow of the Stone of Destiny. Here is where they would make their plea.

"Will he come?" Andahar asked.

"Aye, he will." Derron kept his gaze trained on the tents across the way.

"You sound certain, my lord," Andahar said.

"I am."

He spotted movement and moments later three men trotted toward them. Derron recognized Cormac to the left of the one in the center, the one Derron could only assume was Lord Kieran. He sat tall and straight in the saddle, with dark piercing eyes and hair as black as night and a matching goatee. His tunic was a pale shade of green, his breeches a soft doe-brown ending in dusty black knee-high boots. Derron didn't miss the unmistakable point of his ears that curved out away from his head, indicating he was not a Fae but an Elf.

Once held in high regard at King Urdithane's court, he was now banished to the Unseelie Court for his murderous ways. He came to a halt in front of Derron, leaning casually on the saddle horn as though he were about to greet an old friend.

"Greetings, Lord Derron. To what do I owe the pleasure of this visit?"

"We come with an offer of peace," Derron said. "A truce between us."

Kieran laughed, tossing back his head. "A truce? I cannot say how a truce will do us any good."

"If not a truce, then surrender."

"Ah. You wish to surrender to *me*? I accept."

"No. You will surrender to us." The heat of anger rose in Derron. "You will be arrested for the murder of the Guardians of the Sword of Light, Spear of Lugh and Stone of Destiny. Should you decide to surrender, we can negotiate a more lenient sentence."

Kieran laughed. "I'm surprised you don't wish to avenge the death of your father yourself." He pinned him with that dark glittering gaze. "I would think I'd be on your immediate hit list."

Of course, he was, but Derron wasn't going to reveal that to him here. Not yet. He would exact his revenge on the Dark Elf in due time.

"I'm sure you understand surrender is not an option," Kieran continued.

"If you will not surrender yourself, nor accept the terms of a truce, then we shall have to discuss other alternatives," Derron said.

Kieran's glance went from Derron to the two Elves and then to the humans. "I came to step upon the Stone of Destiny and become High King of the Otherworld. If you choose to get in my way, then I will choose to kill you."

"We are prepared to fight you."

"With the Elves as allies?" He laughed again. "The Elves do not ally themselves with anyone."

"They have with Queen Maeve," Derron replied.

"And what of these humans? There isn't a place for them here in the Otherworld." Kieran spat on the ground, as though saying the very word *human* was distasteful.

Derron was well aware of the hate between those of the Otherworld and humans. Even Queen Maeve had expressed her distaste for them. He found them fascinating with a sense of loyalty he had never seen in any Fae or Elf.

"Aye, we'll be fighting alongside our brothers," Finn said. He leaned one massive forearm on his saddle horn, as though to challenge Kieran.

Derron didn't miss the word *brothers* the Scottish laird managed to slip in. Pride swarmed through him.

"We will defeat you," Derron said.

"You can try," Kieran replied. "But I wouldn't be too certain of that. And because I'm not quite the barbarian you seem to think I am, I propose we meet here at dawn."

A scheduled war. That's what the queen wanted. Less than a day to plan their attack. It would have to be enough.

"Agreed."

"Very well, then. Go back and tell your queen. Let her know I intend to leave no survivors. I intend to kill her myself."

Kieran turned his horse around, gave it a swift kick. All three of them rode back to their camp, leaving clods of dirt and grass in their wake.

"That's it, then," Andahar said. "He intends to go through with it no matter what."

"Let him," Derron said. "I wish we could have gotten more time. Gentlemen, let us return to camp. Tomorrow we fight for the right to live."

Elyne watched Derron ride away with the two Elven princes, her heart in her throat. She hadn't slept the night before and fought the fatigue threatening to overtake her. What the Fae needed was a small victory in this ugly war. Three of their four Guardians were dead. Beheaded by the evil Lord Kieran.

She paced the length of the tent, her mind racing with everything that had happened. The movement soothed her ragged nerves. As Derron rode away to negotiate with the Dark Elf, she knew she couldn't sit back and do nothing. She had to take action.

She was going to get the Treasures back.

The thought struck her hard and fast. Coming back to her with such force, a sharp pain stabbed her in the chest. She halted suddenly, staring out of the tent as a plan formed. She's toyed with the idea before. Now she was certain she would do it.

Elyne knew Derron still had the concealment cloak the High Druid had given them. She also knew he had the small bottle of Faery dust. She could use both of those to hide herself while she crossed enemy lines to retrieve the Treasures.

It was the perfect plan. The dragon would fly her there and back again once she'd found the Treasures. And if she ran into trouble, then what? She would have to improvise since she had returned the dagger Derron had given her.

Princess Elyne forced her feet to be still, standing with her hands clasped behind her back, watching for signs of him and the others returning. Her mother looked at the maps the war council had provided, Gawaine at her side.

So absorbed in her thoughts, it seemed mere minutes between when Derron left and returned. She saw him riding toward the tent with the others right behind. They surrendered their horses to several stable hands and approached the tent at a brisk pace. Queen Maeve looked up expectantly.

"Were you successful?" she asked, not waiting for a greeting.

"We have until tomorrow at dawn," Derron said.

She didn't try to hide her look of disgust.

"It was the best I could do," Derron added.

"Then it will have to be good enough."

They spent the rest of the afternoon planning their attack. Elyne stayed through the meeting, trying to learn all she could about planning a war from her mother, though she secretly hoped she would never have to face it in her reign. Should she ever reign.

Still, she had to know what their plans were so she could make her own. Some troops would be sent directly to the Stone of Destiny, while others confronted Kieran, following Lord Derron and Elven princes into battle. She would have to make her escape before the sun rose, before they would meet in the middle of the field and fight to the death.

Then she had to find the concealment cloak and Faery dust. She knew Derron still had them somewhere in his tent. It would be the only way she could get to the other side, get the Treasures, and return without notice. Mayhap she could search his tent while he slept that night.

After their intense planning session, the queen made sure every Fae, man and Elf was properly fed. The main tent with the

Cauldron was bursting with soldiers. She spied Maggie making her way through the crowd. Elyne waved her over before scanning the multitude for Finn and Sir Drake. They were sitting with Derron, Eldrin and Andahar.

"I'm glad you're here, Maggie," Elyne said.

"Me too," Maggie said. "Elyne, when this is all over, do you think you could get that letter to my father?"

"Of course, I will." Elyne hadn't forgotten about it. She still had it tucked safely away. "That is, if I ever get my powers back." She snuck a glance at her mother, who was in deep conversation with Gawaine.

"Do you think you ever will?"

"I don't know. Mayhap. Truth be told, Mags, I really don't miss them. I suppose I know what it's like to be a human now."

When Maggie didn't respond, she looked at her friend, who was grinning from ear to ear, tears brimming in her eyes.

"What?" Elyne asked.

"You called me Mags," she said. "You've never called me that before."

Elyne waved it away. "A mere slip."

"Maybe, Ellie, you *do* know what it's like to be human."

Maggie flung an arm around her then and hugged her so tight, she thought the human might crush her.

"Well don't get too used to it," Elyne snapped and shoved her away. "I had a weak moment, that's all."

"Right," Maggie said, and gave her a little laugh. "I'll remember that."

Somewhere on the other side of the tent, a group had gotten together with a few instruments and started playing music. It elevated the mood from somber to almost joyful.

"Why don't you dance with Derron?" Maggie suggested. She gave a little nod toward him.

"No." She shook her head.

"Why not?"

"Because we're about to go to war." *And because I'm not ready to face my feelings for him. Not yet.*

"So?" Maggie lifted one shoulder in a half shrug. "I can't think of a better time to ask a man to dance. You may not get another chance."

Elyne knew what she meant. Hearing her say it sent a ripple of fear through her. She knew Maggie was right—that he could be killed tomorrow in battle. She also knew that if she went through with her crazy idea of going behind enemy lines, she could die as well. It was a risk she was willing to take for her kingdom. For Derron.

As this went through Elyne's mind, Prince Andahar approached. He wore a smile on his handsome Elven face and Elyne knew his intent before he even got to her.

"Princess Elyne, would you do me the honor of a dance?" He bowed and held out his hand to her in invitation.

Elyne glanced at Maggie who urged her on with a nod.

"I…" She faltered.

"Are you spoken for, then?" he asked.

Before she could answer, Maggie jumped to her feet, snatched Elyne's hand and pulled her up. "No, she isn't and she'd love to dance with you."

"Maggie!"

"Well you're not. And look at him. He's an Elven prince!" Maggie gave her a nudge toward Andahar. "She'd love to dance with you. She's just shy, is all."

"Maggie," Elyne said through gritted teeth.

"You've been in my arms once. I should like for you to be again," Andahar said.

Maggie's eyes widened. Elyne flushed hot, pinpricks of heat tingling through her. She knew he referred to when he helped her on the footbridge in the Woodlands, but Maggie didn't. Mayhap she would have an opportunity to explain it to her human friend later. But for now, Andahar took her hand in his, his warm fingers closing over hers. He led her to the makeshift dance floor where his sister Allanna danced with Sir Drake. The two made doe eyes at each other and Elyne knew they were both a lost cause.

Still, human and Elf were a forbidden combination. Though there was no law against such a union, it was largely frowned upon by the king and his subjects.

As was Fae and Elf. Yet Andahar took her into his arms and swung her to the music.

"Your sister has taken quite a liking to Sir Drake," Elyne said.

"I've noticed. My father will not be pleased."

"And yet, is there anything wrong with it? Sir Drake is a good man," she said.

"But a *human*." He said it with such distaste, Elyne flinched. Her mother felt much the same way about them yet she tolerated their presence here in the Otherworld at Derron's urging.

"And I am a Fae. I'm sure he would frown upon you dancing with me."

"We are not so different." He said it with a faint smile. That same smile that he gave her as he saved her from certain death on the footbridge.

"Different enough for royal bloodlines," Elyne said.

"A promise would go a long way with my father," he said.

She stared at him. Was he suggesting a betrothal? To ensure she kept *her* promise to King Urdithane about abolishing the Treaty of Separation? She couldn't. Wouldn't. Not when she and Derron were close to reconciling their feelings for each other.

"Mind if I cut in?"

Speak of the devil.

Derron managed to make his way to the two of them and pushed aside the prince before he could answer. Andahar released her and stepped back, his hands up as if in surrender.

"Be my guest, Lord Derron," he said.

Elyne watched him walk away, giving the two of them a backward glance as he left them on the dance floor. Derron took her in his arms, pulling her close as the music changed to something slower, softer. Something that was not a joyful jig.

Derron gave the prince one last scathing look as he walked away and suddenly Elyne understood. She stifled a giggle.

"You're jealous," she said.

"I am not."

"You are. That's why you cut in," she said. "You're jealous of Prince Andahar."

"I didn't like the way he looked at you."

"Which was how exactly?"

"You know how," Derron said.

"Oh, he's harmless," Elyne said. "You shouldn't be intimated by him. Besides, he was there when I spoke to the king."

"Did he help persuade him?" Derron wanted to know.

"No, but he did escort me to and from the king."

Derron's eyes narrowed to slits and Elyne imagined the murderous thoughts going through his mind. She smirked. His jealousy told her that his feelings for her went a lot deeper than he let on. Elyne laughed out loud then.

"Ah, Derron. You have nothing to worry about with Prince Andahar and me. I know we are not well-suited for each other."

"I hope you remember that," he said. "I hope you know too, Princess Elyne, that I am rather fond of you."

Rather fond? She stopped herself from snorting. She followed his lead. "As I am of you, Lord Derron."

The music ended and they stopped moving. He took her hand in his, kissed it. "Let's keep it that way, shall we?"

What was he proposing? Did he want something more than this fake love affair? Did he truly want her for himself? She would be the last fecking one to tell him how she felt. Why couldn't he be the one to initiate that conversation?

Queen Maeve rose from her seat, standing tall and regal, and overlooked the group of men. Everyone quieted and waited for her to speak. Derron laced his fingers with Elyne's, pulling her closer to him.

"You are here because all our lives are at stake. You have volunteered to fight for our right to live. To protect the Seelie Court. I give my gratitude to King Urdithane for sending his Elven men to fight alongside us Fae, something that has not been done in thousands of years."

Derron squeezed her hand tighter as guilt washed over her. The promise she'd made to the king came flooding back to her, haunting her thoughts. How would her mother react when she learned what Elyne had done? How angry would she be? She quickly shoved it aside as the queen continued.

"Some of you will die and for your sacrifice you will be honored in the halls of my palace as well as King Urdithane's. Tomorrow we fight. Tomorrow we destroy the menace who threatens our very existence. For if we do not, the world faces total annihilation from this barbarian. Lord Kieran may be able to take our lives, our Fae Treasures and our kingdoms, but he will never rob us of our spirit. Our determination to survive. Our freedom. We will not go quietly. We will live on." She lifted her goblet then, holding it high. "We *will* win. And we will survive."

The men cheered at her words. Those who had a tankard or goblet held it up in salute and then drank along with the queen.

"Enjoy the rest of your evening for tomorrow Elves, humans and Fae face the Unseelie as one."

Elyne searched for Sir Drake and Finn in the crowd. They too lifted their goblets and drank in salute to the coming fight. Her stomach clenched at the thought of what she intended to do, knowing she had to do it to give them hope.

"Walk with me, princess." Still clutching her hand, Derron led her from the oversized tent into the cool evening. They walked a fair distance before he spoke again. "I want you to make sure your mother and Maggie are safe tomorrow. Take the dragons and get away from here."

"No," she said, using more force than she intended. "I'm staying here. Besides, you know my mother will never listen to me."

"She will if I've already spoken to her. And I have," he said. He stopped, turned her to face him and took her by the shoulders. "Should Kieran breach our line, then you will both be in danger. I want you away from here. I want you safe."

The tenderness in his gaze shredded her heart. "I'm staying, Lord Derron." She gave him a soft smile. "Whatever happens. We are not abandoning the Stone of Destiny."

"Do you understand he will kill you both?"

"Aye, I do. Allanna's vision told us as much. But I am not afraid. If he doesn't find us here, he will hunt us down. Should you and the men lose tomorrow, then my mother and I are as good as dead anyway."

The thought of Derron and the rest of them dead sent a sharp stabbing pain to her heart. She couldn't bear the thought, and if Derron were dead, did she really want to be in this world without him? She already knew that answer. She placed her hands on his chest, leaning toward him.

"You will not fail, though. I know it."

"Promise me if Kieran's men break through, you will leave here. At least promise me that."

Hearing the concern in his voice and seeing the care in his gaze made her want to melt. She should throw propriety and caution and everything out the window and tell him to take her to his tent and make love to her all night. It could be her last chance.

She nodded slowly. "You have my word."

As soon as she said it, she knew it was a lie.

Chapter 20

Elyne made her way back to her own tent after leaving Derron. She feigned fatigue and he made the excuse he had more planning to do for tomorrow. They parted ways without as much as a kiss between them.

It hurt her but she knew it was for the best. She couldn't allow her emotions and feelings for Derron to get in the way of her plan. And she fully intended to go through with it. She still hadn't had a chance to search his tent for the items she needed. She intended to raid his tent once he had fallen asleep. Not exactly a great plan.

"What are you doing here?"

Elyne yelped with her fright, startled at seeing Maggie standing in the center of her tent, arms folded across her chest. She had been so deep in thought she hadn't seen her human friend when she entered.

"What are *you* doing here? Shouldn't you be with Finn?"

"Don't change the subject. I saw you leave with Derron."

"Are you still playing matchmaker?"

"Yes, I am. Why don't you admit you're in love with him?" Maggie asked, propping her hands on her hips. "It's okay to have feelings for him, ya know."

"I can't tell him that," Elyne said. "Not after everything that's happened."

"Oh, you mean everything being him giving you adoring eyes? Him looking at you as though he wants to kiss you every second? And you looking at him like you can't live without him? I *know* he loves you. I know you love him. But, like you, he's too stubborn to admit it." Maggie shook her head in disgust. "Go to him, Ellie. Tell him how you feel. It may be your last chance."

Elyne expelled a heavy breath and sat on the edge of her bed. "If I tell you something, Maggie, you must swear to me you won't tell Derron."

"Another secret? All right." She sounded wary and perched on the bed next to her. "What is it?"

"I plan to get the Treasures back myself."

Her eyebrows rose to her hairline and concert flickered in her eyes. "And how do you plan to do that?"

"I'm taking Aura and flying across enemy lines." It would be simple. That was as far as she'd planned. If something went wrong, she wasn't sure what she'd do. With the azure dragon, though, Elyne should be able to get in and out without detection with the help of the Faery dust.

"Are you mad?" Maggie asked. "You can't go. I won't allow it."

"*You* won't allow it?" Elyne tilted her head to one side and laughed. "My mind is made up. If I can get those Treasures back before the battle in the morning, then Lord Kieran won't stand a chance."

"And what if something goes wrong? What if you're captured? What if—"

"Nothing will go wrong."

"You sound sure about that."

"I am. You swore you wouldn't tell Derron. I need to trust you'll keep your word."

"It's against my better judgment." She folded her arms over her chest and gave Elyne a look of disdain.

"You won't tell him?"

"No. I won't tell Derron. You should."

"If I do, he'll stop me from going."

"And rightly so. You shouldn't do it, Ellie. It's too dangerous."

"I can do this, Maggie."

"You have delusions of grandeur, I think." She shook her head. "If you're determined to go through with it, I guess there's nothing I can say to change your mind."

"No, there isn't."

"Well then, in that case, maybe now would be a great time to tell Derron how you feel."

"Back to that already?"

"I'm determined." She grinned.

"And stubborn. Aye, I know."

Maggie put her arm around Elyne and pushed her to her feet. "Just go. Tell him how you feel."

"In case I die on the morrow, is that it? You think I won't succeed."

"I never said that." Maggie tried her best to look hurt. "And you better not die."

"You implied it."

"If you don't tell Derron you're in love with him, then I will," Maggie snapped. She sounded as though she meant it and in fact stood and took a step toward the tent flap.

Elyne caught her by the arm. "All right! I'll tell him."

"Good. About time you came to your senses." Triumph glowed on her face.

Elyne scowled as she left the tent, determination in her step. But the closer she got to Derron's, the more she lost her nerve. If she told him and he rejected her it would destroy her. But then it would give her all the more reason to take Aura and retrieve the Treasures.

If he didn't reject her and things went as she hoped, when he discovered her missing in the morning, he would be furious. If she returned with two of the Four Treasures, he would forgive her. Going to him now would give her a chance to search for the concealment cloak and the Faery dust.

Her gut told her he wouldn't reject her. Maggie was right. Mayhap it was time to tell Derron her true feelings for him.

Steeling her nerves, she entered his tent and paused. He sat at the small desk, his handsome face aglow in the faint candlelight. He scrawled something with a quill and looked up when she entered. Smiling, he dropped the pen and stood. He scraped his chair backward, the legs raking across the makeshift wood floor.

"I came to see if you needed anything," she said.

He gave her a faint smile. "No. I think all the preparations are made. Our men have been dispatched to pour tar along the backside of Kieran's camp. Then the dragons will light it when the time is right."

"I'm frightened." She hadn't meant to blurt it out. Nor did she intend for that to be the only two words. She thought to add *for you* at the end of that sentence but it didn't come out that way. She halted, unable to continue.

Those two words had so many meanings. She *was* frightened. For her. For him. For the men and Elves and Fae who waited to fight on the morrow. Even for her mother who would be safely tucked away in her own royal tent by now and guarded by several of her best men.

Derron's face softened as he approached her. That same look he had given her not long ago when he made her promise she'd flee if things went wrong. "Don't be."

"How can you be certain of the outcome?" All her earlier bravado melted into a puddle at her feet.

"We fight with all we have. It will have to be enough."

"He has two of the Four Treasures. If we fail—"

"We won't." His hands landed on her shoulders. "You said so yourself."

He sounded certain. She would do her part to help that along when she left in the morning to take back the Sword and the Spear. He had enough burdens as Knight of the Realm, Protector of the Otherworld and Guardian of the Sword of Light. The man had more titles than he knew what to do with.

"I was trying to be brave." Her voice wavered. She didn't want to cry. Not in front of Derron.

"You are brave."

On the morrow, he would lead the Fae of the Light Realm into war. The Elves and the humans would follow. They would fight for him and with him to crush the rebellion.

If she lost him this time, there would be no going back in time to fix things. No help from Maggie to help right things again. If he were mortally wounded, about the best she could hope for was Seamus healing him. She couldn't bear the thought of him dying. She knew now would be the right time to profess her love for him.

"Derron, I…"

She paused, afraid to say the words. To hear the words from her own mouth. How would he respond? Would he say he loved her back? Every indication she had from him since they started this insane journey told her he might. But things had been ugly between them for so long, she wasn't sure if it was truly mended.

"Aye?" He whispered it, encouraging her.

Elyne slipped her hands under his tunic, running up his hardened torso over the cords of muscle, the softness of hair that sprinkled over his chest. She heard his intake of breath at the intimate touch she'd initiated.

"I want to be with you."

He knew what she meant. She didn't have to explain. Fire ignited in his eyes. Fire and desire. Need and want. Love and lust. Everything she wanted. Everything she needed.

"Are you certain?" His voice sounded wary, unsure. His eyes said otherwise.

"I'm more certain of this than anything." Her heart pounded a fast cadence.

His gaze didn't waver as he cupped her face in his hands. He ran a thumb over her lips. Warmth spread through her body as she waited for the kiss.

"I require the bonding. And once it's made, there is no going back. Are you certain you want the bonding with me?"

Past the point of no return, he meant.

She hadn't expected him to demand the bonding and it took her aback for a moment. Her heart had been pattering hard but now slowed to a flutter. Her stomach dropped to her feet. A lump formed in her throat.

Looking at Derron closely, she could see the heartrending tenderness of his gaze and understood he wasn't making a demand. His eyes were soft and still full of desire and need. He was speaking from his heart and asked for hers for forever in the bonding. The binding that could be blessed by only one—the queen. Didn't he know it would not be official? Mayhap he did and he intended to make it official once the war was over. It was his way of claiming her before the battle started.

Without him saying the words, she knew he loved her. Mayhap he wasn't ready to say them, nor was she. But he was ready to bond with her, to choose her as his for the rest of his days. She could not deny him. Not now. Not ever.

He wanted her.

She wanted him.

"I am."

With those two simple words, it sealed their fate together. Derron pulled her into his arms and kissed her as though it would be the last time. Mayhap it would, if things didn't go well when she flew with Aura to retrieve the relics. She shoved aside the voice of guilt niggling at her. No, she would not regret this moment of bonding with Derron. She would memorize every touch, every kiss, every caress. Every second she had with him would be permanently emblazoned on her mind. She would keep it close to her as she went into the enemy's camp.

His mouth was warm and sensual on hers as though he wasn't sure if she really wanted him. She would show him, then. She shoved his tunic upward, breaking the kiss long enough to take it off him. The material fluttered to the ground behind him. He tugged at the laces on the bodice of her dress, untying them and pulling them open.

Her heart…oh, her heart. She had a mixture of joy and fear, desire and want all stabbing through her. She wanted him. *Needed* him. She had waited a lifetime for this moment to finally come and now, here she stood with Derron. He slowly undressed her, taking his time when all she wanted to do was rip off her gown and pull him down to the ground on top of her.

But no. That wouldn't be Derron's style. He would savor the moment. He *did* savor the moment. When her laces were finally free, he slid down her gown, baring her shoulders, but pausing just above her breasts. He kissed each shoulder with his warm, teasing lips.

Her breath was ragged in her throat. Her chest heaving with anticipation. She thought she might go mad as he stood in front of her, shirtless, kissing her shoulders. Then her collarbone. Her neck. Her earlobe. And then he did it all over again on the other side.

"I shall go mad if you don't take me to bed now."

"Patience, my princess. For I have waited an eternity for this."

Unspoken words hung between them. He would take his time, letting his hands memorize her from head to toe. Allowing his lips to taste every inch of her. For there may not be another time. She knew this as well as he.

By the gods, she hoped he didn't die.

And what if she died on her quest to retrieve the Treasures? She wouldn't think about that now. She would think about that on the morrow as she rode on Aura's back. Her eyes closed as he kissed her, his mouth outlining her curves from neck to shoulder and back again.

He had waited an eternity, he said. And she had waited just as long before she finally came to her senses and realized Derron was the Fae for her. The only Fae.

Elyne's knees threatened to buckle as they turned to water beneath her. Her nails dug into his shoulders as he continued his sensual onslaught.

"Say the words." His warm breath was on her collarbone. His tongue dipped to taste her skin. "Say them to me, Elyne."

He wanted her to speak the ancient words of the bonding. The words that would make two hearts one. Even though she knew they would not be truly bonding without the queen's blessing, she would say them anyway. She would freely give him her heart.

"Lord Derron…" Elyne's breath hitched around the words, her eyes suddenly burning with tears that threatened to fall. She didn't want to acknowledge the emotions running high through her and blinked them away. "I bind myself to you. Now and forevermore."

His hands cupped her face again, his gaze meeting hers. And those tears threatened once more. She continued the bonding, speaking the words slowly as she looked into his eyes.

"I bind myself to you until the sun no longer burns. Until the moon no longer glows. Until the Otherworld is no more."

He held her gaze a long silent moment before he repeated the words back to her.

"Princess Elyne, I bind myself to you. Now and forevermore. I bind myself to you until the sun no longer burns. Until the moon no longer glows. Until the Otherworld is no more."

Derron sealed his words with a kiss full of longing and desire.

She could stand the waiting no more and shimmied out of her gown, letting the velvety material pool at her feet. She stood bare before him, her heart beating a ragged tattoo in her chest. When he stepped back to take her in, she refused to look away. She wanted to see the yearning in his face and know it was for her.

He *did* look at her that way. Elyne had longed for that at tourney, had the pang of jealousy when he turned his affections to other women. Couldn't stop the envy of Allanna when he showed her how to properly shoot a bow. Now, all he saw was her. All he wanted was her. She belonged to him.

Derron took her by the hand and led her toward his bed. When this moment came, she had imagined they would be in the palace behind one of the oversized oak doors in a four-poster bed draped with silk. Not under a canvas tent with guards outside or her mother a mere stone's throw away. Now that it was happening, she wouldn't change a thing about it. Somehow, it made it more special. Like the way it should be.

He slid his breeches down and stepped out of them. Taking her by the hand, he led her to the bed. She complied, willingly following him. She lowered to the mattress. He nestled next to her, the weight and heat of him pressing against her.

He cracked a smile and showed off his dimples. "Have I told

you how beautiful you are?"

"You say that now because you have to," she teased. She ran her forefinger over his lips. Lips she always wanted kissing her. "And because I'm in a compromising position with you."

His mouth sipped hers and then he whispered, "Exactly where you should be, my princess."

The words ripped her heart in two. But she couldn't think about that. Not now as his mouth captured hers. Elyne encircled him with her arms, pulled him on top of her and closer than he'd ever been. She pressed her hips closer to his, wiggling against him, a little mewl escaping her.

"Not yet," he said. "I intend to savor every inch of you before I take you."

He did, too. He took his time and she allowed him, savoring the pleasures he had to give her. When they came together, it was as though their bodies were made for each other. As though they were meant to be together, to bond, to become one.

Sweet pleasure bloomed, starting deep in her core and moving outward. Delicious heat waves rippled from head to toe. She was completely attuned to him. She couldn't have loved him any more than she did then.

Derron stilled, his heat pressing into her. He kissed her earlobe before rolling away and settling on his back. He gathered her close, pulling her into his embrace and holding her. He brushed his hand through her hair.

"I thought you wouldn't want me anymore," she said.

"I have always wanted you. Even when you didn't want me. I will always want you." He shifted to slip his hand over her flat stomach. "I suppose that's why I went to the human realm, why I jousted and flirted shamelessly with women."

His words stung, but she knew he spoke the truth. She knew that was why he put his life at risk. She had hurt him, cut him to the core because she hadn't always wanted him. It was something she would spend the rest of her life trying to make up to him.

"Can you forgive me?"

"I forgave you long ago, though you didn't know it."

"When?" She tipped her head back to look up at him. His eyes were dark orbs in the half-light.

"When I broke you out of prison. I couldn't bear the thought of you in that dank place." He tucked a lock of hair behind her ear. "I tried to talk Maeve out of it, but she wouldn't hear of it."

"Once she's made up her mind, she doesn't change it."

"Much like someone else I know."

He smiled. She melted.

"All that is in the past now," he said. "Now, we only have the future to think of."

Aye, the future. She settled against him again, her heart twisting. If there was a future. If she survived. If he survived.

But she would think about that tomorrow. Now, she had him and all night.

Chapter 21

Morning came far too quickly. Elyne wanted the night with Derron to go on forever. They completed their bonding, something those Fae who had chosen each other for all eternity could do. Elyne had allowed Derron to take her body, heart, and soul and accepted her as his life mate as she had accepted him. Should she live through the next few hours, she would deal with the fallout from her mother then. Though Elyne suspected Maeve wouldn't be disappointed at the match.

Lingering in his arms a moment longer, she listened to the silence of the encampment. It seemed no one stirred yet, which was strange since they would be battling it out with Lord Kieran soon enough. The calm before the storm?

Unable to prolong the inevitable, Elyne slipped from him and quickly dressed, making sure not to make a sound to wake him. If he saw her leaving, he would demand to know where she was going and why. She couldn't tell him. At least not until she had returned with the Sword and the Spear.

She still hadn't looked for the cloak or the Faery dust from the High Druid so she would have to do her best to find them now. The cloak was easy to find—Derron had tucked it away in his trunk for safekeeping. She was careful to pack the trunk back exactly, making sure nothing was out of place. The Faery dust, though, was more difficult to find. He had it concealed well and it took precious moments of searching to find it.

The small vial lay on its side under several layers of parchment papers, as though he'd forgotten he had it and tossed it haphazardly on the desk. Snatching it up, she clutched the small corked vial in her hand and glanced over the papers he had been writing the night before.

They were elaborate battle plans, splitting the army in half. Some would be sent behind enemy lines to lay in wait. Others would be headed directly to the Stone of Destiny, while a third group would remain with him and the queen.

He'd drawn a crude map of Kieran's campsite. A thick line labeled "tar" squiggled behind the Dark Elf's encampment. Guilt washed over her, knowing she would be taking one of his weapons. He intended to use the dragons to light the tar, setting his camp on fire and destroying as much of it as possible to give them the advantage.

She glanced one last time at Derron to memorize the sight of him lying on his back, his chest rising and falling in deep sleep. She hoped he would forgive her. Turning, she stepped out of the tent…and smacked into a human wall of over-muscled flesh. Finn towered over her, his silvery eyes glaring down at her.

"Where do ye think yere going, lassie?"

"Shh. Keep your voice down. Derron is still sleeping."

"Aye? Well, then, mayhap I should be waking him."

She lifted her head in her usual snooty response. "You will do no such thing. I have something important to take care of and it's none of your concern." She took a step, but Finn caught her arm.

"That thing wouldna involve flying a wee beastie across enemy lines. Would it?"

Realization trickled through her. Curse that human. Maggie promised she wouldn't tell.

"Oh, aye, she told me," he said, as though reading her thoughts.

"Let me go, Finn. I have to do this."

"*Och*, lassie, have ye taken leave of yere senses? Do ye mean to get yeself killed?"

"I have a plan. I can get there, get the Sword and Spear and get back without incident."

"'Tis no' that easy, lassie. Lord Kieran has beasties on his side, too. He'll see ye coming before ye even make it."

She snorted. "What sort of simple fool do you take me for? I have Faery dust." The vial clutched in her hand would finally come in handy. She held it up to show Finn. "And a concealment cloak."

"Oh, aye? Even so, I canna allow ye to do it."

"You don't get to decide." She poked him in the chest for emphasis. "You're not the boss of me."

Hearing the words come out of her mouth reminded her of Maggie. It sounded exactly like something her human friend would say.

"My Maggie asked me to stop ye. And that's what I mean to

do.”

“This is no concern of Maggie’s or yours. Now let me go before Derron wakes up and finds out what I’m up to.”

“Mayhap I should tell him.” There was an evil glint in his eyes.

“Do you want me to turn back time and make you a ghost again?”

“Dinna try to threaten me. I ken ye have no magic.”

“Not now. But I will.” She jerked her arm free. “Do not interfere in this, Finn. If I can get the Treasures back, there will be less bloodshed.”

“Ye mean to really do this?”

“Aye, I do.”

He sighed. “I canna allow ye to go alone. I’m coming with ye.”

“No, Finn. You can’t come with me. I can’t conceal us both.”

“Ye *are* daft, ye know.” He growled, low and guttural in his chest, and she knew that she’d manage to really anger him. “My Maggie will be unhappy.”

“Tell her I knocked you out.”

Elyne nearly giggled at the *are you kidding me* look he shot her as she gave him a jaunty wave with more confidence than she actually possessed. She appreciated what Maggie intended to do for her. It was her human way—she wanted to make sure everyone was taken care of and not hurt. Plus, the moment she landed here at the Hill of Tara, she’d been playing matchmaker with Elyne and Derron as well as Allanna and Sir Drake. Another one of her human flaws. Everyone had to have a happy ending.

Mayhap she and Derron would, though. If she managed to not get killed.

She hurried through the encampment, pausing long enough to snatch a bunch of wild strawberries off a bush, past the stables where the horses were kept, and to the faery mound where the three dragons made their lair. She paused outside.

“Aura,” she called softly.

The big azure dragon lumbered out a moment later with a snort. Aura nudged Elyne with her head in greeting.

“Hello, my friend.”

You brought a gift?

“Your favorite. Here you go.” She held up the wild strawberries for the dragon.

Dragons loved sweet, wild strawberries. They had slumbered in the shadows far too long, she thought. Elyne, for one, was glad to see them in the skies again. They were gentle beasts unless some unfortunate soul angered them. Elyne patted her nose.

"Are you ready for this, old girl?"

"Old girl" was more accurate than even Elyne probably knew. The dragons lived centuries once they were hatched and Aura had been around a long time. Longer than Queen Maeve even. Their population had been scarce these last few years due to the hunters who'd killed them. Much like the Fae, dragons mated for life and bore only one egg. That was why her mother had sent them to the shadows—for their own protection. Even the Unseelie had their own Dark Dragons who kept to the shadows, though they weren't hunted nearly as much as the ones cherished by the Seelie.

Elyne shivered in the cold morning air as she patted the dragon's nose while she ate the wild strawberries. Sensing her coldness, Aura snorted warm steam to ward off the chill.

It will not be an easy thing we do.

"No, it won't," Elyne agreed.

She had a special connection with the dragon. She had never really believed the lore that dragons could mind-speak, yet it was true. Aura could and often did to Elyne.

Are you certain you wish to do this, my friend?

"Aye, I'm certain. Come on, then. Off we go."

Aura knelt down for her to climb up on her back into the saddle. Gripping the reins in her hand, Elyne took a deep breath and gave her the signal to take flight. The great beast hunched down before launching into the air, the wings flapping as she alighted into the cold morning air.

Holding the reins in one hand and the vial in the other, she used her teeth to pull the cork free, and then spat it out. She hoped the Faery dust would be enough to conceal the two of them as they crossed enemy lines. Elyne tipped the bottle to the side and allowed the powdery blue substance to drift over both of them. She made sure to sprinkle some on Aura's head and behind her toward her tail.

Elyne could feel the Faery dust settle on her skin and her clothes and the subsequent tingling from it. She knew it had been activated and started to work. The two of them would be completely invisible by the time they made it to Kieran's encampment. While in flight, she slipped the cloak over her shoulders, clasped it closed, but left off the hood. She giggled at the thought of her disembodied head bobbing in view.

As they left their camp behind and crossed over the Hill of Tara, Elyne peered down, watching the men for any reaction to the great dragon flying overhead. Nothing. Not one of them looked up as the foot soldiers assembled and the warhorses lined up behind them. Elyne gave a gentle pat on Aura's neck to signal everything was okay.

She saw Kieran's tent toward the back of the encampment, heavily guarded by the Unseelie soldiers. She guessed he kept the Sword and the Spear in there and gave Aura the signal to land behind the tent. It would give her the best access and hopefully she would find what she was looking for. If not, things could get ugly.

The azure dragon turned her body downward, her back legs extended in preparation for landing. Her leathery wings flapped quickly to slow her down before she hit the ground so she wouldn't make a sound. It was as though Aura knew that's what Elyne needed her to do to—be as quiet as possible.

Once the dragon was on the ground, her head lowered and Elyne slid out of the saddle. She paused to pat Aura on the neck.

"I want you to hide in that copse of trees." Elyne pointed to the cluster of greenery behind the dragon. "And don't do anything rash. That's an order."

Aura snorted in response. *Isn't being here rash enough?*

"You know what I mean," she said, exasperated. "Stay hidden. If anything happens to me, you'll need to light the tar and get back to Derron to tell him what happened."

He will not be happy with your decision to come here.

"I'll worry about that later." She patted her nose before giving her a brief hug by laying her head on the scaly skin. The she pulled up the hood on her cloak.

Aura nudged her again for luck before turning and lumbering into the trees. Satisfied the dragon was well-hidden and camouflaged, Elyne watched the hustle of the men who paid neither of them any mind. *Good. The Faery dust is still working.*

She knew there was a time limit on the stuff. But how long it would last was the big question. She hoped she could get in, get the Treasures and get out as quickly as possible. And she was grateful for the cloak. Aura, however, didn't have one to hide her.

Steeling her nerves and tamping down the nausea that roiled in her stomach, she headed for the Unseelie king's tent. As she neared, she could hear him giving final orders to his men before they rushed out to do his bidding. She stopped in front of one of the guards, waved in front of his face to make sure he couldn't see her. He didn't react.

She waited breathless moments, her heart doing a *rat-a-tat* in her chest. She had to wait until the tent was empty before she could go inside and search. Standing there wasted precious moments she didn't have. Finally, Lord Kieran stepped out, a man by his side.

Kieran was dressed richly in his armor—as though he were already king of the Otherworld and victor of the coming war. His gold-plated armor was polished to a high shine and he clinked when he walked. She noted as he walked by, he wore a sword strapped to his side and carried a red-plumed helm under one arm.

What a pompous arse.

"Cormac, you've confirmed the queen is on the battlefield?" he asked.

He knew her mother was there? Of course, he would. He would have spies everywhere, just as the Seelie would.

"Aye, my king. She is there. Heavily guarded, of course. But that's nothing that cannot be remedied."

"Wonderful." He smiled, showing off all his teeth. "Then today I shall claim victory. With the queen dead, no one shall oppose me. And the walls between the human realm and the Otherworld will finally be destroyed."

Anger flooded her. How dare he threaten her mother's life? How dare he think he could kill her and take control?

"You forget about the crown princess, her daughter, my king," Cormac pointed out.

Elyne's heart sped up.

"I forget nothing," Kieran said, his tone hard and unforgiving. "I want her captured alive. With her noble blood, I will make her my bride. It will be the perfect joining of Seelie and Unseelie. Together we can rule the Otherworld."

Over my dead body.

Never would she consent to that. It turned her stomach at the very thought of marrying the vile creature. She would rather slash her wrists than spend one night with him.

"Very good, my king. I will make sure the men understand not to harm the princess."

They continued through the camp, heading toward the front line. But Elyne remained still where she was.

Clenching her fists, she stepped into the Unseelie's tent and stopped short. It was roomy, much bigger than the tents they'd suffered in, with ornate furniture. A writing desk littered with scattered parchment. A quill pen and inkwell on one side. A candelabra on the other. A large bed covered with fine linens and furs. A chest next to that. The floor hosted an animal-skin rug to ward off the cold. Braziers stood in every corner, brightly lit. The tent smelled of death and rot and…sex.

Her stomach threatened to dry heave and she clamped a hand over her mouth. She would do her best to get through the tent without breathing in the awful smells. Spying a chest at the foot of the bed, she fell to her knees and shoved open the lid. Inside were fine tunics, soft leather pants, gloves, vests of animal skin and any number of pieces of clothing. She tossed out every single one of them looking for the Spear and the Sword. Neither was there.

Rising, she spun around, looking for other places to hide the Treasures. She checked under the bed. Then around the desk. They weren't there. And then it occurred to her. *Would Kieran be so stupid as to leave the Treasures lying about in his tent? Of course not. They are someplace secure. Safe.*

She thought back to when he left the tent with Cormac at his side. His ridiculous gold-plated armor, shiny bright. The red-plumed helm under his arm. A sword at his side.

The sword. He has it on his person!

She squeezed her eyes shut, to force the memory clear. What did the hilt look like? She couldn't remember. She would have to get closer to him to find out. With her heart pounding, she left the tent and headed toward the front line where she could find Kieran. If the Faery dust wore off while she was in the camp, she would be safe as long as she wore the cloak.

Elyne found him still giving orders to the men, Cormac still at this side. She made her way through the men, keeping her eyes on the hilt of that sword. It had to be the Sword of Light. It would be like him to be so pompous as to keep it with him. He stopped to talk to a small group of men. She should have been listening for his battle tactics, but she was intent on that sword.

The hilt was just as she remembered from the description. A handle trimmed in gold flowed into a dragon-shaped pommel complete with glittering ruby eyes. The crossguards flared into a pair of golden wings. She had never actually seen the Sword of Light in person but the description she knew from all the lore matched the one in his scabbard. Should he wield it, along with all the other Treasures, he could easily conquer the Otherworld, murder Maeve and take her as an unwilling bride.

Now that I know he has it, how am I supposed to get it off him?

If she tried to remove it, he would know. He would feel her even if he couldn't see her.

As she contemplated this, she noticed the Faery dust drifting from her skin and clothes, forming a shimmery puddle around her. She stood completely still, frozen with her fright.

Too late she saw the squadron of men heading toward her, three wide. She spun, searching for a way out but there were more men coming from the other direction. Trapped. Her heart jumped to her throat as she decided what to do. Her indecision cost her, though, as one of the men bumped her, knocking her off her feet.

She fell backward, throwing her arms out to break her fall. She landed hard, the heels of her hands taking the brunt of her fall. The hood of her cloak fell back and long tendrils of hair spilled out. Glancing down, she saw it had was unclasped and fell open, revealing her gown.

Revealing all of her.

Fecking hell.

"Intruder! My king! Intruder!"

Elyne flushed hot. She could try to flee but swords were already pointed in her direction and all eyes on her. If she tried to run, they would catch her. Her only choice was to sit still and hold her head high.

Her Faery dust had worn off already. She had hoped it would last a lot longer. There she sat in the middle of the Unseelie camp, exposed for all to see.

Lord Kieran's gaze landed on Elyne. A slow smile spread as he stepped closer to her. Several men grabbed her and hauled her to her feet. He looked her over, even fingered a tendril of her blonde hair. She slapped his hand away. He chuckled.

"Well, well. What have we here? Take off that concealment cloak, princess."

Elyne lifted her head higher. When she didn't comply, he gave a nod. One of the men jerked it off her.

"How fortuitous," Kieran said. "Though I'm curious, princess. How did you come to be in my camp?" He glanced around, as though looking for other Seelie. "If you're here, does that mean your Knight of the Realm is nearby?"

"After you murdered his father in cold blood, he became Guardian of the Sword of Light." She wasn't afraid of him. At least, that's what she kept telling herself. She would not allow her fear to show. Not to him. He would take advantage of her, do gods-knew-what to her.

"I stand corrected, your highness." He bowed with a flourish, mocking her. "But Lord Malcolm was most uncooperative. It cost him his life. Mayhap, then, Sir Derron could be so kind as to wield the Sword for me. After I've slaughtered his men and taken him as my prisoner, of course."

"*Lord* Derron will never wield the Sword for you." She put special emphasis on his title to make sure Kieran understood Derron was no longer just a knight. "You haven't won yet."

"How naive you are, princess. I have ten thousand men at my disposal. How many Seelie have you managed to rally? My spies tell me you've recruited *human* knights to help you fight." He shook his head, looking at her with pity in his dark eyes. "How pathetic."

She knew that, even with the Elves, the Seelie army was outnumbered. They would be massacred on the Hill of Tara and it sickened her to think they could lose before they even had a chance. Lord Kieran intended to wipe out as many Fae as he could and what could she do about it?

Get the Sword.

"You have the Sword. I've come for it."

He laughed. "You think you can walk over here and demand it?"

"And the Spear. I want that, too."

"You are a brave one, aren't you? I'm afraid I cannot hand over either of them to you. As it won't matter once your precious army is wiped out. For I have the third Treasure. Isn't that right, Cormac?"

"Aye, my king, you do."

"The Stone of Destiny stands unprotected because you murdered the Guardian."

He pinned her with an icy stare. "I'm not talking about the Stone of Destiny."

Fear trickled through her. He had managed to gain control of the Club of Dagda as well? How? It meant the fourth and last Guardian was also dead. If Derron and her mother failed, then Kieran, holding all three Treasures, would be able to step onto the Stone and proclaim himself High King.

"You're lying," she said. She couldn't—wouldn't—believe it.

"Am I?" He unsheathed the Sword of Light and held it aloft so she could see it. "Cormac, bring the Spear."

Cormac made a motion to someone she couldn't see and moments later the group of men parted to allow two men to come through. One held the Spear of Lugh and handed it to Cormac.

"One of my trusted men has the Club of Dagda and will be bringing it to me shortly. But now you can see I have the two most important—the Spear and the Sword."

Weapons of the Seelie and Unseelie forged long ago. Weapons that when paired with the Club of Dagda and the Stone of Destiny would allow one man to rule the Otherworld.

Her stomach knotted. Not even Derron knew Kieran had the Club, though she wasn't sure she believed it until she saw it for herself in his possession. Still, she had to tell him. To warn him and Maeve of the impending danger.

"So you see, my dear princess, this…war…is all for naught. You will all be slaughtered. And I will rule the Otherworld."

There was one hope left. One way she could get a message back to Derron.

Aura.

The azure dragon would be visible by now, since the Faery dust had worn off. But mayhap she would have enough time to fly back to Derron. If he'd seen Maggie or Finn this morning, they would surely tell him of her plan to get back the Sword. He would know. And seeing Aura flying toward him would reinforce that.

Aura, hear me.

Elyne closed her eyes and concentrated on connecting telepathically to the dragon. Whispering words for her to take flight. To get back to Derron.

"I see the news pains you, my princess," Kieran was saying. "If you cooperate with me, I will allow you to live."

She tried to block out his voice and not allow him to interrupt her thoughts to the dragon.

Aura! Go, now. Back to Derron. Help him fight!

But you, my friend? What of you?

Hearing the low-timbre voice in her head relieved her. The dragon was as yet unharmed. Kieran was giving orders again to his men but she wasn't listening. She was too intent on trying to maintain the contact.

There's nothing you can do for me, Aura. This Unseelie scum will not hurt me. I'll make sure he finds some use for me. Go, now. Please.

Rough hands grabbed Elyne. A sword pointed in her back.

"Tie her up. Make sure she can't get free. And I want guards on her at all times," Kieran said.

So she was to be his prisoner. She could live with that.

As you wish, my friend.

She heard the distant *whomp-whomp* of wings and she knew Aura had taken flight. Elyne looked to the sky, trying to see the dragon as she flew overhead. She caught a glimpse of a flash of blue before there was a flash of flame. And instantly, Elyne knew Aura had followed her instructions.

The tar Derron had secretly laid behind Kieran's camp ignited, engulfing the green landscape into a fiery burst of flame. Fire raced across at breakneck speed through the camp, overtaking tents and killing men who were not fortunate enough to get out of the way. She could hear the beat of Aura's wings as she headed upward into the sky. Men shouted and shot arrows at her. Elyne held her breath, willing the arrows to miss the dragon. Angered by the attack, Aura turned her head, looking directly into the camp. She let loose a burst of bright orange-and-red flames, setting tents on fire, killing men, and nearly singeing Elyne.

"Aura, no!" she shouted before she could stop herself.

The dragon ignored her and dove, releasing another fireball. Men went flying into the air and the smell of charred earth, skin and hair permeated the air around them. Horses and other animals screamed as they were incinerated. Turned to ash in one swift move.

It will give your Seelie a fighting chance. I will tell your mate what has happened. Farewell, my friend.

Aura had evened the odds. How could Elyne repay the dragon for that? If she got out of here alive, she would think of something. She smiled, watching Aura soar away. To freedom.

To Derron.

"You bloody bitch!" Before she knew what was happening,

Kieran was in front of her, jerking her out of the custody of the other guards. He grabbed her by the arms, yanked her toward him. "You came here with a dragon?"

Elyne couldn't help the smug smile that spread on her lips. He released her with a forceful push, making her stumble backward a few steps. Before she could react, he backhanded her so hard, her lip split.

"Cormac! Call Nero!"

"I've already called him, my king," Cormac replied.

And then she saw it. The blackness rose from the ground heading upward toward Aura. The onyx scales glittered gold in the early-morning light. She heard the beating of the wings as it took flight and headed directly for Aura.

Kieran shouted orders to his men, ordering the destruction of the azure dragon. Elyne's heart palpitated hard as she watched the arrows soar into the air toward Aura who flattened her wings against her huge body and did a spiral up, up, up, missing all the projectiles. Elyne's breath caught in her throat as she watched the dragon ascend out of harm's way.

But it wasn't over yet. Elyne got a close-up look at the black dragon as it took flight and chased Aura. It had two sets of wings that thumped against the wind.

Aura, behind you!

She mind-spoke to the dragon, hoping she could hear her.

Do not be afraid, my old friend.

Aura pulled up, her body turning into a crescent as she came to such a quick halt. She turned toward Nero and released several fireballs in quick succession. Nero dodged but not in time. One of the fireballs clipped two of his wings, causing him to screech in horrible pain, the wings smoking from the attack. He faltered, losing control and heading toward the ground. The black dragon landed with a resounding *sha-koom.*

A snort of gray smoke escaped Aura as she turned again, her great wings thumping in the wind as she made for the other side of the camp. Away from Elyne. Toward freedom.

Men screamed. Flames reached for the skies, putting out a thick, black smoke. Elyne glanced toward the destruction, saw Aura had managed to take out nearly half of Kieran's army and injured Nero. Horses ran free back toward the woods, deserting the army.

"I should kill you for that."

He slapped her again, his hand hitting her hard across the cheek and making her head snap to one side. Before she could recover, he punched her on the other side of her face. Her cheekbone exploded in blinding pain. Elyne tumbled to the ground, landing on her hands and knees, her face wet from tears she didn't know she'd shed. He kicked her in the ribs and she fell to her side, gasping for breath, blood on her lips and in her mouth.

"Stop, my king!"

Cormac. Turning her head, she could see him pulling the Unseelie leader away from her, his hands fisted and his face bright red from anger.

"She's not any use to us dead or damaged."

"The only part of her I need intact is her womb. I will beat her face to an unrecognizable bloody pulp to make her understand what she's done to me. To us."

Elyne struggled back to her hands and knees, trying to catch her breath. He'd knocked the wind out of her but she wouldn't let him win. She closed her fist on a handful of dirt, intending to fling it at him. He could beat her all he wanted. He could rape her. He could kill her. But by the gods, she wouldn't go down without a fight.

"May I suggest you take your anger out on the waiting Seelie army, my king?" Cormac's voice was steady and calm. "She may be of some use to us. Especially with Lord Derron."

Kieran jerked his arm free, his piercing gaze still on Elyne. "You may be right, Cormac. See that she's imprisoned in my tent. I'll deal with her later. To the battlefield, my lords."

Kieran stomped away, his armor jingling with every step. Several dozen men followed on his heels, ready for war. Cormac hauled Elyne to her feet, one arm around her shoulders. Her strength gone, she slumped against him.

"Fetch the healer and send him to the king's tent." When no one moved, he shouted, "Now!"

He headed for the tent, helping her along the way. She didn't know why he did it. Nor did she care but she was grateful he had stopped Kieran. Though she knew it would not be the last she'd see of the self-proclaimed king.

"You have sealed your fate with his majesty."

"He is not my king. He will never be my king."

"Be that as it may, princess, he will exact his vengeance on you for killing most of his men."

"And who will exact revenge on him for killing half of *my men*?" she asked. "You don't know what will happen during this battle. You don't know he will win."

They'd arrived at the tent and Cormac lowered her to the bed. She perched on the edge and got a good look at the man for the first time. He was taller than Derron with silvery hair and eyes the color of moonlight. He didn't belong in the Unseelie realm any more than she did and she knew it.

"Who are you?" she blurted. "And why have you aligned yourself with Kieran?"

"Who I am is of no consequence. Lord Kieran will be the one to lead the Otherworld out of this oppression so long ruled by Queen Maeve."

"You called him Lord Kieran, not king as before." He didn't respond, merely gave her a stony stare. She continued. "Do you not believe him to be your true king, then?"

"I believe him to be a born leader."

He was a master at not answering questions. If she could smile without pain, she would.

"My mother has ruled the Otherworld for thousands of years without incident. Our kingdom is prosperous and fair."

"For the Seelie, aye," he agreed. "What about the Unseelie?"

They were evil, vile creatures. But she didn't voice this to Cormac. He was unlike the others with his pale eyes and fair hair. A former Elven ranger? Or mayhap he'd once belonged to the Elves and had been banished. She couldn't decide. He wasn't Fae, that much she knew. But he had the telltale pointed ears of the Elves.

"Long have they been banished to the Dark. I follow Kieran for hope they will be returned to their rightful place in the Light."

They, he said. What stake did he have in this war? What did he hope to gain?

"You are not one of them. You are not Unseelie."

He pressed his lips together and refused to respond. He wouldn't now that the healer had arrived.

"Your patient, healer," he said, nodding toward Elyne. "Make sure she is well cared for."

"Aye, my lord."

Before Elyne could ask him any more questions, Cormac turned on his booted heel and left.

Chapter 22

When Derron woke, he rolled over to find the other side of the bed empty. Blinking his eyes open, he scanned the tent, but Elyne had gone. Her scent lingering on his skin was all that remained of her. That and a small swath of silk she'd tucked inside one of his gauntlets.

He couldn't help but smile. She'd left him a favor as good luck in the coming battle. Despite her absence, it heartened him to see the favor, telling him that she didn't regret anything that had happened the night before.

They had bonded. Pledged their hearts to each other in a vow, each speaking the ancient words. Though neither professed their love for the other, the bonding was still in effect. He waited for her to say it first. When she didn't, he knew that her heart was ready but she was still too afraid to speak the words aloud. He could forgive her for that. He understood. Their relationship had always been a rocky one from the very beginning.

Rolling out of bed, he dressed. He had one last meeting to finalize the plans for their initial attack, and then he'd be ready to take on the Unseelie and Kieran. The queen had emerged from her royal tent dressed in a sapphire gown, her blonde hair flowing freely around her face, giving her the look of a youthful woman instead of a regal queen who had ruled for several centuries.

"I've convened the war council," she said when she saw Derron. "This is a map of the Hill of Tara. We can finalize our strategy."

Nodding, he followed her and her two guards to the center of the camp, where Sir Finian, Gawaine and Sir Drake waited underneath a tattered tent that was more like an awning. They gathered around a scarred wooden table where Maeve rolled out the map.

"Good morrow, gentlemen," she greeted. "I trust you'll appreciate me getting right to it. I've had my council bring me this map of Tara. The Stone of Destiny is where Kieran will make his final stand."

"Has the Club been located yet?" Derron asked.

"The Club is in a safe place," Maeve said. "As is the Guardian. He's been relieved of his burden."

This was news to Derron. "You've known the location of the Club of Dagda? How long? Why have you not told us?"

"I thought it best only Gawaine and I knew," Maeve said. "The Guardian was removed shortly after the Guardian of the Stone of Destiny was found murdered."

"It would have been good to have that information," Derron snapped.

Derron, though, didn't believe the Guardian of the Club was safe. Most likely the man was already dead and the Club in the hands of Lord Kieran. If that were the case, they were doomed once they met in battle. Kieran would destroy every last one of them.

"He still holds the Sword and Spear," Derron pointed out. "If he has the Club, then what's to stop him from stepping onto the Stone of Destiny?"

"We will stop him," Maeve said. "He will need all Four Treasures to proclaim himself High King. That and…" Her voice trailed off, her face paled.

"That and you'd have to be dead," Derron finished for her.

"Which is exactly what he plans," Gawaine put in.

"I'm leaving the protection of the queen to Sir Finian and Sir Drake," Derron said.

"I don't need extra protection," she argued. "My guards will be enough. Send the humans to the battlefield."

"No, my queen. If Lord Kieran tries to get to you, I trust Finn and Drake to keep you from harm."

"I don't need them," she said.

Derron knew her stubbornness was driven by her dislike of humans. "You have no choice. I'm sending them with or without your consent." He turned to Drake and Finn, not waiting for a response from her. "I trust you two knights will guard her with your lives."

"Aye, we will," Finn answered and Drake nodded.

"You will be guarded well, my queen," Derron said. "We will fight and win, despite their numbers. We have the dragons."

"I fear three dragons will not be enough," she said. "They have dragons, too."

He could see the fear in her eyes when she said it. There wasn't much he could do to alleviate her fears for her or himself. They were outmatched and outnumbered. But he would have to worry about that when they were in the midst of battle.

"We will march to the Stone of Destiny and make our final stand there," Derron said. "I took the liberty of sending two thousand men ahead last night, my queen."

"You fool, you've depleted our forces here," Gawaine snapped.

"It was that or risk losing everything. If we're defeated here, then Kieran marches on to the Stone of Destiny. At least there will be a fighting chance it will be protected should he get through us here."

"A wise decision, Lord Derron. I commend you," Maeve said, looking pleased.

"He should have discussed it with the council first, your majesty," Gawaine said, ignoring Derron. "I would have preferred to be informed."

Derron pinned him with a heated stare. He didn't like Gawaine and hadn't since that day in the palace when he'd tried to undermine Derron. He had never voiced his feelings or his suspicions to the queen, and rightfully so. The man was proving to be a problem.

"Lord Derron is Protector of the Realm and Guardian of the Sword of Light. I'd trust him with my life. And have," the queen said, her words icy. "He made the best possible decision in our situation and one I'm grateful for."

"I have another surprise waiting for Lord Kieran. We'll be able to use the dragons effectively against him when—"

A distant explosion interrupted him, the ground vibrating violently. Everyone looked toward the sound and heard shouts in the distance. Derron could see black smoke curling in the air. It was so far away, it had to be on the other side of the field. One of his men came running across the camp and skittered to a halt in front of him, trying to catch his breath.

"Lord Kieran's camp is on fire, my lord," the man gasped.

"What happened?" Derron asked.

"Dragon!" someone else shouted.

Derron glanced up to see the azure dragon coming in for a

landing. Men scattered to get out of her way. She intended to land in the middle of the camp. What was the dragon doing here? She was supposed to be in the mounds with the others. The dragons were their secret weapon. The one thing Kieran wouldn't be expecting.

"Aura. What is she doing here?"

Derron peered at the dragon looking back at him with an intensity he hadn't seen before. It was as though she were trying to convey something to him. He glanced back up at the black smoke curling toward the early morning sky. And suddenly he knew.

"Aura, you set the camp on fire, didn't you?" Derron asked, looking at the dragon.

How did the dragon know he had laid a tar trap in Kieran's camp? He glanced up again, peering at the smoke rising into the air. It was more than one tent on fire. It had to be half the camp.

Aura blinked her eyes and lowered her head as if nodding agreement.

"You helped us." Derron walked toward the dragon, placed his hand on her nose. She snorted. "You might have won the war for us."

He saw Maggie then, running from one of the tents across the field. Her hair bounced behind her, her skirts fluttering as she hurried toward them.

"Did she come back? Is she safe?" Maggie asked on a breath as she came to a halt near the dragon.

"Is who safe?"

"God's teeth," Finn swore under his breath.

Fear trickled through Derron then. He glanced around, looking for Elyne. She was nowhere to be found. Which meant the *she* Maggie must be referring to was…Elyne.

"Bloody hell, what has Elyne done?" he thundered.

"I tried to stop her," Maggie said. She rested her palm against the dragon's neck, who nudged her then as though she were happy to be petted. "I tried to talk her out of it last night."

"Aye, as did I," Finn said.

"But you know how stubborn she is," Maggie continued.

"Lady Margaret, *where* is Elyne?"

"Aye, *where is my daughter*?" the queen asked.

She was captured.

The voice exploded in his head with such force, Derron

stumbled backward a step and nearly doubled over. He looked at the dragon, who blinked and gave him a nod. He had only been mentally connected with Luna once she had chosen him as his rider. Hearing Aura's voice in his head startled him.

"She intended to retrieve the Sword of Light and the Spear of Lugh," Maggie continued, unaware the dragon had spoken in his head.

"By the gods! What the feckin' hell did she think she was doing?" Derron asked.

"Elyne went across enemy lines?" Maeve's face drained of color.

Derron shoved a hand through his hair out of frustration. She had been taken by the worst enemy he'd ever faced. The man who had murdered his father. The man who had tortured the other two Guardians and killed them. The man who would murder the queen and stop at nothing to gain complete control of the Otherworld.

"She was trying to help you regain the advantage," Maggie said.

That's why she'd come to him last night, why she'd asked him to make love to her. Why they had bonded. She *knew* what she was going to do. She had spent her last night with him. In his arms. And now she was gone. Possibly lost forever. But she wanted to give him the most precious gift a Fae could give another—her heart.

She must have known he would be furious when he discovered what she'd done. She would have been right. Had he seen her before she left, he would have stopped her. Tied her up to keep her in the camp if he had to.

Bloody hell.

This made things even more complicated.

"We have to get her back." Maeve's voice quivered with fear. "Lord Kieran knows who she is. He can take her, bond with her, and then—"

"He can't bond with her." Derron's voice was razor sharp, cutting off the queen. He hadn't wanted to tell her like this. He had hoped he and Elyne would break the news to the queen together. At a more appropriate time. Not while she was the enemy's captive and they were about to go to war.

She looked taken aback. "Why not?"

"Because she's already bonded to me."

Silence descended around them, the only sounds those of the

encampment. No one moved a muscle. But he could see Maggie smirking.

"About bloody time," she said. "You two have been pining for each other since the jousting tournament in Middleham."

"God's teeth, woman, was this yere idea?" Finn asked. "Ye canna be playing matchmaker with everyone all the time."

"I merely gave her a gentle nudge in his direction." Maggie blinked, trying to look innocent.

"You've bonded with my daughter, Lord Derron. That is cause for an explanation and I demand one."

"We can discuss this later. Right now, we have to get Elyne back." Derron hushed them all with a wave of his hand.

Kieran intends to kill the queen and take control of the Otherworld, my lord.

Derron heard the dragon's voice in his head again and looked at the beast.

He had ten thousand men before I killed half of them. Still, he intends to slaughter your army.

"We have to protect the queen. Sir Finian, I want you to come with me. Gawaine, I trust you and Sir Drake can guard the queen?"

"I will guard the queen with my life," Sir Drake said.

"As will I," Gawaine said, but he didn't sound all that convincing to Derron.

Which made him suspicious of the man. Derron peered at him, but he masked his true feelings well. His eyes and face were unreadable.

"I'm going with you," Maeve announced.

"The hell you are. The last thing we need is for you to be captured—or worse, killed—while we try to rescue Elyne."

"She is my daughter!"

"And you are the queen. If anything should happen to Elyne, you have to remain in power—"

Derron stopped short of saying *until a suitable heir can be named.* But Queen Maeve knew, as did he, what he meant.

"I know you are correct, Lord Derron. However, I still don't like the idea of sitting idly by while wondering if both of you are either alive or dead."

"I'll stay with you," Maggie said.

Maeve shot her a brief look of disdain before she masked it and nodded with a quick jerk of her head. The queen was not overly fond of humans—as Elyne hadn't been before Maggie won her over. If any human could win over the queen, it would be Maggie.

One of his knights approached. "My lord, Lord Kieran is riding out to midfield."

"Then it begins. Sir Finian, let's go. Let's find Eldrin and face this beast of a man."

"What about Elyne?" Maggie asked, stepping in front of him.

"I'll get her back."

She nodded, reluctantly, though it was clear she didn't like the answer. Maggie touched Finn on his arm and stood on tiptoe to kiss him on the cheek.

"Be careful," she said.

"As my lady wishes."

After finding Eldrin with the other rangers, the three men mounted horses and rode out to greet Lord Kieran.

"I hope ye ken what yere doing," Finn said.

"Aye, I do. I picked a fight with him," Derron said. "He'll never let me get close to his camp without a battle."

"Ye intend to go after the princess yeself?" Finn asked, giving him a sideways glance.

"Aye."

"*Och*, laddie. 'Tis too dangerous."

"I would do anything for her, Finn. Anything."

The admission lingered between them for a long, silent moment as Finn stared at him. Mayhap it was the same for him and Maggie. He would understand. He had to understand.

Derron knew, without a doubt, he was madly in love with Elyne. He would do whatever it took to get her back safe. She belonged to him now and he intended to spend the rest of their immortal eternity together.

Finn nodded. "Aye, then. I canna allow ye to go alone. I'll come with ye."

"As will I," Eldrin said.

"No," Derron said. "I should go alone."

"And if ye fail?" Finn asked. "With the three of us, we stand a better chance of getting in and out with the fair princess."

The knight had a point. He nodded.

Lord Kieran waited in the middle of the field, flanked by two Unseelie soldiers. He wore gold-plated armor, a red plume on the top of his helm, looking like a nothing more than a golden rooster.

"Lord Kieran," Derron greeted.

"Don't you mean *King* Kieran?" he corrected.

"You are not my ruler," Derron said. "Queen Maeve still lives."

"Though not for long," he fired back. "I look forward to killing your queen and taking my rightful place as High King."

Derron noticed the Sword of Light strapped to his side and scowled. His father's sword. Now his sword. And this bloody bastard had it.

"You think because you have the Sword of Light, you can proclaim yourself king." Derron clucked his tongue. "I'm afraid it doesn't work like that."

"I have two Treasures and something else precious to the Guardian of the Sword of Light." Kieran gave him a wolf smile. "The princess and I will become better acquainted very soon."

Derron clenched his fists. "I'm sure Princess Elyne will have something to say about that. She doesn't belong to you."

"On the contrary, she does. She came to me early this morning and waits for me in my tent."

She would not have gone to him willingly, Derron knew. He believed a dragon over Kieran any day.

"She and I will bond and seal the future of the Otherworld."

Derron smirked. He could tell the pompous arse he'd already claimed that right but then what would Kieran do to Elyne? Kill her? She would be useless to him. He tamped down the anger bubbling inside him and turned his smirk into a smile.

"Indeed," Derron said. "I'm sure Queen Maeve will be glad to hear that bit of news."

"I intend to tell her myself," Kieran said. "Right before I slit her throat."

Derron had enough of his threats. "What do you want, Kieran?"

"What I want is for you to vacate this field. Let us ride on to the Stone of Destiny in peace."

"And allow you to step onto the Stone and proclaim yourself High King?" He shook his head. "Never."

"Then you give me no other choice."

"Attack if you will. But I know your army has suffered a huge loss."

Kieran's face grew dark and menacing. "For that, I intend to repay you."

"Do what you must, Kieran. I will do the same."

"So it shall be done."

A dark shadow settled over Kieran's face as he lifted his arms to the skies. The distant rumble started quietly and slowly and then immediately intensified. At first, Derron thought it was the ground that shook but then he realized it wasn't a rumble in the ground—it was a rumble in the sky. Glancing to the heavens, he saw the dark blots moving rapidly toward them. And there, on the ground, a black dragon—the same one he'd seen Cormac riding—limped along with one sickly-looking wing. Above, the swarm of dragons—big and small alike—headed straight for them.

But it was more than dragons. There were other winged creatures, too. Wyvern and harpies and birds with sharp, pointed beaks and razor-like claws. All headed directly for them.

"I did warn you," Kieran said, his tone smug and defiant.

Derron jerked his reins, turning his horse and heading as fast as he could back to their side of the camp. Finn and Eldrin followed, flanking him on either side. Behind him, he could hear more thunder and glanced over his shoulder. Kieran had dispatched his army, headed straight for them. Some held spears in their hands. Others bore swords, the morning sun glinting off the polished steel.

"He's attacking!" Derron shouted. He drew his sword, the metal making a distinctive *shing* as he removed it from the sheath and wielded it. "Eldrin, you and Finn get back to camp! Warn the men!"

Derron yanked the reins of his horse, turning back to face the horde approaching by all sides. Finn ignored his orders, though, and turned his horse around, too.

"What are you doing?"

"Do ye think I'll run from a fight?" he asked, a grin on his face, and then shook his head. "*Och* no, laddie. 'Tis like the melee at tourney, aye?"

Despite the circumstances, Derron let out a laugh. "Aye, you crazy Scotsman. Like the melee. Now with dragons."

"Bring it on," Finn replied.

Eldrin shouted something Derron couldn't hear as he turned back toward their camp at breakneck speed. Derron took that to mean he headed back to rally the troops.

But Derron and Finn were in the middle of the field, about to come face-to-face with the horde before them. There was nothing to do but hold on tight to the reins and attack head-on.

Chapter 23

Maeve allowed Gawaine to grasp her arm and lead her quickly back to her tent, the two remaining humans in tow. She clutched the fabric of her skirt in her fists, keeping the length off the ground to avoid stepping on it in her hurry. How could Elyne do such a foolish thing? How could she think she could accomplish such a task?

Maeve quickly shoved that thought away. Her daughter would return. She would be safe. She would live. And she would someday become queen.

"Sir Drake, you stand guard outside the tent," Gawaine ordered. "I will remain by my queen's side."

"Aye," Drake agreed.

Once inside the tent, Maeve released her skirt and clasped her hands behind her back. She paced the length of the tent, spinning on her toe and turning to go back the other way.

"You should rest, Queen Maeve. There is nothing to be done until Elyne is safe," Maggie said.

"I will not rest until she has returned safely." She paused then, coming to a quick halt in front of the human. She peered at her. "Did you have something to do with this?"

Her eyes widened to huge round disks. "What? No! I had nothing to do with it. You know Elyne, she doesn't listen to anyone. I tried to talk her out of it. So did Finn."

"And her bonding with Lord Derron? Is that your meddling as well?"

The human flushed, her cheeks turning a pale pink. "A blind fool could see how much in love they are with each other."

"That is *not* your concern and I'll thank you to stay out of our affairs."

"Well, I *would* except it's because of Elyne I'm here. It's because of Elyne I found the love of my life. And it's because of *Elyne* Derron even lives."

"Do not speak to me in such an insolent tone, *human*."

"Or what? You can't take my powers away." Maggie crossed her arms over her chest.

Maeve took a warning step toward her. "No, but I *can* have you sent back to your own time. Without your beloved Scotsman."

The color drained from her face. "You wouldn't."

"Aye, I would. And then mayhap you would keep your meddling hands out of our lives."

Now the human woman moved her hands to her hips and leaned forward, her face turning pink again. "I did it because Elyne wouldn't. She loves him dearly. She wants to be with him. And Derron feels the same as she does."

"What do you know of their relationship? I arranged their marriage. I made sure they would spend eternity together. And yet Lord Derron broke the betrothal."

"It was a mistake. He didn't know what he was doing," Maggie snapped.

"One more word, human, and I send you back."

"Ladies, please." Gawaine pinched the bridge of his nose. "Arguing about this will not solve anything. What's done is done. We must move on."

Silence descended between them before Maeve turned on her heel and perched on the edge of a chair. "I do not need a human to babysit me."

"I'm not leaving. I promised Lord Derron."

"As did I," Gawaine said, his hand on the hilt of his sword. "Forgive me, my queen."

"Forgive you for what?" She blinked confusion as she looked at Gawaine.

He pulled his sword then, pointed it directly at her chest. Pinpricks of heat erupted on the back of her neck. There was a sudden sickness in the pit of her stomach. She knew immediately what he intended to do. The man she had trusted with all her council secrets. The man who had willingly become the Guardian of the Club of Dagda.

"How could you?" Her voice was cold as ice. "I trusted you."

Gawaine had been there from the moment Adhamh had been killed. He had been her confidant who consulted with her and helped her make the difficult decisions for her and her kingdom. He had been the one she trusted in a sea of traitors and murderers.

"Aye, you did."

"Your betrayal will never be forgotten." She pressed her lips together, the sickness nearly overtaking her. How could he do this to her?

"What's going on here?" Maggie asked. She looked between the two of them, her head bobbing back and forth.

"Why?" Maeve demanded.

"Lord Kieran came to me, offered me riches and land. Something you've never given me."

"I gave you my life!" She shot to her feet. "I trusted you with it for years."

"Aye, and I thank you for that. It's been very helpful to Lord Kieran."

"He will never give you want you want, Gawaine," Maeve said. "He will use you and kill you once he's done with you. Don't you see that?"

"I'm taking the Club and meeting him at the Stone of Destiny. And you're coming with me."

"No." She sat back down, her arms folded.

"I can kill you here. Now. It makes no difference to me or Kieran," he said. "Though he prefers to kill you himself."

Maeve was aware Maggie edged toward the front of the tent where she knew Sir Drake stood. She refused to look at her directly, though, for fear it would give the human away to Gawaine. She kept her gaze locked on the traitor, trying to control the fear that bubbled up inside her. Gawaine moved closer, the point of his sword a breath from her breastbone.

"What will it be? Will you come with me alive? Or shall I carry your dead body to the Stone?"

"Drake! Help!"

When Maggie shouted, Gawaine swung around to her. His sword arced, slicing across her upper arm. Maggie's sharp intake of breath came as Sir Drake barreled into the tent. He shoved Maggie out of the way, his sword in hand.

Steel clashed against steel as the two men fought against each other. Gawaine wouldn't stand a chance against a seasoned knight such as Sir Drake, Maeve knew. If Kieran won, the Unseelie world would no longer exist. Neither would the Seelie world for that matter. Divided emotions tore through her as she watched the two parry and fight, her stomach clenching in a tight knot.

Where was the Club? Had Gawaine already managed to get it to Kieran?

Maggie rushed to her, clutching her arm, blood streaming through her fingers. She grabbed Maeve with her free hand and pulled her to her feet.

"Come on! We have to get out of here."

She let Maggie drag her out of the tent and into hell.

Chapter 24

"**R**ide through them!" Derron shouted. If they kept riding at breakneck speed, perhaps they could outrun most of the flying creatures.

They had another problem. Four-legged creatures with beady red eyes and sharp-looking teeth were bearing down on them. He recognized them right away. The last thing they needed was to fight off Hell Hounds.

"Now what?" Finn asked.

Derron held his reins in one hand and leaned down with his sword in the other. He swiped back and forth, cutting down two of the hounds. One glance at Finn and he could see the Scotsman doing the same thing. Derron looked behind them and saw with rising hope his army charging after them, cutting down more Hell Hounds in their wake. Overhead, he saw the arrows flying, picking off the smaller flying creatures. The dragons were another matter. They spit fireballs, setting the hillside on fire. There was nothing he could do about that right now. He kept riding, heading directly for Kieran's camp to find Princess Elyne.

Eldrin rode up next to him, his horse frothy from sweat. "Kieran is headed to the Stone of Destiny."

Derron nodded acknowledgement. The men he had sent ahead would face the Dark Elf.

"The Stone, my lord?" Eldrin asked.

"There are men there to greet him."

A snapping Hell Hound charged him, blood matting its fur. Derron swung his sword but missed. The hound sunk its teeth into the back leg of his horse. His destrier bucked, sent him flying to the ground. Derron rolled, narrowly missing the horse falling over on him. The hound turned its attention back to him, snarling and drooling as it advanced. Derron had lost his sword in the fall and fumbled for the dagger on his belt.

He needn't have worried. The hound was beheaded quickly,

blood spurting all over him. Finn had come to the rescue, also unhorsed. He held a hand down to Derron.

"'Tis lucky I happened along when I did," Finn said.

"I owe you my life, my friend."

"Let's get yere princess."

Just as Finn said the words, the world exploded in a bright flash. It knocked them both to the ground as it rumbled beneath them. Derron rolled to his hands and knees. Eldrin was there in an instant, helping him to his feet once again.

"What the bloody hell was that?"

"Kieran's entire camp is on fire, my lord," Eldrin said. He turned to help Finn to his feet. "The whole bloody thing."

He looked to the camp, saw the blaze of fire engulfing the tents and his heart sank into his knotted stomach. *Elyne.* He had to get to her. Unless she was already dead. *No, I will not think that. Kieran wants her alive.* It was the hope he held on to as he barreled across the field.

Derron couldn't find his sword so he snatched one from a dead knight. He took off running toward the camp with one thing on his mind—to save his love.

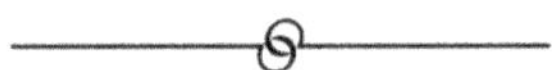

The healer had come and gone, leaving Elyne alone. He had cleaned her wounds carefully yet there wasn't much he could do for her sore ribs. Cormac returned before he'd finished and tied her wrists to the bedpost, leaving her there for Kieran. She would not sit here and wait for the vile Elf to come back and do gods knew what to her. She had to find a way out.

She worked the knots on the rope, but they held fast. Cormac had tied them so tightly they cut into her flesh, leaving raw rope burns. Somewhere in the distance, she heard the explosion and knew something had happened.

Elyne bit her lip. Had Aura come back? Had the dragons been released as her mother intended? What was happening? It drove her mad not to know if Derron was safe. What of her mother? Maggie? Prince Andahar and the other Elves?

She worked the knots again on her wrists, tugging and pulling. But she couldn't loosen them. It was useless, really. All she was doing was shredding her skin.

And then things got worse. She smelled the smoke, saw it leaking under the edge of the tent. Men shouted at each other, but she couldn't make out what they were saying.

The fire must have spread from behind the campsite. She would need to find a way to get out of her bindings quickly. Kieran's tent was toward the back of the campsite, not far from where Aura had ignited everything.

The last thing she needed to do was panic. Panic would get her dead. Dead was not something she wanted to be.

She had someone to live for.

Then she saw the edge of the tent catch fire, the flames eating through the material. Shouting for help wouldn't do her any good—no one would hear her. Aside from that, smoke clogged her throat, making her cough. She buried her face in the coverlet to keep from inhaling more smoke. She jerked on her ropes, trying desperately to get out of them. This wasn't how it was supposed to end. She had to get out.

The skin on her wrists burned with every jerk and yank. She couldn't get them free, no matter how hard she tried. She glanced up to see more of the tent on fire, the flames getting closer and closer. The smoke singed her nose and throat. Tears stung her eyes. There was nothing she could do to get away from it except to bury her face in the material of the bed.

Movement against her wrists made her look up. Cormac sliced off her ropes and then ran from the tent. Not wasting another minute, Elyne hurried after him.

Once outside, everywhere she looked she could see fire. Was this the result of Aura's attack? She didn't think so. Aura had targeted the tar behind the camp but the fire had definitely spread and now consumed everything in its path.

Cormac ran ahead of her, weaving in and out of the flames. Since she didn't know where she was going—and fire consumed every tent around them—she had no choice but to follow him, trying her best to keep up. Undoubtedly, he led her to Kieran but that was better than being burned alive in his tent. But the smoke she inhaled still made her cough, her throat raw. She needed water.

The explosion rocked her to the roots of her hair, making her fall. She landed on her left elbow so hard, it jarred her. It took several minutes before she could orient herself again, her arm now riddled with pain. Whimpering, she rolled to her side, trying to get to her feet.

Cormac was at her side, his hand an iron grip on her upper arm. He hauled her up and then dragged her along behind him as he hurried through the tents.

"No time for rolling on the ground, princess. You're about to be cooked."

"What was that?" Her voice was hoarse and painful as she shouted to him.

"That was Nero," he said.

Nero. The great black dragon. She was too out of breath to ask him any more questions. All she could do was let him drag her through the camp and hope he wasn't taking her to Kieran. If he made a mistake, then she would have a chance to run.

Elyne braved a glance over her right shoulder. Everything behind her was completely consumed in flames. Her left arm hung limp against her side and she was sure she'd broken something. She could barely move it, the pain shooting up to her shoulder. She wanted to cry.

But not now. She wouldn't allow herself to cry. She had to be brave. This was her fault, all of it. Cormac turned a sharp corner, making her stumble. His fingers dug into her arm, keeping her from falling once again. He never slowed his place as he headed through more burning tents, past charred dead men. The smell alone was enough to make her gag.

They passed the last row of tents and finally headed toward the open field. But the field wasn't open at all. It was littered with dead Hell Hounds, knights and dragons. Seelie and Unseelie fought each other. She peered through the men, trying to find Derron. He had to be among them somewhere, fighting for his life. Their lives.

Several men nearby joined Cormac, flanking them and keeping a watchful eye on their surroundings. She knew they were protecting him. Not her.

Overhead, the black dragon flew in a strange, lopsided way. She could tell his wing was injured and he squawked with every awkward flap.

"Nero!"

Cormac shouted the name into the wind and the black dragon turned and looked at them. Her heart rose into her throat as she realized *this* was Nero. He landed with a thud in front of them, stumbling a few feet before coming to a halt in front of Cormac, emitting a pained screech. He shoved her toward the dragon.

"Time to go."

"Where?" she croaked.

"To the Stone of Destiny, princess. To meet your fate."

No. I can't get on that dragon.

She dug in her heels, refusing to go with him but Cormac was stronger. He jerked her, making her stumble and forcing her to follow. He paused beside the dragon, looking at the broken, disfigured wing. He laid his free hand on it, whispered words she couldn't hear and watched the wing heal to perfection.

Nero lifted his head and snorted, gray steam coming out of his nostrils. He let loose a fireball into the sky, as though to say he approved of the healing. All Elyne could do was stare in disbelief at Cormac.

"Who are you?" she whispered.

"It matters not, princess. Now go."

He shoved her toward Nero, making her stumble against the great beast. Then he grasped her under the arms and pushed her upward. She had no choice but to climb upon the dragon's back. But she wasn't going without a fight. If her left arm hadn't been damaged, she could have fought back more. She turned, her right hand fisted as she threw a punch.

Cormac was prepared for that, though, and stopped her with a shove backward. She lost her balance, fell against Nero. He barked disapproval, turning his massive head to look at her with his red eyes, steam curling from his nose.

"Nero, no," he said. "The king wants her alive."

"I would rather die than go with you," she snapped.

"My apologies, princess. That won't be possible. Now get on the dragon."

Before she could retort, she heard her name shouted from a distance. Cormac turned to look over his shoulder. She looked too and saw Finn and Derron running toward her, a sword in each of their hands. Derron's helm was missing and he had blood all over his armor but he appeared to be unscathed despite that. Her heart leapt, seeing him coming for her. She charged toward him, but Cormac caught her by the arm, pulled her to him with a yank.

"Kill him," he ordered the men.

"No!" Elyne shouted. "Derron, look out!"

Cormac turned her and shoved her again toward the dragon.

She craned her neck to see what was happening. One of his Unseelie knights readied an arrow and pointed it directly at Derron. She cried out as he fired the arrow at Derron's head. Finn moved with great speed for a big Scotsman, shoving Derron. The Fae lord stumbled as the arrow slammed into him between his shoulder and breastplate. He lost his balance, his sword dangling by his side.

"Derron!"

Cormac shoved her up onto the dragon's back and mounted behind her. As Nero took to the sky, she glanced down to see Derron fall to his knees, one hand on the arrow sticking out of him. Finn charged toward the three soldiers, taking them out in seconds. That was the last she saw of them as Nero banked and headed toward the Stone of Destiny.

Chapter 25

"I have to get to the Stone of Destiny." Maeve skittered to a halt not far from her tent.

"That's what Kieran wants," Maggie said. "He's baiting you."

"He has my daughter and all Four Treasures," she snapped. "I have to stop him."

"I'm coming with you."

Maeve raised an eyebrow. "You, human?"

"Yes, me. I know you don't like me very much, but Elyne is my friend. If our places were reversed, she'd do the same for me."

"Very well."

Maeve headed through the maze of tents, toward the open field.

"Why can't you sift there?" Maggie asked, her breath hitching as she tried to keep up.

"Because, human, the power at the Stone of Destiny is too strong. It prevents any Fae or Dark Elf to sift to it."

The campsite was mostly deserted as Maeve expected, since Elves and Fae were fighting it out with Kieran and his men. Derron hadn't come back. He must be somewhere in the melee.

Overhead, wyvern and other flying creatures circled the sky. Maeve could see the Hell Hounds snarling and snapping at her men, taking some down. Anger boiled inside her. Kieran had used the creatures against them, something for which she would not stand. She balled her fists then closed her eyes, allowing the power to build inside her. She flung her arms outward, releasing her magic into the wind and commanding it to take out the creatures.

"What are you…oh, God."

Next to her, she could hear the human woman gag. When she opened her eyes, Maggie had turned away, one hand over her mouth.

"You killed them all."

"Aye, I did. Lord Kieran is not as powerful as he thinks."

She took off once more toward the Stone of Destiny, having

killed the creatures and removed that threat.

"Come along, human."

Maggie hurried to join her, her breathing coming in short spurts as she tried hard not to look at the carnage. Maeve had used one of her nastier destructive spells, spilling the guts of wyvern and Hell Hound alike across the field. It smelled like death and decay.

She and Maggie had almost made it to the field when Prince Andahar hurried toward them, his face smeared with dirt and blood, a sword in hand.

"Your majesty, you must go back. It's not safe here for you," he said.

"I'm going to the Stone of Destiny," Maeve said. "Move out of my way."

"You can't go." He put his hands up, as if to shove her backward.

Maeve narrowed her eyes. "You cannot give me orders. Even if you are an Elven prince."

"Maybe there's a reason he's giving you orders," Maggie pointed out.

"Stay out of this, human."

"It's too dangerous," Andahar said. "Kieran has released Hell Hounds and others. You will never make it alive to the Stone of Destiny."

"Oh, aye, I know he has. And I've taken care of them all." She swept her hand across the field behind her to show him her work. "I assure you I will make it to the Stone alive."

A shadow passed over them. Maeve glanced up, saw Ambrielle, the emerald dragon, followed closely by Aura and Luna. She ordered them to land, using the dragon mind-speak. Each one did, squashing the tents around them.

"I'm going."

Maeve charged toward Ambrielle. As she neared, she noticed the dragon had the same riding harness as Aura and Luna. More gifts from the Elves, clearly. She climbed into the saddle on Ambrielle's back and ordered her to take flight.

"You're not leaving without us," Maggie shouted.

As Maeve took to the skies, she saw the human and the prince climb onto the back of Aura. The three dragons headed to the Stone of Destiny together. And as they flew across the sky, Maeve saw the black dragon heading toward it as well.

Nero has your daughter, my queen, Ambrielle said in her mind.

Maeve peered closely at the dragon and caught a glimpse of her daughter's flowing blonde hair so like her own. And behind her, Cormac. The man had kidnapped her daughter and headed directly to the Stone of Destiny. They would all converge there together.

Below them, a bloody battle ensued between Fae, Elf and Unseelie. She briefly wondered if Lord Derron were still alive. If he were, he would be there, too.

And then the battle for the Stone of Destiny would truly begin.

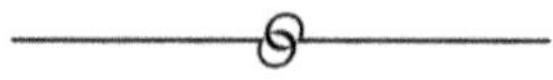

Moments after the arrow buried in his shoulder, a powerful surge went across the land. Dead wyvern, birds and harpies fell out of the sky. The Hell Hounds were no more.

"What was that?" Finn asked.

"Maeve. That's what."

Finn wasted no more time. He hauled Derron to his feet with one hand. "Get up, man. There are more coming."

"He took her."

"Aye, and we'll go after her," Finn said. "He's going to the Stone of Destiny, aye?"

"Aye, most likely."

Derron glanced down at the arrow sticking out of his shoulder. The Unseelie had narrowly missed his head. If it hadn't been for Finn shoving him out of the way, he would be dead.

He knew he couldn't yank it out, or he'd bleed to death before he got to the Stone. He wrapped his fingers around the thin shaft close to his body. Steeling himself, he broke it off, shouting a curse with the pain. He flung aside the butt end of the arrow.

"Ye need tending," Finn said.

"I'll tend to this when Elyne is safe," Derron said. "We need horses."

"Or wee beasties."

Finn's gaze was on the sky. Derron saw the dragons flying in a triangular formation. He suspected the queen to be on the back of the emerald dragon. He couldn't tell who the two riders were with Aura, but he knew it wasn't Elyne. Luna broke away and dove toward them. She spit fireballs, making a charred and fiery path to clear the way to the two men. She left a path of destruction, killing men and beasts easily.

She landed in front of him, bowed her head.

Your servant, Lord Derron.

"Come on, Finn. We've got a ride."

Finn looked dubiously at the dragon. "Ye want me to get on that thing?"

"You can walk if you like," Derron said as he climbed on Luna's back. "It won't be a pleasant one, though."

The ground exploded next to Finn in a fireball as one of the smaller dragons flew by, trying to hit him with its fire. That was enough for Finn as he sprinted across the field to Luna and climbed up behind Derron.

"'Tis not the way I wish to die, on the back of a wee beastie," Finn said in his ear as they took off.

"And you won't," Derron replied.

"I hope yere right, laddie."

Luna's giant wings beat against her body as she struggled to catch up to the other two dragons. She was smaller, though, and had a disadvantage. Derron saw the black dragon approaching seconds before she did. She banked a sharp right to avoid it, but the dragon burped a fireball at her anyway.

"Look out!" Derron wasn't sure if he shouted it at Luna or Finn.

Finn ducked down behind him as the flames went whizzing overhead. The bigger dragon pulled alongside them. Derron's blood boiled when he saw Elyne in front of Cormac. She seemed all right but her face was bruised and he could clearly see a split in her lip in the seconds he managed to make eye contact with her.

Her gaze was apologetic and fearful. She held the reins in front of her so tight, her knuckles were white.

Cormac flashed a brilliant grin as his dragon banked away from them, turning toward the Stone of Destiny.

"Follow them, Luna," Derron ordered.

The silver dragon did, trying hard to keep up with the massive dragon. Ahead, they could see Ambrielle and Aura flying fast toward the Stone. But the black dragon easily caught them, belching fireballs at them along the way. Derron wanted to shout a warning, even though they wouldn't be able to hear.

Ambrielle wobbled from side to side, trying to keep out of the line of fire. Aura fell back, slowing her speed and getting behind

Nero. Derron gritted his teeth as he watched the azure dragon heading straight for it.

"That's Maggie," Finn said, his voice quivering.

And Prince Andahar. Derron saw Maggie's brown hair swept from her face in the wind as the dragon increased her speed. Andahar perched behind her, his sword clasped in his hand and useless. Derron knew what Aura meant to do and he wanted to shout for her to stop.

But it was too late. Steam emitted from Aura's nostrils seconds before she let loose the fire from the depths of her core, growling at Nero in front of her. The black dragon must have sensed it was coming but his big body couldn't react in time. The fire singed his wings.

He screeched, a high-pitched noise that nearly burst Derron's eardrums and made him cringe. He watched, horrified and helpless, as Nero took a dive toward the ground, his princess still very much on the dragon's back.

Elyne's heart sped up when she met Derron's eyes. She wanted to tell him to get away. Go back to the camp. But she knew her lord knight. She knew he would never back down from a fight. When Nero blasted Luna with a fireball, the smaller dragon had managed to bank and get away. Nero then turned his attention to Ambrielle and Maeve. Aura followed close behind Ambrielle. Elyne knew what she had to do.

Take him out, Aura. Fire at him.

Are you certain, princess? She saw Maggie and Prince Andahar riding the dragon and knew her plan could potentially hurt her friends. But she had to try. She had to take out Nero. And if Cormac went with him, then so be it.

Nero sped up, heading for Ambrielle and her mother, spitting fireballs along the way. She gripped the reins tighter.

Get behind us, Aura. Use your fire-magic.

Aura immediately complied, falling back behind them. Elyne crouched down as close to Nero as she could seconds before Aura released her fire, hitting Nero's wings spot on.

His screech rattled the teeth in the back of her head. The dragon faltered, losing control as he headed toward the ground.

Behind her, Cormac stiffened, his arms tightening around her and his hands gripping the reins. She didn't know if the dragon would land or crash but she braced herself for either.

Elyne held her breath when Nero hit the ground. He tried to land on his hind legs but they immediately gave out. He stumbled, wobbled on his massive legs and started the long fall to the ground. It unseated both of them. She slipped off the back of the dragon and held her breath as she fell to the ground. She tucked her bad arm against her body, hoping to save it from further injury but it was really no use. Time seemed to halt as she watched the ground speed toward her.

When she landed, it knocked the wind out of her. She didn't know where Cormac had gone. Didn't even care. She lay on the cold ground, staring up at the pinkish sky and taking a mental inventory of her body. She was momentarily disoriented, her brain not functioning properly as she tried to feel everything that hurt. Somewhere in the distance, she could swear she heard Derron calling her, but she couldn't focus and she couldn't turn her head. It took all her focus to breathe.

Elyne thought she heard the clang of steel against steel. Men screaming. She smelled death and it made her stomach turn. She finally rolled to her right side, still cradling her left arm against her body.

"Elyne!"

Maggie appeared in her line of vision, running toward her. Her face was pale, her hair flying.

"Are you all right? Tell me you're all right."

She could think the words, but she couldn't form them. She couldn't tell Maggie that she was fine, that she intended to stand up and walk to the Stone of Destiny and stop Lord Kieran herself. She lay on her side and peered up at her.

"We have to find the healer," Maggie said. "Andahar, help me get her to her feet. Allanna, go find the healer."

No healer. I must get to the Stone.

Gentle hands slipped under her arms and pulled her to her feet. Andahar on one side. Maggie on the other. She was certain her head might swivel off her shoulders any second now. It took all her strength to keep it steady. She scanned the field, looking for Derron as Andahar and Maggie walked her away.

"Where's…Derron?"

"He tried to kill Cormac."

Elyne wasn't sure if that was Maggie or Andahar who answered. *Was Cormac dead? Had Derron succeeded?*

A pang of sorrow went through her. Why, she wasn't sure. The man had saved her from certain death in Kieran's burning tent, but only to turn her over to Kieran.

Why then did she feel sorrow for him?

Because he showed kindness when Kieran would have bludgeoned me to death. Because he got me out of the burning tent.

A part of her thought he truly meant her no harm. Yet she couldn't prove that. Not now. Not if the man was dead.

"Stone…Destiny…" Elyne croaked. Her throat was raw and painful.

"No, you're not going there. It's too dangerous." That was Maggie.

"I have…to. My mother…"

"She can take care of herself. She has Derron and Finn to protect her."

Mayhap she did. But Kieran intended to murder her. He would do anything to get her out of his way so he could become High King.

The ground suddenly buckled, a large fissure splitting the earth in two. Maggie gasped. Allanna shrieked. When had the Elven girl joined them? They halted, stumbled back a few steps and waited for the rumbling to cease. But the rumbling didn't stop. It surrounded them, the ground shuddering and quaking beneath their feet.

This was a place of magic. A sacred place. A place where all the High Kings and Queens had been proclaimed. Where her mother had been crowned. Where she would one day be crowned.

No more.

"What is that?" Allanna's high-pitched voice squealed with the razor-sharp edge of fear.

Elyne knew what it was and it sent terror rippling through her. She saw pale-blue bleeding into the normally pink sky over the Stone of Destiny.

Aye, she knew what it was, indeed.

The walls of the Otherworld were coming down.

Chapter 26

Queen Maeve watched, helpless, as the great black dragon crashed to the ground. Her heart clotted in her throat as her daughter tumbled from his back, Cormac right behind her. There was nothing she could do.

"Land, Ambrielle. Now!"

The emerald dragon complied and even before she had completely gotten to the ground, Maeve slid out of the saddle and sprinted toward her daughter.

The soldiers flanked her before she realized they were even there. They were not the Elves and not her Fae soldiers. These were Unseelie. They all held swords pointed at her, giving her no choice but to halt in front of them.

"Let me pass."

"I'm afraid they can't do that, your majesty." She knew that smarmy voice. Kieran walked toward her, a smug smile on his face.

"You bloody bastard."

"It's good to see you, too, Maeve. How long has it been? Thousands of years by my calendar."

"You mean when you murdered my husband in cold blood?" She tilted her chin up, looking down her nose at him. "Aye, I'd say it's been a few thousand years."

His expression turned dark, forbidding. "I must ask you to come with me, Maeve."

"No. I will never give power to you."

"Not willingly, no." He gave a nod to one of his men behind her. Seconds later, there was cold steel against her throat. He held a hand out to her as if to invite her along. "Allow us to escort you to the Stone of Destiny."

"Why don't you kill me now and get it over with?" she asked through gritted teeth.

"Because I want you to live long enough to see the future of your world."

"How kind of you."

"Oh, aye. I thought so. And I need your blood on the Stone of Destiny. I'm sure you know that."

She did, but she had hoped Kieran didn't. Clearly, he'd been reading up on his Fae lore. There was one hope left in her—that he hadn't learned how to use the Four Treasures together. It would be the only thing that could save them from this doom.

Maeve had no choice but to follow Kieran and his men up the gentle slope of the hill. From her vantage point, she could see the top of the giant stone monolith.

Once they crested the hill, the entire stone came into view. It stood about ten feet tall, the circumference too big for anyone to wrap arms around and flat on the top. Where the future ruler would stand. Stone steps carved into the surface spiraled around, heading up and up to the flat surface to the Place of Crowning.

Dead men—hers and his—littered the ground, bleeding the lush green scarlet. Few were left standing. The Unseelie who managed to survive had captured the Elves and the Fae, holding them prisoner.

Nearly her entire army had been wiped out. It made her heart hurt to see so many dead.

"Bring me the Club," Kieran ordered.

A man came forward, holding the Club in his hand. As she watched him, she realized with some dismay it was Gawaine. A very bloody and beaten Gawaine. He had an ugly cut over his eye, blood staining the side of his face and his neck. His clothes were filthy. The knuckles of the hand holding the Club purple and black. One eye was swollen shut.

She smiled. Sir Drake had made things difficult for Gawaine. She quickly scanned the area, looking for the human knight, but not finding him. Had he died trying to protect her?

Gawaine paused next to Kieran, who unsheathed the Sword of Light. The bastard had been carrying it on him the entire time and she hadn't noticed. The sword glowed faintly and she realized he must have learned how to wield it, how to become undefeatable in battle. That would explain all the dead men. All *her* dead men.

Three of the Four Treasures were together and Maeve could feel the magic humming between them. All it would take was one drop of her blood spilled. The dagger at her throat pressed harder into her skin.

"Where is Cormac?"

"He was riding Nero, my king, when the dragon was taken down," Gawaine said.

"Find him. Bring him to me at once."

The screech of a dragon at the bottom of the hill made Maeve cringe. Nero must still be alive and fighting with the other three. It was a horrible sound.

"You will never succeed, Kieran," she taunted, trying to buy more time.

"I've come this far, haven't I? All I need is the Spear."

And my blood.

She focused her gaze on Gawaine, who looked as though he might faint any moment. He wobbled on his feet.

"I'm disappointed to see you on the other side, Gawaine."

"Do not answer her," Kieran snapped.

"After all the time you served me, I thought I knew you better than that," she continued. "Now I find you are nothing but a servant of evil. Know this. You will be banished to the Dark Realm."

"That's very presumptuous of you, Queen Maeve. There will not be a Dark Realm much longer."

Kieran stepped toward her, much closer than she liked. He clamped his icy fingers around her wrist, held out her hand and placed the tip of the Sword of Light against her pale skin between thumb and forefinger. She knew what he meant to do and tried to jerk her hand away, but his iron grip held fast. His fingers dug into her skin, holding her steady.

"And now I will unleash my wrath."

"No…"

She whimpered the word as he sliced open her hand. Blood streamed from the wound. The magic in the Sword of Light hummed louder now, her blood dripping to the ground. The Stone of Destiny lit up in a soft yellow glow. And the pain in her heart increased to an indeterminable amount.

Beneath their feet, the ground rumbled. Looking up, she could see the earth move in waves, as though it were the sea. Her heart pounded and she was acutely aware of the throbbing pain in her hand and the cold steel pressing into her neck. Bile rose to clump in the back of her throat. Hot tears stung her eyes as the ground cracked open.

"The walls are coming down, your majesty. And you can do nothing to stop it."

She clenched her fist, watching the blood stream off her hand, dripping to the ground. The world crumbled around her with every drop that landed in the green earth.

Behind her there was a commotion but she couldn't turn to see what it was. She heard the scuffle. And then she sensed the presence of the Spear of Lugh. Cormac must have arrived. She tried to turn her head a scant inch to see, but the blade didn't yield.

He stumbled into her line of vision, covered in blood from head to toe. But he clasped the Spear tightly in one hand as he headed for Kieran. The magic between the Four Treasures hummed through her veins. Her blood seared hot, boiling through her.

The veil between human world and the Otherworld evaporated at the Stone of Destiny, disappearing as though it had never existed. The sky became a blended color of pink and blue, each one vying to dominate the other. The ground, once so lush and green, turned brown and cracked. Fissured as the Otherworld became one with the human world.

Kieran gave a nod to the soldier behind her, who released her and removed the dagger from her throat.

"Come, my queen. Let us climb the steps of the Stone of Destiny and proclaim me High King together."

With his hand still clamped on her wrist, he dragged her toward the Stone. The Sword of Light glowed bright white now. Cormac and Gawaine fell in step with them as they walked toward the steps. Kieran shoved her in front of him and gave her a rough push toward the stairs. Pulling her to a stop, he put the Sword in the small of her back.

"There is one more piece of business we must take care of. Cormac, if you please."

Cormac placed a hand on her arm. A tingling sensation went up to her shoulder and then spread through her entire body. Shocking her. Turning her cold. Normally she could feel her magic swirling with warmth throughout her body but now it stilled inside. She could only sense a few wisps. What had he done?

"Cormac has cast a hold spell on you. It will prevent you from striking us with any of your magic should you be foolish enough to make an attempt."

Maeve glanced at the man, hiding the surprise that flickered through her. Who was he? And how did she not know he was a magic user until now?

Kieran jabbed the Sword in her back. "Up, your majesty."

She took the first step, her heart palpitating, a sickness in the pit of her belly. Then the second and the third. She'd stopped counting by the time they reached the Place of Crowning, knowing what would come next. Knowing he would kill her there and take over the Otherworld. Even though she wanted to cry, tears would not come. Her anguish had turned numb, leaving her unfeeling for the future that awaited her.

On the top of the Stone of Destiny, at the Place of Crowning, she paused at the edge, looked down at the dirty, bloodied faces upturned to her. Her men looked defeated, disappointed. Kieran's men wore nothing but expectant looks, waiting for the world to be theirs.

Maeve had failed.

But mayhap there was still something she could do. She would not allow Kieran to steal her throne *and* her magic. No. Despite the hold spell keeping her magic in check, she sensed the few warm tendrils floating through her that she could grasp. She would have to concentrate but she knew she could do it. She would transfer all her power to Elyne. Now. At least the Seelie who remained would still have a chance to survive. Derron would protect Elyne, Maeve knew. After all, she had finally accomplished one selfless act by trying to retrieve the Treasures, even though it had nearly gotten her killed. She was worthy. And if Maeve died here and now, she had every confidence Elyne would carry on as queen with Derron at her side.

Closing her eyes, she thought of her daughter. She envisioned her, tried to place her on the battlefield. It took a few precious seconds, but she found her. Sensed her presence and knew where she was. Elyne was badly injured. Maeve would make sure her strength returned and she would be able to continue to fight against the darkness. In her head, she chanted the ancient spell and gathered her magic, sending every drop of magic from her to Elyne. When the transfer was complete, she opened her eyes and smiled.

It was done. She'd rendered herself completely defenseless.

Kieran stood behind her. Cormac to her left and Gawaine to

her right. Beneath their feet, the Stone of Destiny glowed bright, the light pulsating in recognition of her as the queen, the rightful ruler of the Otherworld.

"Even if you kill me here, Kieran, there is still an heir that will take my place."

"I have the Treasures," he said. "Once you are dead, I will proclaim myself High King and then the fate of your daughter no longer concerns me. I will give her to my men. They will do with her as they wish."

Maeve clenched her fists. Derron would never let the barbarians lay a finger on her, she was sure of it. But as High King, wielding the Sword of Light, he could do whatever he wished. Derron would have to come up with a miracle to keep her safe.

Elyne would be raped, murdered. The Otherworld would be left to ruin at the hands of this monster. But there was still hope.

"Any last words you wish to share? Care to beg for your life?"

She remained silent, staring across the cracked world. Her broken world.

"No? Well then, let's get started, shall we?" Kieran asked. "We will begin with your death."

He lifted the sword over his head. Gawaine and Cormac followed suit with their Treasures. Under his breath, Maeve could hear Kieran whispering the ancient words. The words that allowed him to become High King on the Place of Crowning.

The Stone of Destiny hummed under their feet, emitting a pleasant warmth that spread through them—the Stone prepared to recognize the one true ruler. The one who could wield the Treasures. She couldn't allow this to happen. And since no one was riding to her rescue, it was time to take matters into her own hands.

Glancing around, she took note of the over-six-foot drop. The top of the Stone was barely big enough for the four of them. There wouldn't be much room to maneuver. She would have to be quick, as she had no choice but to fight.

She could probably take out Gawaine first. With his injuries, he wouldn't have much fight left in him. She took a deep breath and then shoved Gawaine as hard as she could. He stumbled, trying to maintain his balance. The Club in his hand flailed, Kieran's spell suddenly broken. The Stone beneath their feet reacted by dimming, the warm humming dissipating.

Before she could give Gawaine another shove, arms went

around her in a viselike grip. Cormac held her against him, the Spear still clutched in one hand. She could use that as a weapon, if she could get her hand on it.

Chaos broke out below. She couldn't see what was happening but she knew there was some type of commotion. Men shouted at each other and she was certain she could hear the screams of others.

Gawaine managed to regain his footing and turned to her, his bloodied face looking like a menacing mask as he advanced one step toward her. Her heart in her throat, she leaned back into Cormac and lifted her feet off the ground, kicking at Gawaine.

Her feet made contact with his chest. He stumbled backward. This time he was unable to regain his footing and tumbled off the side of the Stone of Destiny. She heard the sickening thump when he hit the ground. Bile rose in her throat.

"Bitch!"

Kieran growled in fierce frustration, his fists clenched as he peered over the edge of the Stone of Destiny. One of the Four Treasures was now on the ground. Maeve struggled with Cormac, trying to break his hold. It did no good. Kieran reeled on her and his fist connected with her cheekbone. Her face exploded in blinding white pain.

"He's dead."

Maeve whimpered, yet when she spoke, her voice remained steady. "I can't say I'm sorry to see him go."

"Show her."

Cormac stepped to the edge and bent to allow her to see. Gawaine's head had the misfortune of hitting a well-placed rock at the foot of the Stone of Destiny. Blood seeped from the death blow. His body was twisted in an awkward position—his legs at angles that defied the norm—and the Club still clenched in his hand.

"Kill her," Kieran said, his gaze remaining on the queen.

With those two words, her blood turned to ice and she knew she was about to die.

Chapter 27

"Look!"

Maggie's voice cut into Elyne's thoughts. Her friend pointed to the top of the Stone of Destiny where her mother, Kieran, Cormac and Gawaine stood.

The Place of Crowning.

"My mother," she croaked. "He'll kill her."

"Not if I can help it."

With all the strength she could muster, she turned her head and saw Derron flanked by Finn, Sir Drake, Eldrin and Prince Andahar. They lived.

"Time to reclaim what is rightfully ours," Derron said. "Maggie, get her out of here. She needs medical attention."

Seeing Derron sent a surge of relief and a renewed strength through her. When Maggie tried to take her by the hand, she pushed her away. Something warmed her from the inside out. All her aches and pains disappeared. Her arm no longer hurt. A familiar tingling sensation spiraled within her, spreading from deep within outward. Her fingertips tingled. The roots of her hair prickled. Even her feet tickled.

A slow smile spread on her face. *My magic. I have it back.*

Her mother must have reversed her decision and returned it.

"No. I'm coming. You can't make me stay. And I feel fine."

"Stubborn girl. You nearly got yourself killed going over there."

She flushed. Of course he knew.

"You're staying away from him," Derron said, his tone holding an edge of finality.

Elyne shook her head as she followed him and the rest up the slope to the Stone of Destiny. Even Maggie and Allanna came along. No one wanted to be left behind and who could blame them? Unseelie still crawled all over the Hill of Tara looking for their next kill.

They crested the hill and Allanna shrieked. Glancing up, Elyne saw her mother shove then kick Gawaine off the Place of Crowning. He plunged toward the ground, his head cracking on a rock. She squeezed her eyes shut as he landed. When she opened them again, he was dead, the Club of Dagda still clasped in his hand.

"The Club, Derron. He has the Club."

But Derron was already running toward him. Despite feeling more energetic, Elyne hadn't regained enough strength to run. Maggie clasped her by the arm and helped her. Finn and Sir Drake joined Derron as they headed for the Club, trying to get to it before another Unseelie.

As Derron ran toward the dead man, a power bolt flashed from Kieran, striking him down. Elyne shrieked, her knees threatening to turn to water as Derron went down in a heap. He wasn't moving. Finn shouted something to Drake, who kneeled beside the Knight of the Realm while the Scotsman continued toward the Club.

Another power bolt flashed, narrowly missing Finn. Elyne heard the sharp intake of Maggie's breath.

"Take me to Derron."

"It's too dangerous," Maggie said. "He'll kill you."

"I don't care! Take me to Derron. Now."

Elyne forced her feet to walk, and then trot toward her beloved. She had to see if he was all right. Drake wouldn't know what to do for him. Neither did she for that matter but she had to get to him.

Another flash of light. The magic hit Finn. Maggie emitted a strangled cry. He paused long enough to get his bearings, and then continued toward the Club.

"He'll kill him," Maggie squeaked, the fear evident in her voice.

"Finn will be fine. He's too stubborn to die," Elyne said through gritted teeth.

Maggie bit her thumbnail as she watched and Elyne could tell it took all her strength not to dash toward him.

Ahead, Finn had claimed the Club of Dagda and held it, looking up at Kieran in defiance. The Dark Elf was far from pleased. He sent another bolt of magic downward, hitting Finn square in the chest. The Scot stumbled backward a step. When he regained his footing, he merely extended his middle finger before turning and fighting off the men who tried to attack him and take back the Club.

Beside her, Maggie laughed in a high-pitched squeak. "I love my husband! I taught him that gesture, you know."

Elyne took her attention off the Place of Crowning long enough to tend Derron. His armor was charred and blood caked his neck.

"Gods, Derron," she muttered. Then to Drake, "Go find my mother's healer, Seamus."

"He's barely breathing," Drake said.

"Go find him!" she shouted.

Drake blinked and rose, hurrying to do her bidding. Elyne cradled Derron's head in her lap, brushing away golden hair from his forehead.

"Don't you dare die on me, Derron. Do you hear me?"

His lids fluttered open. His sharp blue eyes peered back up at her. "Elyne, what happened?"

"Kieran. That's what happened. Stay still. Drake has gone to fetch the healer."

"There's no time for that."

He shoved her away and rolled to his side, pushing to a sitting position. Derron sat back on his heels, shaking his head to clear it.

"No, Derron. You can't go."

"It may be too late already," Maggie said.

They all followed her gaze to the Place of Crowning. Kieran's eye caught Elyne's. His cold stare stayed on her for a long moment and then she could see the rage flood his face. He shoved Cormac out of the way, who had been struggling with Maeve. When she was free, she tried to get to the stairs, but Kieran snatched her by the hair, yanking her back toward him, putting the Sword of Light at her throat.

"No!"

Elyne's stomach twisted in a knot as she watched the man hold her mother there, the sword digging into the skin. He barked an order to Cormac, who turned and barreled down the steps. Then Kieran said something to Maeve, leaning toward her so she would be sure to hear. His lips were a scant inch from her face. Too many emotions passed through Elyne. Everything from anger to fear to horror. Time stood still as she watched the next events unfold in slow motion.

The blood drained from Maeve's face. Kieran continued to speak in her ear. Elyne heard the *whoosh* of something next to her and realized what it was when the arrow buried itself in Kieran's arm. The same arm holding the Sword of Light against Maeve's neck.

Next to Elyne, Allanna lowered the bow with a smug look on her youthful face.

Kieran released Maeve. He shouted something, his cursing lost in the wind. Maeve stumbled away from him, taking a few seconds to get her bearings before she turned on him and shoved with all her might.

His face registered shock then anger. The arm with the arrow went limp, the Sword falling from his grasp. As he fell backward, Kieran reached for the queen and snatched her as he plummeted off the Stone of Destiny.

Elyne shrieked. Derron was already running toward them, Finn behind him. Allanna nocked another arrow in her bow but Elyne stopped her, putting her hand on her arm.

"No, you could hit the queen."

Elyne ran hard to catch up to the two knights. She could see Kieran rise to his feet. How was the man still alive? Anger flared through Elyne as she watched him. He broke off the arrow still sticking out of his arm and flung it aside, his face a mask of hate and horror. As Derron approached him, Kieran casually leaned down and retrieved the Sword of Light, as though he had all the time in the world, standing between them and her mother. Elyne's heart sank to her toes. Derron hadn't made it to the Sword in time.

"The Sword of Light does not belong to you," Derron said.

"I have as much right to it as you do," Kieran retorted. His cold gaze paused on each one of the knights. "Brought your human friend, did you?"

Cormac reappeared from behind the Stone of Destiny, the Club of Dagda in one hand, the Spear of Lugh in the other.

"You may as well surrender yourself. We have the Treasures," Kieran taunted.

"Not for long."

The men attacked each other. Derron's sword clanged against Kieran's while Finn went after Cormac. The Sword of Light glowed brightly and Elyne knew the Dark Elf would be undefeatable now. Elyne couldn't have felt more helpless as she stood there, watching the two fight it out.

You have the power.

An unfamiliar voice punctured her mind. She shook her head. Was she hearing things? It wasn't Aura's voice she'd heard in her head. It was a woman's.

Cormac attacked Finn with the Spear. Finn fought back, blocking him with the Club, but Elyne could tell he was losing his strength with every hit he received and every hit he absorbed from the Treasures. They were far more powerful than he.

Elyne, you have the power. Destroy the Dark Elf.

Again, the voice in her head. Clenching her fists, she looked past the men fighting and pinned her gaze on her mother's body. Was she alive? Was her body broken? Could she still be saved? She couldn't tell from where she stood and she couldn't get to her. But she would have to try.

As she took a step toward Maeve, someone grabbed her, pulled her to him and put a knife to her throat. Fear pulsed through her, then irritation. How dare someone stop her from getting to her mother? Something inside her boiled, tingled, rose to the surface and before she realized what was happening, a bright light exploded from her, shoving away her would-be assailant.

Elyne spun around, looking behind her. The Unseelie solider lay dead, his body still smoking from where she'd singed him with her magic. And then she knew. It was her mother's voice she heard in her head, telling her she had the power to destroy Kieran. Her confidence swelling, she knew what she had to do.

Other Unseelie tried to attack her, but they were no match for her. She easily shoved them off, killing them as she walked with a purposeful stride toward the Dark Elf. When she got close, she paused, stared him down.

"I command you to return the Sword of Light," she said.

All movement ceased and all eyes were on her. When Derron looked at her, his eyes went wide. Kieran laughed.

"You cannot command me, your highness. Once I've finished with your Faery boyfriend, I intend to kill you."

She remained unruffled by his words, but her anger increased. "You've lost, Kieran. Return the Treasures."

"Elyne?" Derron sounded far away, as though he wasn't sure who he was looking at or what he was seeing. "What's going on?"

"You think to frighten me with your Faery tricks?" Kieran shook his head. "I am not afraid of you."

"You should be."

She sent all the anger and hatred she had toward Kieran. A bright bolt of magic loosed toward him and he stumbled backward, the Sword of Light hanging limp in his hand. He held it up, tried to charge her but she released more punching magic. It pulsed from her, pounded against his armored chest, the flash so blinding she had to shield her eyes. Something sizzled and cracked and she could see the fissure in the steel across his breastplate.

Kieran looked down and then back up at her. He opened his mouth—she thought to scream but she heard no sound. His mouth went slack-jawed. As though it hung by nothing more than a thread. He stumbled backward, his arms now hanging by his sides in a sickly manner. He looked like a puppet controlled by unseen forces. His legs didn't seem to work. His knees wobbled, threatening to buckle. The skin peeled off his bones, loosely hanging. Blood oozed out of his eyes, nose and ears.

"You will never harm us again." Elyne's words were a whisper on the wind. A shudder through the air. "I avenge the death of my father and Lord Derron's."

The final bright flash blinded her, burning the sight right out of her eyes, and took every ounce of energy she had remaining. Releasing the magic felt like a punch in the gut and sent her flying. When the light faded, she was left with a raging headache and she realized she was on the ground, looking up at the pink-and-blue sky and wondering what exactly had happened.

She heard men shouting and smelled blood and death, burned hair and skin. But she couldn't move. She could barely breathe. And then Derron was at her side, kneeling next to her, looking down at her. Worry lines creased his forehead. His face was smudged with dirt and coated with sweat. Blood was still on his neck and armor.

"Are you all right? Are you hurt?"

"My mother…is she…?" But she couldn't finish. Her mouth had become desert dry.

"She's wounded, but she'll be fine as soon as we find the healer. Prince Andahar and Eldrin have her under their guard. Allanna has gone to fetch Seamus. Elyne, you were glowing." He slid his arm under her shoulders, lifted her into his lap. He brushed tendrils of hair off her pounding forehead.

"Glowing?" She blinked, trying to comprehend what he meant. "I was glowing?"

"Aye, glowing. I've never seen anything like it. None of us have. What happened to you? What did you do?"

"My mother returned my magic. I used it to attack Kieran." When she tried to sit up, the world tipped on its axis and she quickly lay back down with a groan. He held her steady.

"Easy, princess."

"Where is Kieran? What happened to him?"

"He's dead." Derron glanced back up to where Kieran had been. "And you don't want to see the body."

Sudden tears flooded her eyes, blurring her vision. Tears of relief her mother was still alive, that their kingdom would be safe. The realm was still broken, though, and that was something they would have to work to repair. It would take time to heal the Otherworld, to close the fractures that had erupted throughout the Dark and Light Realms.

She slipped her arms around his neck and pulled him down close. He smelled of blood and sweat, but even so underneath all that she could still discern his woodsy scent.

"You came for me."

"I will always come for you." His words were muffled against her hair as he buried his face there. "I would die for you."

Her heart tripped. Aye, she knew he would. She knew he would go to the ends of the world for her. He would give her anything she wanted, including the sun, the moon and the stars. She hugged him tighter.

"I know."

Elyne pulled away, looking into his eyes and she knew *this* was the moment. It was now or never. She couldn't stop the tears streaming down her face. She didn't want to. She placed a hand on each cheek, leaned into him.

"I will always love you."

"You'd better." He said it with a smile. "You're stuck with me, princess. I'm glad you finally came to your senses."

"Me? What about you? Chasing everything in a dress at tourney."

"Oh, you had to bring that up?" He rolled his eyes. "That was to make you jealous. Did it work?" He flashed a wicked grin.

She punched him. "Why couldn't you just say, 'I love you, too'?"

His face softened, turning serious. "I love you, too, princess. I thought you always knew."

His mouth brushed against hers as he said it, making her heart smile and her stomach flip. Aye, she'd known for a while his true feelings. But he had never said it.

Until now.

Chapter 28

Elyne sat in the main tent, at the head of the table with Lord Vaughan, Lord Roderick, Derron, Lord Aldun and all who remained of the High Council. Lord Vaughan had requested her presence. She had never attended these meetings, had never had an interest. But now she knew that would have to change.

"While the queen convalesces, it is up to you, Princess Elyne, to rule in her stead," Lord Vaughan said. "What is your first order, your highness?"

This was not news Elyne had wanted to hear, though she knew he was right. With the death of Gawaine, there was no one to counsel her. She glanced at Derron who gave her a knowing nod toward Lord Vaughan.

"My first order is to appoint you High Councilor, Lord Vaughan."

He bowed his head low. "You have my gratitude, your highness, for appointing me to such a prestigious position."

"Aye, well, don't let it go to your head like Gawaine. Tell me what needs to be done."

"If you will permit me, princess?" Derron asked. When she nodded, he continued. "The Queen's Palace is still overrun by Unseelie. Allow me to take the remainder of the army to regain control of it."

"Granted. When do you intend to depart?"

"As soon as this meeting is completed, princess," Derron said.

"Good. As soon as the Queen's Palace is secured and my mother can be moved, I want to return there." *I'm tired of living in tents.*

"What of the prisoners?" Lord Roderick asked.

She considered this. She didn't particularly want them dead. But she didn't want to release them either for fear those loyal to Kieran would attempt to cause more problems for the Seelie. They didn't need more problems. "What do we normally do with them?"

"It would be appropriate to imprison them and then convict them of their war crimes," Lord Vaughan said. "We can continue to keep them under guard until we move to the Queen's Palace and then put them behind the wards in the prison."

"Do that, then."

"Banishing them to the Dark Realm is no longer an option with the Barrier destroyed," Lord Aldun pointed out. "How do you intend to convict them?"

"We can decide that once we return to the Queen's Palace," Elyne said. She turned back to Vaughan. "What has become of Cormac?"

She knew she shouldn't be concerned with him after he'd attempted to murder her and the queen. He was a traitor to the realm. But he had saved her from certain death. For that, she owed him at least one small favor in return.

"He's imprisoned with the others, my princess," Lord Vaughan said.

"I wish to see him once this meeting has concluded."

"Why?" Derron demanded. He leaned toward her on his forearm, giving her a piercing look.

"He is neither Dark Elf nor Fae, Lord Derron," she said. "He spared my life. I want to know why."

"He is a criminal." Derron's voice was terse, his words razor sharp. "He was also Kieran's second in command. I'll not allow you to see him."

She stared him down. "You can accompany me if you wish. But I intend to speak with him."

He clenched his jaw, the muscles ticking, and she knew she'd angered him. If he wanted to play protector, that was fine by her. He *was* Protector of the Otherworld and Knight of the Realm, after all.

"Very well, princess."

"What of the Treasures?" she asked Derron.

"I have the Sword of Light, princess." He rested his hand on the hilt of the Sword. "New Guardians will need to be appointed for the Stone of Destiny, the Club of Dagda and the Spear of Lugh."

"None of them had heirs?"

"No, your highness," Lord Vaughan said.

She knit her brow and looked at Lord Vaughan for counsel.

"What happens in that instance, then?"

"The queen may select a noble whom she deems valiant, honorable and trustworthy," he replied.

Since she had no idea who that would be… "I'd rather leave that decision to my mother. In the interim, I would like Prince Andahar to act as Guardian of the Spear of Lugh and Lord Eldrin as Guardian of the Club of Dagda. I will ask Prince Andahar to leave a garrison here to protect the Stone of Destiny until a Guardian can be appointed."

The men of the High Council stared at her with disbelief on their faces. Derron smiled.

"Your highness, they are…Elves." Lord Aldun scrunched his nose in distaste.

"They have proven their loyalty to my mother and the Fae. They are valiant, honorable, and trustworthy."

"It's simply not done, Princess Elyne," Lord Vaughan put in. "An Elf as Guardian?" He shook his head. "It would be quite controversial."

"This is my decision." Elyne gave him a pointed look. "I expect it to be done."

He bowed his head low. "As you wish, princess."

"Anything else?" she asked, looking at each of the men's faces around the table.

"The dragons, your highness," Lord Vaughan said. "What do you intend to do with them?"

"I intend to do nothing with them."

"Forgive me, Princess Elyne, but they are dangerous—" Lord Aldun said.

She cut him off. "My mother told me she would not put them back into shadow. I intend to honor that."

"And the black dragon? What becomes of it? That beast is a menace," Aldun said.

"That beast was under the control of Lord Kieran and you'll leave Nero alone by my command."

Aldun clenched his fist but didn't argue further. Lord Vaughan cleared his throat.

"One last thing, your highness. What of the humans?"

"Maggie, Finn and Sir Drake are welcome here for as long as they wish," Elyne said. "They are our honored guests as the Elven princes and princess are our honored guests."

"Queen Maeve will want them returned at once," Aldun said.

"Queen Maeve will have bigger things to worry about than the humans, I should think," Elyne said. She immediately shifted gears, thinking of the most important things that needed to be addressed. "And so do I. What are we doing about the walls of the Otherworld and the Barrier?" Why hadn't anyone broached the subject yet?

"The Barrier is completely destroyed, your highness," Vaughan said. "It will take the magic of the High Druid to replace it."

"Then why hasn't anyone sent for him or sifted him here?"

"We will do that at once, of course, your highness," Vaughan said. He scratched a note with a quill pen on a piece of parchment. "As for the walls of the Otherworld, your mother is the only one powerful enough who can put them back up."

That presented a problem since her mother was completely out if at the moment. "What of the human realm bleeding into ours? What do we do about that?"

"There are a few areas affected," Vaughan continued. "As I understand it, any standing stone structure on the human side is a direct portal to the Otherworld."

"But I saw the blue sky of the human realm merging with our pink sky. What of that?"

"Only we can see that. Not those in the human realm."

Was he saying they, the humans, were unaware the walls had fallen? "Whom can we send to protect these areas to keep humans from wandering into the Otherworld?"

"This is a question the High Druid can answer," Vaughan continued. "I believe he can send his druids to these areas."

"Then make it so as quickly as possible." Elyne stood and all the men rose after her out of respect. "Thank you, gentlemen, for your time. I believe this concludes our meeting. Lord Derron, would you care to escort me to see Cormac?"

He gave her a nod and followed her out of the tent. "I don't like this, Elyne."

"You don't have to like it," she said. "Maggie, Finn and Sir Drake can stay as long as they want. As for the Guardian Elves, I'm sure my mother will disagree with my decision but she can reverse it once she's able to take her place as queen again."

"I was talking about Cormac, but now that you mention it, when do you intend to tell her about the Treaty of Separation?"

With the reminder of her promise to King Urdithane, Elyne's heart stuttered in her chest.

"You *do* intend to tell her?" he asked.

"Aye, I do. But not until she's managed to recover."

Guilt washed over her. Guilt and shame. She had lied to Queen Maeve. Mayhap by omission, but lied nonetheless. Her mother would not be pleased. Nor would she be pleased with her decision to allow the Elves to act as Guardians of their most sacred Treasures.

I'll think about that on the morrow.

"I still don't understand why you have this need to speak to the man who nearly murdered you and your mother."

"Because I don't believe he would have done it willingly. Kieran had some hold on him. He is not evil, Derron."

"You don't know that. You can't."

"He *healed* Nero when his wing was damaged. I saw him do it."

"He healed a dragon. That doesn't make him a nice guy."

She sighed. "Derron, he could have left me to die in that burning tent. But he didn't. He cut me free and got me out of there. Alive."

"Aye, to deliver you to Kieran. The man should be executed." Derron slipped a protective arm around her shoulders as they walked.

"I'll keep your suggestion in mind," she said.

The prisoners were kept in a makeshift cage that was nothing more than crudely built walls outside their encampment. It was heavily guarded by Fae and Elf. When they arrived, Elyne ordered Cormac brought to her. The Elf guarding the gate shouted the order and moments later, two soldiers brought Cormac, his wrists shackled.

He still had dirt and dried blood on his face. His tunic was ripped. His pants were tattered. He'd lost his boots. He gave her a stony look, unmoved by her visit.

"Princess Elyne requested to speak to you. Show some respect." One of the guards slapped him hard in the back of the head.

"Stop," she ordered. "Leave us."

"But, princess…?"

"Leave us. Lord Derron will remain with me."

The two soldiers scuttled back to the gate but not before the one who hit him spit on his bare feet. She made a mental note to reprimand him later.

Elyne gave Cormac a hard look. "I asked you once before. Now I want an answer. Who are you?"

"I am no one, princess," he replied, his voice monotone. His gaze on her, but not seeing her.

"You told me in the tent you didn't want to see Kieran crowned king. Why?"

He remained silent. Derron pulled the Sword of Light and pointed it at his throat. "The crown princess asked you a question. You *will* answer."

His dead eyes flickered to Derron then back to Elyne. "She wants an answer? I'll give her one. Kieran is—was—the only person who can release my family." His words were harsh, gravelly.

"Your…family?" Of all the answers she expected, that was not one of them.

"Aye, my family. He imprisoned them when they refused to help his rebellion. To save their lives, I agreed to assist him. I gave him my money and my magic. I found spells for him. I unlocked Fae secrets for him. I did his bidding. He knew where they were and *you killed him*." He looked past her now, to something in the distance, as though remembering.

She *had* killed Kieran. And with that, she'd destroyed Cormac's hope of ever seeing his family again.

"Shall I go on?" He blinked sightless eyes, still not looking at her. "Kieran tortured my wife and three children to the point of death. If I hadn't agreed to help him on his quest, he would have surely killed them. I am no traitor to the Fae." At last, Cormac's gaze returned to her face, the dead look now a blaze of fiery anger. "I have never been a traitor to the Fae."

Derron sized him up, giving him a good once-over. "Who are you then? Are you part of the Dark Realm?"

"No. I am not," Cormac agreed. "I am a Fomorian. I am sure, princess, you are familiar with our race."

The Fomorians had been defeated by the Tuatha dé Danann eons ago. They were a godlike magical race all but wiped out by the Tuatha. She was surprised to know they still lived and thrived—but where she had no idea.

"I see your surprise, princess," he said.

"I swear to you, I will find out where they are," Elyne said.

"And I will have them released and brought back to you. You will be reunited."

"Elyne—" Derron started, but Cormac interrupted.

"I will hold you to that promise, princess." Cormac's gaze turned hard, threatening. She could feel the heat from that look and knew would or she would be at his mercy.

Derron snatched her by the arm and shouted for the guards to return the prisoner to the cell.

"Let me go, Derron."

"No." He dragged her as far from there as possible. "Have you lost your mind? You cannot make such a promise to *him*."

"Why not?" She stopped, refusing to take one more step.

"You don't owe him anything, Elyne."

"No," she said. "But I intend to help him. Whether you approve of this or not."

"You don't even know where to look for them."

"No," she agreed. "But you're going to help me."

He looked taken aback. "Am I? Why would I do that?"

"Because you love me and you would do anything for me." She gave him a winning smile.

Derron sighed. "Aye, I would. And I hate that you know it. It's against my better judgment and your mother can never know, but I'll help you. I'll find the Fomorians."

She kissed him on the cheek. "Thank you, love."

Chapter 29

Once Elyne had Derron's promise to help her find Cormac's family, she sent him off to conquer the Queen's Palace. Finn, Drake, Eldrin, and Prince Andahar insisted on joining him. Maggie gave her husband a kiss for luck. Elyne couldn't help but see the young Elven princess, Allanna, give Sir Drake an adoring look. While sitting in his saddle, he clasped her hand and bid her farewell, promising her he'd come back to her safely.

Elyne idly wondered who would break the news to Allanna that falling in love with a human would never be accepted by her father.

Two days later, the victorious Derron, Elves and humans returned. They'd retaken the palace without much resistance. All the servants had been killed by Kieran's men, but the palace hadn't sustained as much damage as first thought. It would be easy to rebuild. He'd left part of the army behind to protect it in their absence until they could return.

Four days after that, Queen Maeve finally regained consciousness and immediately asked to see her daughter. It was with some trepidation Elyne approached her mother's tent, her heart beating wildly in her chest.

"I'll come with you," Derron said.

Elyne took a deep breath and entered.

"The princess and Knight of the Realm, your majesty," Seamus announced.

Queen Maeve sat upright in her bed, her blonde hair combed to a high shine. Her hand was bandaged where Kieran had sliced her open. Her face held a sickly pallor but her eyes were alert and she looked like the steely Queen of the Otherworld had always looked. Regal. Beautiful. Foreboding.

"I understand you have taken my place while I recover," Maeve said, her powder-blue eyes fixed on her daughter.

Elyne shifted from one foot to the other, trying hard not to squirm under that gaze. "I have."

"These were not the circumstances under which I would have wanted you to take command, my daughter. However, I am glad you have accepted the responsibility so readily." She looked at Derron. "Are the Four Treasures secured?"

"Aye, your majesty."

"And Guardians? Have they been appointed?" Her gaze swung back to Elyne.

Elyne lifted her chin a notch, knowing she would have to stand her ground. "I have appointed several men to act as Guardians until you select more appropriate ones."

"And who might they be?" She clasped her hands in her lap, as though she already knew the answer but wanted to hear it directly from Elyne.

"Prince Andahar and Lord Eldrin have agreed to guard the Club and Spear."

Her gaze remained steady as she looked at her, her face impassive. "Elves, Elyne? You've entrusted Elves with our sacred Treasures?"

"Aye, Mother, I have."

"I suppose they did help save the Otherworld from certain doom," Maeve said. "I'm pleased they have agreed to continue to assist the Fae in our current plight until the walls can fully be reinstated and the council can reconvene. Who will guard the Stone of Destiny?"

"Prince Andahar agreed to have a garrison stationed here until you can appoint someone more appropriate to guard the Stone."

"More Elves. At least you had some good sense and didn't choose the humans." Maeve sighed and shook her head in disbelief. "The Otherworld truly is broken. I will owe King Urdithane a great debt of gratitude. Please thank Prince Andahar and Lord Eldrin for me."

"Of course."

Elyne nearly fainted. Of all the reactions she'd expected from her mother *that* was not one of them. Why hadn't Maeve given her the icy stare she expected? Or spoken to her with a condescending tone, telling her what an imbecile she was by appointing Elves?

"Seamus has filled me in on most of the details. I understand Kieran's spell to break down the walls didn't work."

"That's right," Elyne said. "There are portals to the human realm through standing stone structures such as the Stone of

Destiny. Humans will find them if they know where to look."

"'Tis good we didn't suffer as much damage as I first thought," she said. "There are many other matters that must be discussed but we can do that another time. Now I wish to talk to you about your behavior, Princess Elyne."

This was what she'd expected from her mother.

"You broke out of Fae prison—albeit with help." She pinned Derron with a disapproving look before turning back to Elyne. "You stole the dragon and headed across enemy lines to risk your life. Among other things."

Elyne held her head high. Her mother hadn't listed all the other crimes she'd committed. Had Maeve forgiven her for them? *She still doesn't know about the deal I made with the king of the Elves. How furious will she be when she learns of that?* "I did."

"You exhibited bravery and a sense of selflessness I have never seen in you. There is hope for you yet as a ruler." She paused, as though searching for the right words. "As I stood on the Stone of Destiny, I knew I was going to die. I was certain Kieran would kill me, absorb my magic and proclaim himself High King." Her gaze glittered with tears. "I knew if I died, he would come after you and even Lord Derron wouldn't be able to stop him. That is why I transferred all my magic to you, Elyne. I knew if you had it, you and Lord Derron could defeat him. And you did."

Elyne stared at her in disbelief, her mother's words repeating over and over in her head. All her magic? Elyne received *all the queen's magic?* Thinking back on it now, she remembered the tingling sensation she had when the magic returned. The way the aches and pains suddenly disappeared. The voice she'd heard in her head, telling her she had the power.

"I have never been more proud of you than I am now," Maeve said.

A lump formed in Elyne's throat. She swallowed hard around it, trying to stave off the tears that wanted to erupt. Next to her, Derron slipped his hand in hers and squeezed. She'd forgotten he was there and now she glanced his way. The glow of his smile warmed her, reassured her. For the first time in her life, her mother approved of her, told her she was proud of her.

"Thank you, Mother," she whispered.

Maeve cleared her throat then. "I'm not finished yet. Once I've regained my strength, I will take my powers back from you. Until such time, I hope you will take care of them."

"I will."

"There is another matter I need to discuss with you both. I understand you and Lord Derron have bonded." She glanced between the two of them, the threat of tears gone almost as quickly as they appeared.

How did she find out about that? Maeve didn't wait for a reply before continuing.

"It is quite possibly what saved you from certain bonding with Kieran. For that, I am eternally grateful, Lord Derron. However, you bonded without my consent or knowledge."

"I have the right to choose whom I wish, Mother," Elyne said.

"You do. I would have blessed you, had you come to me beforehand. Now that it's done..." She paused, looking at them both. "All that is left to do is have the appropriate bonding ceremony in the sacred halls of the Queen's Palace to make it official."

Elyne had no words. She was stunned to silence. Again.

Derron slipped an arm around her and hugged her. "As you wish, my queen."

"It seems foolish you didn't bond sooner. Why we had to go through the breaking of the betrothal, I know not. At least you've both come to your senses at last."

"Thank you, your majesty," Lord Derron said.

Elyne was perfectly content to allow him to speak for her.

"We will, of course, have to reconvene the Council and rebuild the Queen's Palace. I trust you two can occupy your time wisely. By wisely, I mean help close the portals of the Otherworld and contain the Unseelie. I look to you, Lord Derron, as Knight of the Realm, Protector of the Otherworld and Guardian of the Sword of Light to take care of that."

"We have already begun the process, your majesty."

Elyne finally found her voice. "I've appointed Lord Vaughan as the new High Councilor."

"He would have been my choice as well. Seamus tells me we can move back to the Queen's Palace in another day or two. I'm confident the two of you can handle everything until I've mended." Maeve leaned back into the pillows of the bed and closed her eyes.

Elyne recognized that as a dismissal. She and Derron left Queen Maeve to rest. As they walked away, silence pressed between them.

Elyne could sense Derron had something on his mind.

"What is it?" she asked. "I know you want to say something."

"You didn't tell her about the promise you made to King Urdithane."

"No, I didn't. She seemed in good humor. I should have."

"No," Derron said and stopped her. He turned to her, his hands on her shoulders. "You did the right thing. We'll tell her once we've returned to the Queen's Palace and she's well. Prince Andahar and Lord Eldrin will go with us and they can help convince her why the Treaty of Separation should be abolished."

"I hope you're right, Derron. What do we do in the meantime?"

"In the meantime?" There was a mischievous glint in his eyes as his lips brushed her brow. "We enjoy each other's company." He nibbled her earlobe. "I have a lot to discuss with you about that stunt you pulled."

Her heart pounded in anticipation as she feigned innocence. "What stunt?"

"Don't pretend you don't know what I'm talking about." His heated breath cascaded over her neck, warm lips on her skin as he tasted her erratic pulse. "Never do that again. You could have been killed. I could have lost you."

"I won't, my lord." She slipped her arms around his neck. "You didn't lose me. And now you have me forever."

"Aye, princess, indeed I do. I will love and protect you. Forever."

And he sealed his promise with a kiss.

Realm of Honor Cast of Characters

The Humans

Sir Finian "Finn" McCullough: Scottish knight

Maggie Chase McCullough: Finn's wife

Sir Drake Attenborough: English knight and jousting hero

Henry Chase: Maggie's father

The Fae

Princess Elyne: crown princess of the Fae Otherworld

Lord Derron: Knight of the Realm, Protector of the Otherworld

Queen Maeve: ruler of the Otherworld and the Seelie Court

Lord Roderick: member of the High Council

Lord Aldun: member of the High Council

Lord Vaughan: member of the High Council

Seamus: healer for the Fae

King Adhamh: the queen's husband who was murdered

Morrigan: Goddess of War

Lord/Dark King Kieran: dark elf bent on human and Otherworld domination

Lord Gawaine: Queen Maeve's high councilor

Dark King Fergus mac Delbaith: dark king of the Unseelie court

Lord Pwyll: Guardian of the Stone of Destiny

Lord Malcolm: Guardian of the Sword of Light and Derron's father

Lord Llewelyn: Guardian of the Club of Dagda

Lord Udrich: Guardian of the Spear of Lugh

The Elves

King Urdithane emar'Rudul: ruler of the Wood Elves

Andahar emar'Rudul: crown prince of the Woodlands Elven throne

Leopold: Wood Elves royal advisor

Eldrin emar'Rudul: brother to Andahar, Elven ranger

Allanna emar'Rudul: sister to Andahar and Elven Princess

Lord Navin emar'Rudul: brother to Andahar, Woodlands Gatekeeper

Lord-Regent Marath: Wood Elves liege lord

Lord Randir: Fire Elf and Laerwen's betrothed

Laerwen emer'Aranhil Bloodfire: Fire Elf and Princess of the Hin'dar Rhule

Hiram: Laerwen's royal advisor

Lady Talaiel: ruler of the Skye Elves

Turin: healer for the Skye Elves

Brom: healer for the Wood Elves

Lord Malack: one of the noble Wood Elves

Queen Lucinda and King Aleron: ruler of the Fire Elves

The Fomorians

Cormac: Fomorian mage forced to help Kieran

Lorcann: Fomorian mage

The Dragons

Ambrielle: the emerald dragon

Aura: the azure dragon

Luna: the silver dragon

Nero: the black dragon

Moon dragons: silver dragons of the Skye Elves

The Realms

Fae Otherworld: home of the Fae, includes Seelie and Unseelie Courts

Woodlands: a humid forest region and home of the Wood Elves
Hin'dar Rhule: dry, arid volcanic region and home of the Fire Elves
Skye Realm in the clouds: home of the Skye Elves and the moon dragons

Human Realm: home for Maggie and Finn

Underworld: where Morrigan was banished

The Races

The Fae: also known as Faeries, a race of magical beings who can alter time and travel from their realm to the human realm.

Fire Elves: Elves who live in the volcanic realm known as the Hin'dar Rhule. Their bodies can withstand the hottest heat of the fires, but the lava is still deadly to them. They seek help from the Wood Elves when the Fomorians destroy their home.

Fomorians: an ancient race of vile creatures who wreak havoc. They were banished to a watery prison but one powerful Fomorian mage managed to break out and free his people so they could rampage once more.

Skye Elves: a reclusive Elven race living among the clouds with their moon dragons. The legend of the Skye Elves says one is as strong as ten men and they are undefeatable in battle.

Wood Elves: Elves who live in the trees of the Woodlands and who had a long-standing Treaty of Separation with the Fae, dividing the two races. The Treaty has since been abolished, uniting the two and allowing them to work together to defeat the evil in the realm.

Sign up and get your free book!

I love interacting with readers and the best way to do that is through email. Sign up for my VIP Reader's List and get a free book, notifications of upcoming releases, join the review team and much, much more. It's a great way for me to connect with you!

You can get the free book by signing up at:
https://www.subscribepage.com/_VIP

Your privacy is important to me. I will never sell or share your email address.

Did you enjoy this book? You can make a difference!

Reviews are an indie author's most powerful marketing tool. Honest reviews help us get noticed by other readers and increase vis- ibility in the marketplace. It's the best way for indie authors like me to be discovered by fabulous readers like you.

If you enjoyed this book, I would be ever so grateful if you could spend a few minutes leaving a review at your favorite e-retailer. It can be as short as you like. And if you're interested in joining my re- view team, email me a note to let me know! I personally answer every email I receive.

Thank you very much!

ALSO BY MICHELLE MILES

Dream Walker
Call of the Dark

Age of Wizards
In the Tower of the Wizard King
On the Hunt for the Wizard King

A Ransom & Fortune Adventure
Highland Fling, Vol 1
Dead of Winter, Vol 2
The Citadel, Vol 3
Lord of the Underworld, Vol 4

Dragon Protectors
Desiring the Dragon Lord
Seducing the Dragon Knight
Tempting Her Dragon Bodyguard

Guardians of Atlantis
Tempting Eden
Seducing Eve
Ravishing Helene
Guardians of Atlantis Box Set

Realm of Honor
One Knight Only
Only for a Knight
A Knight to Remember
A Knight Like No Other
Shadows of the Knight

Coffee House Chronicles
Talk Dirty to Me
Nice Girls Do
Have Yourself a Merry Little Latte
Take Me I'm Yours
Sex, Lust & Martinis

Forever Yours
A Little Taste of Heaven

Shorts and Anthologies
A Dance Among the Faeries, Short Story
Eorwulf, Short Story
The Soul of Sharah, Short Story
Sinfully Sweet, Short Story
Flights of Fantasy: A Collection of Short Stories

Watch for more at www.michellemiles.net

About the Author

Michelle Miles believes in fairy tales, true love and magic. She is the award-winning author of the epic fantasy, IN THE TOWER OF THE WIZARD KING, as well as the fantasy romance series, REALM OF HONOR, featuring knights and their ladies fair, and the paranormal dragon-shifter romance series, DRAGON PROTECTORS.

In her spare time, she enjoys listening to music, reading, cross-stitching and watching movies. Even though she's a native Texan, she loves castles, dragons, fairies and elves and is an avid Game of Thrones fan. She can be found online at Facebook, Twitter, Instagram, Pinterest, and Goodreads.